1 MONTH OF
FREE
READING

at

www.ForgottenBooks.com

By purchasing this book you are eligible for one month membership to ForgottenBooks.com, giving you unlimited access to our entire collection of over 700,000 titles via our web site and mobile apps.

To claim your free month visit:
www.forgottenbooks.com/free792787

ISBN 978-0-483-62928-8
PIBN 10792787

CIHM
Microfiche
Series
(Monographs)

ICMH
Collection d
microfiches
(monographi

flan Institute for Historical Microreproductions / Institut canadien de microreprodu

Technical and Bibliographic Notes / Notes techniques et bibliographiques

Institute has attempted to obtain the best original available for filming. Features of this copy which be bibliographically unique, which may alter any images in the reproduction, or which may change the usual method of filming, are below.

L'Institut a microfilmé le meil lui a été possible de se procurer exemplaire qui sont peut-être bibliographiques, qui peuvent reproduite, ou qui peuvent exig dans la méthode normale de film ci-dessous.

Coloured covers/
Couverture de couleur

Covers damaged/
Couverture endommagée

Covers restored and/or laminated/
Couverture restaurée et/ou pelliculée

Cover title missing/
Le titre de couverture manque

Coloured maps/
Cartes géographiques en couleur

Coloured ink (i.e. other than blue or black)/
Encre de couleur (i.e. autre que bleue ou noire)

Coloured plates and/or illustrations/
Planches et/ou illustrations en couleur

Bound with other material/
Relié avec d'autres documents

Tight binding may cause shadows or distortion along interior margin/
La reliure serrée peut causer de l'ombre ou de la distortion le long de la marge intérieure

Blank leaves added during restoration may appear within the text. Whenever possible, these have been omitted from filming/
Il se peut que certaines pages blanches ajoutées lors d'une restauration apparaissent dans le texte, mais, lorsque cela était possible, ces pages n'ont pas été filmées.

☐ Coloured pages/
Pages de couleur

☑ Pages damaged/
Pages endommagées

☐ Pages restored and/or lam
Pages restaurées et/ou pelli

☑ Pages discoloured, stained
Pages décolorées, tachetées

☐ Pages detached/
Pages détachées

☑ Showthrough/
Transparence

☑ Quality of print varies/
Qualité inégale de l'impress

☐ Continuous pagination/
Pagination continue

☐ Includes index(es)/
Comprend un (des) index

Title on header taken from:
Le titre de l'en-tête provien

☐ Title page of issue/
Page de titre de la livraison

☐ Caption of issue/
Titre de départ de la livrai

☐ Masthead/
Générique (périodiques) de

Additional comments:/   343-346 are bound in twice.

L'exemplaire filmé fut reproduit grâce à la générosité de:

Bibliothèque nationale du Canada

Les images suivantes ont été reproduites avec le plus grand soin, compte tenu de la condition et de la netteté de l'exemplaire filmé, et en conformité avec les conditions du contrat de filmage.

Les exemplaires originaux dont la couverture en papier est imprimée sont filmés en commençant par le premier plat et en terminant soit par la dernière page qui comporte une empreinte d'impression ou d'illustration, soit par le second plat, selon le cas. Tous les autres exemplaires originaux sont filmés en commençant par la première page qui comporte une empreinte d'impression ou d'illustration et en terminant par la dernière page qui comporte une telle empreinte.

Un des symboles suivants apparaîtra sur la dernière image de chaque microfiche, selon le cas: le symbole ➔ signifie "A SUIVRE", le symbole ▼ signifie "FIN".

Les cartes, planches, tableaux, etc., peuvent être filmés à des taux de réduction différents. Lorsque le document est trop grand pour être reproduit en un seul cliché, il est filmé à partir de l'angle supérieur gauche, de gauche à droite, et de haut en bas, en prenant le nombre d'images nécessaire. Les diagrammes suivants illustrent la méthode.

1

2

MICROCOPY RESOLUTION TEST CHART

(ANSI and ISO TEST CHART No. 2)

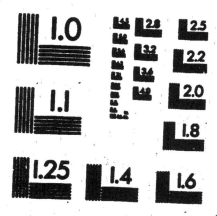

APPLIED IMAGE Inc

1653 East Main Street
Rochester, New York 14809   USA
(716) 482 – 0300 – Phone
(716) 288 – 5989 – Fax

To Father
  From Art
  Xmas 191

450U

lot Can Ed

The
MOONLIT WAY

Novels By Robert W. Chambers

The Laughing Girl
The Restless Sex
Barbarians
The Dark Star
The Girl Philippa
Who Goes There!
Athalie
The Business of Life
The Gay Rebellion
The Streets of Ascalon
The Common Law
The Fighting Chance
The Younger Set
The Danger Mark
The Firing Line
Japonette
Quick Action
The Adventures of
    A Modest Man
Anne's Bridge
Between Friends
The Better Man
Police!!!
Some Ladies in Haste
The Tree of Heaven
The Tracer of Lost
    Persons
The Hidden Children

The Moonlit Way
Cardigan
The Reckoning
The Maid-at-Arms
Ailsa Paige
Special Messenger
The Haunts of Men
Lorraine
Maids of Paradise
Ashes of Empire
The Red Republic
Blue-Bird Weather
A Young Man in a
    Hurry
The Green Mouse
Iole
The Mystery of Choice
The Cambric Mask
The Maker of Moons
The King in Yellow
In Search of the
    Unknown
The Conspirators
A King and a Few
    Dukes
In the Quarter
Outsiders

140 H

HIS STRAINED GAZE SOUGHT TO FIX ITSELF ON THIS FACE
(PAGE 325)

The
MOONLIT WAY

A Novel

BY
ROBERT W. CHAMBERS
AUTHOR OF
"THE COMMON LAW," "THE FIGHTING CHANCE," ETC.

ILLUSTRATED BY
A. I. KELLER

TORONTO
GEORGE J. McLEOD, LIMITED
PUBLISHERS
1919

TO

MY FRIEND

FRANK HITCHCOCK.

CONTENTS

CONTENTS

LIST OF ILLUSTRATIONS

THE MOONLIT WAY

PROLOGUE

CLAIRE-DE-LUNE

THERE was a big moon over the Bosphorus; the limpid waters off Seraglio Point glimmered; the Golden Horn was like a sheet of beaten silver inset with topaz and ruby where lanterns on rusting Turkish warships dyed the tarnished argent of the flood. Except for these, and the fixed lights on the foreign guard-ships and on a big American steam yacht, only a pale and nebulous shoreward glow betrayed the monster city.

Over Pera the full moon's lustre fell, silvering palace, villa, sea and coast; its rays glimmered on bridge and wharf, bastion, tower arsenal, and minarette, transforming those big, sprawling, ramshackle blotches of architecture called Constantinople into that shadowy, magnificent enchantment of the East, which all believe in, but which exists only in a poet's heart and mind.

Night veiled the squalour of Balat, and its filth, its meanness, its flimsy sham. Moonlight made of Galata a marvel, ennobling every bastard dome, every starved façade, every unlovely and attenuated minarette, and invested with added charm each really lovely ruin, each tower, palace, mosque, garden wall and balcony, and every crenelated battlement, where the bronze bulk of

1

ancient cannon slanted, outlined in silver under the Prophet's moon.

Tiny moving lights twinkled on the Galata Bridge; pale points of radiance dotted Scutari; but the group of amazing cities called Constantinople lay almost blotted out under the moon.

Darker at night than any capital in the world, its huge, solid and ancient shapes bulking gigantic in the night, its noble ruins cloaked, its cheap filth hidden, its flimsy Coney Island aspect transfigured and the stylographic-pen architecture of a hundred minarettes softened into slender elegance, Constantinople lay dreaming its immemorial dreams under the black shadow of the Prussian eagle.

The German Embassy was lighted up like a Pera café; the drawing-rooms crowded with a brilliant throng where sashes, orders, epaulettes and sabre-tache glittered, and jewels blazed and aigrettes waved under the crystal chandeliers, accenting and isolating sombre civilian evening dress, which seemed mournful, rusty, and out of the picture, even when plastered over with jewelled stars.

Few Turkish officials and officers were present, but the disquieting sight of German officers in Turkish uniforms was not uncommon. And the Count d'Eblis, Senator of France, noted this phenomenon with lively curiosity, and mentioned it to his companion, Ferez Bey.

Ferez Bey, lounging in a corner with Adolf Gerhardt, for whom he had procured an invitation, and flanked by the Count d'Eblis, likewise a guest aboard the rich German-American banker's yacht, was very much in his element as friend and mentor.

For Ferez Bey knew everybody in the Orient—knew

when to cringe, when to be patronising, when to fawn, when to assert himself, when to be servile, when impudent.

He was as impudent to Adolf Gerhardt as he dared be, the banker not knowing the su' tler shades and differences; he was on an equality with the French senator, Monsieur le Comte d'Eblis because he knew that d'Eblis dared not resent his familiarity.

Otherwise, in that brilliant company, Ferez Bey was a jackal—and he knew it perfectly—but a valuable jackal; and he also knew that.

So when the German Ambassador spoke pleasantly to him, his attitude was just sufficiently servile, but not overdone; and when Von-der-Hohe Pasha, in the uniform of a Turkish General of Division, graciously exchanged a polite word with him during a moment's easy gossip with the Count d'Eblis, Ferez Bey writhed moderately under the honour, but did not exactly squirm.

To Conrad von Heimhols he ventured to present his German-American patron, Adolf Gerhardt, and the thin young military attaché condescended in his Prussian way to notice the introduction.

"Saw your yacht in the harbour," he admitted stiffly. "It is astonishing how you Americans permit no bounds to your somewhat noticeable magnificence."

"She's a good boat, the *Mirage*," rumbled Gerhardt, in his bushy red beard, "but there are plenty in America finer than mine."

"Not many, Adolf," insisted Ferez, in his flat, Eurasian voice—"not ver' many anyw'ere so fine like your *Mirage*."

"I saw none finer at Kiel," said the attaché, staring at Gerhardt through his monocle, with the habitual insolence and disapproval of the Prussian junker. "To me it exhibits bad taste"—he turned to the Count d'Eblis—"particularly when the *Meteor* is there."

"Where?" asked the Count.

"At Kiel. I speak of Kiel and the ostentation of certain foreign yacht owners at the recent regatta."

Gerhardt, redder than ever, was still German enough to swallow the meaningless insolence. He was not getting on very well at the Embassy of his fellow countrymen. Americans, properly presented, they endured without too open resentment; for German-Americans, even when millionaires, their contempt and bad manners were often undisguised.

"I'm going to get out of this," growled Gerhardt, who held a good position socially in New York and in the fashionable colony at Northbrook. "I've seen enough puffed up Germans and over-embroidered Turks to last me. Come on, d'Eblis——"

Feres detained them both:

"Surely," he protested, "you would not miss Nihla!"

"Nihla?" repeated d'Eblis, who had passed his arm through Gerhardt's. "Is that the girl who set St. Petersburg by the ears?"

"Nihla Quellen," rumbled Gerhardt. "I've heard of her. She's a dancer, isn't she?"

Feres, of course, knew all about her, and he drew the two men into the embrasure of a long window.

It was not happening just exactly as he and the German Ambassador had planned it together; they had intended to let Nihla burst like a flaming jewel on the vision of d'Eblis and blind him then and there.

Perhaps, after all, it was better drama to prepare her entrance. And who but Feres was qualified to prepare that entrée, or to speak with authority concerning the history of this strange and beautiful young girl who had suddenly appeared like a burning star in the East, had passed like a meteor through St. Petersburg, leaving several susceptible young men—notably the Grand Duke Cyril—mentally unhinged and hopelessly dissatisfied with fate.

"It is ver' fonny, d'Eblis—une histoire chic, vous saves! Figures vous——"

"Talk English," growled Gerhardt, eyeing the serene progress of a pretty Highness, Austrian, of course, surrounded by gorgeous uniforms and empressement.

"Who's that?" he added.

Feres turned; the gorgeous lady snubbed him, but bowed to d'Eblis.

"The Archduchess Zilka," he said, not a whit abashed. "She is a ver' great frien' of mine."

"Can't you present me?" enquired Gerhardt, restlessly; "—or you, d'Eblis—can't you ask permission?"

The Count d'Eblis nodded inattentively, then turned his heavy and rather vulgar face to Feres, plainly interested in the "histoire" of the girl, Nihla.

"What were you going to say about that dancer?" he demanded.

Feres pretended to forget, then, apparently recollecting:

"Ah! Apropos of Nihla? It is a ver' piquant storee —the storee of Nihla Quellen. Zat is not 'er name. No! Her name is Dunois—Thessalie Dunois."

"French," nodded d'Eblis.

"Alsatian," replied Feres slyly. "Her fathaire was captain—Achille Dunois?—you know——?"

"What!" exclaimed d'Eblis. "Do you mean that notorious fellow, the Grand Duke Cyril's hunting cheetah?"

"The same, dear frien'. Dunois is dead—his bullet head was crack open, doubtless by so i' ladee's angree husban'. There are a few thousan' roubles—not more—to stan' between some kind gentleman and the prettee Nihla. You see?" he added to Gerhardt, who was listening without interest, "—Dunois, if he was the Gran' Duke's cheetah, kept all such merry gentlemen from his charming daughtaire."

Gerhardt, whose aspirations lay higher, socially, than a dancing girl, merely grunted. But d'Eblis, whose aspirations were always below even his own level, listened with visibly increasing curiosity. And this was according to the programme of Ferez Bey and Excellenz. As the Hun has it, "according to plan."

"Well," enquired d'Eblis heavily, "did Cyril get her?"

"All St. Petersburg is still laughing at heem," replied the voluble Eurasian. "Cyril indeed launched her. And that was sufficient—yet, that first night she storm St. Petersburg. And Cyril's reward? Listen, d'Eblis, they say she slapped his sillee face. For me, I don't know. That is the storee. And he was ver' angree, Cyril. You know? And, by God, it was what Gerhardt calls a 'raw deal.' Yess? Figurez vous!—this girl, déjà lancée—and her fathaire the Grand Duke's hunting cheetah, and her mothaire, what? Yes, mon ami, a 'andsome Géorgianne, caught quite wild, they say, by Prince Haledine! For me, I believe it. Why not? . . . And then the beautiful Géorgianne, she fell to Dunois—on a bet?—a service rendered?—gratitude of Cyril?—— Who knows? Only that Dunois must marry her. And Nihla is their daughtaire. Voilà!"

"Then why," demanded d'Eblis, "does she make such a fuss about being grateful? I hate ingratitude, Ferez. And how can she last, anyway? To dance for the German Ambassador in Constantinople is all very well, but unless somebody launches her properly—in Paris—she'll end in a Pera café.

Ferez held his peace and listened with all his might.

"I could do that," added d'Eblis.

"Please?" inquired Ferez suavely.

"Launch her in Paris."

The programme of Excellenz and Ferez Bey was certainly proceeding as planned.

But Gerhardt was becoming restless and dully irritated as he began to realise more and more what caste meant to Prussians and how insignificant to these people was a German-American multimillionaire. And Ferez realised that he must do something.

There was a Bavarian Baroness there, uglier than the usual run of Bavarian baronesses; and to her Ferez nailed Gerhardt, and wriggled free himself, making his way amid the gorgeous throngs to the Count d'Eblis once more.

"I left Gerhardt planted," he remarked with satisfaction; "by God, she is uglee like camels—the Baroness von Schaunitz! Nev' mind. It is nobility; it is the same to Adolf Gerhardt."

"A homely woman makes me sick!" remarked d'Eblis. "Eh, mon Dieu!—one has merely to look at these ladies to guess their nationality! Only in Germany can one gather together such a collection of horrors. The only pretty ones are Austrian."

Perhaps even the cynicism of Excellenz had not realised the perfection of this setting, but Ferez, the nimble witted, had foreseen it.

Already the glittering crowds in the drawing rooms were drawing aside like jewelled curtains; already the stringed orchestra had become mute aloft in its gilded gallery.

The gay tumult softened; laughter, voices, the rustle

7

of silks and fans, the metallic murmur of drawing room equipment died away. Through the increasing stillness, from the gilded gallery a Thessalonian reed began skirling like a thrush in the underbrush.

Suddenly a sand-coloured curtain at the end of the east room twitched open, and a great desert ostrich trotted in. And, astride of the big, excited, bridled bird, sat a young girl, controlling her restless mount with disdainful indifference.

"Nihla!" whispered Ferez, in the large, fat ear of the Count d'Eblis. The latter's pallid jowl reddened and his pendulous lips tightened to a deep-bitten crease across his face.

To the weird skirling of the Thessalonian pipe the girl, Nihla, put her feathered steed through its absurd paces, aping the haute-école.

There is little humour in your Teuton; they were too amazed to laugh; too fascinated, possibly by the girl herself, to follow the panicky gambols of the reptile-headed bird.

The girl wore absolutely nothing except a Yashmak and a zone of blue jewels across her breasts and hips.

Her childish throat, her limbs, her slim, snowy body, her little naked feet were lovely beyond words. Her thick dark hair flew loose, now framing, now veiling an oval face from which, above the gauzy Yashmak's edge, two dark eyes coolly swept her breathless audience.

But under the frail wisp of cobweb, her cheeks glowed pink, and two full red lips parted deliciously in the half-checked laughter of confident, reckless youth.

Over hurdle after hurdle she lifted her powerful, half-terrified mount; she backed it, pirouetted, made

VINLA FOR HER FLATHEAD DIED CERTIFIED THROUGH ITS ABSURD FACES

it squat, leap, pace, trot, run with wings half spread and neck stretched level.

She rode sideways, then kneeling, standing, then poised on one foot; she threw somersaults, faced to the rear, mounted and dismounted at full speed. And through the frail, transparent Yashmak her parted red lips revealed the glimmer of teeth and her childishly engaging laughter rang delightfully.

Then, abruptly, she had enough of her bird; she wheeled, sprang to the polished parquet, and sent her feathered steed scampering away through the sand-coloured curtains, which switched into place again immediately.

Breathless, laughing that frank, youthful, irresistible laugh which was to become so celebrated in Europe, Nihla Quellen strolled leisurely around the circle of her applauding audience, carelessly blowing a kiss or two from her slim finger-tips, evidently quite unspoiled by her success and equally delighted to please and to be pleased.

Then, in the gilded gallery the strings began; and quite naturally, without any trace of preparation or self-consciousness, Nihla began to sing, dancing when the fascinating, irresponsible measure called for it, singing again as the sequence occurred. And the enchantment of it all lay in its accidental and detached allure—as though it all were quite spontaneous—the song a passing whim, the dance a capricious afterthought, and the whole thing done entirely to please herself and give vent to the sheer delight of a young girl, in her own overwhelming energy and youthful spirits.

Even the Teuton comprehended that, and the applause grew to a roar with that odd undertone of ani-

mal menace always to be detected when the German
herd is gratified and expresses pleasure en masse.

But she wouldn't stay, wouldn't return. Like one
of those beautiful Persian cats, she had lingered long
enough to arouse delight. Then she went, deaf to recall, to persuasion, to caress—indifferent to praise, to
blandishment, to entreaty. Cat and dancer were similar; Nihla, like the Persian puss, knew when she had
had enough. That was sufficient for her: nothing
could stop her, nothing lure her to return.

Beads of sweat were glistening upon the heavy features of the Count d'Eblis. Von-der-Goltz Pasha,
strolling near, did him the honour to remember him,
but d'Eblis seemed dazed and unresponsive; and the
old Pasha understood, perhaps, when he caught the
beady and expressive eyes of Ferez fixed on him in
exultation.

"Whose is she?" demanded d'Eblis abruptly. His
voice was hoarse and evidently out of control, for he
spoke too loudly to please Ferez, who took him by
the arm and led him out to the moonlit terrace.

"Mon pauvere ami," he said soothingly, "she is
actually the propertee of nobodee at present. Cyril,
they say, is following her—quite ready for anything—
marriage——"

"What!"

Ferez shrugged:

"That is the gosseep. No doubt som' man of wealth,
more acceptable to her——"

"I wish to meet her!" said d'Eblis.

"Ah! That is, of course, not easee——"

"Why?"

Ferez laughed:

"Ask yo'self the question again! Excellenz and his
guests have gone quite mad ovaire Nihla——"

"I care nothing for them," retorted d'Eblis thickly; "I wish to know her. . . . I wish to know her! . . . *Do you understand?*"

After a silence, Ferez turned in the moonlight and looked at the Count d'Eblis.

"And your newspapaire—*Le Mot d'Ordre?*"

"Yes. . . . If you get her for me."

"You sell to me for two million francs the control stock in *Le Mot d'Ordre?*"

"Yes."

"An' the two million, eh?"

"I shall use my influence with Gerhardt. That is all I can do. If your Emperor chooses to decorate him— something—the Red Eagle, third class, perhaps——"

"I attend to those," smiled Ferez. "Hit's ver' fonny, d'Eblis, how I am thinking about those Red Eagles all time since I know Gerhardt. I spik to Von-der-Golts de votre part, si vous le voulez? Oui? Alors——"

"Ask her to supper aboard the yacht."

"God knows——"

The Count d'Eblis said through closed teeth:

"There is the first woman I ever really wanted in all my life! . . . I am standing here now waiting for her—waiting to be presented to her now."

"I spik to Von-der-Goltz Pasha," said Ferez; and he slipped through the palms and orange trees and vanished.

For half an hour the Count d'Eblis stood there, motionless in the moonlight.

She came about that time, on the arm of Ferez Bey, her father's friend of many years.

And Ferez left her there in the creamy Turkish moonlight on the flowering terrace, alone with the Count d'Eblis.

When Feres came again, long after midnight, with Excellenz on one arm and the proud and happy Adolf Gerhardt on the other, the whole cycle of a little drama had been played to a conclusion between those two shadowy figures under the flowering almonds on the terrace—between this slender, dark-eyed girl and this big, bulky, heavy-visaged man of the world.

And the man had been beaten and the girl had laid down every term. And the compact was this: that she was to be launched in Paris; she was merely to borrow any sum needed, with privilege to acquit the debt within the year; that, if she ever came to care for this man sufficiently, she was to become only one species of masculine property—a legal wife.

And to every condition—and finally even to the last, the man had bowed his heavy, burning head.

"D'Eblis!" began Gerhardt, almost stammering in his joy and pride. "His highness tells me that I am to have an order—an Imperial d-decoration——"

D'Eblis stared at him out of unseeing eyes; Nihla laughed outright, alas, too early wise and not even troubling her lovely head to wonder why a decoration had been asked for this burly, bushy-bearded man from nowhere.

But within his sinuous, twisted soul Feres writhed exultingly, and patted Gerhardt on the arm, and patted d'Eblis, too—dared even to squirm visibly closer to Excellenz, like a fawning dog that fears too much to venture contact in his wriggling demonstrations.

"You take with you our pretty wonder-child to Paris to be launched, I hear," remarked Excellenz, most affably, to d'Eblis. And to Nihla: "And upon a yacht fit for an emperor, I understand. Ach! Such a going forth is only heard of in the Arabian Nights. Eh

12

bien, ma petite, go West, conquer, and reign! It is
a prophecy!"

And Nihla threw back her head and laughed her full-
throated laughter under the Turkish moon.

Later, Ferez, walking with the Ambassador, replied
humbly to the curt question:

"Yes, I have become his jackal. But always at the
orders of Excellenz."

Later still, aboard the *Mirage*, Ferez stood alone
by the after-rail, staring with ratty eyes at the black-
ness beyond the New Bridge.

"Oh, God, be merciful!" he whispered. He had often
said it on the eve of crime. Even an Eurasian rat has
emotions. And Ferez had been in love with Nihla many
years, and was selling her now at a price—selling her
and Adolf Gerhardt and the Count d'Eblis and France
—all he had to barter—for he had sold his soul too long
ago to remember even what he got for it.

The silence seemed more intense for the sounds that
made it audible. From the unlighted cities on the
seven hills came an unbroken howling of dogs; transparent waves of the limpid Bosphorus slapped the ves-
sel's sides, making a mellow and ceaseless clatter. Far
away beyond Galata Quay, in the inner reek of unseen
Stamboul, the notes of a Turkish flute stole out across
the darkness, where some Tzigane—some unseen wretch
in rags—was playing the melancholy song of Mourad.
And, mournfully responsive to the reedy complaint
of a homeless wanderer from a nation without a home,
the homeless dogs of Islam wailed their miserere under
the Prophet's moon.

The tragic wolf-song wavered from hill to hill; from
the Fields of the Dead to the Seven Towers, from

Kassim to Tophane, seeming to swell into one dreadful, endless plaint:

"My God, why hast Thou forsaken me?"

"And me!" muttered Ferez, shivering in the windy vapours from the Black Sea, which already dampened his face with their creeping summer chill.

"Ferez!"

He turned slowly. Swathed in a white wool bernous, Nihla stood there in the foggy moonlight.

"Why?" she enquired, without preliminaries and with the unfeigned curiosity of a child.

He did not pretend to misunderstand her in French:

"Thou knowest, Nihla. I have never touched thy heart. I could do nothing for thee——"

"Except to sell me," she smiled, interrupting him in English, without the slightest trace of accent.

But Ferez preferred the refuge of French:

"Except to launch thee and make possible thy career," he corrected her very gently.

"I thought you were in love with me?"

"I have loved thee, Nihla, since thy childhood."

"Is there anything on earth or in paradise, Ferez, that you would not sell for a price?"

"I tell thee——"

"Zut! I know thee, Ferez!" she mocked him, slipping easily into French. "What was my price? Who pays thee, Colonel Ferez? This big, shambling, world-wearied Count, who is, nevertheless, afraid of me? Did he pay thee? Or was it this rich American, Gerhardt? Or was it Von-der-Goltz? Or Excellenz?"

"Nihla! Thou knowest me——"

Her clear, untroubled laughter checked him:

"I know you, Ferez. That is why I ask. That is why I shall have no reply from you. Only my wits can ever answer me any questions."

She stood laughing at him, swathed in her white wool, looming like some mocking spectre in the misty moonlight of the after-deck.

"Oh, Ferez," she said in her sweet, malicious voice, "there was a curse on Midas, too! You play at high finance; you sell what you never had to sell, and you are paid for it. All your life you have been busy selling, re-selling, bargaining, betraying, seeking always gain where only loss is possible—loss of all that justifies a man in daring to stand alive before the God that made him! . . . And yet—that which you call love—that shadowy emotion which you have also sold to-night—I think you really feel for me. . . . Yes, I believe it. . . . But it, too, has its price. . . . *What was that price, Ferez?*"

"Believe me, Nihla——"

"Oh, Ferez, you ask too much! No! Let me tell you, then. The price was paid by that American, who is not one but a German."

"That is absurd!"

"Why the Red Eagle, then? And the friendship of Excellenz? What is he then, this Gerhardt, but a millionaire? Why is nobility so gracious then? What does Gerhardt give for his Red Eagle?—for the politeness of Excellenz?—for the crooked smile of a Bavarian Baroness and the lifted lorgnette of Austria? What does he give for me? Who buys me after all? Enver? Talaat? Hilmi? Who sells me? Excellenz? Vonder-Goltz? You? And who pays for me? Gerhardt, who takes his profit in Red Eagles and offers me to d'Eblis for something in exchange to please Excellenz —and you? And what, at the end of the bargaining, does d'Eblis pay for me—pay through Gerhardt to you, and through you to Excellenz, and through Excellenz to the Kaiser Wilhelm II——"

Ferez, showing his teeth, came close to her and spoke very softly:

"See how white is the moonlight off Seraglio Point, my Nihla! . . . It is no whiter than those loveliest ones who lie fathoms deep below these little silver waves. . . . Each with her bowstring snug about her snowy neck. . . . As fair and young, as warm and fresh and sweet as thou, my Nihla."

He smiled at her; and if the smile stiffened an instant on her lips, the next instant her light, dauntless laughter mocked him.

"For a price," she said, "you would sell even Life to that old miser, Death! Then listen what you have done, little smiling, whining jackal of his Excellency! I go to Paris and to my career, certain of my happy destiny, sure of myself! For my opportunity I pay if I choose—pay what I choose—when and where it suits me to pay!——"

She slipped into French with a little laugh:

"Now go and lick thy fingers of whatever crumbs have stuck there. The Count d'Eblis is doubtless licking his. Good appetite, my Ferez! Lick away lustily, for God does not temper the jackal's appetite to his opportunities!"

Ferez let his level gaze rest on her in silence.

"Well, trafficker in Eagles, dealer in love, vendor of youth, merchant of souls, what strikes you silent?"

But he was thinking of something sharper than her tongue and less subtle, which one day might strike her silent if she laughed too much at Fate.

And, thinking, he showed his teeth again in that noiseless snicker which was his smile and laughter too.

The girl regarded him for a moment, then deliberately mimicked his smile:

"The dogs of Stamboul laugh that way, too," she

said, baring her pretty teeth. "What amuses you? Did the silly old Von-der-Golts Pasha promise you. also, a dish of Eagle?—old Von-der-Golts with his spectacles an inch thick and nothing living within what he carries about on his two doddering old legs! There's a German!—who died twenty years ago and still walks like a damned man—jingling his iron crosses and mumbling his gums! Is it a resurrection from 1870 come to foretell another war? And why are these Prussian vultures gathering here in Stamboul? Can you tell me, Ferez?—these Prussians in Turkish uniforms! Is there anything dying or dead here, that these buzzards appear from the sky and alight? Why do they crowd and huddle in a circle around Constantinople? Is there something dead in Persia? Is the Bagdad railroad dying? Is Enver Bey at his last gasp? Is Talaat? Or perhaps the savoury odour comes from the Yildiz——"

"Nihla! Is there nothing sacred—nothing thou fearest on earth?"

"Only old age—and thy smile, my Ferez. Neither agrees with me." She stretched her arms lazily.

"Allons," she said, stifling a pleasant yawn with one slim hand, "—my maid will wake below and miss me; and then the dogs of Stamboul yonder will hear a solo such as they never heard before. . . . Tell me, Ferez, do you know when : are to weigh anchor?"

"At sunrise."

"It is the same to me,"—she yawned again—"my maid is aboard and all my luggage. And my Ferez, also. . . . Mon dieu! And what will Cyril have to say when he arrives to find me vanished! It is, perhaps, well for us that we sha" ` at sea!"

Her quick laughter pea¹ l with a careless

gesture of salute, friendly and contemptuous; and her white bernous faded away in the moonlit fog.

And Ferez Bey stood staring after her out of his near-set, beady eyes, loving her, desiring her, fearing her, unrepentant that he had sold her, wondering whether the day might dawn when he would find it best to kill her for the prosperity and peace of mind of the only living being in whose service he never tired— himself.

I

A SHADOW DANCE

THREE years later Destiny still wore a rosy face for Nihla Quellen. And, for a young American of whom Nihla had never even heard, Destiny still remained the laughing jade he had always known, beckoning him ever nearer, with the coquettish promise of her curved forefinger, to fame and wealth immeasurable.

Seated now on a moonlit lawn, before his sketching easel, this optimistic young man, whose name was Barres, continued to observe the movements of a dim white figure which had emerged from the villa opposite, and was now stealing toward him across the dew-drenched grass.

When the white figure was quite near it halted, holding up filmy skirts and peering intently at him.

"May one look?" she inquired, in that now celebrated voice of hers, through which ever seemed to sound a hint of hidden laughter.

"Certainly," he replied, rising from his folding camp stool.

She tiptoed over the wet grass, came up beside him, gazed down at the canvas on his easel.

"Can you really see to paint? Is the moon bright enough?" she asked.

"Yes. But one has to be familiar with one's palette."

19

"Oh. You seem to know yours quite perfectly, monsieur."

"Enough to mix colours properly."

"I didn't realise that painters ever actually painted pictures by moonlight."

"It's a sort of hit or miss business, but the notes made are interesting," he explained.

"What do you do with these moonlight studies?"

"Use them as notes in the studio when a moonlight picture is to be painted."

"Are you then a realist, monsieur?"

"As much of a realist as anybody with imagination can be," he replied, smiling at her charming, moonlit face.

"I understand. Realism is merely honesty plus the imagination of the individual."

"A delightful *mot*, madam——"

"Mademoiselle," she corrected him demurely. "Are you English?"

"American."

"Oh. Then may I venture to converse with you in English?" She said it in exquisite English, entirely without accent.

"You *are* English!" he exclaimed under his breath. .

"No. . . . I don't know what I am. . . . Isn't it charming out here? What particular view are you painting?"

"The Seine, yonder."

She bent daintily over his sketch, holding up the skirts of her ball-gown.

"Your sketch isn't very far advanced, is it?" she inquired seriously.

"Not very," he smiled.

They stood there together in silence for a while,

looking out over the moonlit river to the misty, tree-covered heights.

Through lighted rows of open windows in the elaborate little villa across the lawn came lively music and the distant noise of animated voices.

"Do you know," he ventured smilingly, "that your skirts and slippers are soaking wet?"

"I don't care. Isn't this June night heavenly?" She glanced across at the lighted house. "It's so hot and noisy in there; one dances only with discomfort. A distaste for it all sent me out on the terrace. Then I walked on the lawn. Then I beheld you! . . . Am I interrupting your work, monsieur? I suppose I am." She looked up at him naïvely.

He said something polite. An odd sense of having seen her somewhere possessed him now. From the distant house came the noisy American music of a two-step. With charming grace, still inspecting him out of her dark eyes, the girl began to move her pretty feet in rhythm with the music.

"Shall we?" she inquired mischievously. . . . "Unless you are too busy——"

The next moment they were dancing together there on the wet lawn, under the high lustre of the moon, her fresh young face and fragrant figure close to his.

During their second dance she said serenely:

"They'll raise the dickens if I stay here any longer. Do you know the Comte d'Eblis?"

"The Senator? The numismatist?"

"Yes."

"No, I don't know him. I am only a Latin Quarter student."

"Well, he is giving that party. He is giving it for me—in my honour. That is his villa. And I"—

she laughed—"am going to marry him—*perhaps!*
this a delightful escapade of mine?"

"Isn't it rather an indiscreet one?" he asked
ingly.

"Frightfully. But I like it. How did you hap
to pitch your easel on his lawn?"

"The river and the hills—their composition appeal
to me from here. It is the best view of the Seine."

"Are you glad you came?"

They both laughed at the mischievous question.

During their third dance she became a little app
hensive and kept looking over her shoulder toward th
house.

"There's a man expected there," she whispered, "Fe
ez Bey. He's as soft-footed as a cat and he alway
prowls in my vicinity. At times it almost seems t
me as though he were slyly watching me—as though he
were employed to keep an eye on me."

"A Turk?"

"Eurasian. . . . I wonder what they think of my
absence? Alexandre—the Comte d'Eblis—won't like
it."

"Had you better go?"

"Yes; I ought to, but I won't. . . . Wait a moment!" She disengaged herself from his arms. "Hide
your easel and colour-box in the shrubbery, in case
anybody comes to look for me."

She helped him strap up and fasten the telescope-
easel; they placed the paraphernalia behind the blossoming screen of syringa. Then, coming together, she
gave herself to him again, nestling between his arms
with a little laugh; and they fell into step once more
with the distant dance-music. Over the grass their
united shadows glided, swaying, gracefully interlocked

22

—moon-born phantoms which dogged their light young feet. . . .

A man came out on the stone terrace under the Chinese lanterns. When they saw him they hastily backed into the obscurity of the shrubbery.

"Nihla!" he called, and his heavy voice was vibrant with irritation and impatience.

He was a big man. He walked with a bulky, awkward gait—a few paces only, out across the terrace.

"Nihla!" he bawled hoarsely.

Then two other men and a woman appeared on the terrace where the lanterns were strung. The woman called aloud in the darkness:

"Nihla! Nihla! Where are you, little devil?" Then she and the two men with her went indoors, laughing and skylarking, leaving the bulky man there alone.

The young fellow in the shrubbery felt the girl's hand tighten on his coat sleeve, felt her slender body quiver with stifled laughter. The desire to laugh seized him, too; and they clung there together, choking back their mirth while the big man who had first appeared waddled out across the lawn toward the shrubbery, shouting:

"Nihla! Where are you then?" He came quite close to where they stood, then turned, shouted once or twice and presently disappeared across the lawn toward a walled garden. Later, several other people came out on the terrace, calling, "Nihla, Nihla," and then went indoors, laughing boisterously.

The young fellow and the girl beside him were now quite weak and trembling with suppressed mirth.

They had not dared venture out on the lawn, although dance music had begun again.

"Is it your name they called?" he asked, his eyes very intent upon her face.

"Yes, Nihla."

"I recognise you now," he said, with a little thrill of wonder.

"I suppose so," she replied with amiable indifference. "Everybody knows me."

She did not ask his name; he did not offer to enlighten her. What difference, after all, could the name of an American student make to the idol of Europe, Nihla Quellen?

"I'm in a mess," she remarked presently. "He will be quite furious with me. It is going to be most disagreeable for me to go back into that house. He has really an atrocious temper when made ridiculous."

"I'm awfully sorry," he said, sobered by her seriousness.

She laughed:

"Oh, pouf! I really don't care. But perhaps you had better leave me now. I've spoiled your moonlight picture, haven't I?"

"But think what you have given me to make amends!" he replied.

She turned and caught his hands in hers with adorable impulsiveness:

"You're a sweet boy—do you know it! We've had a heavenly time, haven't we? Do you really think you ought to go—so soon?"

"Don't you think so, Nihla?"

"I don't want you to go. Anyway, there's a train every two hours——"

"I've a canoe down by the landing. I shall paddle back as I came——"

"A canoe!" she exclaimed, enchanted. "Will you take me with you?"

24

"To Paris?"

"Of course! Will you?"

"In your ball-gown?"

"I'd adore it! Will you?"

"That is an absolutely crazy suggestion," he said.

"I know it. The world is only a big asylum. There's a path to the river behind these bushes. Quick—pick up your painting traps——"

"But, Nihla, dear——"

"Oh, please! I'm dying to run away with you!"

"To Paris?" he demanded, still incredulous that the girl really meant it.

"Of course! You can get a taxi at the Pont-au-Change and take me home. Will you?"

"It would be wonderful, of course——"

"It will be paradise!" she exclaimed, slipping her hand into his. "Now, let us run like the dickens!"

In the uncertain moonlight, filtering through the shrubbery, they found a hidden path to the river; and they took it together, lightly, swiftly, speeding down the slope, all breathless with laughter, along the moonlit way.

In the suburban villa of the Comte d'Eblis a wine-flushed and very noisy company danced on, supped at midnight, continued the revel into the starlit morning hours. The place was a jungle of confetti.

Their host, restless, mortified, angry, perplexed by turns, was becoming obsessed at length with dull premonitions and vaguer alarms.

He waddled out to the lawn several times, still wearing his fancy gilt and tissue cap, and called:

"Nihla! Damnation! Answer me, you little fool!"

He went down to the river, where the gaily painted row-boats and punts lay, and scanned the silvered flood, tortured by indefinite apprehensions. About dawn he started toward the weed-grown, slippery river-stairs for the last time, still crowned with his tinsel cap; and there in the darkness he found his aged boatman, fishing for gudgeon with a four-cornered net suspended to the end of a bamboo pole.

"Have you see anything of Mademoiselle Nihla?" he demanded, in a heavy, unsteady voice, tremulous with indefinable fears.

"Monsieur le Comte, Mademoiselle Quellen went out in a canoe with a young gentleman."

"W-what is that you tell me?" faltered the Comte d'Eblis, turning grey in the face.

"Last night, about ten o'clock, M'sieu le Comte. I was out in the moonlight fishing for eels. She came down to the shore—took a canoe yonder by the willows. The young man had a double-bladed paddle. They were singing."

"They—they have not returned?"

"No, M'sieu le Comte——"

"Who was the—man?"

"I could not see——"

"Very well." He turned and looked down the dusky river out of light-coloured, murderous eyes. Then, always awkward in his gait, he retraced his steps to the house. There a servant accosted him on the terrace:

"The telephone, if Monsieur le Comte pleases——"

"Who is calling?" he demanded with a flare of fury.

"Paris, if it pleases Monsieur le Comte."

The Count d'Eblis went to his own quarters, seated himself, and picked up the receiver:

"Who is it?" he asked thickly.

"Max Freund."

"What has h-happened?" he stammered in sudden terror.

Over the wire came the distant reply, perfectly clear and distinct:

"Ferez Bey was arrested in his own house at dinner last evening, and was immediately conducted to the frontier, escorted by Government detectives. . . . Is Nihla with you?"

The Count's teeth were chattering now. He managed to say:

"No, I don't know where she is. She was dancing. Then, all at once, she was gone. Of what was Colonel Ferez suspected?"

"I don't know. But perhaps we might guess."

"Are *you* followed?"

"Yes."

"By—by whom?"

"By Souchez. . . . Good-bye, if I don't see you. I join Ferez. And look out for Nihla. She'll trick you yet!"

The Count d'Eblis called:

"Wait, for God's sake, Max!"—listened; called again in vain. "The one-eyed rabbit!" he panted, breathing hard and irregularly. His large hand shook as he replaced the instrument. He sat there as though paralysed, for a moment or two. Mechanically he removed his tinsel cap and thrust it into the pocket of his evening coat. Suddenly the dull hue of anger dyed neck, ears and temple:

"By God!" he gasped. "What is that she-devil trying to do to me? What has she *done!*"

After another moment of staring fixedly at nothing, he opened the table drawer, picked up a pistol and poked it into his breast pocket.

Then he rose, heavily, and stood looking out of the window at the paling east, his pendulous under lip a-quiver.

THE first sunbeams had already gilded her bedroom windows, barring the drawn curtains with
light, when the man arrived. He was still wearing his disordered evening dress under a light overcoat; his soiled shirt front was still crossed by the red
ribbon of watered silk; third class orders striped his
breast, where also the brand new Turkish sunburst
glimmered.

A sleepy maid in night attire answered his furious
ringing; the man pushed her aside with an oath and
strode into the semi-darkness of the corridor. He was
nearly six feet tall, bulky; but his legs were either
too short or something else was the matter with them,
for when he walked he waddled, breathing noisily from
the ascent of the stairs.

"Is your mistress here?" he demanded, hoarse with
his effort.

"Y-yes, monsieur——"

"When did she come in?" And, as the scared and
bewildered maid hesitated: "Damn you, answer me!
When did Mademoiselle Quellen come in? I'll wring
your neck if you lie to me!"

The maid began to whimper:

"Monsieur le Comte—I do not wish to lie to
you. . . . Mademoiselle Nihla came back with the
dawn——"

"Alone?"

28

The maid wrung her hands:

"Does Monsieur le Comte m-mean to harm her?"

"Will you answer me, you snivelling cat!" he panted between his big, discoloured teeth. He had fished out a pistol from his breast pocket, dragging with it a silk handkerchief, a fancy cap of tissue and gilt, and some streamers of confetti which fell to the carpet around his feet.

"Now," he breathed in a half-strangled voice, "answer my questions. Was she alone when she came in?"

"N-no."

"Who was with her?"

"A———"

"A man?"

The maid trembled violently and nodded.

"What man?"

"M-Monsieur le Comte, I have never before beheld him———"

"You lie!"

"I do not lie! I have never before seen him, Monsieur le———"

"Did you learn his name?"

"No———"

"Did you hear what they said?"

"They spoke in English———"

"What!" The man's puffy face went flabby white, and his big, badly made frame seemed to sag for a moment. He laid a large fat hand flat against the wall, as though to support and steady himself, and gazed dully at the terrified maid.

"Is the man there—in there now—with her?" demanded the Comte d'Eblis heavily.

"No, monsieur."

"Gone?"

"Oh, Monsieur le Comte, the young man stayed but a moment——"

"Where were they? In her bedroom?"

"In the salon. I—I served a pâté—a glass of wine—and the young gentleman was gone the next minute——"

A dull red discoloured the neck and features of the Count.

"That's enough," he said; and waddled past her along the corridor to the furthest door; and wrenched it open with one powerful jerk.

In the still, golden gloom of the drawn curtains, now striped with sunlight, a young girl suddenly sat up in bed.

"Alexandre!" she exclaimed in angry astonishment.

"You slut!" he said, already enraged again at the mere sight of her. "Where did you go last night!"

"What are you doing in my bedroom?" she demanded, confused but flushed with anger. "Leave it! Do you hear!——" She caught sight of the pistol in his hand and stiffened.

He stepped nearer; her dark, dilated gaze remained fixed on the pistol.

"Answer me," he said, the menacing roar rising in his voice. "Where did you go last night when you left the house?"

"I—I went out—on the lawn."

"And then?"

"I had had enough of your party: I came back to Paris."

"And *then?*"

"I came here, of course."

"Who was with you?"

Then, for the first time, she began to comprehend. She swallowed desperately.

"Who was your companion?" he repeated.

"A—man."

"You brought him here?"

"He—came in—for a moment."

"Who was he?"

"I—never before saw him."

"You picked up a man in the street and brought him here with you?"

"N-not on the street——"

"Where?"

"On the lawn—while your guests were dancing——"

"And you came to Paris with him?"

"Y-yes."

"Who was he?"

"I don't know——"

"If you don't name him, I'll kill you!" he yelled, losing the last vestige of self-control. "What kind of story are you trying to tell me, you lying drab! You've got a lover! Confess it!"

"I have not!"

"Liar! So this is how you've laughed at me, mocked me, betrayed me, made a fool of me! You!—with your fierce little snappish ways of a virgin! You with your dangerous airs of a tiger-cat if a man so much as laid a finger on your vicious body! So Mademoiselle-Don't-touch-me had a lover all the while. Max Freund warned me to keep an eye on you!" He lost control of himself again; his voice became a hoarse shout: "Max Freund begged me not to trust you! You filthy little beast! Good God! Was I crazy to believe in you—to talk without reserve in your presence! What kind of im-

becile was I to offer you marriage because I was crazy
enough to believe that there was no other way to possess you! You—a Levantine dancing girl—a common
painted thing of the public footlights—a creature of
brasserie and cabaret! And you posed as Mademoiselle
Nitouche! A novice! A devotee of chastity! And, by
God, your devilish ingenuity at last persuaded me that
you actually were what you said you were. And all
Paris knew you were fooling me—all Paris was laughing in its dirty sleeve—mocking me—spitting on
me——"

"All Paris," she said, in an unsteady voice, "gave
you credit for being my lover. And I endured it. And
you knew it was not true. Yet you never denied it.
. . . But as for me, I never had a lover. When I told
you that I told you the truth. And it is true to-day
as it was yesterday. Nobody believes it of a dancing
girl. Now, you no longer believe it. Very well, there
is no occasion for melodrama. I tried to fall in love
with you: I couldn't. I did not desire to marry you.
You insisted. Very well; you can go."

"Not before I learn the name of your lover of last
night!" he retorted, now almost beside himself with
fury, and once more menacing her with his pistol. "I'll
get that much change out of all the money I've lavished
on you!" he yelled. "Tell me his name or I'll kill
you!"

She reached under her pillow, clutched a jewelled
watch and purse, and hurled them at him. She twisted
from her arm a gemmed bracelet, tore every flashing
ring from her fingers, and flung them in a handful
straight at his head.

"There's some more change for you!" she panted.
"Now, leave my bedroom!"

"I'll have that man's name first!"

The girl laughed in his distorted face. He was within an ace of shooting her—of firing point-blank into the lovely, flushed features, merely to shatter them, destroy, annihilate. He had the desire to do it. But her breathless, contemptuous laugh broke that impulse—relaxed it, leaving it flaccid. And after an interval something else intervened to stay his hand at the trigger—something that crept into his mind; something he had begun to suspect that she knew. Suddenly he became convinced that she *did* know it—that she believed that he dared not kill her and stand the investigation of a public trial before a *juge d'instruction*—that he could not afford to have his own personal affairs scrutinised too closely.

He still wanted to kill her—shoot her there where she sat in bed, watching him out of scornful young eyes. So intense was his need to slay—to disfigure, brutalise this girl who had mocked him, that the raging desire hurt him physically. He leaned back, resting against the silken wall, momentarily weakened by the violence of passion. But his pistol still threatened her.

No; he dared not. There was a better, surer way to utterly destroy her,—a way he had long ago prepared,—not expecting any such contingency as this, but merely as a matter of self-insurance.

His levelled weapon wavered, dropped, held loosely now. He still glared at her out of pallid and blood-shot eyes in silence. After a while:

"You hell-cat," he said slowly and distinctly. "Who is your English lover? Tell me his name or I'll beat your face to a pulp!"

"I have no English lover."

"Do you think," he went on heavily, disregarding her reply, "that I don't know why you chose an Englishman? You thought you could blackmail me, didn't you?"

"How?" she demanded wearily.

Again he ignored her reply:

"Is he one of the Embassy?" he demanded. "Is he some emissary of Grey's? Does he come from their intelligence department? Or is he only a police jackal? Or some lesser rat?"

She shrugged; her night-robe slipped and she drew it over her shoulder with a quick movement. And the man saw the deep blush spreading over face and throat.

"By God!" he said, "you *are* an actress! I admit it. But now you are going to learn something about real life. You think you've got me, don't you?—you and your Englishman? Because I have been fool enough to trust you—hide nothing from you—act frankly and openly in your presence. You thought you'd get a hold on me, so that if I ever caught you at your treacherous game you could defy me and extort from me the last penny! You thought all that out—very thriftily and cleverly—you and your Englishman between you—didn't you?"

"I don't know what you mean."

"Don't you? Then why did you ask me the other day whether it was not German money which was paying for the newspaper which I bought?"

"The *Mot d'Ordre*?"

"Certainly."

"I asked you that because Ferez Bey is notoriously in Germany's pay. And Ferez Bey financed the affair. You said so. Besides, you and he discussed it before me in my own salon."

"And you suspected that I bought the *Mot d'Ordre* with German money for the purpose of carrying out German propaganda in a Paris daily paper?"

"I don't know why Ferez Bey gave you the money to buy it."

"He did not give me the money."

"You said so. Who did?"

"*You!*" he fairly yelled.

"W-what!" stammered the girl, confounded.

"Listen to me, you rat!" he said fiercely. "I was not such a fool as you believed me to be. I lavished money on you; you made a fortune for yourself out of your popularity, too. Do you remember endorsing a cheque drawn to your order by Ferez Bey?"

"Yes. You had borrowed every penny I possessed. You said that Ferez Bey owed you as much. So I accepted his cheque——"

"That cheque paid for the *Mot d'Ordre*. It is drawn to your order; it bears your endorsement; the *Mot d'Ordre* was purchased in your name. And it was Max Freund who insisted that I take that precaution. Now, try to blackmail me!—you and your English spy!" he cried triumphantly, his voice breaking into a squeak.

Not yet understanding, merely conscious of some vague and monstrous danger, the girl sat motionless, regarding him intently out of beautiful, intelligent eyes.

He burst into laughter, made falsetto by the hysteria of sheer hatred:

"That's where you are now!" he said, leering down at her. "Every paper I ever made you sign incriminates you; your cancelled cheque is in the same packet; your *dossier* is damning and complete. You didn't know that Ferez Bey was sent across the frontier yesterday, did you? Your English spy didn't inform you last night, did he?"

"N-no."

"You lie! You *did* know it! That was why you

stole away last night and met your jackal—to sell him something besides yourself, this time! You knew they had arrested Ferez! I don't know how you knew it, but you did. And you told your lover. And both of you thought you had me at last, didn't you?"

"I—what are you trying to say to me—do to me?" she stammered, losing colour for the first time.

"Put you where you belong—you dirty spy!" he said with grinning ferocity. "If there is to be trouble, I've prepared for it. When they try you for espionage, they'll try you as a foreigner—a dancing girl in the pay of Germany—as my mistress whom Max Freund and I discover in treachery to France, and whom I instantly denounce to the proper authorities!"

He shoved his pistol into his breast pocket and put on his marred silk hat.

"Which do you think they will believe—you or the Count d'Eblis?" he demanded, the nervous leer twitching at his heavy lips. "Which do you think they will believe—your denials and counter-accusations against me, or Max Freund's corroboration, and the evidence of the packet I shall now deliver to the authorities—the packet containing every cursed document necessary to convict you!—you filthy little——"

The girl bounded from her bed to the floor, her dark eyes blazing:

"Damn you!" she said. "Get out of my bedroom!"

Taken aback, he retreated a pace or two, and, at the furious menace of the little clenched fist, stepped another pace out into the corridor. The door crashed in his face; the bolt shot home.

In twenty minutes Nihla Quellen, the celebrated and adored of European capitals, crept out of the street door. She wore the dress of a Finistère peasant; her hair was grey, her step infirm.

The *commissaire*, two *agents de police*, and a Government detective, one Souchez, already on their way to identify and arrest her, never even glanced at the shabby, infirm figure which hobbled past them on the sidewalk and feebly mounted an omnibus marked Gare du Nord.

For a long time Paris was carefully combed for the dancer, Nihla Quellen, until more serious affairs occupied the authorities, and presently the world at large. For, in a few weeks, war burst like a clap of thunder over Europe, leaving the whole world stunned and reeling. The dossier of Nihla Quellen, the dancing girl, was tossed into secret archives, together with the dossier of one Ferez Bey, an Eurasian, now far beyond French jurisdiction, and already very industrious in the United States about God knows what, in company with one Max Freund.

As for Monsieur the Count d'Eblis, he remained a senator, an owner of many third-rate decorations, and of the *Mot d'Ordre*.

And he remained on excellent terms with everybody at the Swedish, Greek, and Bulgarian legations, and the Turkish Embassy, too. And continued in cipher communication with Max Freund and Ferez Bey in America.

Otherwise, he was still president of the Numismatic Society of Spain, and he continued to add to his wonderful collection of coins, and to keep up his voluminous numismatic correspondence.

He was growing stouter, too, which increased his spinal waddle when he walked; and he became very prosperous financially, through fortunate "operations," as he explained, with one Bolo Pasha.

He had only one regret to interfere with his sleep and his digestion; he was sorry he had not fired his pistol into the youthful face of Nihla Quellen. He should have avenged himself, taken his chances, and above everything else he should have destroyed her beauty. His timidity and caution still caused him deep and bitter chagrin.

For nearly a year he heard absolutely nothing concerning her. Then one day a letter arrived from Feres Bey through Max Freund, both being in New York. And when, using his key to the cipher, he extracted the message it contained, he had learned, among other things, that Nihla Quellen was in New York, employed as a teacher in a school for dancing.

The gist of his reply to Feres Bey was that Nihla Quellen had already outlived her usefulness on earth, and that Max Freund should attend to the matter at the first favourable opportunity.

III

ON the edge of evening she came out of the Palace
of Mirrors and crossed the wet asphalt, which
already reflected primrose lights from a clearing western sky.

A few moments before, he had been thinking of her,
never dreaming that she was in America. But he knew
her instantly, there amid the rush and clatter of the
street, recognised her even in the twilight of the passing storm—perhaps not alone from the half-caught
glimpse of her shadowy, averted face, nor even from
that young, lissome figure so celebrated in Europe.
There is a sixth sense—the sense of nearness to what
is familiar. When it awakes we call it premonition.

The shock of seeing her, the moment's exciting incredulity, passed before he became aware that he was
already following her through swarming metropolitan
throngs released from the toil of a long, wet day in
early spring.

Through every twilit avenue poured the crowds;
through every cross-street a rosy glory from the west
was streaming; and in its magic he saw her immortally
transfigured, where the pink light suffused the cross-
ings, only to put on again her lovely mortality in the
shadowy avenue.

At Times Square she turned west, straight into the
dazzling fire of sunset, and he at her slender heels, not
knowing why, not even asking it of himself, not thinking, not caring.

A third figure followed them both.

The bronze giants south of them stirred, swung their great hammers against the iron bell; strokes of the hour rang out above the din of Herald Square, inaudible in the traffic roar another square away, lost, drowned out long before the pleasant bell-notes penetrated to Forty-second Street, into which they both had turned.

Yet, as though occultly conscious that some hour had struck on earth, significant to her, she stopped, turned, and looked back—looked quite through him, seeing neither him nor the one-eyed man who followed them both—as though her line of vision were the East itself, where, across the grey sea's peril, a thousand miles of cannon were sounding the hour from the North Sea to the Alps.

He passed her at her very elbow—aware of her nearness, as though suddenly close to a young orchard in April. The girl, too, resumed her way, unconscious of him, of his youthful face set hard with controlled emotion.

The one-eyed man followed them both.

A few steps further and she turned into the entrance to one of those sprawling, pretentious restaurants, the sham magnificence of which becomes grimy overnight. He halted, swung around, retraced his steps and followed her. And at his heels two shapes followed them very silently—her shadow and his own—so close together now, against the stucco wall that they seemed like Destiny and Fate linked arm in arm.

The one-eyed man halted at the door for a few moments. Then he, too, went in, dogged by his sinister shadow.

The red sunset's rays penetrated to the rotunda and were quenched there in a flood of artificial light; and there their sun-born shadows vanished, and three strange new shadows, twisted and grotesque, took their places.

She continued on into the almost empty restaurant, looming dimly beyond. He followed; the one-eyed man followed both.

The place into which they stepped was circular, centred by a waterfall splashing over concrete rocks. In the ruffled pool goldfish glimmered, nearly motionless, and mandarin ducks floated, preening exotic plumage. A wilderness of tables surrounded the pool, set for the expected patronage of the coming evening. The girl seated herself at one of these.

At the next table he found a place for himself, entirely unnoticed by her. The one-eyed man took the table behind them. A waiter presented himself to take her order; another waiter came up leisurely to attend to him. A third served the one-eyed man. There were only a few inches between the three tables. Yet the girl, deeply preoccupied, paid no attention to either man, although both kept their eyes on her.

But already, under the younger man's spellbound eyes, an odd and unforeseen thing was occurring: he gradually became aware that, almost imperceptibly, the girl and the table where she sat, and the sleepy waiter who was taking her orders, were slowly moving nearer to him on a floor which was moving, too.

He had never before been in that particular restaurant, and it took him a moment or two to realise that the floor was one of those trick floors, the central part of which slowly revolves.

Her table stood on the revolving part of the floor, his upon fixed terrain; and he now beheld her moving toward him, as the circle of tables rotated on its axis, which was the waterfall and pool in the middle of the restaurant.

A few people began to arrive—theatrical people, who are obliged to dine early. Some took seats at tables placed upon the revolving section of the floor, others preferred the outer circles, where he sat in a fixed position.

Her table was already abreast of his, with only the circular crack in the floor between them; he could easily have touched her.

As the distance began to widen between them, the girl, her gloved hands clasped in her lap, and studying the table-cloth with unseeing gaze, lifted her dark eyes —looked at him without seeing, and once more gazed through him at something invisible upon which her thoughts remained fixed—something absorbing, vital; perhaps tragic—for her face had become as colourless, now, as one of those translucent marbles, vaguely warmed by some buried vein of rose beneath the snowy surface.

Slowly she was being swept away from him—his gaze following—hers lost in concentrated abstraction.

He saw her slipping away, disappearing behind the noisy waterfall. Around him the restaurant continued to fill, slowly at first, then more rapidly after the orchestra had entered its marble gallery.

The music began with something Russian, plaintive at first, then beguiling, then noisy, savage in its brutal precision—something sinister—a trampling melody that was turning into thunder with the throb of doom all through it. And out of the vicious, Asiatic clangour, from behind the dash of too obvious waterfalls, glided the girl he had followed, now on her way toward him again, still seated at her table, still gazing at nothing out of dark, unseeing eyes.

42

It seemed to him an hour before her table approached his own again. Already she had been served by a waiter—was eating.

He became aware, then, that somebody had also served him. But he could not even pretend to eat, so preoccupied was he by her approach.

Scarcely seeming to move at all, the revolving floor was steadily drawing her table closer and closer to his. She was not looking at the strawberries which she was leisurely eating—did not lift her eyes as her table swept smoothly abreast of his.

Scarcely aware that he spoke aloud, he said:

"Nihla—Nihla Quellen! . . ."

Like a flash the girl wheeled in her chair to face him. She had lost all her colour. Her fork had dropped and a blood-red berry rolled over the table-cloth toward him.

"I'm sorry," he said, flushing. "I did not mean to startle you——"

The girl did not utter a word, nor did she move; but in her dark eyes he seemed to see her every sense concentrated upon him to identify his features, made shadowy by the lighted candles behind his head.

By degrees, smoothly, silently, her table swept nearer, nearer, bringing with it her chair, her slender person, her dark, intelligent eyes, so unsmilingly and steadily intent on him.

He began to stammer:

"—Two years ago—at—the Villa Tresse d'Or—on the Seine. . . . And we promised to see each other—in the morning——"

She said coolly:

"My name is Thessalie Dunois. You mistake me for another."

"No," he said, in a low voice, "I am not mistaken."

43

Her brown eyes seemed to plunge their clear regard into the depths of his very soul—not in recognition, but in watchful, dangerous defiance.

He began again, still stammering a trifle:

"—In the morning, we were to—to meet—at eleven —near the fountain of Marie de Médicis—unless you do not care to remember——"

At that her gaze altered swiftly, melted into the exquisite relief of recognition. Suspended breath, released, parted her blanched lips; her little guardian heart, relieved of fear, beat more freely.

"Are you Garry?"

"Yes."

"I know you now," she murmured. "You are Garret Barres, of the rue d'Eryx . . . You are Garry!" A smile already haunted her dark young eyes; colour was returning to lip and cheek. She drew a deep, noiseless breath.

The table where she sat continued to slip past him; the distance between them was widening. She had to turn her head a little to face him.

"You do remember me then, Nihla?"

The girl inclined her head a trifle. A smile curved her lips—lips now vivid but still a little tremulous from the shock of the encounter.

"May I join you at your table?"

She smiled, drew a deeper breath, looked down at the strawberry on the cloth, looked over her shoulder at him.

"You owe me an explanation," he insisted, leaning forward to span the increasing distance between them.

"Do I?"

"Ask yourself."

After a moment, still studying him, she nodded as

though the nod answered some silent question of her own:

"Yes, I owe you one."

"Then may I join you?"

"My table is more prudent than I. It is running away from an explanation." She fixed her eyes on her tightly clasped hands, as though to concentrate thought. He could see only the back of her head, white neck and lovely dark hair.

Her table was quite a distance away when she turned, leisurely, and looked back at him.

"May I come?" he asked.

She lifted her delicate brows in demure surprise.

"I've been waiting for you," she said amiably.

The one-eyed man had never taken his eyes off them.

IV

DUSK

SHE had offered him her hand; he had bent over it, seated himself, and they smilingly exchanged the formal banalities of a pleasantly renewed acquaintance.

A waiter laid a cover for him. She continued to concern herself, leisurely, with her strawberries.

"When did you leave Paris?" she enquired.

"Nearly two years ago."

"Before war was declared?"

"Yes, in June of that year."

She looked up at him very seriously; but they both smiled as she said:

"It was a momentous month for you then—the month of June, 1914?"

"Very. A charming young girl broke my heart in 1914; and so I came home, a wreck—to recuperate."

At that she laughed outright, glancing at his youthful, sunburnt face and lean, vigorous figure.

"When did *you* come over?" he asked curiously.

"I have been here longer than you have. In fact, I left France the day I last saw you."

"The same day?"

"I started that very same day—shortly after sunrise. I crossed the Belgian frontier that night, and I sailed for New York the morning after. I landed here a week later, and I've been here ever since. That, monsieur, is my history."

46

"You've been here in New York for two years!" he repeated in astonishment. "Have you really left the stage then? I supposed you had just arrived to fill an engagement here."

"They gave me a try-out this afternoon."

"*You!* A try-out!" he exclaimed, amazed.

She carelessly transfixed a berry with her fork:

"If I secure an engagement I shall be very glad to fill it . . . and my stomach, also. If I don't secure one—well—charity or starvation confronts me."

He smiled at her with easy incredulity.

"I had not heard that you were here!" he repeated. "I've read nothing at all about you in the papers——"

"No. . . . I am here incognito. . . . I have taken my sister's name. After all, your American public does not know me."

"But——"

"Wait! I don't wish it to know me!"

"But if you——"

The girl's slight gesture checked him, although her smile became humorous and friendly:

"Please! We need not discuss my future. Only the past!" She laughed: "How it all comes back to me now, as you speak—that crazy evening of ours together! What children we were—two years ago!"

Smilingly she clasped her hands together on the table's edge, regarding him with that winning directness which was a celebrated part of her celebrated personality; and happened to be natural to her.

"Why did I not recognise you immediately?" she demanded of herself, frowning in self-reproof. "I *am* stupid! Also, I have, now and then, thought about you——" She shrugged her shoulders, and again her face faltered subtly:

"Much has happened to distract my memories," she

47

added carelessly, impaling a strawberry, "—since you and I took the key to the fields and the road to the moon—like the pair of irresponsibles we were that night in June."

"Have you really had trouble?"

Her slim figure straightened as at a challenge, then became adorably supple again; and she rested her elbows on the table's edge and took her cheeks between her hands.

"Trouble?" she repeated, studying his face. "I don't know that word, trouble. I don't admit such a word to the honour of my happy vocabulary."

They both laughed a little.

She said, still looking at him, and at first speaking as though to herself:

"Of course, you are that same, delightful Garry! My youthful American accomplice! . . . Quite unspoiled, still, but very, very irresponsible . . . like all painters—like all students. And the mischief which is in me recognised the mischief in you, I suppose. . . . I *did* surprise you that night, didn't I? . . . And what a night! What a moon! And how we danced there on the wet lawn until my skirts and slippers and stockings were drenched with dew! . . . And how we laughed! Oh, that full-hearted, full-throated laughter of ours! How wonderful that we have lived to laugh like that! It is something to remember after death. Just think of it!—you and I, absolute strangers, dancing every dance there in the drenched grass to the music that came through the open windows. . . . And do you remember how we hid in the flowering bushes when my sister and the others came out to look for me? How they called, 'Nihla! Nihla! Little devil, where are you?' Oh, it *was* funny—funny! And to see *him* come out on the lawn—do you remember? He looked so fat and stupid and anxious and bad-tempered! And you and I expiring with stifled laughter! And he, with his sash, his decorations and his academic palms! He'd have shot us both, you know. . . ."

They were laughing unrestrainedly now at the memory of that impossible night a year ago; and the girl seemed suddenly transformed into an irresponsible gamine of eighteen. Her eyes grew brighter with mischief and laughter—laughter, the greatest magician and doctor emeritus of them all! The immortal restorer of youth and beauty.

Bluish shadows had gone from under her lower lashes; her eyes were starry as a child's.

"Oh, Garry," she gasped, laying one slim hand across his on the table-cloth, "it was one of those encounters —one of those heavenly accidents that reconcile one to living. . . . I think the moon had made me a perfect lunatic. . . . Because you don't yet know what I risked. . . . Garry! . . . It ruined me—ruined me utterly—our night together under the June moon!"

"What!" he exclaimed, incredulously.

But she only laughed her gay, undaunted little laugh:

"It was worth it! Such moments are worth anything we pay for them! I laughed; I pay. What of it?"

"But if I am partly responsible I wish to know——"

"You shall know nothing about it! As for me, I care nothing about it. I'd do it again to-night! That is living—to go forward, laugh, and accept what comes —to have heart enough, gaiety enough, brains enough to seize the few rare dispensations that the niggardly gods fling across this calvary which we call life! *That,* that alone is living; the rest is making the endless stations on bleeding knees."

"Yet, if I thought——" he began, perplexed and trou-, bled, "——if I thought that through my folly——"

"Folly! *Non pas!* Wisdom! Oh, my blessed accomplice! And do you remember the canoe? Were we indeed quite mad to embark for Paris on the moonlit Seine, you and I?—I in evening gown, soaked with dew to the knees!—you with your sketching block and easel! *Quelle déménagement en famille!* Oh, Garry, my friend of gayer days, was that really folly! No, no, no, it was infinite wisdom; and its memory is helping me to live through this very moment!"

She leaned there on her elbows and laughed across the cloth at him. The mockery began to dance again and glimmer in her eyes:

"After all I've told you," she added, "you are no wiser, are you? You don't know why I never went to the Fountain of Marie de Médicis—whether I forgot to go—whether I remembered but decided that I had had quite enough of you. You don't know, do you?"

He shook his head, smiling. The girl's face grew gradually serious:

"And you never heard anything more about me?" she demanded.

"No. Your name simply disappeared from the billboards, kiosques, and newspapers."

"And you heard no malicious gossip? None about my sister, either?"

"None."

She nodded:

"Europe is a senile creature which forgets overnight. *Tant mieux.* . . . You know, I shall sing and dance under my sister's name here. I told you that, didn't I?"

"Oh! That would be a great mistake——"

"Listen! Nihla Quellen disappeared—married some fat bourgeois, died, perhaps,"—she shrugged,—"anything you wish, my friend. Who cares to listen to what is said about a dancing girl in all this din of war? Who is interested?"

It was scarcely a question, yet her eyes seemed to make it so.

"Who cares?" she repeated impatiently. "Who remembers?"

" I have remembered you," he said, meeting her intently questioning gaze.

"You? Oh, you are not like those others over there. Your country is not at war. You still have leisure to remember. But they forget. They haven't time to remember anything—anybody—over there. Don't you think so?" She turned in her chair unconsciously, and gazed eastward. "—They have forgotten me over there—" And her lips tightened, contracted, bitten into silence.

The strange beauty of the girl left him dumb. He was recalling, now, all that he had ever heard concerning her. The gossip of Europe had informed him that, though Nihla Quellen was passionately and devotedly French in soul and heart, her mother had been one of those unmoral and lovely Georgians, and her father an Alsatian, named Dunois—a French officer who entered the Russian service ultimately, and became a hunting cheetah for the Grand Duke Cyril, until himself hunted into another world by that old bag of bones on the pale and shaky nag. His daughter took the name of Nihla Quellen and what money was left, and made her début in Constantinople.

As the young fellow sat there watching her, all the petty gossip of Europe came back to him—anecdotes, panegyrics, eulogies, scandals, stage chatter, Quarter "divers," paid réclames—all that he had ever read and heard about this notorious young girl, now seated there across the table, with her pretty head framed by slender, unjewelled fingers. He remembered the gems she had worn that June night, a year ago, and their magnificence.

"Well," she said, "life is a pleasantry, a jest, a bon-mot flung over his shoulder by some god too drunk with nectar to invent a better joke. Life is an Olympian epigram made between immortal yawns. What do you think of my epigram, Garry?"

"I think you are just as clever and amusing as I remember you, Nihla."

"Amusing to you, perhaps. But I don't entertain myself very successfully. I don't think poverty is a very funny joke. Do you?"

"Poverty!" he repeated, smiling his unbelief.

She smiled too, displayed her pretty, ringless hands humorously, for his inspection, then framed her oval face between them again and made a deliberate grimace.

"All gone," she said. "I am, as you say, here on my uppers."

"I can't understand, Nihla——"

"Don't try to. It doesn't concern you. Also, please forget me as Nihla Quellen. I told you that I've taken my sister's name, Thessalie Dunois."

"But all Europe knows you as Nihla Quellen——"

"Listen!" she interrupted sharply. "I have troubles enough. Don't add to them, or I shall be sorry I met you again. I tell you my name is Thessa. Please remember it."

"Very well," he said, reddening under the rebuke.

She noted the painful colour in his face, then looked elsewhere, indifferently. Her features remained expressionless for a while. After a few moments she looked around at him again, and her smile began to glimmer:

"It's only this," she said; "the girl you met once in

your life—the dancing singing-girl they knew over there—is already an episode to be forgotten. End her career any way you wish, Garry,—natural death, suicide—or she can repent and take the veil, if you like —or perish at sea—only end her. . . ; Please?" she added, with the sweet, trailing inflection characteristic of her.

He nodded. The girl smiled mischievously.

"Don't nod your head so owlishly and pretend to understand. You don't understand. Only two or three people do. And I hope they'll believe me dead, even if you are not polite enough to agree with them."

"How can you expect to maintain your incognito?" he insisted. "There will be plenty of people in your very first audience——"

"I had a sister, did I not?"

"*Was* she your sister?—the one who danced with you—the one called Thessa?"

"No. But the play-bills said she was. Now, I've told you something that nobody knows except two or three unpleasant devils——" She dropped her arms on the table and leaned a trifle forward:

"Oh, pouf!" she said. "Don't let's be mysterious and dramatic, you and I. I'll tell you: I gave that woman the last of my jewels and she promised to disappear and leave her name to me to use. It was my own name, anyway, Thessalie Dunois. Now, you know. Be as discreet and nice as I once found you. Will you?"

"Of course."

" 'Of course,' " she repeated, smiling, and with a little twitch of her shoulders, as though letting fall a burdensome cloak. "Allons! With a free heart, then! I am Thessalie Dunois; I am here; I am poor—don't be frightened! I shall not borrow——"

"That's rotten, Thessa!" he said, turning very red.

"Oh, go lightly, please, my friend Garry. I have no claim on you. Besides, I know men——"

"You don't appear to!"

"Tiens! Our first quarrel!" she exclaimed, laughingly. "This is indeed serious——"

"If you need aid——"

"No, I don't! Please, why do you scowl at me? Do you then wish I needed aid? Yours? Allez, Monsieur Garry, if I did I'd venture, perhaps, to say so to you. Does that make amends?" she added sweetly.

She clasped her white hands on the cloth and looked at him with that engaging, humorous little air which had so easily captivated her audiences in Europe—that, and her voice with the hint of recklessness ever echoing through its sweetness and youthful gaiety.

"What are you doing in New York?" she asked. "Painting?"

"I have a studio, but——"

"But no clients? Is that it? Pouf! Everybody begins that way. I sang in a café at Dijon for five francs and my soup! At Rennes I nearly starved. Oh, yes, Garry, in spite of a number of obliging gentlemen who, like you, offered—first aid——"

"That is absolutely rotten of you, Thessa. Did I ever——"

"No! For goodness' sake let me jest with you without flying into tempers!"

"But——"

"Oh, pouf! I shall not quarrel with you! Whatever you and I were going to say during the next ten minutes shall remain unsaid! . . . Now, the ten minutes are over; now, we're reconciled and you are in good humour again. And now, tell me about yourself, your painting—in other words, tell me the things about yourself that would interest a friend."

"Are you?"

"Your friend? Yes, I am—if you wish."

"I do wish it."

"Then I am your friend. I once had a wonderful evening with you. . . . I'm having a very good time now. You were *nice* to me, Garry. I really was sorry not to see you again."

"At the fountain of Marie de Médicis," he said reproachfully.

"Yes. Flatter yourself, monsieur, because I did *not* forget our rendezvous. I might have forgotten it easily enough—there was sufficient excuse, God knows—a girl awakened by the crash of ruin—springing out of bed to face the end of the world without a moment's warning—yes, the end of all things—death, too! Tenez, it was permissible to forget our rendezvous under such circumstances, was it not? But—I did *not* forget. I thought about it in a dumb, calm way all the while—even while *he* stood there denouncing me, threatening me, noisy, furious—with the button of the Legion in his lapel—and an ugly pistol which he waved in the air—" She laughed:

"Oh, it was not at all gay, I assure you. . . . And even when I took to my heels after he had gone—for it was a matter of life or death, and I hadn't a minute to lose—oh, very dramatic, of course, for I ran away in disguise and I had a frightful time of it leaving France! Well, even then, at top speed and scared to death, I remembered the fountain of Marie de Médicis, and you. Don't be too deeply flattered. I remembered these items principally because they had caused my downfall."

"I? I caused——"

"No. *I* caused it! It was I who went out on the lawn. It was I who came across to see who was painting by moonlight. That began it—seeing you there—in moonlight bright enough to read by—bright enough to paint by. Oh, Garry—and you were *so* good-looking! It was the moon—and the way you smiled at me. And they all were dancing inside, and *he* was so big and fat and complacent, dancing away in there! . . . And so I fell a prey to folly."

"Was it really our escapade that—that ruined you?"

"Well—it was partly that. Pouf! It is over. And I am here. So are you. It's been nice to see you. . . . Please call our waiter." She glanced at her cheap, leather wrist watch.

As they rose and left the dining-room, he asked her if they were not to see each other again. A one-eyed man, close behind them, listened for her reply.

She continued to walk on slowly beside him without answering, until they reached the rotunda.

"Do you wish to see me again?" she enquired abruptly.

"Don't you also wish it?"

"I don't know, Garry. . . . I've been annoyed in New York—bothered—seriously. . . . I can't explain, but somehow—I don't seem to wish to begin a friendship with anybody. . . ."

"Ours began two years ago."

"Did it?"

"Did it not, Thessa?"

"Perhaps. . . . I don't know. After all—it doesn't matter. I think—I think we had better say good-bye—until some happy hazard—like to-day's encounter—" She hesitated, looked up at him, laughed:

"Where is your studio?" she asked mischievously.

The one-eyed man at their heels was listening.

V

THERE was a young moon in the southwest—a slender tracery in the April twilight—curved high over his right shoulder as he walked northward and homeward through the flare of Broadway.

His thoughts were still occupied with the pleasant excitement of his encounter with Thessalie Dunois; his mind and heart still responded to the delightful stimulation. Out of an already half-forgotten realm of romance, where, often now, he found it increasingly difficult to realise that he had lived for five happy years, a young girl had suddenly emerged as bodily witness, to corroborate, revive, and refresh his fading faith in the reality of what once had been.

Five years in France!—France with its clear sun and lovely moon; it silver-grey cities, its lilac haze, its sweet, deep greenness, its atmosphere of living light!—France, the dwelling-place of God in all His myriad aspects—in all His protean forms! France, the sanctuary of Truth and all her ancient and her future liberties; France, blossoming domain of Love in Love's million exquisite transfigurations, wherein only the eye of faith can recognise the winged god amid his camouflage!

Wine-strong winds of the Western World, and a pitiless Western sun which etches every contour with terrible precision, leaving nothing to imagination—no deli-

cate mystery to rest and shelter souls—had swept away
and partly erased from his mind the actuality of those
five past years.

Already that past, of which he had been a part, was
becoming disturbingly unreal to him.   Phantoms
haunted its ever-paling sunlight; its scenes were fading; its voices grew vague and distant; its hushed
laughter dwindled to a whisper, dying like a sigh.

Then, suddenly, against that misty tapestry of tinted
spectres, appeared Thessalie Dunois in the flesh!—
straight out of the phantom-haunted void had stepped
this glowing thing of life! Into the raw reek and familiar dissonance of Broadway she had vanished. Small
wonder that he had followed her to keep in touch with
the vanishing past, as a sleeper, waking against his will,
strives still to grasp the fragile fabric of a happy
dream.

Yet, in spite of Thessalie, in spite of dreams, in spite
of his own home-coming, and the touch of familiar
pavements under his own feet, the past, to Barres, was
utterly dead, the present strange and unreal, the future
obscure and all aflame behind a world afire with war.

For two years, now, no human mind in America had
been able to adjust itself to the new heaven and the
new earth which had sprung into lurid being at the
thunderclap of war.

All things familiar had changed in the twinkling of
an eye; all former things had passed away, leaving the
stunned brain of humanity dulled under the shock.

Slowly, by degrees, the world was beginning to realise
that the civilisation of Christ was being menaced once
again by a resurgence from that ancient land of legend
where the wild Hun denned;—that again the endless
hordes of barbarians were rushing in on Europe out
of their Eastern fastnesses—hordes which filled the

shrinking skies with their clamour, vaunting the might of Baal, cheering their antichrist, drenching the knees of their own red gods with the blood of little children.

It seemed impossible for Americans to understand that these things could be—were really true—that the horrors the papers printed were actualities happening to civilised people like themselves and their neighbours.

Out of their own mouths the German tribes thundered their own disgrace and condemnation, yet America sat dazed, incredulous, motionless. Emperor and general, professor and junker, shouted at the top of their lungs the new creed, horrible as the Black Mass, reversing every precept taught by Christ.

Millions of Teuton mouths cheered fiercely for the new religion—Frightfulness; worshipped with frantic yells the new trinity—Wotan, Kaiser and Brute Strength.

Stunnned, blinded, deafened, the Western World, still half-paralysed, stirred stiffly from its inertia. Slowly, mechanically, its arteries resumed their functions; the reflex, operating automatically, started trade again in its old channels; old habits were timidly resumed; minds groped backward, searching for severed threads which connected yesterday with to-day—groped, hunted, found nothing, and, perplexed, turned slowly toward the smoke-choked future for some reason for it all—some outlook.

There was no explanation, no outlook—nothing save dust and flame and the din of Teutonic hordes trampling to death the Son of Man.

So America moved about her worn, deep-trodden and familiar ways, her mind slowly clearing from the cataclysmic concussion, her power of vision gradually returning, adjusting itself, little by little, to this new heaven and new earth and this hell entirely new.

The *Lusitania* went down; the Great Republic merely quivered. Other ships followed; only a low murmur of pain came from the Western Colossus.

But now, after the second year, through the thickening nightmare the Great Republic groaned aloud; and a new note of menace sounded in her drugged and dreary voice.

And the thick ears of the Hun twitched and he paused, squatting belly-deep in blood, to listen.

Barres walked homeward. Somewhere along in the 40's he turned eastward into one of those cross-streets originally built up of brownstone dwelling houses, and now in process of transformation into that architectural and commercial miscellany which marks the transition stage of the metropolis anywhere from Westchester to the sea.

Altered for business purposes, basements displayed signs and merchandise of bootmakers, dealers in oriental porcelains, rare prints, silverware; parlour windows modified into bay windows, sheeted with plate-glass, exposed, perhaps, feminine headgear, or an expensive model gown or two, or the sign of a real-estate man, or of an upholsterer.

Above the parlour floors lived people of one sort or another; furnished and unfurnished rooms and suites prevailed; and the brownstone monotony was already indented along the building line by brand-new constructions of Indiana limestone, behind the glittering plate-glass of which were to be seen reticent displays of artistic furniture, modern and antique oil paintings, here and there the lace-curtained den of some superior ladies' hair-dresser, where beautifying also was accomplished at a price, alas!

Halfway between Sixth Avenue and Fifth, on the

north side of the street, an enterprising architect had purchased half a dozen squatty, three-storied houses, set back from the sidewalk behind grass-plots. These had been lavishly stuccoed and transformed into abodes for those irregulars in the army of life known as "artists."

In the rear the back fences had been levelled; six corresponding houses on the next street had been purchased; a sort of inner court established, with a common grass-plot planted with trees and embellished by a number of concrete works of art, battered statues, sundials, and well-curbs.

Always the army of civilisation trudges along screened, flanked, and tagged after by life's irregulars, who cannot or will not conform to routine. And these are always roaming around seeking their own cantonments, where, for a while, they seem content to dwell at the end of one more aimless étape through the world —not in regulation barracks, but in regions too unconventional, too inconvenient to attract others.

Of this sort was the collection of squatty houses, forming a "community," where, in the neighbourhood of other irregulars, Garret Barres dwelt; and into the lighted entrance of which he now turned, still exhilarated by his meeting with Thessalie Dunois.

The architectural agglomeration was known as Dragon Court—a faïence Fu-dog above the electric light over the green entrance door furnishing that priceless idea—a Fu-dog now veiled by mesh-wire to provide against the indiscretions of sparrows lured thither by housekeeping possibilities lurking among the dense screens of Japanese ivy covering the façade.

Larry Soane, the irresponsible superintendent, always turned gardener with April's advent in Dragon Court, contributions from its denizens enabling him to pepper a few flower-beds with hyacinths and tulips, and later with geraniums. These former bulbs had now gratefully appeared in promising thickets, and Barres saw the dark form of the handsome, reckless-looking Irishman fussing over them in the lantern-lit dusk, while his little daughter, Dulcie, kneeling on the dim grass, caressed the first blue hyacinth blossom with thin, childish fingers.

Barres glanced into his letter-box behind the desk, above which a drop-light threw more shadows than illumination. Little Dulcie Soane was supposed to sit under it and emit information, deliver and receive letters, pay charges on packages, and generally supervise things when she was not attending school.

There were no letters for the young man. He examined a package, found it contained his collars from the laundry, tucked them under his left arm, and walked to the door looking out upon the dusky interior court.

"Soane," he said, "your garden begins to look very fine." He nodded pleasantly to Dulcie, and the child responded to his friendly greeting with the tired but dauntless smile of the young who are missing those golden years to which all childhood has a claim.

Dulcie's three cats came strolling out of the dusk across the lamplit grass—a coal black one with sea-green eyes, known as "The Prophet," and his platonic mate, white as snow, and with magnificent azure-blue eyes which, in white cats, usually betokens total deafness. She was known as "The Houri" to the irregulars of Dragon Court. The third cat, unanimously but misleadingly christened "Strindberg" by the dwellers in Dragon Court, has already crooked her tortoise-shell tail and was tearing around in eccentric circles or darting halfway up trees in a manner characteristic, and possibly accounting for the name, if not for the sex.

"Thim cats of the kid's," observed Soane, "do be scratchin' up the plants all night long—bad cess to thim! Barrin' thim three omadhauns yonder, I'd show ye a purty bed o' poisies, Misther Barres. But Sthrin'-berg, God help her, is f'r diggin' through to China."

Dulcie impulsively caressed the Prophet, who turned his solemn, incandescent eyes on Barres. The Houri also looked at him, then, intoxicated by the soft spring evening, rolled lithely upon the new grass and lay there twitching her snowy tail and challenging the stars out of eyes that matched their brilliance.

Dulcie got up and walked slowly across the grass to where Barres stood:

"May I come to see you this evening?" she asked, diffidently, and with a swift, sidelong glance toward her father.

"Ah, then, don't be worritin' him!" grumbled Soane. "Hasn't Misther Barres enough to do, what with all thim idees he has slitherin' in his head, an' all the books an' learnin' an' picters he has to think of—whithout the likes of you at his heels every blessed minute, day an' night!——"

"But he always lets me——" she remonstrated.

"G'wan, now, and lave the poor gentleman be! Quit your futtherin' an' muttherin'. G'wan in the house, ye little scut, an' see what there is f'r ye to do!——"

"What's the matter with you, Soane?" interrupted Barres good-humouredly. "Of course she can come up if she wants to. Do you feel like paying me a visit, Dulcie, before you go to bed?"

"Yes," she nodded diffidently.

"Well, come ahead then, Sweetness! And whenever you want to come you say so. Your father knows well enough I like to have you."

He smiled at Dulcie; the child's shy preference for his society always had amused him. Besides, she was always docile and obedient; and she was very sensitive, too, never outwearing her welcome in his studio, and always leaving without a murmur when, looking up from book or drawing he would exclaim cheerfully: "Now, Sweetness! Time's up! Bed for yours, little lady!"

It had been a very gradual acquaintance between them—more than two years in developing. From his first pleasant nod to her when he first came to live in Dragon Court, it had progressed for a few months, conservatively on her part, and on his with a detached but kindly interest born of easy sympathy for youth and loneliness.

But he had no idea of the passionate response he was stirring in the motherless, neglected child—of what hunger he was carelessly stimulating, what latent qualities and dormant characteristics he was arousing.

Her appearance, one evening, in her night-dress at his studio doorway, accompanied by her three cats, began to enlighten him in regard to her mental starvation. Tremulous, almost at the point of tears, she had asked for a book and permission to remain for a few moments in the studio. He had rung for Selinda, ordered fruit, cake, and a glass of milk, and had installed Dulcie upon the sofa with a lapful of books. That was the beginning.

But Barres still did not entirely understand what particular magnet drew the child to his studio. The place was full of beautiful things, books, rugs, pictures, fine old furniture, cabinets glimmering with porcelains, ivories, jades, Chinese crystals. These all, in minutest detail, seemed to fascinate the girl. Yet, after giving her permission to enter whenever she desired, often while reading or absorbed in other affairs, he became conscious of being watched; and, glancing up, would frequently surprise her sitting there very silently, with an open book on her knees, and her strange grey eyes intently fixed on him.

Then he would always smile and say something friendly; and usually forget her the next moment in his absorption of whatever work he had under way.

Only one other man inhabiting Dragon Court ever took the trouble to notice or speak to the child—James Westmore, the sculptor. And he was very friendly in his vigorous, jolly, rather boisterous way, catching her up and tossing her about as gaily and irresponsibly as though she were a rag doll; and always telling her he was her adopted godfather and would have to chastise her if she ever deserved it. Also, he was always urging her to hurry and grow up, because he had a wedding present for her. And though Dulcie's smile was friendly, and Westmore's nonsense pleased the shy child, she merely submitted, never made any advance.

Barres's ménage was accomplished by two specimens of mankind, totally opposite in sex and colour: Selinda, a blonde, slant-eyed, and very trim Finn, doing duty as maid; and Aristocrates W. Johnson, lately employed in the capacity of waiter on a dining-car by the New York Central Railroad—tall, dignified, graceful, and Ethiopian—who cooked as daintily as a débutante trifling with culinary duty, and served at table with the languid condescension of a dilettante and wealthy amateur of domestic arts.

Barres ascended the two low, easy flights of stairs and unlocked his door. Aristocrates, setting the table in the dining-room, approached gracefully and relieved his master of hat, coat, and stick.

Half an hour later, a bath and fresh linen keyed up his already lively spirits; he whistled while he tied his tie, took a critical look at himself, and, dropping both hands into the pockets of his dinner jacket, walked out into the big studio, which also was his living-room.

There was a piano there; he sat down and rattled off a rollicking air from the most recent spring production, beginning to realise that he was keyed up for something livelier than a solitary dinner at home.

His hands fell from the keys and he swung around on the piano stool and looked into the dining-room rather doubtfully.

"Aristocrates!" he called.

The tall pullman butler sauntered gracefully in.

Barres gave him a telephone number to call. Aristocrates returned presently with the information that the lady was not at home.

"All right. Try Amsterdam 6706. Ask for Miss Souval."

But Miss Souval, also, was out.

Barres possessed a red-leather covered note-book; he went to his desk and got it; and under his direction Aristocrates called up several numbers, reporting adversely in every case.

It was a fine evening; ladies were abroad or preparing to fulfil engagements wisely made on such a day as this had been. And the more numbers he called up the lonelier the young man began to feel.

Thessalie had not given him either her address or telephone number. It would have been charming to have her dine with him. He was now thoroughly inclined for company. He glanced at the empty dining-room with aversion.

"All right; never mind," he said, dismissing Aristocrates, who receded as lithely as though leading a cake-walk.

"The devil," muttered the young fellow. "I'm not going to dine here alone. I've had too happy a day of it."

He got up restlessly and began to pace the studio. He knew he could get some man, but he didn't want one. However, it began to look like that or a solitary dinner.

So after a few more moments' scowling cogitation he went out and down the stairs, with the vague idea of inviting some brother painter—any one of the regular irregulars who inhabited Dragon Court.

Dulcie sat behind the little desk near the door, head bowed, her thin hands clasped over the closed ledger, and in her pallid face the expressionless dullness of a child forgotten.

"Hello, Sweetness!" he said cheerfully.

She looked up; a slight colour tinted her cheeks, and she smiled.

"What's the matter, Dulcie?"

"Nothing."

"Nothing? That's a very dreary malady—nothing. You look lonely. Are you?"

"I don't know."

"You don't know whether you are lonely or not?" he demanded.

"I suppose I am," she ventured, with a shy smile.

"Where is your father?"

"He went out."

"Any letters for me—or messages?"

"A man—he had one eye—came. He asked who you are."

"What?"

"I think he was German. He had only one eye. He asked your name."

"What did you say?"

"I told him. Then he went away."

Barres shrugged:

"Somebody who wants to sell artists' materials," he concluded. Then he looked at the girl: "So you're lonely, are you? Where are your three cats? Aren't they company for you?"

"Yes. . . ."

"Well, then," he said gaily, "why not give a party for them? That ought to amuse you, Dulcie."

The child still smiled; Barres walked on past her a pace or two, halted, turned irresolutely, arrived at some swift decision, and came back, suddenly understanding that he need seek no further—that he had discovered his guest of the evening at his very elbow.

"Did you and your father have your supper, Dulcie?"

"My father went out to eat at Grogan's."

"How about you?"

"I can find something."

"Why not dine with me?" he suggested.

The child stared, bewildered, then went a little pale.

"Shall we have a dinner party for two—you and I, Dulcie? What do you say?"

She said nothing, but her big grey eyes were fixed on him in a passion of inquiry.

"A real party," he repeated. "Let the people get their own mail and packages until your father returns. Nobody's going to sneak in, anyway. Or, if that won't do, I'll call up Grogan's and tell your father to come back because you are going to dine in my studio with me. Do you know the telephone number? Very well; get Grogan's for me. I'll speak to your father."

Dulcie's hand trembled on the receiver as she called up Grogan's; Barres bent over the transmitter:

"Soane, Dulcie is going to take dinner in my studio with me. You'll have to come back on duty, when you've eaten." He hung up, looked at Dulcie and laughed.

"I wanted company as much as you did," he confessed. "Now, go and put on your prettiest frock, and we'll be very grand and magnificent. And afterward we'll talk and look at books and pretty things—and maybe we'll turn on the Victrola and I'll teach you to dance—" He had already begun to ascend the stairs:

"In half an hour, Dulcie!" he called back; "—and you may bring the Prophet if you like. . . . Shall I ask Mr. Westmore to join us?"

"I'd rather be all alone with you," she said shyly.

He laughed and ran on up the stairs.

In half an hour the electric bell rang very timidly. Aristocrates, having been instructed and rehearsed, and, loftily condescending to his rôle in a kindly comedy to be played seriously, announced: "Miss Soane!" in his most courtly manner.

Barres threw aside the evening paper and came forward, taking both hands of the white and slightly frightened child.

"Aristocrates ought to have announced the Prophet, too," he said gaily, breaking the ice and swinging Dulcie around to face the open door again.

The Prophet entered, perfectly at ease, his eyes of living jade shining, his tail urbanely hoisted.

Dulcie ventured to smile; Barres laughed outright; Aristocrates surveyed the Prophet with toleration mingled with a certain respect. For a black cat is never without occult significance to a gentleman of colour.

With Dulcie's hand still in his, Barres led her into the living-room, where, presently, Aristocrates brought a silver tray upon which was a glass of iced orange juice for Dulcie, and a "Bronnix," as Aristocrates called it, for the master.

"To your health and good fortune in life, Dulcie," he said politely.

The child gazed mutely at him over her glass, then, blushing, ventured to taste her orange juice.

When she finished, Barres drew her frail arm through his and took her out, seating her. Ceremonies began in silence, and the master of the place was not quite sure whether the flush on Dulcie's face indicated unhappy embarrassment or pleasure.

He need not have worried: the child adored it all. The Prophet came in and gravely seated himself on a neighbouring chair, whence he could survey the table and seriously inspect each course.

"Dulcie," he said, "how grown-up you look with your bobbed hair put up, and your fluffy gown."

She lifted her enchanted eyes to him:

"It is my first communion dress. . . . I've had to make it longer for a graduation dress."

"Oh, that's so; you're graduating this summer!"

"Yes."

"And what then?"

"Nothing." She sighed unconsciously and sat very still with folded hands, while Aristocrates refilled her glass of water.

She no longer felt embarrassed; her gravity matched Aristocrates's; she seriously accepted whatever was offered or set before her, but Barres noticed that she ate it all, merely leaving on her plate, with inculcated and mathematical precision, a small portion as concession to good manners.

They had, toward the banquet's end, water ices, bonbons, French pastry, and ice cream. And presently a slight and blissful sigh of repletion escaped the child's red lips. The symptoms were satisfactory but unmistakable; Dulcie was perfectly feminine; her capacity had proven it.

The Prophet's stately self-control in the fragrant vicinity of nourishment was now to be rewarded: Barres conducted Dulcie to the studio and installed her among cushions upon a huge sofa. Then, lighting a cigarette, he dropped down beside her and crossed one knee over the other.

"Dulcie," he said in his lazy, humorous way, "it's a funny old world any way you view it."

"Do you think it is always funny?" inquired the child, her deep, grey eyes on his face.

He smiled:

"Yes, I do; but sometimes the joke in on one's self. And then, although it is still a funny world, from the world's point of view, you, of course, fail to see the humour of it. . . . I don't suppose you understand."

"I do," nodded the child, with the ghost of a smile.

"Really? Well, I was afraid I'd been talking nonsense, but if you understand, it's all right."

They both laughed.

"Do you want to look at some books?" he suggested.

"I'd rather listen to you."

He smiled:

"All right. I'll begin at this corner of the room and tell you about the things in it." And for a while he rambled lazily on about old French chairs and Spanish chests, and the panels of Mille Fleur tapestry which hung behind them; the two lovely pre-Raphael panels in their exquisite ancient frames; the old Venetian velvet covering triple choir-stalls in the corner; the ivory-

MICROCOPY RESOLUTION TEST CHART

(ANSI and ISO TEST CHART No. 2)

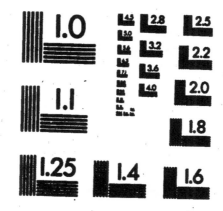

APPLIED IMAGE Inc

1653 East Main Street
Rochester, New York   14609   USA
(716) 482 - 0300 - Phone
(716) 288 - 5989 - Fax

toned marble figure on its wood and compos pedestal, where tendrils and delicate foliations of water gilt had become slightly irridescent, harmonising with the patine on the ancient Chinese garniture flanking a mantel clock of dullest gold.

About these things, their workmanship, the histories of their times, he told her in his easy, unaccented voice, glancing sideways at her from time to time to note how she stood it.

But she listened, fascinated, her gaze moving from the object discussed to the man who discussed it; her slim limbs curled under her, her hands clasped around a silken cushion made from the robe of some Chinese princess.

Lounging there beside her, amused, humorously flattered by her attention, and perhaps a little touched, he held forth a little longer.

"Is it a nice party, so far, Dulcie?" he concluded with a smile.

She flushed, found no words, nodded, and sat with lowered head as though pondering.

"What would you rather do if you could do what you want to in the world, Dulcie?"

"I don't know."

"Think a minute."

She thought for a while.

"Live with you," she said seriously.

"Oh, Dulcie! That is no sort of ambition for a growing girl!" he laughed; and she laughed, too, watching his every expression out of grey eyes that were her chiefest beauty.

"You're a little too young to know what you want yet," he concluded, still smiling. "By the time that bobbed mop of red hair grows to a proper length, you'll know more about yourself."

"Do you like it up?" she enquired naïvely.

"It makes you look older."

"I want it to."

"I suppose so," he nodded, noticing the snowy neck which the new coiffure revealed. It was becoming evident to him that Dulcie had her own vanities—little pathetic vanities which touched him as he glanced at the reconstructed first communion dress and the drooping hyacinth pinned at the waist, and the cheap white slippers on a foot as slenderly constructed as her long and narrow hands.

"Did your mother die long ago, Dulcie?"

"Yes."

"In America?"

"In Ireland."

"You look like her, I fancy—" thinking of Soane.

"I don't know."

Barres had heard Soane hold forth in his cups on one or two occasions—nothing more than the vague garrulousness of a Celt made more loquacious by the whiskey of one Grogan—something about his having been a gamekeeper in his youth, and that his wife— "God rest her!"—might have held up her head with "anny wan o' thim in th' Big House."

Recollecting this, he idly wondered what the story might have been—a young girl's perverse infatuation for her father's gamekeeper, perhaps—a handsome, common, ignorant youth, reckless and irresponsible enough to take advantage of her—probably some such story—resembling similar histories of chauffeurs, riding-masters, grooms, and coachmen at home.

The Prophet came noiselessly into the studio, stopped at sight of his little mistress, twitched his tail reflectively, then leaped onto a carved table and calmly began his ablutions.

Barres got up and wound up the Victrola. Then he kicked aside a rug or two.

"This is to be a real party, you know," he remarked. "You don't dance, do you?"

"Yes," she said diffidently, "a little."

"Oh! That's fine!" he exclaimed.

Dulcie got off the sofa, shook out her reconstructed gown. When he came over to where she stood, she laid her hand in his almost solemnly, so overpowering had become the heavenly sequence of events. For the rite of his hospitality had indeed become a rite to her. Never before had she stood in awe, enthralled before such an altar as this man's hearthstone. Never had she dreamed that he who so wondrously served it could look at such an offering as hers—herself.

But the miracle had happened; altar and priest were accepting her; she laid her hand, which trembled, in his; gave herself to his guidance and to the celestial music, scarcely seeing, scarcely hearing his voice.

"You dance delightfully," he was saying; "you're a born dancer, Dulcie. I do it fairly well myself, and I ought to know."

He was really very much surprised. He was enjoying it immensely. When the Victrola gave up the ghost he wound it again and came back to resume. Under his suggestions and tutelage, they tried more intricate steps, devious and ambitious, and Dulcie, unterrified by terpsichorean complications, surmounted every one with his whispered coaching and expert aid.

Now it came to a point where time was not for him. He was too interested, enjoying it too genuinely.

Sometimes, when they paused to enable him to resurrect the defunct music in the Victrola, they laughed at the Prophet, who sat upon the ancient carved table, gravely surveying them. Sometimes they rested because he thought she ought to—himself a trifle pumped —only to find, to his amasement, that he need not be solicitous concerning her.

A tall and ancient clock ringing midnight from clear, uncompromising bells, brought Barres to himself.

"Good Lord!" he exclaimed, "this won't do! Dear child, I'm having a wonderful time, but I've got to deliver y⁻u to your father!"

He drew her arm through his, laughingly pretending horror and haste; she fled lightly along beside him as he whisked her through the hall and down the stairs.

A candle burned on the desk. Soane sat there, asleep, and odorous of alcohol, his flushed face buried in his arms.

But Soane was what is known as a "sob-souse"; never ugly in his cups, merely inclined to weep over the immemorial wrongs of Ireland.

He woke up when Barres touched his shoulder, rubbed his swollen eyes and black, curly head, gazed tragically at his daughter:

"G'wan to bed, ye little scut!" he said, getting to his feet with a terrific yawn.

Barres took her hand:

"We've had a wonderful party, haven't we, Sweetness?"

"Yes," whispered the child.

The next instant she was gone like a ghost, through the dusky, whitewashed corridor where distorted shadows trembled in the candlelight.

"Soane," said Barres, "this won't do, you know. They'll sack you if you keep on drinking."

The man, not yet forty, a battered, middle-aged byproduct of hale and reckless vigour, passed his hands over his temples with the dignity of a Hibernian Hamlet:

"The harp that wanst through Tara's halls—" he began; but memory failed; and two tears—by-products, also, of Grogan's whiskey—sparkled in his reproachful eyes.

"I'm merely telling you," remarked Barres. "We all like you, Soane, but the landlord won't stand for it."

"May God forgive him," muttered Soane. "Was there ever a landlord but he was a tyrant, too?"

Barres blew out the candle; a faint light above the Fu-dog outside, over the street door, illuminated the stone hall.

"You ought to keep sober for your little daughter's sake," insisted Barres in a low voice. "You love her, don't you?"

"I do that!" said Soane—"God bless her and her poor mother, who could hould up her pretty head with anny wan till she tuk up with th' like o' me!"

His brogue always increased in his cups; devotion to Ireland and a lofty scorn of landlords grew with both.

"You'd better keep away from Grogan's," remarked Barres.

"I had a bite an' a sup at Grogan's. Is there anny harrm in that, sorr?"

"Cut out the 'sup,' Larry. Cut out that gang of bums at Grogan's, too. There are too many Germans hanging out around Grogan's these days. You Sinn Feiners or Clan-na-Gael, or whatever you are, had better manage your own affairs, anyway. The old-time Feinans stood on their own sturdy legs, not on German beer-skids."

"Wisha then, sorr, d'ye mind th' ould song they sang in thim days:

"*Then up steps Bonyparty*
An' takes me by the hand,
And how is ould Ireland,
And how does she shtand?
It's a poor, disthressed country
As ever yet was seen,
And they're hangin' men and women
For the wearing of the green!

Oh, the wearing of the——"

"That'll do," said Barres drily. "Do you want to wake the house? Don't go to Grogan's and talk about Ireland to any Germans. I'll tell you why; we'll probably be at war with Germany ourselves within a year, and that's a pretty good reason for you Irish to keep clear of all Germans. Go to bed!"

VI

ONE warm afternoon late in spring, Dulcie Soane, returning from school to Dragon Court, found her father behind the desk, as usual, awaiting his daughter's advent, to release him from duty.

A tall, bony man with hectic and sunken cheeks and only a single eye was standing by the desk, earnestly engaged in whispered conversation with her father.

He drew aside instantly as Dulcie came up and laid her school books on the desk. Soane, already redolent of Grogan's whiskey, pushed back his chair and got to his feet.

"G'wan in f'r a bite an' a sup," he said to his daughter, "while I talk to the gintleman."

So Dulcie went slowly into the superintendent's dingy quarters for her mid-day meal, which was dinner; and between her and a sloppy scrub-woman who cooked for them, she managed to warm up and eat what Soane had left for her from his own meal.

When she returned to the desk in the hall, the one-eyed man had gone. Soane sat on the chair behind the desk, his face over-red and shiny, his heels drumming the devil's tattoo on the tessellated pavement.

"I'll be at Grogan's," he said, as Dulcie seated herself in the ancient leather chair behind the desk telephone, and began to sort the pile of mail which the postman evidently had just delivered.

"Very well," she murmured absently, turning around

78

and beginning to distribute the letters and parcels in the various numbered compartments behind her. Soane slid off his chair to his feet and straightened up, stretching and yawning.

"Av anny wan tilliphones to Misther Barres," he said, "listen in."

"What!"

"Listen in, I'm tellin' you. And if it's a lady, ask her name first, and then listen in. And if she says her name is Quellen or Dunois, mind what she says to Misther Barres."

"Why?" enquired Dulcie, astonished.

"Becuz I'm tellin' ye!"

"I shall not do that," said the girl, flushing up.

"Ah, bother! Sure, there's no harm in it, Dulcie! Would I be askin' ye to do wrong, asthore? Me who is your own blood and kin? Listen then: 'Tis a woman what do be botherin' the poor young gentleman, an' I'll not have him f'r to be put upon. Listen, m'acushla, and if airy a lady tilliphones, or if she comes futtherin' an' muttherin' around here, call me at Grogan's and I'll be soon dishposen' av the likes av her."

"Has she ever been here—this lady?" asked the girl, uncertain and painfully perplexed.

"Sure has she! Manny's the time I've chased her out," replied Soane glibly.

"Oh. What does she look like?"

"God knows—annything ye don't wish f'r to look like yourself! Sure, I disremember what make of woman she might be—her name's enough for you. Call me up if she comes or rings. She may be a dangerous woman, at that," he added, "so speak fair to her and listen in to what she says."

Dulcie slowly nodded, looking at him hard.

Soane put on his faded brown hat at an angle, fished

a cigar with a red and gold band from his fancy but soiled waistcoat, scratched a match on the seat of his greasy pants, and sauntered out through the big, white-washed hallway into the street, with a touch of the swagger which always characterised him.

Dulcie, both hands buried in her ruddy hair and both thin elbows on the desk, sat poring over her school books.

Graduation day was approaching; there was much for her to absorb, much to memorise before then.

As she studied she hummed to herself the air of the quaint song which she was to sing at her graduation exercises. That did not interfere with her concentration; but as she finished one lesson, cast aside the book, and opened another to prepare the next lesson, vaguely happy memories of her evening party with Barres came into her mind to disturb her thoughts, tempting her to reverie and the delicious idleness she knew only when alone and absorbed in thoughts of him.

But she resolutely put him out of her mind and opened her book.

The hall clock ticked loudly through the silence; slanting sun rays fell through the street grille, across the tessellated floor where flies crawled and buzzed.

The Prophet sat full in a bar of sunlight and gravely followed the movements of the flies as though specialising on the study of those amazing insects.

Tenants of Dragon Court passed out or entered at intervals, pausing to glance at their letter-boxes or requesting their keys.

Westmore came down the eastern staircase, like an avalanche, with a cheery:

"Hello, Dulcie! Any letters? All right, old dear! If you see Mr. Mandel, tell him I'll be at the club!"

Corot Mandel came in presently, and she gave him Westmore's message.

"Thanks," he said, not even glancing at the ⸺n figure in the shabby dress too small for her. And, af.er peering into his letter-box, he went away with the indolent swing of a large and powerful plantigrade, gasing fixedly ahead of him out of heavy, oriental eyes, and twisting up his jet black, waxed moustache.

A tall, handsome girl called and enquired for Mr. Trenor. Dulcie returned her amiable smile, unhooked the receiver, and telephoned up. But nobody answered from Esmé Trenor's apartment, and the girl, whose name was Damaris Souval, and whose profession varied between the stage and desultory sitting for artists, smiled once more on Dulcie and sauntered out in her very charming summer gown.

The shabby child looked after her through the sunny hallway, the smile still curving her lips—a sensitive, winning smile, untainted by envy. Then she resumed her book, serenely clearing her youthful mind of vanity and desire for earthly things.

Half an hour later Esmé Trenor sauntered in. His was a sensative nature and fastidious, too. Dinginess, obscurity—everything that was shabby, tarnished, humble in life, he consistently ignored. He had ignored Dulcie Soane for three years: he ignored her now.

He glanced indifferently into his letter-box as he passed the desk. Dulcie said, with the effort it always required for her to speak to him:

"Miss Souval called, but left no message."

Trenor's supercilious glance rested on her for the fraction of a second, then, with a bored nod, he continued on his way and up the stairs. And Dulcie returned to her book.

The desk telephone rang: a Mrs. Helmund desired

to speak to Mr. Trenor. Dulcie switched her on, rested her chin on her hand, and continued her reading.

Some time afterward the telephone rang again.

"Dragon Court," said Dulcie, mechanically.

"I wish to speak to Mr. Barres, please."

"Mr. Barres has not come in from luncheon."

"Are you sure?" came the pretty, feminine voice.

"Quite sure," replied Dulcie. "Wait a minute——"

She called Barres's apartment; Aristocrates answered and confirmed his master's absence with courtly effusion.

"No, he is not in," repeated Dulcie. "Who shall I say called him?"

"Say that Miss Dunois called him up. If he comes in, say that Miss Thessalie Dunois will come at five to take tea with him. Thank you. Good-bye."

Startled to hear the very name against which her father had warned her, Dulcie found it difficult to reconcile the sweet voice that came to her over the wire with the voice of any such person her father had described.

Still a trifle startled, she laid aside the receiver with a disturbed glance toward the wrought-iron door at the further end of the hall.

She had no desire at all to call up her father at Grogan's and inform him of what had occurred. The mere thought of surreptitious listening in, of eavesdropping, of informing, reddened her face. Also, she had long since lost confidence in the somewhat battered but jaunty man who had always neglected her, although never otherwise unkind, even when intoxicated.

No, she would neither listen in nor inform on anybody at the behest of a father for whom, alas, she had no respect, merely those shreds of conventional feeling which might once have been filial affection, but had become merely an habitual solicitude.

No, her character, her nature refused such obedience. If there was trouble between the owner of the unusually sweet voice and Mr. Barres, it was their affair, not hers, not her father's.

This settled in her mind, she opened another book and turned the pages slowly until she came to the lesson to be learned.

It was hard to concentrate; her thoughts were straying, now, to Barres.

And, as she leaned there, musing above her dingy school book, through the grilled door at the further end of the hall stepped a young girl in a light summer gown—a beautiful girl, lithe, graceful, exquisitely groomed—who came swiftly up to the desk, a trifle pale and breathless:

"Mr. Barres? He lives here?"

"Yes."

"Please announce Miss Dunois."

Dulcie flushed deeply under the shock:

"Mr.—Mr. Barres is still out——"

"Oh. Was it you I talked to over the telephone?" asked Thessalie Dunois.

"Yes."

"Mr. Barres has not reutrned?"

"No."

Thessalie bit her lip, hesitated, turned to go. And at the same instant Dulcie saw the one-eyed man at the street door, peering through the iron grille.

Thessalie saw him, too, stiffened to marble, stood staring straight at him.

He turned and went away up the street. But Dulcie, to whom the incident signified nothing in particular except the impudence of a one-eyed man, was not prepared

for the face which Thessalie Dunois turned toward her.
Not a vestige of colour remained in it, and her dark
eyes seemed feverish and too large.

"You need not give Mr. Barres any message from
me," she said in an altered voice, which sounded strained
and unsteady. "Please do not even say that I came
or mention my name. . . . May I ask it of you?"

Dulcie, very silent in her surprise, made no reply.

"Please may I ask it of you?" whispered Thessalie.
"Do you mind not telling anybody that I was here?"

"If—you wish it."

"I do. May I trust you?"

"Y-yes."

"Thank you—" A bank bill was in her gloved fingers; intuition warned her; she took another swift look
at Dulcie. The child's face was flaming scarlet.

"Forgive me," whispered Thessalie. . . . "And
thank you, dear—" She bent over quickly, took Dulcie's hand, pressed it, looking her in the eyes.

"It's all right," she whispered. "I am not asking
you to do anything you shouldn't. Mr. Barres will
understand it all when I write to him. . . . Did you
see that man at the street door, looking through the
grating?"

"Yes."

"Do you know who he is?" whispered Thessalie.

"No."

"Have you never before seen him?"

"Yes. He was here at two o'clock talking to my
father."

"Your father?"

"My father's name is Lawrence Soane. He is superintendent of Dragon Court."

"What is your name?"

"Dulcie Soane."

Thessalie still held her hand tightly. Then with a quick but forced smile, she pressed it, thanking the girl for her consideration, turned and walked swiftly through the hall out into the street.

Dulcie, dreaming over her closed books in the fading light, vaguely uneasy lest her silence might embrace the faintest shadow of disloyalty to Barres, looked up quickly at the sound of his familiar footsteps on the pavement.

"Hello, little comrade," he called to her on his way to the stairs. "Didn't we have a jolly party the other evening? I'm going out to another party this evening, but I bet it won't be as jolly as ours!"

The girl smiled happily.

"Any letters, Sweetness?"

"None, Mr. Barres."

"All the better. I have too many letters, too many visitors. It leaves me no time to have another party with you. But we shall have another, Dulcie—never fear. That is," he added, pretending to doubt her receptiveness of his invitation, "if you would care to have another with me."

She merely looked at him, smiling deliciously.

"Be a good child and we'll have another!" he called back to her, running on up the western staircase.

Around seven o'clock her father came in, steady enough of foot but shiny-red in the face and maudlin drunk.

"That woman was here," he whined, "an' ye never called me up! I am b-bethrayed be me childer—wurra the day——"

"Please, father! If any one sees you——"

"An' phwy not! Am I ashamed o' the tears I shed?

No, I am not. No Irishman need take shame along av the tears he sheds for Ireland—God bless her where she shtands!—wid the hob-nails av the crool tyrant foreninst her bleeding neck an'——"

"Father, please——"

"That woman I warned ye of! She was here! 'Twas the wan-eyed lad who seen her——"

Dulcie rose and took him by his arm. He made no resistance; but he wept while she conducted him bedward, as the immemorial wrongs of Ireland tore his soul.

VII

THE tremendous tragedy in Europe, now nearing the end of the second act, had been slowly shaking the drowsy Western World out of its snug slumber of complacency. Young America was already sitting up in bed, awake, alert, listening. Older America, more difficult to convince, rolled solemn and interrogative eyes toward Washington, where the wooden gods still sat nodding in a row, smiling vacuously at destiny out of carved and painted features. Eyes had they but they saw not, ears but they heard not; neither spake they through their mouths.

Yet, they that made them were no longer like unto them, for many an anxious idolator no longer trusted in them. For their old God's voice was sounding in their ears.

The voice of a great ex-president, too, had been thundering from the wilderness; lesser prophets, endowed, however, with intellect and vision, had been warning the young West that the second advent of Attila was at hand; an officer of the army, inspired of God, had preached preparedness from the market places and had established for its few disciples an habitation; and a great Admiral had died of a broken heart because his lips had been officially sealed—the wisest lips that ever told of those who go down to the sea in ships.

Plainer and plainer in American ears sounded the

87

mounting surf of that blood-red sea thundering against the frontiers of Democracy; clearer and clearer came the discordant clamour of the barbaric hordes; louder and more menacing the half-crazed blasphemies of their chief, who had given the very name of the Scourge of God to one among the degenerate litter he had sired.

Garret Barres had been educated like any American of modern New York type. Harvard, then five years abroad, and a return to his native city revealed him as an ambitious, receptive, intelligent young man, deeply interested in himself and his own affairs, theoretically patriotic, a good citizen by intention, an affectionate son and brother, and already a pretty good painter of the saner species.

A modest income of his own enabled him to bide his time and decline pot-boilers. A comparatively young father and an even more youthful mother, both of sporting proclivities, together with a sister of the same tastes, were his preferred companions when he had time to go home to the family rooftree in northern New York. His lines, indeed, were cast in pleasant places. Beside still waters in green pastures, he could always restore his city-tarnished soul when he desired to retire for a while from the battleground of endeavour.

The city, after all, offered him a world-wide battlefield; for Garret Barres was by choice a painter of thoroughbred women, of cosmopolitan men—a younger warrior of the brush imbued with the old traditions of those great English captains of portraiture, who recorded for us the mo.e brilliant human truths of the seventeenth and eighteenth centuries.

From their stately canvases aglow, the eyes of the lovely dead look out at us; the eyes of ambition, of

pride, of fatuous complacency; the haunted eyes of
sorrow; the clear eyes of faith.   Out of the past they
gaze—those who once lived—deathlessly recorded by
Van Dyck, Lely, Kneller; by Gainsborough, Reynolds,
Hoppner, Lawrence, Raeburn; or consigned to a dignified destiny by Stuart, Sully, Inman, and Vanderlyn.

When Barres returned to New York after many
years, he found that the aspect of the city had not
altered very greatly.   The usual dirt, disorder, and
municipal confusion still reigned; subways were being
dug, but since the memory of man runneth, the streets
of the metropolis have been dug up, and its market
places and byways have been an abomination.
  The only visible excitement, however, was in the war
columns of the newspapers, and, sometimes, around
bulletin boards where wrangling groups were no uncommon sight, citizens and aliens often coming into ver-
bal   collision—sometimes   physical—promptly   suppressed by bored policemen.
  There was a "preparedness" parade; thousands of
worthy citizens marched in it, nervously aware, now,
that the Great Republic's only mobile military division
was on the Mexican border, where also certain Guard
regiments were likely to be directed to reinforce the
regulars—pet regiments from the city, among whose
corps of officers and enlisted men everybody had some
friend or relative.
  But these regiments had not yet entrained.   There
were few soldiers to be seen on the streets.   Khaki
began to be noticeable in New York only when the
Plattsburg camps opened.   After that there was an in-
terim of the usual dull, unaccented civilian monotony,
mitigated at rare intervals by this dun-coloured ebb
and flow from Plattsburg.

Like the first vague premonitions of a nightmare the first ominous symptoms of depression were slowly possessing hearts already uneasy under two years' burden of rumours unprintable, horrors incredible to those aloof and pursuing the peaceful tenor of their ways.

A growing restlessness, unbelief, the incapacity to understand—selfishness, rapacity, self-righteousness, complacency, cowardice, even stupidity itself were being jolted and shocked into something resembling a glimmer of comprehension as the hunnish U-boats, made ravenous by the taste of blood, steered into western shipping lanes like a vast shoal of sharks.

And always thicker and thicker came the damning tales of rape and murder, of cowardly savagery, brutal vileness, degenerate bestiality—clearer, nearer, distinctly audible, the sigh of a ravaged and expiring civilisation trampled to obliteration by the slavering, ferocious swine of the north.

Fires among shipping, fires amid great stores of cotton and grain destined for France or England, explosions of munitions of war ordered by nations of the Entente, the clumsy propaganda or impudent sneers of German and pro-German newspapers; reports of German meddling in Mexico, in South America, in Japan; more sinister news concerning the insolent activities of certain embassies—all these were beginning to have their logical effect among a fat and prosperous people which simply could not bear to be aroused from pleasant dreams of brotherhood to face the raw and hellish truth.

"For fifty years," remarked Barres to his neighbour, Esmé Trenor, also a painter of somewhat eccentric portraits, "our national characteristic has been a capacity for absorbing bunk and a fixed determination to kid ourselves. There really is a war, Trenor, old top, and we're going to get into it before very long."

Trenor, a tall, tired, exquisitely groomed young Lian, who once had painted a superficially attractive portrait of a popular débutante, and had been overwhelmed with fashionable orders ever since, was the adored of women. He dropped one attenuated knee over the other and lighted an attenuated cigarette.

"Fancy anybody bothering enough about anything to fight over it!" he said languidly.

"We're going to *war*, Trenor," repeated Barres, jamming his brushes into a bowl of black soap. "That's my positive conviction."

"Yours is so disturbingly positive a nature," remonstrated the other. "Why ever raise a row? Nothing positive is of any real importance—not even opinions."

Barres, vigorously cleaning his brushes in turpentine and black soap, glanced around at Trenor, and in his quick smile there glimmered a hint of good-natured malice. For Esmé Trenor was notoriously anything except positive in his painting, always enveloping a lack of technical knowledge with a veil of camouflage. Behind this pretty veil hid many defects, perhaps even deformities—protected by vague, indefinite shadows and the effrontery of an adroit exploiter of the restless sex.

But Esmé Trenor was both clever and alert. He had not even missed that slight and momentary glimmer of good-humoured malice in the pleasant glance of Barres. But, like his more intelligent prototype, Whistler, it was impossible to know whether or not discovery ever made any particular difference to him. He tucked a lilac-bordered handkerchief a little deeper into his cuff, glanced at his jewelled wrist-watch, shook the long ash from his cigarette.

"To be positive in anything," he drawled, "is an effort; effort entails exertion; exertion is merely a degree of violence; violence engenders toxins; toxins dull the intellect. Quod erat, dear friend. You see?"

"Oh, yes, I see," nodded Barres, always frankly amused at Trenor and his ways.

"Well, then, if you see——" Trenor waved a long, bony, over-manicured hand, expelled a ring or two of smoke, meditatively; then, in his characteristically languid voice: "To be positive closes the door to further observation and pulls down the window shades. Nothing remains except to go to bed. Is there anything more uninteresting than to go to bed? Is there anything more depressing than to know all about something?"

"You do converse like an ass sometimes," remarked Barres.

"Yes—sometimes. Not now, Barres. I don't desire to know all about anybody or anything. Fancy my knowing all about art, for example!"

"Yes, fancy!" repeated Barres, laughing.

"Or about anything specific—a woman, for example!" He shrugged wearily.

"If you meet a woman and like her, don't you want to know all there is to know about her?" inquired Barres.

"I should say not!" returned the other with languid contempt. "I don't wish to know anything at all about her."

"Well, we differ about that, old top."

"Religiously. A woman can be only an incidental amusement in one's career. You don't go to a musical comedy twice, do you? And any woman will reveal herself sufficiently in one evening."

"Nice, kindly domestic instincts you have, Trenor."

"I'm merely fastidious," returned the other, dropping his cigarette out of the open window. He rose, yawned, took his hat, stick and gloves.

"Bye," he said languidly. "I'm painting Elsena Helmund this morning."

Barres said, with good-humoured envy:

"I've neither commission nor sitter. If I had, you bet I'd not stand there yawning at my luck."

"It is you who have the luck, not I," drawled Trenor. "I give a portion of my spiritual and material self with every brush stroke, while you remain at liberty to flourish and grow fat in idleness. I perish as I create; my life exhausts itself to feed my art. What you call my good luck is my martyrdom. You see, dear friend, how fortunate you are?"

"I see," grinned Barres. "But will your spiritual nature stand such a cruel drain? Aren't you afraid your morality may totter?"

"Morality," mused Esmé, going; "that is one of those early Gothic terms now obsolete, I believe——"

He sauntered out with his hat and gloves and stick, still murmuring:

"Morality? Gothic—very Gothic—"

Barres, still amused, sorted his wet brushes, dried them carefully one by one on a handful of cotton waste, and laid them in a neat row across the soapstone top of his palette-table.

"Hang it!" he muttered cheerfully. "I could paint like a streak this morning if I had the chance—"

He threw himself back in his chair and sat there smoking for a while, his narrowing eyes fixed on a great window which opened above the court. Soft spring breezes stirred the curtains; sparrows were noisy out there; a strip of cobalt sky smiled at him over the opposite chimneys; an April cloud floated across it.

He rose, walked over to the window and glanced down into the court. Several more hyacinths were now in blossom. The Prophet dozed majestically, curled up on an Italian garden seat. Beside him sprawled the snow white Houri, stretched out full length in the sun, her wonderful blue eyes following the irrational gambols of the tortoise-shell cat, Strindberg, who had gone loco, as usual, and was tearing up and down trees, prancing sideways with flattened ears and crooked tail, in terror at things invisible, or digging furiously toward China amid the hyacinths.

Dulcie Soane came out into the court presently and expostulated with Strindberg, who suffered herself to be removed from the hyacinth bed, only to make a hysterical charge on her mistress's ankles.

"Stop it, you crazy thing!" insisted Dulcie, administering a gentle slap which sent the cat bucketing and corvetting across the lawn, where the eccentric course of a dead leaf, blown by the April wind, instantly occupied its entire intellectual vacuum.

Barres, leaning on the window-sill, said, without raising his voice:

"Hello, Dulcie! How are you, after our party?"

The child looked up, smiled shyly her response through the pale glory of the April sunshine.

"What are you doing to-day?" he inquired, with casual but friendly interest.

"Nothing."

"Isn't there any school?"

"It's Saturday."

"That's so. Well, if you're doing nothing you're

just as busy as I am," he remarked, smiling down at her where she stood below his window.

"Why don't you paint pictures?" ventured the girl diffidently.

"Because I haven't any orders. Isn't that sad?"

"Yes. . . . But you could paint a picture just to please yourself, couldn't you?"

"I haven't anybody to paint from," he explained with amiable indifference, lazily watching the effect of alternate shadow and sunlight on her upturned face.

"Couldn't you find—somebody?" Her heart had suddenly begun to beat very fast.

Barres laughed:

"Would you like to have your portrait painted?"

She could scarcely find voice to reply:

"Will you—let me?"

The slim young figure down there in the April sunshine had now arrested his professional attention. With detached interest he inspected her for a few moments; then:

"You'd make an interesting study, Dulcie. What do you say?"

"Do—do you mean that you *want* me?"

"Why—yes! Would you like to pose for me? It's pin-money, anyway. Would you like to try it?"

"Y-yes."

"Are you quite sure? It's hard work."

"Quite—sure——" she stammered. The little flushed face was lifted very earnestly to his now, almost beseechingly. "I am quite sure," she repeated breathlessly.

"So you'd really like to pose for me?" he insisted in smiling surprise at the girl's visible excitement. Then he added abruptly: "I've half a mind to give you a job as my private model!"

Through the rosy confusion of her face her grey eyes were fixed on him with a wistful intensity, almost painful. For into her empty heart and starved mind had suddenly flashed a dazzling revelation. Opportunity was knocking at her door. Her chance had come! Perhaps it had been inherited from her mother —God knows!—this deep, deep hunger for things beautiful—this passionate longing for light and knowledge.

Mere contact with such a man as Barres had already made endurable a solitary servitude which had been subtly destroying her child's spirit, and slowly dulling the hunger in her famished mind. And now to aid him—to feel that he was using her—was to arise from her rags of ignorance and emerge upright into the light which filled that wonder-house wherein he dwelt, and on the dark threshold of which her lonely little soul had crouched so long in silence.

She looked up almost blindly at the man who, in careless friendliness, had already opened his door to her, had permitted her to read his wonder-books, had allowed her to sit unreproved and silent from sheer happiness, and gaze unsatiated upon the wondrous things within the magic mansion where he dwelt.

And now to serve this man; to aid him, to creep into the light in which he stood and strive to learn and see!—the thought already had produced a delicate intoxication in the child, and she gazed up at Barres from the sunny garden with her naked soul in her eyes. Which confused, perplexed, and embarrassed him.

"Come on up," he said briefly. "I'll tell your father over the 'phone."

She entered without a sound, closed the door which

he had left open for her, advanced across the thick-meshed rug. She still wore her blue gingham apron; her bobbed hair, full of ruddy lights, intensified the whiteness of her throat. In her arms she cradled the Prophet, who stared solemnly at Barres out of depthless green eyes.

"Upon my word," thought Barres to himself, "I believe I have found a model and an uncommon one!"

Dulcie, watching his expression, smiled slightly and stroked the Prophet.

"I'll paint you that way! Don't stir," said the young fellow pleasantly. "Just stand where you are, Dulcie. You're quite all right as you are——" He lifted a half-length canvas, placed it on his heavy easel and clamped it.

"I feel exactly like painting," he continued, busy with his brushes and colours. "I'm full of it to-day. It's in me. It's got to come out. . . . And you certainly are an interesting subject—with your big grey eyes and bobbed red hair—oh, quite interesting constructively, too—as well as from the colour point."

He finished setting his palette, gathered up a handful of brushes:

"I won't bother to draw you except with a brush——"

He looked across at her, remained looking, the pleasantly detached expression of his features gradually changing to curiosity, to the severity of increasing interest, to concentrated and silent absorption.

"Dulcie," he presently concluded, "you are so unusually interesting and paintable that you make me think very seriously. . . . And I'm hanged if I'm going to waste you by slapping a technically adequate sketch of you onto this nice new canvas . . . which might give me pleasure while I'm doing it . . . and might even tickle my vanity for a week . . . and then be laid away to gather dust . . . and be covered over next year and used for another sketch. . . . No. . . . No! . . . You're worth more than that!"

He began to pace the place to and fro, thinking very hard, glancing around at her from moment to moment, where she stood, obediently immovable on the blue meshed rug, clasping the prophet to her breast.

"Do you want to become my private model?" he demanded abruptly. "I mean seriously. Do you?"

"Yes."

"I mean a real model, from whom I can ask anything?"

"Oh, yes, please," pleaded the girl, trembling a little.

"Do you understand what it means?"

"Yes."

"Sometimes you'll be required to wear few clothes. Sometimes none. Did you know that?"

"Yes. Mr. Westmore asked me once."

"You didn't care to?"

"Not for him."

"You don't mind doing it for me?"

"I'll do anything you ask me," she said, trying to smile and shivering with excitement.

"All right. It's a bargain. You're my model, Dulcie. When do you graduate from school?"

"In June."

"Two months! Well—all right. Until then it will be a half day through the week, and all day Saturdays and Sundays, if I require you. You'll have a weekly salary——" He smiled and mentioned the figure, and the girl blushed vividly. She had, it appeared, expected nothing.

"Why, Dulcie!" he exclaimed, immensely amused.

"You didn't intend to come here and give me all your time for nothing, did you?"

"Yes."

"But why on earth should you do such a thing for me?"

She found no words to explain why.

"Nonsense," he continued; "you're a business woman now. Your father will have to find somebody to cook for him and take the desk when he's out at Grogan's. Don't worry; I'll fix it with him. . . . By the way, Dulcie, supposing you sit down."

She found a chair and took the Prophet onto her lap.

"Now, this will be very convenient for me," he went on, inspecting her with increasing satisfaction. "If I ever have any orders—any sitters—you can have a vacation, of course. Otherwise, I'll always have an interesting model at hand—I've got chests full of wonderful costumes—genuine ones——" He fell silent, his eyes studying her. Already he was planning half a dozen pictures, for he was just beginning to perceive how adaptable the girl might be. And there was about her that indefinable something which, when a painter discovers it, interests him and arouses his intense artistic curiosity.

"You know," he said musingly, "you are something more than pretty, Dulcie. . . . I could put you in eighteenth century clothes and you'd look logical. Yes, and in seventeenth century clothes, too. . . . I could do some amusing things with you in oriental garments. . . . A young Herodiade. . . . Calypso. . . . Theodora. . . . She was a child, too, you know. There's a portrait with bobbed hair—a young girl by Van Dyck. . . . You know you are quite stimulating to me, Dulcie. You excite a painter's imagination.

It's rather odd," he added naïvely, "that I never discovered you before; and I've known you over two years."

He had seated himself on the sofa while discoursing. Now he got up, touched a bell twice. The Finnish maid, Selinda, with her high cheek-bones, frosty blue eyes and colourless hair, appeared in cap and apron.

"Selinda," he said, "take Miss Dulcie into my room. In a long, leather Turkish box on the third shelf of my clothes closet is a silk and gold costume and a lot of jade jewelry. Please put her into it."

So Dulcie Soane went away with her cat in her arms, beside the neat and frosty-eyed Selinda; and Barres opened a portfolio of engravings, where were gathered the lovely aristocrats of Van Dyck and Rubens and Gainsborough and his contemporaries—a charmingly mixed company, separated by centuries and frontiers, yet all characterised by a common *something*—some inexplicable similarity which Barres recognised without defining.

"It's rather amusing," he murmured, "but that kid, Dulcie, seems to remind me of these people—somehow or other. . . . One scarcely looks for qualities in the child of an Irish janitor. . . . I wonder who her mother was. . . ."

When he looked up again Dulcie was standing there on the thick rug. On her naked feet were jade bracelets, jade-set rings on her little toes; a cascade of jade and gold falling over her breasts to the straight, narrow breadth of peacock hue which fell to her ankles. And on her childish head, clasping the ruddy bobbed hair, glittered the jade-incrusted diadem of a fairy princess of Cathay.

The Prophet, gathered close to her breast, stared

back at Barres with eyes that dimmed the splendid jade about him.

"That settles it," he said, the tint of excitement rising in his cheeks. "I *have* discovered a model and a wonder! And right here is where I paint my winter Academy—right here and right now! . . . And I call it 'The Prophets.' Climb up on that model stand and squat there cross-legged, and stare at me—straight at me—the way your cat stares! . . . There you are. That's right! Don't move. Stay put or I'll come over and bow-string you!—you little miracle!"

"Do—you mean me?" faltered Dulcie.

"You bet, Sweetness! Do you know how beautiful you are? Well, never mind——" He had begun already to draw with a wet brush, and now he relapsed into absorbed silence.

The Prophet watched him steadily. The studio became intensely still.

VIII

THE studio door bell rang while Barres was at breakfast one morning late in June. Aristocrates leisurely answered the door, but shut it again immediately and walked out into the kitchenette without any explanation.

Selinda removed the breakfast cover and fetched the newspaper. Later, Aristocrates, having washed his master's brushes, brought them into the studio mincingly, upon a silver service-salver.

"No letters?" inquired Barres, glancing up over the morning paper and laying aside his cigarette.

"No letters, suh. No co'espondence in any shape, fo'm or manner, suh."

"Anybody to see me?" inquired Barres, always amused at Aristocrates' flights of verbiage.

"Nobody, suh, excusin' a persistless 'viduality inquihin' fo' you, suh."

"What persistless individuality was that?" asked Barres.

"A ve'y or-nary human objec', suh, pahshially afflicted with one bad eye."

"That one-eyed man? He's been here several times, hasn't he? Why does he come?"

"Fo' commercial puhposes, suh."

"Oh, a pedlar?"

"He mentions a desiah, suh, to dispose, commercially, of vahious impo'ted materials requiahed by ahtists."

"YOU LITTLE MIRACLE!"

"Didn't you show him the sign in the hall, 'No pedlars allowed'?"

"Yaas, suh."

"What did he say?"

"I would not demean myse'f to repeat what this human objec' said, suh."

"And what did you do then?"

"Mistuh Barres, suh, I totally igno'hed that man," replied Aristocrates languidly.

"Quite right. But you tell Soane to enforce the rule against pedlars. Every day there are two or three of them ringing at the studio, trying to sell colours, laces, or fake oriental rugs. It annoys me. Selinda can't hear the bell and I have to leave my work and open the door. Tell that persistless one-eyed man to keep away. Tell Soane to bounce him next time he enters Dragon Court. Do you understand?"

"Yaas, suh. But Soane, suh, he's a might friendly Irish. He's spo'tin' 'round Grogan's nights, 'longa this here one-eyed 'viduality. Yaas, suh. I done seen 'em co-gatherin' on vahious occasionalities."

"Oho!" commented Barres. "It's graft, is it? This one-eyed pedlar meets Soane at Grogan's and bribes him with a few drinks to let him peddle colours in Dragon Court! That's the Irish of it, Aristocrates. I began to suspect something like that. All right. I'll speak to Soane myself. . . . Leave the studio door open; it's warm in here."

The month of May was now turning somewhat sultry as it melted into June. Every pivot-pane in the big studio window had been swung wide open. The sun had already clothed every courtyard tree with dense and tender foliage; hyacinth and tulip were gone and Soane's subscription geraniums blazed in their place like beds of coals heaped up on the grass plot of Dragon Court.

But blue sky, sunshine of approaching summer, gentle winds and freshening rains brought only restlessness to New Yorkers that month of May.

Like the first two years of the war, the present year seemed strange, unreal; its vernal breezes brought no balm, its blue skies no content. The early summer sunlight seemed almost uncanny in a world where, beyond the sea, millions of men at arms swayed ceaselessly under sun and moon alike, interlocked in one gigantic death grip!—a horrible and blood-drenched human chain of butchery stretching half around the earth.

Into every Western human eye had come strange and subtle shadows which did not depart with moments of forgetful mirth, intervals of self-absorption, hours filled with familiar interests—the passions, hopes, perplexities of those years which were now no more.

Those years of yesterdays! A vast and depthless cleft already divided them from to-day. They seemed as remote as dusty centuries—those days of an ordered and tranquil world—those days of little obvious faiths unshattered—even those days of little wars, of petty local strifes, of an almost universal calm and peace and trust in brotherhood and in the obligations of civilisation.

Familiar yesterday had vanished, its creeds forgotten. It was already decades away, and fading like a legend in the ever-increasing glare of the red and present moment.

And the month of May seemed strange, and its soft skies and sun seemed out of place in a world full of dying—a world heavy with death—a western world aloof from the raging hell beyond the seas, yet already tense under the distant threat of three continents in flames—and all a-quiver before the deathly menace of that horde of blood-crazed demons still at large, still unsubdued, still ranging the ruins of the planet which they had so insanely set on fire.

Entire nations were still burning beyond the ocean; other nations had sunk into cinders. Over the Eastern seas the furnace breath began to be felt along the out-thrust coast lines of the Western World. Inland, not yet; but every seaward city became now conscious of that first faint warning wave of heat from hell. Millions of ears strained to catch the first hushed whisper of the tumult. Silent in its suspense the Great Republic listened. Only the priesthood of the deaf and wooden gods continued voluble. But Israel had already begun to lift up its million eyes; and its ancient faith began to glow again; and its trust was becoming once more a living thing—the half-forgotten trust of Israel in that half-forgotten Lord, who, in the beginning, had been their helper and their shield.

Through the open studio door came Dulcie Soane. The Prophet followed at her slender heels, gently waving an urbane tail.

After his first smiling greeting—he always rose, advanced, and took her hand with that pleasant appearance of formality so adored by femininity, youthful or mature—he resumed his seat and continued to write his letters.

These finished, he stamped them, rang for Aristocrates, picked up his palette and brushes, and pulled out the easel upon which was the canvas for the morning.

Dulcie, still in the hands of Selinda, had not yet

emerged. The Prophet sat upright on the carved table, motionless as a cat of ebony with green-jewelled eyes.

"Well, old sport," said Barres, stepping across the rug to caress the cat, "you and your pretty mistress begin to look very interesting on my canvas."

The Prophet received the blandishments with dignified gratitude. A discreet and feathery purring filled the room as Barres stroked the jet black, silky fur.

"Fine cat, you are," commented the young man, turning as Dulcie entered.

She laid one hand on his extended arm and sprang lightly to the model stand. And the next moment she was seated—a slim, gemmed thing glimmering with imperial jade from top to toe.

Barres laid the Prophet in her arms, stepped back while Dulcie arranged the docile cat, then retreated to his canvas.

"All right, Sweetness?"

"All right," replied the child happily. And the morning séance was on.

Barres was usually inclined to ramble along conversationally in his pleasant, detached way while at work, particularly if work went well.

"Where were we yesterday, Dulcie? Oh, yes; we were talking about the Victorian era and its art; and we decided that it was not the barren desert that the ultra-moderns would have us believe. That's what we decided, wasn't it?"

"*You* decided," she said.

"So did you, Dulcie. It was a unanimous decision. Because we both concluded that some among the Victorians were full of that sweet, clean sanity which alone endures. You recollect how our decision started?"

"Yes. It was about my new pleasure in Tennyson, Browning, Morris, Arnold, and Swinburne."

"Exactly. Victorian poets, if sometimes a trifle stilted and self-conscious, wrote nobly; makers of Victorian prose displayed qualities of breadth, imagination and vision and a technical cultivation unsurpassed. The musical compositions of that epoch were melodious and sometimes truly inspired; never brutal, never vulgar, never degenerate. And the Victorian sculptors and painters—at first perhaps austerely pedantic—became, as they should be, recorders of the times and customs of thought, bringing the end of the reign of a great Queen to an admirable renaissance."

Dulcie's grey eyes never left his. And if she did not quite understand every word, already the dawning familiarity with his vocabulary and a general comprehension of his modes of self-expansion permitted her to follow him.

"A great Queen, a great reign, a great people," he rambled on, painting away all the while. "And if in that era architecture declined toward its lowest level of stupidity, and if taste in furniture and in the plastic, decorative, and textile arts was steadily sinking toward its lowest ebb, and if Mrs. Grundy trudged the Empire, paramount, dull and smugly ferocious, while all snobbery saluted her and the humble grovelled before her dusty brogans, yet, Dulcie, it was a great era.

"It was great because its faith had not been radically impaired; it was sane because Germany had not yet inoculated the human race with its porcine political vulgarities, its bestial degeneracy in art. . . . And if, perhaps, the sentimental in British art and literature predominated, thank God it had not yet been tainted with the stark ugliness, the swinish nakedness, the ferocious leer of things Teutonic!"

He continued to paint in silence for a while. Presently the Prophet yawned on Dulcie's knees, displaying a pink cavern.

"Better rest," he said, nodding smilingly at Dulcie. She released the cat, who stretched, arched his back, yawned again gravely, and stalked away over the velvety Eastern carpet.

Dulcie got up lithely and followed him on little jade-encrusted, naked feet.

A box of bon-bons lay on the sofa; she picked up Rossetti's poems, turned the leaves with jewel-laden fingers, while with the other hand she groped for a bon-bon, her grey eyes riveted on the pages before her.

During these intervals between poses it was the young man's custom to make chalk sketches of the girl, recording swiftly any unstudied attitude, any unconscious phase of youthful grace that interested him.

Dulcie, in the beginning, diffidently aware of this, had now become entirely accustomed to it, and no longer felt any responsibility to remain motionless while he was busy with red chalk or charcoal.

When she had rested sufficiently, she laid aside her book, hunted up the Prophet, who lazily endured the gentle tyranny, and resumed her place on the model stand.

And so they worked away all the morning, until luncheon was served in the studio by Aristocrates; and Barres in his blouse, and Dulcie in her peacock silk, her jade, and naked feet, gravely or lightly as their moods dictated, discussed an omelette and a pot of tea or chocolate, and the ways and manners and customs of a world which Dulcie now was discovering as a brand new and most enchanting planet.

IX

HER DAY

JUNE was ending in a very warm week. Work in the studio lagged, partly because Dulcie, preparing for graduation, could give Barres little time; partly because, during June, that young man had been away spending the week-ends with his parents and his sister at Foreland Farms, their home.

From one of these visits he returned to the city just in time to read a frantic little note from Dulcie Soane:

"DEAR MR. BARRES, please, *please* come to my graduation. I do want *somebody* there who knows me. And my father is not well. Is it too much to ask of you? I hadn't the courage to speak to you about it when you were here, but I have ventured to write because it will be so lonely for me to graduate without having anybody there I know.

"DULCIE SOANE."

It was still early in the morning; he had taken a night train to town.

So when he had been freshened by a bath and change of linen, he took his hat and went down stairs.

A heavy, pasty-visaged young woman sat at the desk in the entrance hall.

"Where is Soane?" he inquired.

"He's sick."

"*Where* is he?"

"In bed," she replied indifferently. The woman's manner just verged on impertinence. He hesitated, then walked across to the superintendent's apartments and entered without knocking.

Soane, in his own room, lay sleeping off the consequences of an evening at Grogan's. One glance was sufficient for Barres, and he walked out.

On Madison Avenue he found a florist, selected a bewildering bouquet, and despatched it with a hasty note, by messenger, to Dulcie at her school. In the note he wrote:

"I shall be there. Cheer up!"

He also sent more flowers to his studio, with pencilled orders to Aristocrates.

In a toy-shop he found an appropriate decoration for the centre of the lunch table.

Later, in a jeweller's, he discovered a plain gold locket, shaped like a heart and inset with one little diamond. A slender chain by which to suspend it was easily chosen; and an extra payment admitted him to the emergency department where he looked on while an expert engraved upon the locket: "Dulcie Soane from Garret Barres," and the date.

After that he went into the nearest telephone booth and called up several people, inviting them to dine with him that evening.

It was nearly ten o'clock now. He took his little gift, stopped a taxi, and arrived at the big brick high-school just in time to enter with the last straggling parents and family friends.

The hall was big and austerely bare, except for the ribbons and flags and palms which decorated it. It was hot, too, though all the great blank windows had been swung open wide.

The usual exercises had already begun; there were speeches from Authority; prayers by Divinity; choral effects by graduating pulchritude.

The class, attired in white, appeared to average much older than Dulcie. He could see her now, in her reconstructed communion dress, holding the big bouquet which he had sent her, one madonna lily of which she had detached and pinned over her breast.

Her features were composed and delicately flushed; her bobbed hair was tucked up, revealing the snowy neck.

One girl after another advanced and read or spoke, performing the particular parlour trick assigned her in the customary and perfectly unremarkable manner characteristic of such affairs.

Rapturous parental demonstrations greeted each effort; piano, violin and harp filled in nobly. A slight haze of dust, incident to pedalistic applause, invaded the place; there was an odour of flowers in the heated atmosphere.

Glancing at a programme which he had found on his seat, Barres read: "Song: Dulcie Soane."

Looking up at her where she sat on the stage, among her comrades in white, he noticed that her eyes were busy searching the audience—possibly for him, he thought, experiencing an oddly pleasant sensation at the possibility.

The time at length arrived for Dulcie to do her parlour trick; she rose and came forward, clasping the big, fragrant bouquet, prettily flushed but self-possessed. The harp began a little minor prelude—something Irish and not very modern. Then Dulcie's pure, untrained voice stole winningly through the picked harp-strings' hesitation:

"Heart of a colleen,
Where do you roam?
Heart of a colleen,

111

Far from your home?
Laden with love you stole from her breast!
Wandering dove, return to your nest!

Sodgers are sailin'
Away to the wars;
Ladies are wailin'
Their woe to the stars;
Why is the heart of you straying so soon——
Heart that was part of you, Eileen Aroon?

Lost to a sodger,
Gone is my heart!
Lost to a sodger,
Now we must part——
I and my heart——for it journeys afar
Along with the sodgers who sail to the war!

Tears that near blind me
My pride shall dry,——
Wisha! don't mind me!.
Lave a lass cry!
Only a sodger can whistle the tune
That coaxes the heart out of Eileen Aroon!"

And Dulcie's song ended.

Almost instantly the audience had divined in the
words she sang a significance which concerned them—
a warning—perhaps a prophecy. The 69th Regiment
of New York infantry was Irish, and nearly every seat
in the hall held a relative of some young fellow serving
in its ranks.

The applause was impulsive, stormy, persistent; the
audience was demanding the young girl's recall; the
noise they made became overwhelming, checking the
mediating music and baffling the next embarrassed graduate, scheduled to read an essay, and who stood there
mute, her manuscript in her hand.

Finally the principal of the school arose, went over to Dulcie, and exchanged a few words with her. Then he came forward, hand lifted in appeal for silence.

"The music and words of the little song you have just heard," he said, "were written, I have just learned, by the mother of the girl who sang them. They were written in Ireland a number of years ago, when Irish regiments were sent away for over-seas service. Neither words nor song have ever been published. Miss Soane found them among her mother's effects.

"I thought the story of the little song might interest you. For, somehow, I feel—as I think you all feel —that perhaps the day may come—may be near— when the hearts of our women, too, shall be given to their soldiers—sons, brothers, fathers—who are 'sailin' away to the wars.' But if that time comes—which God avert!—then I know that every man here will do his duty. . . . And every woman. . . . And I know that:

> 'Tears that near blind you,
> Your pride shall dry!——' "

He paused a moment:

"Miss Soane has prepared no song to sing as an encore. In her behalf, and in my own, I thank you for your appreciation. Be kind enough to permit the exercises to proceed."

And the graduating exercises continued.

Barres waited for Dulcie. She came out among the first of those departing, walking all alone in her reconstructed white dress, and carrying his bouquet. When she caught sight of him, her face became radiant and she made her way toward him through the crowd, seeking his outstretched hand with hers, clinging to it in a passion of gratitude and emotion that made her voice tremulous:

"My bouquet—it is so wonderful! I love every flower in it! Thank you with all my heart. You are so kind to have come—so kind to me—so k-kind——"

"It is I who should be grateful, Dulcie, for your charming little song," he insisted. "It was fascinating and exquisitely done."

"Did you really like it?" she asked shyly.

"Indeed I did! And I quite fell in love with your voice, too—with that trick you seem to possess of conveying a hint of tears through some little grace-note now and then. . . . And there *were* tears hidden in the words; and in the melody, too. . . . And to think that your mother wrote it!"

"Yes."

After a short interval of silence he released her hand.

"I have a taxi for you," he said gaily. "We'll drive home in state."

The girl flushed again with surprise and gratitude:

"Are—are *you* coming, too?"

"Certainly I'm going to take you home. Don't you belong to me?" he demanded laughingly.

"Yes," she said. But her forced little smile made the low-voiced answer almost solemn.

"Well, then!" he said cheerfully. "Come along. What's mine I look after. We'll have lunch together in the studio, if you are too proud to pose for a poor artist this afternoon."

At this her sensitive face cleared and she laughed happily.

"The pride of a high-school graduate!" he commented, as he seated himself beside her in the taxicab. "Can anything equal it?"

"Yes."

"What?"

"Her pride in your—friendship," she ventured.

Which unexpected reply touched and surprised him.

"You dear child!" he said; "I'm proud of your friendship, too. Nothing ought to make a man prouder than winning a young girl's confidence."

"You are so kind," she sighed, touching the blossoms in her bouquet with slender fingers that trembled a little. For she would have offered him a flower from it had she found courage; but it seemed presumptuous and she dropped her hand into her lap again.

Aristocrates opened the door for them: Selinda took her away.

Barres had ordered flowers for the table. In the middle of it a doll stood, attired in academic cap and gown, the Stars and Stripes in one hand, in the other a green flag bearing a gold harp.

When Dulcie came in she stopped short, enchanted at the sight of the decorated table. But when Aristocrates opened the kitchen door and her three cats came trotting in, she was overcome.

For each cat wore a red, white and blue cravat on which was pinned a silk shamrock; and although Strindberg immediately keeled over on the rug and madly attacked her cravat with her hind toes, the general effect remained admirable.

Aristocrates seated Dulcie. Upon her plate was the box containing chain and locket. And the girl cast a swift, inquiring glance across the centre flowers at Barres.

"Yes, it's for you, Dulcie," he said.

She turned quite pale at sight of the little gift. After a silence she leaned on the table with both elbows, shading her face with her hands.

He let her alone—let the first tense moment in her youthful life ebb out of it; nor noticed, apparently, the furtive and swift touch of her best handkerchief to her closed eyes.

Aristocrates brought her a little glass of frosted orange juice. After an interval, not looking at Barres, she sipped it. Then she took the locket and chain from the satin-lined box, read the inscription, closed her lids for a second's silent ecstasy, opened them looking at him through rapturous tears, and with her eyes still fixed on him lifted the chain and fastened it around her slender neck.

The luncheon then proceeded, the Prophet gravely. assisting from the vantage point of a neighbouring chair, the Houri, more emotional, promenading earnestly at the heels of Aristocrates. As for Strindberg, she possessed neither manners nor concentration, and she alternately squalled her desires for food or frisked all over the studio, attempting complicated maneuvres with every curtain-cord and tassel within reach.

Dulcie had found her voice again—a low, uncertain, tremulous little voice when she tried to thank him for the happiness he had given her—a clearer, firmer voice when he dexterously led the conversation into channels more familiar and serene.

They talked of the graduating exercises, of her part in them, of her classmates, of education in general.

She told him that since she was quite young she had learned to play the piano by remaining for an hour every day after school, and receiving instruction from a young teacher who needed a little extra pin money.

As for singing, she had had no instruction. Her voice had never been tried, never been cultivated.

"We'll have it tried some day," he said casually.

But Dulcie shook her head, explaining that it was an expensive process and not to be thought of.

"How did you pay for your piano lessons?" he asked.

"I paid twenty-five cents an hour. My mother left a little money for me when I was a baby. I spent it all that way."

"Every bit of it?"

"Yes. I had $500. It lasted me seven years—from the time I was ten to now."

"*Are* you seventeen? You don't look it."

"I know I don't. My teachers tell me that my mind is very quick but my body is slow. It annoys me to be mistaken for a child of fifteen. And I have to dress that way, too, because my dresses still fit me and clothes are very expensive."

"Are they?"

Dulcie became confidential and loquacious:

"Oh, very. You don't know about girls' clothes, I suppose. But they cost a very great deal. So I've had to wear out dresses I've had ever since I was fourteen and fifteen. And so I can't put up my hair because it would make my dresses look ridiculous; and that renders the situation all the worse—to be obliged to go about with bobbed hair, you see? There doesn't seem to be any way out of it," she ended, with a despairing little laugh, "and I was seventeen last February!"

"Cheer up! You'll grow old fast enough. And now you're going to have a jolly little salary as my model, and you ought to be able to buy suitable clothes. Oughtn't you?"

She did not answer, and he repeated the question. And drew from her, reluctantly, that her father, so far, had absorbed what money she had earned by posing.

A dull red gathered under the young man's cheek-bones, but he said carelessly:

"That won't do. I'll talk it over with your father. I'm very sure he'll agree with me that you should bank your salary and draw out what you need for your personal expenses."

Dulcie sat silent over her fruit and bon-bons. Reaction from the keen emotions of the day had, perhaps, begun to have their effect.

They rose and reseated themselves on the sofa, where she sat in the corner among gorgeous Chinese cushions, her reconstructed dress now limp and shabby, the limp madonna lily hanging from her breast.

It had been for her the happiest day of her life. It had dawned the loneliest, but under the magic of this man's kindness the day was ending like a day in Paradise.

To Dulcie, however, happiness was less dependent upon receiving than upon giving; and like all things feminine, mature and immature, she desired to serve where her heart was enlisted—began to experience the restless desire to give. What? And as the question silently presented itself, she looked up at Barres:

"Could I pose for you?"

"On a day like this! Nonsense, Dulcie. This is your holiday."

"I'd really like to—if you want me——"

"No. Curl up here and take a nap. Slip off your gown so you won't muss it and ask Selinda for a kimono. Because you're going to need your gown this evening," he added smilingly.

"Why? *Please* tell me why?"

"No. You've had enough excitement. Tell Selinda to give you a kimono. Then you can lie down in my room if you like. Selinda will call you in plenty of time. And after that I'll tell you how we're going to bring your holiday to a gay conclusion."

She seemed disinclined to stir, curled up there, her eyes brilliant with curiosity, her lips a trifle parted in a happy smile. She lay that way for a few moments, looking up at him, her fingers caressing the locket, then she sat up swiftly.

"Must I take a nap?"

"Certainly."

She sprang to her feet, flashed past him, and disappeared in the corridor.

"Don't forget to wake me!" she called back.

"I won't forget!"

When he heard her voice again, conversing with Selinda, he opened the studio door and went down stairs.

Soane, rather the worse for wear, was at the desk, and, standing beside him, was a one-eyed man carrying two pedlar's boxes under his arms. They both looked around quickly when Barres appeared. Before he reached the desk the one-eyed man turned and walked out hastily into the street.

"Soane," said Barres, "I've one or two things to say to you. The first is this: if you don't stop drinking and if you don't keep away from Grogan's, you'll lose your job here."

"Musha, then, Misther Barres——"

"Wait a moment; I'm not through. I advise you to stop drinking and to keep away from Grogan's. That's the first thing. And next, go on and graft as much as you like, only warn your pedlar-friends to keep away from Studio No. 9. Do you understand?"

"F'r the love o' God——"

"Cut out the injured innocence, Soane. I'm telling you how to avoid trouble, that's all."

"Misther Barres, sorr! As God sees me——"

119

"I can see you, too. I want you to behave, Soane. This is friendly advice. That one-eyed pedlar who just beat it has been bothering me. Other pedlars come ringing at the studio and interrupt and annoy me. You know the rules. If the other tenants care to stand for it, all right. But I'm through. Is that plain?"

"It is, sorr," said the unabashed delinquent. The faintest glimmer of a grin came into his battered eyes. "Sorra a wan o' thim ever lays a hand to No. 9 bell or I'll have his life!"

"One thing more," continued Barres, smiling in spite of himself at the Irish of it all. "I am paying Dulcie a salary——"

"Wisha then——"

"Stop! I tell you that she's in my employment on a salary. Don't ever touch a penny of it again."

"Sure the child's wages——"

"No, they *don't* belong to the father. Legally, perhaps, but the law doesn't suit me. So if you take the money that she earns, and blow it in at Grogan's, I'll have to discharge her because I won't stand for what you are doing."

"Would you do that, Mr. Barres?"

"I certainly would."

The Irishman scratched his curly head in frank perplexity.

"Dulcie needs clothes suitable to her age," continued Barres. "She needs other things. I'm going to take charge of her savings so don't you attempt to tamper with them. You wouldn't do such a thing, anyway, Soane, if this miserable drink habit hadn't got a hold on you. If you don't quit, it will down you. You'll lose your place here. You know that. Try to brace up. This is a rotten deal you're giving your-self and your daughter."

Soane wept easily. He wept now. Tearful volu-bility followed—picturesque, lit up with Hibernian flashes, then rambling, and a hint of slyness in it which kept one weeping eye on duty watching Barres all the while.

"All right; behave yourself," concluded Barres. "And, Soane, I shall have three or four people to din-ner and a little dancing afterward. I want Dulcie to enjoy her graduating dance."

"Sure, Misther Barres, you're that kind to the child——"

"*Somebody* ought to be. Do you know that there was nobody she knew to see her graduate to-day, ex-cepting myself?"

"Oh, the poor darling! Sure, I was that busy——"

"Busy sleeping off a souse," said Barres drily. "And by the way, who is that stolid, German-looking girl who alternates with you here at the desk?"

"Miss Kurtz, sorr."

"Oh. She seems stupid. Where did you dig her up?"

"A fri'nd o' mine riccominds her highly, sorr."

"Is that so? Who is he? One of your German ped-lar friends at Grogan's? Be careful, Soane. You Sinn Feiners are headed for trouble."

He turned and mounted the stairs. Soane looked after him with an uneasy expression, partly humorous.

"Ah, then, Mr. Barres," he said, "don't be both-erin' afther the likes of us poor Irish. Is there anny harrm in a sup o' beer av a Dootchman pays?"

Barres looked back at him:

"A one-eyed Dutchman?"

"Ah, g'wan, sorr, wid yer hokin' an' jokin'! Is it

graft ye say? An' how can ye say it, sorr, knowin' me as ye do, Misther Barres?"

The impudent grin on the Irishman's face was too much for the young man. He continued to mount the stairs, laughing.

X

A S he entered the studio he heard the telephone ringing. Presently Selinda marched in:

"A lady, sir, who will not giff her name, desires to spik to Mr. Barres."

"I don't talk to anonymous people," he said curtly.

"I shall tell her, sir?"

"Certainly. Did you make Miss Dulcie comfortable?"

"Yess, sir."

"That's right. Now, take that dress of Miss Dulcie's, go out to some shop on Fifth Avenue, buy a pretty party gown of similar dimensions, and bring it back with you. Take a taxi both ways. Wait— take her stockings and slippers, too, and buy her some fine ones. And some underwear suitable." He went to a desk, unlocked it, and handed the maid a flat packet of bank-notes. "Be sure the things are nice," he insisted.

Selinda, starched, immaculate, frosty-eyed, marched out. She returned a few moments later, wearing jacket and hat.

"Sir, the lady on the telephone hass called again. The lady would inquire of Mr. Barres if perhaps he has recollection of the Fountain of Marie de Médicis."

Barres reddened with surprise and pleasure:

"Oh! Yes, indeed, I'll speak to *that* lady. Hang up

the service receiver, Selinda." And he stepped to the studio telephone.

"Nihla?" he exclaimed in a low, eager voice.

"C'est moi, Thessa! Have you a letter from me?"

"No, you little wretch! Oh, Thessa, you're certainly a piker! Fancy my not hearing one word from you since April!—not a whisper, not a sign to tell me that you are alive——"

"Garry, hush! It was not because I did not wish to see you——"

"Yes, it was! You knew bally well that I hadn't your address and that you had mine! Is that what you call friendship?"

"You don't understand what you are saying. I wanted to see you. It has been impossible——"

"You are not singing and dancing anywhere in New York. I watched the papers. I even went to the Palace of Mirrors to enquire if you had signed with them there."

"Wait! Be careful, please!——"

"Why?"

"Be careful what you say over the telephone. For my sake, Garry. Don't use my former name or say anything to identify me with any place or profession. I've been in trouble. I'm in trouble still. Had you no letter from me this morning?"

"No."

"That is disquieting news. I posted a letter to you last night. You should have had it in your morning mail."

"No letter has come from you. I had no letters at all in the morning mail, and only one or two important business letters since."

"Then I'm deeply worried. I shall have to see you unless that letter is delivered to you by evening."

"Splendid! But you'll have to come to me, Thessa. I've invited a few people to dine here and dance afterwards. If you'll dine with us, I'll get another man to balance the table. Will you?"

After a moment she said:

"Yes. What time?"

"Eight! This is wonderful of you, Thessa!" he said excitedly. "If you're in trouble we'll clear it up between us. I'm so happy that you will give me this proof of friendship."

"You dear boy," she said in a troubled voice. "I should be more of a friend if I kept away from you."

"Nonsense! You promise, don't you?"

"Yes. . . . . Do you realise that to-night another summer moon is to witness our reunion? . . . I shall come to you once more under a full June moon. . . . And then, perhaps, no more. . . . Never. . . . Unless after the world ends I come to you through shadowy outer space—a ghost drifting—a shred of mist across the moon, seeking you once more!——"

"My poor child," he said laughing, "you must be in no end of low spirits to talk that way."

"It does sound morbid. But I have plenty of courage, Garry. I shall not snivel on the starched bosom of your evening shirt when we meet. Donc, à bientôt, monsieur. Soyez tranquille! You shall not be ashamed of me among your guests."

"Fancy!" he laughed happily. "Don't worry, Thessa. We'll fix up whatever bothers you. Eight o'clock! Don't forget!"

"I am not likely to," she said.

Until Selinda returned from her foray along Fifth Avenue, Barres remained in the studio, lying in his arm-chair, still possessed by the delightful spell, still excited by the prospect of seeing Thessalie Dunois again, here, under his own roof.

But when the slant-eyed and spotlessly blond Finn arrived, he came back out of his retrospective trance.

"Did you get some pretty things for Miss Soane?" he enquired.

"Yess, sir, be-ootiful." Selinda deposited on the table a sheaf of paid bills and the balance of the bank-notes. "Would Mr. Barres be kind enough to inspect the clothes for Miss Soane?"

"No, thanks. You say they're all right?"

"Yess, sir. They are heavenly be-ootiful."

"Very well. Tell Aristocrates to lay out my clothes after you have dressed Miss Dulcie. There will be two extra people to dinner. Tell Aristocrates. Is Miss Dulcie still asleep?"

"Yess, sir."

"All right. Wake her in time to dress her so she can come out here and give me a chance——" He glanced at the clock "Better wake her now, Selinda. It's time for her to dress and evacuate my quarters. I'll take forty winks here until she's ready."

Barres lay dozing on the sofa when Dulcie came in.

Selinda, enraptured by her own efficiency in grooming and attiring the girl, marched behind her, unable to detach herself from her own handiwork.

From crown to heel the transfiguration was absolute—from the point of her silk slipper to the topmost curl on the head which Selinda had dressed to perfection.

For Selinda had been a lady's maid in great houses, and also had a mania for grooming herself with the minute and thorough devotion of a pedigreed cat. And Dulcie emerged from her hands like some youthful sea-nymph out of a bath of foam, snowy-sweet as some fresh and slender flower.

With a shy courage born with her own transfiguration, she went to Barres, where he lay on the sofa, and bent over him.

She had made no sound; perhaps her nearness awoke him, for he opened his eyes.

"Dulcie!" he exclaimed.

"Do I please you?" she whispered.

He sat up abruptly.

"You wonderful child!" he said, frankly astonished. Whereupon he got off the sofa, walked all around her inspecting her.

"What a get-up! What a girl!" he murmured. "You lovely little thing, you astound me! Selinda, you certainly know a thing or two. Take it from me, you do Miss Soane and yourself more credit in your way than I do with paint and canvas."

Dulcie blushed vividly; the white skin of Selinda also reddened with pleasure at her master's enthusiasm.

"Tell Aristocrates to fix my bath and lay out my clothes," he said. "I've guests coming and I've got to hustle!" And to Dulcie: "We're going to have a little party in honour of your graduation. That's what I have to tell you, dear. Does it please you? Do your pretty clothes please you?"

The girl, overwhelmed, could only look at him. Her lips, vivid and slightly parted, quivered as her breath came irregularly. But she found no words—nothing to say except in the passionate gratitude of her grey eyes.

"You dear child," he said gently. Then, after a moment's silence, he eased the tension with his quick smile: "Wonder-child, go and seat yourself very carefully, and be jolly careful you don't rumple your frock, because I want you to astonish one or two people this evening."

Dulcie found her voice:

"I—I'm so astonished at myself that I don't seem real. I seem to be somebody else—long ago!" She stepped close to him, opened her locket for his inspection, holding it out to him as far as the chain permitted. It framed a miniature of a red-haired, grey-eyed girl of sixteen.

"Your mother, Dulcie?"

"Yes. How perfectly it fits into my locket! I carry it always in my purse."

"It might easily be yourself, Dulcie," he said in a low voice. "You are her living image."

"Yes. That is what astonishes me. To-night, for the first time in my life, it occurred to me that I look like this girl picture of my mother."

"You never thought so before?"

"Never." She stood looking down at the laughing face in the locket for a few moments, then, lifting her eyes to his:

"I've been made over, in a day, to look like this. . . . You did it!"

"Nonsense! Selinda and her curling iron did it."

They laughed a little.

"No," she said, "you have made me. You began to make me all over three months ago—oh, longer ago than that!—you began to remake me the first time you ever spoke to me—the first time you opened your door to me. That was nearly two years ago. And ever since I have been slowly becoming somebody quite new—inside and outside—until to-night, you see, I begin to look like my mother." She smiled at him, drew a deep breath, closed the locket, dropped it on her breast.

"I mustn't keep you," she said. "I wanted to show

the picture—so you can understand what you have done for me to make me look like that."

When Barres returned to the studio, freshened and groomed for the evening, he found Dulcie at the piano, playing the little song she had sung that morning, and singing the words under her breath. But she ceased as he came up, and swung around on the piano-stool to confront him with the most radiant smile he had ever seen on a human face.

"What a day this has been!" she said, clasping her hands tightly. "I simply cannot make it seem real."

He laughed:

"It isn't ended yet, either. There's a night to every day, you know. And your graduation party will begin in a few moments."

"I know. I'm fearfully excited. You'll stay near me, won't you?"

"You bet! Did I tell you who . coming? Well, then, you won't feel strange, becaus I've merely asked two or three men who live in Dragon Court—men you see every day—Mr. Trenor, Mr. Mandel, and Mr. Westmore."

"Oh," she said, relieved.

"Also," he said, "I have asked Miss Souval—that tall, pretty girl who sometimes sits for Mr. Trenor—Damaris Souval. You remember her?"

"Yes."

"Also," he continued, "Mr. Mandel wishes to bring a young married woman who has developed a violent desire for the artistic and informal, but who belongs in the Social Register." He laughed. "It's all right if Corot Mandel wants her. Her name is Mrs. Helmund—Elsena Helmund. Mr. Trenor is painting her."

Dulcie's face was serious but calm.

"And then, to even the table," concluded Barres smilingly, "I invited a girl I knew long ago in Paris. Her name is Thessalie Dunois; and she's very lovely to look upon, Dulcie. I am very sure you will like her."

There was a silence; then the electric bell rang in the corridor, announcing the arrival of the first guest. As Barres rose, Dulcie laid her hand on his arm—a swift, involuntary gesture—as though the girl were depending on his protection.

The winning appeal touched him and amused him, too.

"Don't worry, dear," he said. "You'll have the prettiest frock in the studio—if you need that knowledge to reassure you——"

The corridor door opened and closed. Somebody went into his bedroom with Selinda—that being the only available cloak-room for women.

XI

"THESSALIE DUNOIS! This is charming of you!" said Barres, crossing the studio swiftly and taking her hand in both of his.

"I'm so glad to see you, Garry—" she looked past him across the studio at Dulcie, and her voice died out for a moment. "Who is that girl?" she enquired under her breath.

"I'll present you——"

"Wait. *Who* is she?"

"Dulcie Soane——"

"*Soane?*"

"Yes. I'll tell you about her later——"

"In a moment, Garry." Thessalie looked across the room at the girl for a second or two longer, then turned a troubled, preoccupied gaze on Barres. "Have you a letter from me? I posted it last night."

"Not yet."

The door-bell rang. He could hear more guests entering the corridor beyond. A faint smile—the forced smile of courage—altered Thessalie's features now, until it became a fixed and pretty mask.

"Contrive to give me a moment alone with you this evening," she whispered. "My need is great, Garry."

"Whenever you say! Now?"

"No. I want to talk to that young girl first."

They walked over to where Dulcie stood by the piano, silent and self-possessed.

"Thessa," he said, "this is Miss Soane, who graduated from high school to-day, and in whose honour I am giving this little party." And to Dulcie he said: "Miss Dunois and I were friends when I lived in France. Please tell her about your picture, which you and I are doing." He turned as he finished speaking, and went forward to welcome Esmé Trenor and Damaris Souval, who happened to arrive together.

"Oh, the cunning little girl over there!" exclaimed the tall and lovely Damaris, greeting Barres with cordial, outstretched hands. "Where did you find such an engaging little thing?"

"You don't recognise her!" he asked, amused.

"I? No. Should I?"

"She's Dulcie Soane, the girl at the desk downstairs!" said Barres, delighted. "This is her party. She has just graduated from high school, and she——"

"Belongs to Barres," interrupted Esmé Trenor in his drawling voice. "Unusual, isn't she, Damaris?—logical anatomy, ornamental, vague development; nice lines, not obvious—like yours, Damaris," he added impudently. Then waving his lank hand with its overpolished nails: "I like the indefinite accented with one ripping value. Look at that hair!—lac and burnt orange rubbed in, smeared, then wiped off with the thumb! You follow the intention, Barres?"

"You talk too much, Esmé," interrupted Damaris tartly. "Who is that lovely being talking to the little Soane girl, Garry?"

"A friend of my Paris days—Thessalie Dunois——" Again he checked himself to turn and greet Corot Mandel, subtle creator and director of exotic spectacles—another tall and rather heavily built man, with a mop of black and shiny hair, a monocle, and sanguine features slightly oriental.

With Corot Mandel had come Elsena Helmund—an attractive woman of thoroughbred origin and formal environment, and apparently fed up with both. For she frankly preferred "grades" to "registered stock," and she prowled through every art and theatrical purlieu from the Mews to Westchester, in eternal and unquiet search for an antidote to the sex-ennui which she erroneously believed to be an intellectual necessity for self-expression.

"Who is that winning child with red hair?" she enquired, nodding informal recognition to the other guests, whom she already knew. "Don't tell me," she added, elevating a quizzing glass and staring at Dulcie, "that this engaging infant has a history already! It isn't possible, with that April smile in her child eyes!"

"You bet she hasn't a history, Elsena," said Barres, frowning; "and I'll see that she doesn't begin one as long as she's in my neighbourhood."

Corot Mandel, who had been heavily inspecting Dulcie through his monocle, now stood twirling it by its frayed and greasy cord:

"I could do something for her—unless she's particularly yours, Barres?" he suggested. "I've seldom seen a better type in New York."

"You idiot. Don't you recognise her? She's Dulcie Soane! You could have picked her yourself if you'd had any flaire."

"Oh, hell," murmured Mandel, disgusted. "And I thought I possessed flaire. Your private property, I suppose?" he added sourly.

"Absolutely. Keep off!"

"Watch me," murmured Corot Mandel, with a wry face, as they moved forward to join the others and be presented to the little guest of the evening.

Westmore came in at the same moment—a short,

blond, vigorous young man, who knew everybody except Thessalie, and proceeded to smash the ice in characteristic fashion:

"Dulcie! You beautiful child! How are you, duckey?"—catching her by both hands,—"a little salute for Nunky? Yes?"—kissing her heartily on both cheeks. "I've a gift for you in my overcoat pocket. We'll sneak out and get it after dinner!" He gave her hands a hearty squeeze, turned to the others: "I ought to have been Miss Soane's godfather. So I appointed myself as such. Where are the cocktails, Garry?"

Road-to-ruin cocktails were served—frosted orange juice for Dulcie. Everybody drank her health. Then Aristocrates gracefully condescended to announce dinner. And Barres took out Dulcie, her arm resting light as a snowflake on his sleeve.

There were flowers everywhere in the dining-room; table, buffet, curtains, lustres were gay with early blossoms, exhaling the haunting scent of spring.

"Do you like it, Dulcie?" he whispered.

She merely turned and looked at him, quite unable to speak, and he laughed at her brilliant eyes and flushed cheeks, and, dropping his right hand, squeezed hers.

"It's your party, Sweetness—all yours! You must have a good time every minute!" And he turned, still smiling, to Thessalie Dunois on his left:

"It's quite wonderful, Thessa, to have you here—to be actually seated beside you at my own table. I shall not let you slip away from me again, you enchanting ghost!—and leave me with a dislocated heart."

"Garry, that sounds almost sentimental. We're not, you know."

"How do I know? You never gave me a chance to be sentimental."

She laughed mirthlessly:

"Never gave you a chance? And our brief but head-long career together, monsieur? What was it but a continuous cataract of chances?"

"But we were laughing our silly heads off every minute! I had no opportunity."

That seemed to amuse her and awaken the ever-latent humour in her.

"Opportunity," she observed demurely, "should be created and taken, not shyly awaited with eyes rolled upward and a sucked thumb."

They both laughed outright. Her colour rose; the old humorous challenge was in her eyes again; the subtle mask was already slipping from her features, revealing them in all their charming recklessness.

"You know my creed," she said; "to go forward—laugh—and accept what Destiny sends you—still laughing!" Her smile altered again, became, for a moment, strange and vague. "God knows that is what I am doing to-night," she murmured, lifting her slim glass, in which the gush of sunny bubbles caught the candle-light. "To Destiny—whatever it may be! Drink with me, Garry!"

Around them the chatter and vivacity increased, as Damaris ended a duel of wit with Westmore and pre-pared for battle with Corot Mandel. Everybody seemed to be irresponsibly loquacious except Dulcie, who sat between Barres and Esmé Trenor, a silent, smiling, reserved little listener. For Barres was still conversationally involved with Thessalie, and Esmé Trenor, languid and detached, being entirely ignored by Damaris, whom he had taken out, awaited his own proper modicum of worship from his silent little neigh-bour on his left—which tribute he took for granted was his sacred due, and which, hitherto, he had invariably received from woman.

But nobody seemed to be inclined to worship; Demaris scarcely deigned to notice him, his impudence, perhaps, still rankling. Thessalie, laughingly engaged with Barres, remained oblivious to the fashionable portrait painter. As for Eleena Helmund, that youthful matron was busily pretending to comprehend Corot Mandel's covert orientalisms, and secretly wondering whether they were, perhaps, as improper as Westmore kept whispering to her they were, urging her to pick up her skirts and run.

Esmé Trenor permitted a few weary but slightly disturbed glances to rest on Dulcie from time to time, but made no effort to entertain her.

And she, on her part, evinced no symptoms of worshipping him. And all the while he was thinking to himself:

"Can this be the janitor's daughter? Is she the same rather soiled, impersonal child whom I scarcely ever noticed—the thin, immature, negligible little drudge with a head full of bobbed red hair?"

His lack of vision, of finer discernment, deeply annoyed him. Her lack of inclination to worship him, now that she had the God-sent opportunity, irritated him.

"The silly little bounder," he thought, "how can she sit beside me without timidly venturing to entertain me?"

He stole another profoundly annoyed glance at Dulcie. The child was certainly beautiful—a slim, lovely, sensitive thing of qualities so delicate that the painter of pretty women became even more surprised and chagrined that it had taken Barres to discover this desirable girl in the silent, shabby child of Larry Soane.

Presently he lurched part way toward her in his chair, and looked at her with bored but patronising encouragement.

"Talk to me," he said languidly.

Dulcie turned and looked at him out of uninterested grey eyes.

"What?" she said.

"Talk to me," he repeated pettishly.

"Talk to yourself," retorted Dulcie, and turned again to listen to the gay nonsense which Damaris and Westmore were exchanging amid peals of general laughter.

But Esmé Trenor was thunderstruck. A deep and painful colour stained his pallid features. Never before had mortal woman so flouted him. It was unthinkable. It really wouldn't do. There must be some explanation for this young girl's monstrous attitude toward offered opportunity.

"I say," he insisted, still very red, "are you bashful, by any chance?"

Dulcie slowly turned toward him again:

"Sometimes I am bashful; not now."

"Oh. Then wouldn't you like to talk to me?"

"I don't think so."

"Fancy! And why not, Dulcie?"

"Because I haven't anything to say to you."

"Dear child, that is the incentive to all conversation —lack of anything to say. You should practise the art of saying nothing politely."

"You should have practised it enough to say good morning to me during these last five years," said Dulcie gravely.

"Oh, I say! You're rather severe, you know! You were just a little thing running about underfoot!—I'm sorry you feel angry——"

"I do not. But how can I have anything to talk to you about, Mr. Trenor, when you have never even noticed me all these years, although often I have handed you your keys and your letters."

"It was quite stupid of me. I'm sorry. But a man, you see, doesn't notice children——"

"Some men do."

"You mean Mr. Barres! That *is* unkind. Why rub it in, Dulcie? I'm rather an interesting fellow, after all."

"Are you?" she asked absently.

Her honest indifference to him was perfectly apparent to Esmé Trenor. This would never do. She must be subdued, made sane, disciplined!

"Do you know," he drawled, leaning lankly nearer, dropping both arms on the cloth, and fixing his heavy-lidded eyes intensely on her, "—do you know—do you guess, perhaps, why I never spoke to you in all these years?"

"You did not trouble yourself to speak to me, I imagine."

"You are wrong. I was *afraid!*" And he stared at her pallidly.

"Afraid?" she repeated, puzzled.

He leaned nearer, confidential, sad:

"Shall I tell you a precious secret, Dulcie? I am a coward. I am a slave of fear. I am afraid of beauty! Isn't that a very strange thing to say? Can you understand the subtlety of that indefinable psychology? Fear is an emotion. Fear of the beautiful is still a subtler emotion. Fear, itself, is beautiful beyond words. Beauty is Fear. Fear is Beauty. Do you follow me, Dulcie?"

"No," said the girl, bewildered.

Esmé sighed:

"Some day you will follow me. It is my destiny to be followed, pursued, haunted by loveliness impotently seeking to express itself to me, while I, fearing it, dare only to express my fear with brush and pencil! . . . When shall I paint you?" he added with sad benevolence.

"What?"

"When shall I try to interpret upon canvas my subtle fear of you?" And, as the girl remained mute: "When," he explained languidly, "shall I appoint an hour for you to sit to me?"

"I am Mr. Barres's model," she said, flushing.

"I shall have to arrange it with him, then," he nodded, wearily.

"I don't think you can."

"Fancy! Why not?"

"Because I do not wish to sit to anybody except Mr. Barres," she said candidly, "and what you paint does not interest me at all."

"Are you familiar with my work?" he asked incredulously.

She shook her head, shrugged, and turned to Barres, who had at last relinquished Thessalie to Westmore.

"Well, Sweetness," he said gaily, "do you get on with Esmé Trenor?"

"He talked," she said in a voice perfectly audible to Esmé.

Barres glanced toward Esmé, secretly convulsed, but that young apostle of Fear had swung one thin leg over the other and was now presenting one shoulder and the back of his head to them both, apparently in delightful conversation with Elsena Helmund, who was fed up on him and his fears.

"You must always talk to your neighbours at dinner," insisted Barres, still immensely amused. "Esmé

is a very popular man with fashionable women, Dulcie,
—a painter in much demand and much adored. . . .
Why do you smile?"

Dulcie smiled again, deliciously.

"Anyway," continued Barres, "you must now give
the signal for us to rise by standing up. I'm so proud
of you, Dulcie, darling!" he added impulsively; "—and
everybody is mad about you!"

"You made me—" she laughed mischievously, "—out
of a rag and a bone and a hank of hair!"

"You made yourself out of nothing, child! And
everybody thinks you delightful."

"Do *you?*"

"You dear girl!—of course I do. Does it make such
a difference to you, Dulcie—my affection for you?"

"Is it—*affection?*"

"It certainly is. Didn't you know it?"

"I didn't—know—what it was."

"Of course it is affection. Who could be with you
as I have been and not grow tremendously fond of
you?"

"Nobody ever did except you. Mr. Westmore was
always nice. But—but you are so kind—I can't express—I—c-can't——" Her emotion checked her.

"Don't try, dear!" he said hastily. "We're going
in to have a jolly dance now. You and I begin it together. Don't you let any other fellow take you
away!"

She looked up, laughed blissfully, gazing at him
with brilliant eyes a little dimmed.

"They'll all be at your heels," he said, beginning to
comprehend the beauty he had let loose on the world,
"—every man-jack of them, mark my prophecy! But
ours is the first dance, Dulcie. Promise?"

"I do. And I promise you the next—please——"

"Well, I'm host," he said doubtfully, and a trifle taken aback. "We'll have some other dances together, anyway. But I couldn't monopolise you, Sweetness."

The girl looked at him silently, then her grey, intelligent eyes rested directly on Thessalie Dunois.

"Will you dance with her?" she asked gravely.

"Yes, of course. And with the others, too. Tell me, Dulcie, did you find Miss Dunois agreeable?"

"I—don't—know."

"Why, you ought to like her. She's very attractive."

"She is quite beautiful," said the girl, watching Thessalie across his shoulder.

"Yes, she really is. What did you and she talk about?"

"Father," replied Dulcie, determined to have no further commerce with Thessalie Dunois which involved a secrecy excluding Barres. "She asked me if he were not my father. Then she asked me a great many stupid questions about him. And about Miss Kurtz, who takes the desk when father is out. Also, she asked me about the mail and whether the postman delivered letters at the desk or in the box outside, and about the tenants' mail boxes, and who distributed the letters through them. She seemed interested," added the girl indifferently, "but I thought it a silly subject for conversation."

Barres, much perplexed, sat gazing at Dulcie in silence for a moment, then recollecting his duty, he smiled and whispered:

"Stand up, now, Dulcie. You are running this show."

The girl flushed and rose, and the others stood up. Barres took her to the studio door, then returned to the table with the group of men.

"Well," he exclaimed happily, "what do you fellows think of Soane's little girl now? Isn't she the sweetest thing you ever heard of?"

"A peach!" said Westmore, in his quick, hearty voice. "What's the idea, Garry? Is it to be her career, this posing business? And where is it going to land her? In the Winter Garden?"

"Where is it going to land *you!*" added Esmé impudently.

"Why, I don't know, myself," replied Barres, with a troubled smile. "The little thing always appealed to me—her loneliness and neglect, and—and something about the child—I can't define it——"

"Possibilities?" suggested Mandel viciously. "Take it from me, you're some picker, Garry."

"Perhaps. Anyway, I've given her the run of my place for the last two years and more. And she has been growing up all the while, and I didn't notice it. And suddenly, this spring, I discovered her for the first time. . . . And—well, look at her to-night!"

"She's your private model, isn't she?" persisted Mandel.

"Entirely," replied Barres drily.

"Selfish dog!" remarked Westmore, with his lively, wholesome laugh. "I once asked her to sit for me— more out of good nature than anything else. And a jolly fine little model she ought to make you, Garry. She's beginning to acquire a figure."

"She's quite wonderful that way, too," nodded Barres.

"Undraped?" inquired Esmé.

"A miracle," nodded Barres absently. "Paint is becoming inadequate. I shall model her this summer. I tell you I have never seen anything to compare to her. Never!"

"What else will you do with her?" drawled Esmé. "You'll go stale on her some day, of course. Am I next?"

"*No!* . . . I don't know what she'll do. It begins to look like a responsibility, doesn't it? She's such a fine little girl," explained Barres warmly. "I've grown quite fond of her—interested in her. Do you know she has an excellent mind? And nice, fastidious instincts? She *thinks* straight. That souse of a father of hers ought to be jailed for the way he neglects her."

"Are you thinking of adopting her?" asked Trenor, with the faintest of sneers, which escaped Barres.

"Adopt a *girl?* Oh, Lord, no! I can't do anything like that. Yet—I hate to think of her future, too . . . unless somebody looks out for her. But it isn't possible for *me* to do anything for her except to give her a good job with a decent man——"

"Meaning yourself," commented Mandel, acidly.

"Well, I *am* decent," retorted Barres warmly, amid general laughter. "You fellows know what chances she might take with some men," he added, laughing at his own warm retort.

Esmé and Corot Mandel nodded piously, each perfectly aware of what chance any attractive girl would run with his predatory neighbour.

"To shift the subject of discourse—that girl, Thessalie Dunois," began Westmore, in his energetic way, "is about the cleverest and prettiest woman I've seen in New York outside the theatre district."

"I met her in France," said Barres, carelessly. "She really is wonderfully clever."

"I shall let her talk to me," drawled Esmé, flicking at his cigarette. "It will be a liberal education for her."

Mandel's slow, oriental eyes blinked contempt; he

caressed his waxed moustache with nicotine-stained fingers:

"I am going to direct an out-of-door spectacle—a sort of play—not named yet—up your way, Barres—at Northbrook. It's for the Belgians. . . . If Miss Dunois—unless," he added sardonically, "you have her reserved, also——"

"Nonsense! You cast Thessalie Dunois and she'll make your show for you, Mandel!" exclaimed Barres. "I know and I'm telling you. Don't make any mistake: there's a girl who can make good!"

"Oh. Is she a professional?"

It was on the tip of Barres's tongue to say "Rather!" But he checked himself, not knowing Thessalie's wishes concerning details of her incognito.

"Talk to her about it," he said, rising.

The others laid aside cigars and followed him into the studio, where already the gramophone was going and Aristocrates and Selinda were rolling up the rugs.

Barres and Dulcie danced until the music, twice revived, expired in husky dissonance, and a new disc was substituted by Westmore.

"By heaven!" he said, "I'll dance this with my godchild or I'll murder you, Garry. Back up, there!— you soulless monopolist!" And Dulcie, half laughing, half vexed, was swept away in Westmore's vigorous arms, with a last, long, appealing look at Barres.

The latter danced in turn with his feminine guests, as in duty bound—in pleasure bound, as far as concerned Thessalie.

"And to think, to *think*," he repeated, "that you and I, who once trod the moonlit way, June-mad, moon-mad, should be dancing here together once more!"

"Alas," she said, "though this is June again, moon

and madness are lacking. So is the enchanted river and your canoe. And so is that gay heart of mine— that funny, careless little heart which was once my comrade, sending me into a happy gale of laughter every time it counselled me to folly."

"What is the matter, Thessa?"

"Garry, there is so much the matter that I don't know how to tell you. . . . And yet, I have nobody else to tell. . . . Is that maid of yours German?"

"No, Finnish."

"You can't be certain," she murmured. "Your guests are all American, are they not?"

"Yes."

"And the little Soane girl? Are her sympathies with Germany?"

"Why, certainly not! What gave you that idea, Thessa?"

The music ran down; Westmore, the indefatigable, still keeping possession of Dulcie, went over to wind up the gramophone.

"Isn't there some place where I could be alone with you for a few minutes?" whispered Thessalie.

"There's a balcony under the middle window. It overlooks the court."

She nodded and laid her hand on his arm, and they walked to the long window, opened it, and stepped out.

Moonlight fell into the courtyard, silvering everything. Down there on the grass the Prophet sat, motionless as a black sphinx in the lustre of the moon.

Thessalie looked down into the shadowy court, then turned and glanced up at the tiled roof just above them, where a chimney rose in silhouette against the pale radiance of the sky.

Behind the chimney, flat on their stomachs, lay two men who had been watching, through an upper ven-

145

tilating pane of glass, the scene in the brilliantly lighted studio below them.

The men were Soane and his crony, the one-eyed pedlar. But neither Thessalie nor Barres could see them up there behind the chimney.

Yet the girl, as though some unquiet instinct warned her, glanced up at the eaves above her head once more, and Barres looked up, too.

"What do you see up there?" he inquired.

"Nothing. . . . There could be nobody up there to listen, could there?"

He laughed:

"Who would want to climb up on the roof to spy on you or me——"

"Don't speak so loud, Garry——"

"What on earth is the trouble?"

"The same trouble that drove me out of France," she said in a low voice. "Don't ask me what it was. All I can tell you is this: I am followed everywhere I go. I cannot make a living. Whenever I secure an engagement and return at the appointed time to fill it, something happens."

"What happens?" he asked bluntly.

"They repudiate the agreement," she said in a quiet voice. "They give no reasons; they simply tell me that they don't want me. Do you remember that evening when I left the Palace of Mirrors?"

"Indeed, I do——"

"That was only one example. I left with an excellent contract, signed. The next day, when I returned, the management took my contract out of my hands and tore it up."

"What! Why, that's outrageous——"

"Hush! That is only one instance. Everywhere it is the same. I am accepted after a try-out; then, without apparent reason, I am told not to return."

"You mean there is some conspiracy——" he began incredulously, but she interrupted him with a white hand over his, nervously committing him to silence:

"Listen, Garry! Men have followed me here from Europe. I am constantly watched in New York. I cannot shake off this surveillance for very long at a time. Sooner or later I become conscious again of curious eyes regarding me; of features that all at once become unpleasantly familiar in the throng. After several encounters in street or car or restaurant, I recognise these. Often and often instinct alone warns me that I am followed; sometimes I am so certain of it that I take pains to prove it."

"Do you prove it?"

"Usually."

"Well, what the devil——"

"Hush! I seem to be getting into deeper trouble than that, Garry. I have changed my residence so many, many times!—but every time people get into my room when I am away and ransack my effects. . . . And now I never enter my room unless the landlady is with me, or the janitor—especially after dark."

"Good Lord!——"

"Listen! I am not really frightened. It isn't fear, Garry. That word isn't in my creed, you know. But it bewilders me."

"In the name of common sense," he demanded, "what reason has anybody to annoy you——"

Her hand tightened on his:

"If I only knew who these people are—whether they are agents of the Count d'Eblis or of the—the French Government! But I can't determine. They steal letters directed to me; they steal letters which I write and mail with my own hands. I wrote to you yesterday, because I—I felt I couldn't stand this persecution—any—longer——"

Her voice became unsteady; she waited, gripping his hand, until self-control returned. When she was mistress of herself again, she forced a smile and her tense hand relaxed.

"You know," she said, "it is most annoying to have my little love-letter to you intercepted."

But his features remained very serious:

"When did you mail that letter to me?"

"Yesterday evening."

"From where?"

"From a hotel."

He considered.

"I ought to have had it this morning, Thessa. But the mails, lately, have been very irregular. There have been other delays. This is probably an example."

"At latest," she said, "you should have my letter this evening."

"Y-yes. But the evening is young yet."

After a moment she drew a light sigh of relief, or perhaps of apprehension, he was not quite sure which.

"But about this other matter—men following and annoying you," he began.

"Not now, Garry. I can't talk about it now. Wait until we are sure about my letter——"

"But, Thessa——"

"Please! If you don't receive it before I leave, I shall come to you again and ask your aid and advice——"

"Will you come *here?*"

"Yes. Now take me in. . . . Because I am not quite certain about your maid—and perhaps one other person——"

His expression of astonishment checked her for a

148

moment, then the old irresistible laughter rang out sweetly in the moonlight.

"Oh, Garry! It is funny, isnt' it!—to be dogged and hunted day and night by a pack of shadows! If I only knew who casts them!"

She took his arm gaily, with that little, courageous lifting of the head:

"Allons! We shall dance again and defy the devil! And you may send your servant down to see whether my letter has arrived—not that maid with slanting eyes!—I have no confidence in her—but your marvellous major-domo, Garry——"

Her smile was bright and untroubled as she stepped back into the studio, leaning on his arm.

"You dear boy," she whispered, with the irresponsible undertone of laughter ringing in her voice, "thank you for bothering with my woes. I'll be rid of them soon, I hope, and then—perhaps—I'll lead you another dance along the moonlit way!"

On the roof, close to the chimney, the one-eyed man and Soane peered down into the studio through the smeared ventilator.

In the studio Dulcie's first party was drawing to an early but jolly end.

She had danced a dozen times with Barres, and her heart was full of sheerest happiness—the unreasoning bliss which asks no questions, is endowed with neither reason nor vision—the matchless delight which fills the candid, unquestioning heart of Youth.

Nothing had marred her party for her, not even the importunity of Esmé Trenor, which she had calmly disregarded as of no interest to her.

True, for a few moments, while Barres and Thessalie were on the balcony outside, Dulcie had become a trifle subdued. But the wistful glances she kept casting toward the long window were free from meaner taint; neither jealousy nor envy had ever found lodging in the girl's mind or heart. There was no room to let them in now.

Also, she was kept busy enough, one man after another claiming her for a dance. And she adored it —even with Trenor, who danced extremely well when he took the trouble. And he was taking it now with Dulcie; taking a different tone with her, too. For if it were true, as some said, that Esmé Trenor was three-quarters charlatan, he was no fool. And Dulcie began to find him entertaining to the point of a smile or two, as her spontaneous tribute to Esmé's efforts.

That languid apostle said afterward to Mandel, where they were lounging over the piano:

"Little devil! She's got a mind of her own, and she knows it. I've had to make efforts, Corot!—efforts, if you please, to attract her mere attention. I'm exhausted!—never before had to make any efforts— never in my life!"

Mandel's heavy-lidded eyes of a big bird rested on Dulcie, where she was seated. Her gaze was lifted to Barres, who bent over her in jesting conversation.

Mandel, watching her, said to Esmé:

"I'm always ready to *train*—that sort of girl; always on the lookout for them. One discovers a specimen once or twice in a decade. . . . Two or three in a lifetime: that's all."

"Train them?" repeated Esmé, with an indolent smile. "Break them, you mean, don't you?"

"Yes. The breaking, however, is usually mutual. However, that girl could go far under my direction."

"Yes, she could go as far as hell."

"I mean artistically," remarked Mandel, undisturbed.

"As what, for example?"

"As anything. After all, I *have* flaire, even if it failed me this time. . But now I see. It's there, in her —what I'm always searching for."

"What may that be, dear friend?"

"What Westmore calls 'the goods.' "

"And just what are they in her case?" inquired Esmé, persistent as a stinging gnat around a pachyderm.

"I don't know—a voice, maybe; maybe the dramatic instinct—genius as a dancer—who knows? All that is necessary is to discover it—whatever it may be—and then direct it."

"Too late, O philanthropic Pasha!" remarked Esmé with a slight sneer. "I'd be very glad to paint her, too, and become good friends with her—so would many an honest man, now that she's been discovered—but our friend Barres, yonder, isn't likely to encourage either you or me. So"—he shrugged, but his languid gaze remained on Dulcie—"so you and I had better kiss all hope good-bye and toddle home."

Westmore and Thessalie still danced together; Mrs. Helmund and Damaris were trying new steps in new dances, much interested, indulging in much merriment. Barres watched them casually, as he conversed with Dulcie, who, deep in an armchair, never took her eyes from his smiling face.

"Now, Sweetness," he was saying, "it's early yet, I know, but your party ought to end, because you are coming to sit for me in the morning, and you and I ought to get plenty of sleep. If we don't, I shall have an unsteady hand, and you a pair of sleepy eyes. Come on, ducky!" He glanced across at the clock:

"It's very early yet, I know," he repeated, "but you

and I have had rather a long day of it. And it's been
a very happy one, hasn't it, Dulcie?"

As she smiled, the youthful soul of her itself seemed
to be gazing up at him out of her enraptured eyes.

"Fine!" he said, with deepest satisfaction. "Now,
you'll put your hand on my arm and we'll go around
and say good-night to everybody, and then I'll take
you down stairs."

So she rose and placed her hand lightly on his arm,
and together they made her adieux to everybody, and
everybody was cordially demonstrative in thanking her
for her party.

So he took her down stairs to her apartment, off
the hall, noticing that neither Soane nor Miss Kurts
was on duty at the desk, as they passed, and that a
pile of undistributed mail lay on the desk.

"That's rotten," he said curtly. "Will you have to
change your clothes, sort this mail, and sit here until
the last mail is delivered?"

"I don't mind," she said.

"But I wanted you to go to sleep. Where is Miss
Kurts?"

"It is her evening off."

"Then your father ought to be here," he said, irritated, looking around the big, empty hallway.

But Dulcie only smiled and held out her slim hand:

"I couldn't sleep, anyway. I had really much rather
sit here for a while and dream it all over again. Good-
night. . . . Thank you—I can't say what I feel—but
m-my heart is very faithful to you, Mr. Barres—will
always be—while I am alive . . . because you are my
first friend."

He stooped impulsively and touched her hair with
his lips:

"You dear child," he said, "I *am* your friend."

Halfway up the western staircase he called back:
"Ring me up, Dulcie, when the last mail comes!"

"I will," she nodded, almost blindly.

Out of her lovely, abashed eyes she watched him
mount the stairs, her cheeks a riot of surging colour.
It was some few minutes after he was gone that she
recollected herself, turned, and, slowly traversing the
east corridor, entered her bedroom.

Standing there in darkness, vaguely silvered by reflected moonlight, she heard through her door ajar the
guests of the evening descending the western staircase;
heard their gay adieux exchanged, distinguished Esmé's
impudent drawl, Westmore's lively accents, Mandel's
voice, the easy laughter of Damaris, the smooth, affected tones of Mrs. Helmund.

But Dulcie listened in vain for the voice which had
haunted her ears since she had left the studio—the
lovely voice of Thessalie Dunois.

If this radiant young creature also had departed
with the other guests, she had gone away in silence.
. . . *Had* she departed? Or was she still lingering
upstairs in the studio for a little chat with the most
wonderful man in the world? . . . A very, very beautiful girl. . . . And the most wonderful man in the
world. Why should they not linger for a little chat
together after the others had departed?

Dulcie sighed lightly, pensively, as one whose happiness lies in the happiness of others. To be a witness
seemed enough for her.

For a little while longer she remained standing there
in the silvery dusk, quite motionless, thinking of Barres.

The Prophet lay asleep, curled up on her bed; her
alarm clock ticked noisily in the darkness, as though
to mimic the loud, fast rhythm of her heart.

At last, and as in a dream, she groped for a match,

lighted the gas jet, and began to disrobe. Slowly, dreamily, she put from her slender body the magic garments of light—*his* gift to her.

But under these magic garments, clothing her new-born soul, remained the radiant rainbow robe of that new dawn into which this man had led her spirit. Did it matter, then, what dingy, outworn clothing covered her, outside?

Clad once more in her shabby, familiar clothes, and bedroom slippers, Dulcie opened the door of her dim room, and crept out into the whitewashed hall, moving as in a trance. And at her heels stalked the Prophet, softly, like a lithe shape that glides through dreams.

Awaiting the last mail, seated behind the desk on the worn leather chair, she dropped her linked fingers into her lap, and gazed straight into an invisible world peopled with enchanting phantoms. And, little by little, they began to crowd her vision, throng all about her, laughing, rosy wraiths floating, drifting, whirling in an endless dance. Everywhere they were invading the big, silent hall, where the candle's grotesque shadows wavered across whitewashed wall and ceiling. Drowsily, now, she watched them play and sway around her. Her head drooped; she opened her eyes.

The Prophet sat there, staring back at her out of depthless orbs of jade, in which all the wisdom and mysteries of the centuries seemed condensed and concentrated into a pair of living sparks.

XII

THE LAST MAIL

THE last mail had not yet arrived at Dragon Court.

Five people awaited it—Dulcie Soane, behind the desk in the entrance hall, already wandering drowsily with Barres along the fairy borderland of sleep; Thessalie Dunois in Barres' studio, her rose-coloured evening cloak over her shoulders, her slippered foot tapping the dance-scarred parquet; Barres opposite, deep in his favourite arm-chair, chatting with her; Soane on the roof, half stupid with drink, watching them through the ventilator; and, lurking in the moonlit court, outside the office window, the dimly sinister figure of the one-eyed man. He wore a white handkerchief over his face, with a single hole cut in it. Through this hole his solitary optic was now fixed upon the back of Dulcie's drowsy head.

As for the Prophet, perched on the desk top, he continued to gaze upon shapes invisible to all things mortal save only such as he.

The postman's lively whistle aroused Dulcie. The Prophet, knowing him, observed his advent with indifference.

"Hello, girlie," he said;—he was a fresh-faced and flippant young man. "Where's Pop?" he added, depositing a loose sheaf of letters on the desk before her and sketching in a few jig steps with his feet.

"I don't know," she murmured, patting with one slim hand her pink and yawning lips, and watching him unlock the post-box and collect the outgoing mail. He lingered a moment to caress the Prophet, who endured it without gratitude.

"You better go to bed if you want to grow up to be a big, sassy girl some day," he advised Dulcie. "And hurry up about it, too, because I'm going to marry you if you behave." And, with a last affable caress for the Prophet, the young man went his way, singing to himself, and slamming the iron grille smartly behind him.

Dulcie, rising from her chair, sorted the mail, sleepily tucking each letter and parcel into its proper pigeon-hole. There was a thick letter for Barres. This she held in her left hand, remembering his request that she call him up when the last mail arrived.

This she now prepared to do—had already reseated herself, her right hand extended toward the telephone, when a shadow fell across the desk, and the Prophet turned, snarled, struck, and fled.

At the same instant grimy fingers snatched at the letter which she still held in her left hand, twisted it almost free of her desperate clutch, tore it clean in two at one violent jerk, leaving her with half the letter still gripped in her clenched fist.

She had not uttered a sound during the second's struggle. But instantly an ungovernable rage blazed up in her at the outrage, and she leaped clean over the desk and sprang at the throat of the one-eyed man.

His neck was bony and muscular; she could not compass it with her slender hands, but she struck at it furiously, driving a sound out of his throat, half roar, half cough.

"Give me my letter!" she breathed. "I'll kill you

156

if you don't!" Her furious little hands caught his clenched fist, where the torn letter protruded, and she tore at it and beat upon it, her teeth set and her grey Irish eyes afire.

Twice the one-eyed man flung her to her knees on the pavement, but she was up again and clinging to him before he could tear free of her.

"My letter!" she gasped. "I shall kill you, I tell you—unless you return it!"

His solitary yellow eye began to glare and glitter as he wrenched and dragged at her wrists and arms about him.

"Schweinstück!" he panted. "Let los, mioche de malheur! Eh! Los!—or I strike! No? Also! Attrape!—sale gallopin!——"

His blow knocked her reeling across the hall. Against the whitewashed wall she collapsed to her knees, got up half stunned, the clang of the outer grille ringing in her very brain.

With dazed eyes she gazed at the remnants of the torn letter, still crushed in her rigid fingers. Bright drops of blood from her mouth dripped slowly to the tessellated pavement.

Reeling still from the shock of the blow, she managed to reach the outer door, and stood swaying there, striving to pierce with confused eyes the lamplit darkness of the street. There was no sign of the one-eyed man. Then she turned and made her way back to the desk, supporting herself with a hand along the wall.

Waiting a few moments to control her breathing and her shaky limbs, she contrived finally to detach the receiver and call Barres. Over the wire she could hear the gramophone playing again in the studio.

"Please may I come up?" she whispered.

"Has the last mail come? Is there a letter for me?" he asked.

"Yes. . . . I'll bring you w-what there is—if you'll let me?"

"Thanks, Sweetness! Come right up!" And she heard him say: "It's probably your letter, Thessa. Dulcie is bringing it up."

Her limbs and body were still quivering, and she felt very weak and tearful as she climbed the stairway to the corridor above.

The nearer door of his apartment was open. Through it the music of the gramophone came gaily; and she went toward it and entered the brilliantly illuminated studio.

Soane, who still lay flat on the roof overhead, peeping through the ventilator, saw her enter, all dishevelled, grasping in one hand the fragments of a letter. And the sight instantly sobered him. He tucked his shoes under one arm, got to his stockinged feet, made nimbly for the scuttle, and from there, descending by the service stair, ran through the courtyard into the empty hall.

"Be gorry," he muttered, "thot dommed Dootchman has done it now!" And he pulled on his shoes, crammed his hat over his ears, and started east, on a run, for Grogan's.

Grogan's was still the name of the Third Avenue saloon, though Grogan had been dead some years, and one Frans Lehr now presided within that palace of cherrywood, brass and pretzels.

Into the family entrance fled Soane, down a dim hallway past several doors, from behind which sounded voices joining in guttural song; and came into a rear room.

The one-eyed man sat there at a small table, piecing together fragments of a letter.

"Arrah, then," cried Soane, "phwat th' devil did ye do, Max?"

The man barely glanced at him.

"Vy iss it," he enquired tranquilly, "you don'd vatch Nihla Quellen by dot wentilator some more?"

"I axe ye," shouted Soane, "what t'hell ye done to Dulcie!"

"Vat I haff done already yet?" queried the one-eyed man, not looking up, and continuing to piece together the torn letter. "Vell, I tell you, Soane; dot kid she keep dot letter in her handt, und I haff to grab it. Sacré saligaud de malheur! Dot letter she tear herself in two. Pas de chance! Your kid she iss mad like tigers! Voici—all sat resta me de la sacré-nom-de sacréminton de lettre——"

"Ah, shut up, y'r Dootch head-cheese!—wid y'r gillipin' gallopin' gabble!" cut in Soane wrathfully. "D'ye mind phwat ye done? It's not petty lar_ _, ye omadhoun!—it's highway robbery ye done—bad cess to ye!"

The one-eyed man shrugged:

"Pourtant, I must haff dot letter——" he observed, undisturbed by Soane's anger; but Soane cut him short again fiercely:

"You an' y'r dommed letter! Phwat do you care if I'm fired f'r this night's wurruk? Y'r letter, is it? An' what about highway robbery, me bucko! An' me off me post! How'll I be explaining that? Ah, ye sicken me entirely, ye Dootch square-head! Now, phwat'll I say to them? Tell me that, Max Freund! Phwat'll I tell th' aygent whin he comes runnin'? Phwat'll I tell th' po-lice? Arrah, phwat't'hell de you

care, anyway!" he shouted. "I've a mind f'r to knock
the block off ye——"

"You shall say to dot agent you haff gone out to
smell," remarked Max Freund placidly.

"Smell, is it? Smell what, ye dom——"

"You smell some smoke. You haff fear of fire. You
go out to see. Das iss so simble, ach! Take shame,
you Irish Sinn Fein! You behave like rabbits!" He
pointed to his arrangement of the torn letter on the
table: "Here iss sufficient already—regardes! Look
once!" He laid one long, soiled and bony finger on
the fragments: "Read it vat iss written!"

"G'wan, now!"

"I tell you, read!"

Soane, still cursing under his breath, bent over the
table, reading as Freund's soiled finger moved:

"Fein plots," he read. "German agents . . . disloyal propa . . . explo . . . bomb fac . . . shipping
munitions to . . . arms for Ireland can be . . . destruction of interned German li . . . disloyal newspapers which . . . controlled by us in Pari . . . Feres
Bey . . . bankers are duped. . . . I need your advi
. . . bounded day and ni . . . d'Eblis or Govern . . .
not afraid of death but indignant . . . Sinn Fei——"

Soane's scowl had altered, and a deeper red stained
his brow and neck.

"Well, by God!" he muttered, jerking up a chair
from behind him and seating himself at the table, but
never taking his fascinated eyes off the torn bits of
written paper.

Presently Freund got up and went out. He returned in a few moments with a large sheet of wrap-
ping paper and a pot of mucilage. On this paper, with
great care, he arranged the pieces of the torn letter,

neatly gumming each bit and leaving a space between it and the next fragment.

"To fill in iss the job of Louis Sendelbeck," remarked Freund, pasting away industriously. "Is it not time we learn how much she knows—this Nihla Quellen? Iss she sly like mice? I ask it."

Soane scratched his curly head

"Be gorry," he said, "av that purty girrl is a Frinch spy she don't look the parrt, Max."

Freund waved one unclean hand:

"Vas iss it to look like somedings? Nodding! Also, you Sinn Fein Irish talk too much. Why iss it in Belfast you march mit drums und music? To hold our tongues und vatch vat iss we Germans learn already first! Also! Sendelbeck shall haff his letter."

"An' phwat d'ye mean to do with that girrl, Max?"

"Vatch her! Vy you don'd go back by dot wentilator already?"

"Me? Faith, I'm done f'r th' evenin', an' I thank God I wasn't pinched on the leads!"

"Vait I catch dot Nihla somevares," muttered Freund, regarding his handiwork.

"Ye'll do no dirty thrick to her? Th' Sinn Fein will shtand f'r no burkin', mind that!"

"Ach, wass!" grunted Freund; "iss it your business vat iss done to somebody by Ferez? If you Irish vant your rifles und machine guns, leaf it to us Germans und dond speak nonsense aboud nodding!" He leaned over and pushed a greasy electric button: "Now ve drink a glass bier. Und after, you go home und vatch dot girl some more."

"Av Misther Barres an' th' yoong lady makes a holler, they'll fire me f'r this," snarled Soane.

"Sei ruhig, mon vieux! Nihla Quellen keeps like a mouse quiet! Und she keeps dot yoong man quiet!

You see! No, no! Not for Nihla to make some foolishness und publicity. French agents iss vatching fo her too—l'affaire du *Mot d'Ordre*. She iss vat yo say, 'in Dutch'! Iss she, vielleicht, a German spy In France they believe it. Iss she a French spy? Ach Possibly some day; not yet! And it iss for us Germa to know always vat she iss about. Dot iss my aff not yours, Soane."

A heavy jowled man in a soiled apron brought tw big mugs of beer and retired on felt-slippered feet.

"Hoch!" grunted Freund, burying his nose in frothing mug.

Soane, wasting no words, drank thirstily. After long pull he shoved aside his sloppy stein, rose, ca tiously unlatched the shutter of a tiny peep-hole in th wall, and applied one eye to it.

"Bad luck!" he muttered, "there do be was av thin secret service lads drinkin' at the bar! I'll not g home yet, Max."

"Dot big vone?" inquired Freund, mildly interested

"That's the buck! Him wid th' phony whiskers an' th' Dootch getup!"

"Vell, vot off it? Can he do somedings?"

"And how should I know phwat that lad can do t th' likes o' me, or phwat the divil brings him here a all, at all! Sure, he's been around these three night running——"

Freund laughed his contempt for all things Amer ican, including police and secret service, and wiped hi chin with the back of his hand.

"Look, once, Soane! Do these Yankees know va it iss a police, a gendarme, a military intelligence! Vat they call secret service, wass iss it? I ask it! Schweinerei! Dummheit! Fantoches! Imbeciles! O the Treasury they haff a secret service; of the Jus

tice Department also another; and another of the
Army, and yet another of the Posts! Vot kind of
foolish system iss it?—mitout no minister, no chef, no
centre, no head, no organisation—und everybody interfering in vot efferybody iss doing und nobody knowing vot nobody is doing—ach wass! Je m'en moque—
I make mock myself at dot secret service which iss too
dam dumm!" He yawned. "Trop bête," he added in-
distinctly.

Soane, reassured, lowered the shutter, came back to
the table, and finished his beer with loud gulps.

"Lave us go up to the lodge till he goes out," he
suggested. "Maybe th' boys have news o' thim rifles."

Freund yawned again, nodded, and rose, and they
went out to an unlighted and ill-smelling back stairway. It was so narrow that they had to ascend in
single file.

Half way up they set off a hidden bell, by treading
on some concealed button under foot; and a man,
dressed only in undershirt and trousers, appeared at
the top of the stairs, silhouetted against a bright light
burning on the wall behind him.

"Oh, all right," he said, recognising them, and turned
on his heel carelessly, pocketing a black-jack.

They followed to a closed door, which was made
out of iron and painted like quartered oak. In the wall
on their right a small shutter slid back noiselessly, then
was closed without a sound; and the iron door opened
very gently in their faces.

The room they entered was stifling—all windows being closed—in spite of a pair of electric fans whirling
and droning on shelves. Some perspiring Germans were
playing skat over in a corner. One or two other men
lounged about a centre table, reading Irish and German newspapers published in New York, Chicago, and

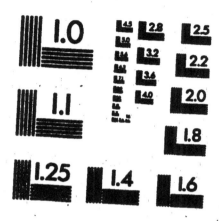

APPLIED IMAGE Inc

1653 East Main Street
Rochester, New York   14609   USA
(716) 482 – 0300 – Phone
(716) 288 – 5989 – Fax

Milwaukee. There were also on file there copies of th
Evening Mail, the *Evening Post*, a Chicago paper, an
a pile of magazines, including numbers of *Pearson'*
The Fatherland, *The Masses*, and similar publication

Two lithograph portraits hung side by side ove
the fireplace—Robert Emmet and Kaiser Wilhelm II
Otherwise, the art gallery included photographs of Vo
Hindenburg, Von Bissing, and the King of Greece.

A large map, on which the battle-line in Europe had
been pricked out in red pins, hung on the wall. Also
a map of New York City, on a very large scale; another
map of New York State; and a map of Ireland. A
dumb-waiter, on duty and astonishingly noiseless, slid
into sight, carrying half a dozen steins of beer and
some cheese sandwiches, just as Soane and Freund entered the room, and the silent iron door closed behind
them of its own accord and without any audible click.

The man who had met them on the stairs, in undershirt and trousers, went over to the dumb-waiter, scrib-
bled something on a slate which hung inside the shelf,
set the beer and sandwiches beside the skat players,
and returned to seat himself at the table to which
Freund and Soane had pulled up cane-bottomed chairs.

"Well," he said, in rather a pleasant voice, "did you
get that letter, Max?"

Freund nodded and leisurely sketched in the episode
at Dragon Court.

The man, whose name was Franz Lehr, and who had
been born in New York of German parents, listened
with lively interest to the narrative. But he whistled
softly when it ended:

"You took a few chances, Max," he remarked. "It's
all right, of course, because you got away with it,
but——" He whistled again, thoughtfully.

"Sendelbeck must haff his letter. Yess? Also!"

"Certainly. I guess that was the only way—if she was really going to take it up to young Barres. And I guess you're right when you conclude that Nihla won't make any noise about it and won't let her friend, Barres, either."

"Sure, I'm right," grunted Freund. "We got the goots on her now. You bet she's scared. You tell Ferez—yess?"

"Don't worry; he'll hear it all. You got that letter on you?"

Freund nodded.

"Hand it to Hochstein"—he half turned on his rickety chair and addressed a squat, bushy-haired man with very black eyebrows and large, angry blue eyes— "Louis, Max got that letter you saw Nihla writing in the Hotel Astor. Here it is——" taking the pasted fragments from Freund and passing them over to Hochstein. "Give it to Sendelbeck, along with the blotter you swiped after she left the writing room. Dave Sendelbeck ought to fix it up all right for Ferez Bey."

Hochstein nodded, shoved the folded brown paper into his pocket, and resumed his cards.

"Is thim rifles——" began Soane; but Lehr laid a hand on his shoulder:

"Now, listen! They're on the way to Ireland now. I told you that. When I hear they're landed I'll let you know. You Sinn Feiners don't understand how to wait. If things don't happen the way you want and when you want, you all go up in the air!"

"An' how manny hundred years would ye have us wait f'r to free th' ould sod!" retorted Soane.

"You'll not free it with your mouth," retorted Lehr. "No, nor by drilling with banners and arms in Cork and Belfast, and parading all over the place!"

"Is—that—so?"

"You bet it's so! The way to make England sick to stick her in the back, not make faces at her across Irish Channel. If your friends in the Clan-na-G and your poets and professors who call themsel Sinn Feiners, will quit their childish circus playing an trust us, we'll show you how to make the Lion yowl.

"Ah, bombs an' fires an' shtrikes is all right, to An' proppygandy is fine as far as it goes. But Clan-na-Gael is all afire f'r to start the shindy in land——"

"You start it," interrupted Lehr, "before you're really ready, and you'll see where it lands the Clan-na-Gael and the Sinn Fein! I tell you to leave it to Berlin!"

"An' I tell ye lave it to the Clan-na-Gael!" retorted Soane, excitedly. "Musha——"

"For why you yell?" yawned Freund, displaying a very yellow fang. "Dot big secret service slob, he iss in the bar hinunter. Perhaps he hear you if like a pig you push forth cries."

Lehr raised his eyebrows; then, carelessly:

"He's only a State agent. Johnny Klein is keeping an eye on him. What does that big piece of cheese expect to get by hanging out in my bar?"

Freund yawned again, appallingly; Soane said:

"I wonder is that purty Frinch girrl agin us Irish?"

"What does she care about the Irish?" replied Lehr. "Her danger to us lies in the fact that she may blab about Ferez to some Frenchman, and that he may believe her in spite of all the proof they have in Paris against her. Max," he added, turning to Freund, "it's funny that Ferez doesn't do something to her."

"I haff no orders."

"Maybe you'll get 'em when Ferez reads that letter.

He's certainly not going to let that girl go about blabbing and writing letters——"

Soane struck the table with doubled fist:

"Ye'll do no vi'lence to anny wan!" he cut in. "The Sinn Fein will shtand for no dirrty wurruk in America! Av you set fires an' blow up plants, an' kidnap ladies, an' do murther, g'wan, ye Dootch scuts!—it's your business, God help us!—not ours.

"All we axe of ye is machine-goons, an' rifles, an' ships to land them; an' av ye don't like it, phway th' divil d'ye come botherin' th' likes of us Irish wid y'r proppygandy! Sorra the day," he added, "I tuk up wid anny Dootchman at all at all——"

Lehr and Freund exchanged expressionless glances. The former dropped a propitiating hand on Soane's shoulder.

"Can it," he said good-humouredly. "We're trying to help you Irish to what you want. You want Irish independence, don't you? All right. We're going to help you get it——"

A bell rang; Lehr sprang to his feet and hastened out through the iron door, drawing his black-jack from his hip pocket as he went.

He returned in a few moments, followed by a very good-looking but pallid man in rather careless evening dress, who had the dark eyes of a dreamer and the delicate features of a youthful acolyte.

He saluted the company with a peculiarly graceful gesture, which recognition even the gross creatures at the skat table returned with visible respect.

Soane, always deeply impressed by the presence of Murtagh Skeel, offered his chair and drew another one to the table.

Skeel accepted with a gently preoccupied smile, and seated himself gracefully. All that is chivalrous, romantic, courteous, and brave in an Irishman seemed to be visibly embodied in this pale man.

"I have just come," he said, "from a dinner at Sherry's. A common hatred of England brought together the dozen odd men with whom I have been in conference. Ferez Bey was there, the military attachés of the German, Austrian, and Turkish embassies, one or two bankers, officials of certain steamship lines, and a United States senator."

He sipped a glass of plain water which Lehr had brought him, thanked him, then turning from Soane to Lehr:

"To get arms and munitions into Ireland in substantial quantities requires something besides the U-boats which Germany seems willing to offer.

"That was fully discussed to-night. Not that I have any doubt at all that Sir Roger will do his part skilfully and fearlessly——"

"He will that!" exclaimed Soane, "God bless him!"

"Amen, Soane," said Murtagh Skeel, with a wistful and involuntary upward glance from his dark eyes. Then he laid his hand of an aristocrat on Soane's shoulder. "What I came here to tell you is this: I want a ship's crew."

"Sorr?"

"I want a crew ready to mutiny at a signal from me and take over their own ship on the high seas."

"Their own ship, sorr?"

"Their own ship. That is what has been decided. The ship to be selected will be a fast steamer loaded with arms and munitions for the British Government. The Sinn Fein and the Clan-na-Gael, between them, are to assemble the crew. I shall be one of that crew. Through powerful friends, enemies to England, it will

be made possible to sign such a crew and put it aboard
the steamer to be seized:

"Her officers will, of course, be British. And I
am afraid there may be a gun crew aboard. But that
is nothing. We shall take her over when the time
comes—probably off the Irish coast at night. Now,
Soane, and you, Lehr, I want you to help recruit a
picked crew, all Irish, all Sinn Feiners or members of
the Clan-na-Gael.

"You know the sort. Absolutely reliable, fearless,
and skilled men devoted soul and body to the cause for
which we all would so cheerfully die. . . . Will you
do it?"

There was a silence. Soane moistened his lips reflectively. Lehr, intelligent, profoundly interested,
kept his keen, pleasant eyes on Murtagh Skeel. Only
the droning electric fans, the rattle of a newspaper, the
slap of greasy cards at the skat table, the slobber-
ing gulp of some Teuton, guzzling beer, interrupted the
sweltering quiet of the room.

"Misther Murtagh, sorr," said Soane with a light,
careless laugh, "I've wan recruit f'r to bring ye."

"Who is he?"

"Sure, it's meself, sorr—av ye'll sign the likes o'
me."

"Thanks; of course," said Skeel, with one of his
rare smiles, and taking Soane's hand in comradeship.

"I'll go," said Lehr, coolly; "but my name won't do.
Call me Grogan, if you like, and I'll sign with you,
Mr. Skeel."

Skeel pressed the offered hand:

"A splendid beginning," he said. "I wanted you
both. Now, see what you can do in the Sinn Fein
and Clan-na-Gael for a crew which, please God, we
shall require very soon!"

XIII

WHEN Dulcie had entered the studio that evening, her white face smeared with blood and a torn letter clutched in her hand, the gramophone was playing a lively two-step, and Barres and Thessalie Dunois were dancing there in the big, brilliantly lighted studio, all by themselves.

Thessalie caught sight of Dulcie over Barres's shoulder, hastily slipped out of his arms, and hurried across the polished floor.

"What is the matter?" she asked breathlessly, a fearful intuition already enlightening her as her startled glance travelled from the blood on Dulcie's face to the torn fragments of paper in her rigidly doubled fingers.

Barres, coming up at the same moment, slipped a firm arm around Dulcie's shoulders.

"Are you badly hurt, dear? What has happened?" he asked very quietly.

She looked up at him, mute, her bruised mouth quivering, and held out the remains of the letter. And Thessalie Dunois caught her breath sharply as her eyes fell on the bits of paper covered with her own handwriting.

"There was a man hiding in the court," said Dulcie. "He wore a white cloth over his face and he came up behind me and tried to snatch your letter out of my hand; but I held fast and he only tore it in two."

170

Barres stared at the sheaf of torn paper, lying crumpled up in his open hand, then his amazed gaze rested on Thessalie:

"Is this the letter you wrote to me?" he inquired.

"Yes. May I have the remains of my letter?" she asked calmly.

He handed over the bits of paper without a word, and she opened her gold-mesh bag and dropped them in.

There was a moment's silence, then Barres said:

"Did he strike you, Dulcie?"

"Yes, when he thought he couldn't get away from me."

"You hung on to him?"

"I tried to."

Thessalie stepped closer, impulsively, and framed Dulcie's pallid, blood-smeared face in both of her cool, white hands.

"He has cut your lower lip inside," she said. And, to Barres: "Could you get something to bathe it?"

Barres went away to his own room. When he returned with a finger-bowl full of warm water, some powdered boric acid, cotton, and a soft towel, Dulcie was lying deep in an arm-chair, her lids closed; and Thessalie sat beside her on one of the padded arms, smoothing the ruddy, curly hair from her forehead.

She opened her eyes when Barres appeared, giving him a clear but inscrutable look. Thessalie gently washed the traces of battle from her face, then rinsed her lacerated mouth very tenderly.

"It is just a little cut," she said. "Your lip is a trifle swelled."

"It is nothing," murmured Dulcie.

"Do you feel all right?" inquired Barres anxiously.

"I feel sleepy." She sat erect, always with her grey eyes on Barres. "I think I will go to bed." She stood up, conscious, now, of her shabby clothes and slippers; and there was a painful flush on her face as she thanked Thessalie and bade her a confused good-night.

But Thessalie took the girl's hand and retained it.

"Please don't say anything about what happened," she said. "May I ask it of you as a very great favour?"

Dulcie turned her eyes on Barres in silent appeal for guidance.

"Do you mind not saying anything about this affair," he asked, "as long as Miss Dunois wishes it?"

"Should I not tell my father?"

"Not even to him," replied Thessalie gently. "Because it won't ever happen again. I am very certain of that. Will you trust my word?"

Again Dulcie looked at Barres, who nodded.

"I promise never to speak of it," she said in a low, serious voice.

Barres took her down stairs. At the desk she pointed out, at his request, the scene of recent action. Little by little he discovered, by questioning her, what a dogged battle she had fought there alone in the whitewashed corridor.

"Why didn't you call for help?" he asked.

"I don't know. . . . . I didn't think of it. And when he got away I was dizzy from the blow."

At her bedroom door he took both her hands in his. The gas-jet was still burning in her room. On the bed lay her pretty evening dress.

"I'm so glad," she remarked naïvely, "that I had on my old clothes."

He smiled, drew her to him, and lightly smoothed the thick, bright hair from her brow.

"You know," he said, "I am becoming very fond of you, Dulcie. You're such a splendid girl in every way. . . . We'll always remain firm friends, won't we?"

"Yes."

"And in perplexity and trouble I want you to feel that you can always come to me. Because—you do like me, don't you, Dulcie?"

For a moment or two she sustained his smiling, questioning gaze, then laid her cheek lightly against his hands, which still held both of hers imprisoned. And for one exquisite instant of spiritual surrender her grey eyes closed. Then she straightened herself up; he released her hands; she turned slowly and entered her room, closing the door very gently behind her.

In the studio above, Thessalie, still wearing her rose-coloured cloak, sat awaiting him by the window.

He crossed the studio, dropped onto the lounge beside her, and lighted a cigarette. Neither spoke for a few moments. Then he said:

"Thessa, don't you think you had better tell me something about this ugly business which seems to involve you?"

"I can't, Garry."

"Why not?"

"Because I shall not take the risk of dragging you in."

"Who are these people who seem to be hounding you?"

"I can't tell you."

"You trust me, don't you?"

She nodded, her face partly averted:

"It isn't that. And I had meant to tell you something concerning this matter—tell you just enough so that I might ask your advice. In fact, that is what

I wrote you in that letter—being rather scared and desperate. . . . But half my letter to you has been stolen. The people who stole it are clever enough to piece it out and fill in what is missing——"

She turned impulsively and took his hands between her own. Her face had grown quite white.

"How much harm have I done to you, Garry? Have I already involved you by writing as much as I did write? I have been wondering. . . . I couldn't bear to bring anything like that into your life——"

"Anything like what?" he asked bluntly. "Why don't you tell me, Thessa?"

"No. It's too complicated—too terrible. There are elements in it that would shock and disgust you. . . . And perhaps you would not believe me——"

"Nonsense!"

"The Government of a great European Power does not believe me to be honest!" she said very quietly. "Why should you?"

"Because I know you."

She smiled faintly:

"You're such a dear," she murmured. "But you talk like a boy. What do you really know about me? We have met just three times in our entire lives. Do any of those encounters really enlighten you? If you were a business man in a responsible position, could you honestly vouch for me?"

"Don't you credit me with common sense?" he insisted warmly.

She laughed:

"No, Garry, dear, not with very much. Even I have more than you, and that is saying very little. We are inclined to be irresponsible, you and I—inclined to take the world lightly, inclined to laugh, inclined to tread the moonlit way! No, Garry, neither you nor I possess very much of that worldly caution born of hardened wisdom and sharpened wits."

She smiled almost tenderly at him and pressed his hands between her own.

"If I had been worldly wise," she said, "I should never have danced my way to America through summer moonlight with you. If I had been wiser still, I should not now be an exile, my political guilt established, myself marked for destruction by a great European Power the instant I dare set foot on its soil."

"I supposed your trouble to be political," he nodded.

"Yes, it is." She sighed, looked at him with a weary little smile. "But, Garry, I am not guilty of being what that nation believes me to be."

"I am very sure of it," he said gravely.

"Yes, you would be. You'd believe in me anyway, even with the terrible evidence against me. . . . I don't suppose you'd think me guilty if I tell you that I am not—in spite of what they might say about me—might prove, apparently."

She withdrew her hands, clasped them, her gaze lost in retrospection for a few moments. Then, coming to herself with a gesture of infinite weariness:

"There is no use, Garry. I should never be believed. There are those who, base enough to entrap me, now are preparing to destroy me because they are cowardly enough to be afraid of me while I am alive. Yes, trapped, exiled, utterly discredited as I am today, they are still afraid of me."

"Who are you, Thessa?" he asked, deeply disturbed.

"I am what you first saw me—a dancer, Garry, and nothing worse."

"It seems strange that a European Government should desire your destruction," he said.

"If I really were what this Government believes me to be, it would not seem strange to you."

She sat thinking, worrying her under lip with delicate white teeth; then:

"Garry, do you believe that your country is going to be drawn into this war?"

"I don't know what to think," he said bitterly. "The *Lusitania* ought to have meant war between us and Germany. Every brutal Teutonic disregard of decency since then ought to have meant war—every unarmed ship sunk by their U-boats, every outrage in America perpetrated by their spies and agents ought to have meant war. I don't know how much more this Administration will force us to endure—what further flagrant insult Germany means to offer. They've answered the President's last note by canning Von Tirpitz and promising, conditionally, to sink no more unarmed ships without warning. But they all are liars, the Huns. So that's the way matters stand, Thessa, and I haven't the slightest idea of what is going to happen to my humiliated country."

"Why does not your country prepare?" she asked.

"God knows why. Washington doesn't believe in it, I suppose."

"You should build ships," she said. "You should prepare plans for calling out your young men."

He nodded indifferently:

"There was a preparedness parade. I marched in it. But it only irritated Washington. Now, finally, the latest Mexican insult is penetrating official stupidity, and we are mobilising our State Guardsmen for service on the border. And that's about all we are doing. We are making neither guns nor rifles; we are building no ships; the increase in our regular army is of little account; some of the most vital of the great

176

national departments are presided over by rogues, clowns, and fools—pacifists all!—stupid, dull, grotesque and impotent. And you ask me what my country is going to do. And I tell you that I don't know. For real Americans, Thessa, these last two years have been years of shame. For we should have armed and mobilised when the first rifle-shot cracked across the Belgian frontier at Longwy; and we should have declared war when the first Hun set his filthy hoof on Belgian soil.

"In our hearts we real Americans know it. But we had no leader—nobody of faith, conviction, vision, action, to do what was the only thing to do. No; we had only talkers to face the supreme crisis of the world—only the shallow noise of words was heard in answer to God's own summons warning all mankind that hell's deluge was at hand."

The intense bitterness of what he said had made her very grave. She listened silently, intent on his every expression. And when he ended with a gesture of hopelessness and disgust, she sat gazing at him out of her lovely dark eyes, deep in reflection.

"Garry," she said at length, "do you know anything about the European systems of intelligence?"

"No—only what I read in novels."

"Do you know that America, to-day, is fairly crawling with German spies?"

"I suppose there are some here."

"There are a hundred thousand paid German spies within an hour's journey of this city."

He looked up incredulously.

"Let me tell you," she said, "how it is arranged here. The German Ambassador is the master spy in America. Under his immediate supervision are the so-called diplomatic agents—the personnel of the embassy and members of the consular service. These people do not class themselves as agents or as spies; they are the directors of spies and agents.

"Agents gather information from spies who perform the direct work of investigating. Spies usually work alone and report, through local agents, to consular or diplomatic agents. And these, in turn, report to the Ambassador, who reports to Berlin.

"It is all directed from Berlin. The personal source of all German espionage is the Kaiser. He is the supreme master spy."

"Where have you learned these things, Thessa?" he asked in a troubled voice.

"I have learned, Garry."

"Are you—a spy?"

"No."

"Have you been?"

"No, Garry."

"Then how——"

"Don't ask me; just listen. There are men here in your city who are here for no good purpose. I do not mean to say that merely because they seek also to injure me—destroy me, perhaps,—God knows what they wish to do to me!—but I say it because I believe that your country will declare war on Germany some day very soon. And that you ought to watch these spies who move everywhere among you!

"Germany also believes that war is near. And this is why she strives to embroil your country with Japan and Mexico. That is why she discredits you with Holland, with Sweden. It is why she instructs her spies here to set fires in factories and on ships, blow up powder mills and great industrial plants which are manufacturing munitions for the Allies of the Triple Entente.

"America may doubt that there is to be war between her and Germany, but Germany does not doubt it.

"Let me tell you what else Germany is doing. She is spreading insidious propaganda through a million disloyal Germans and pacifist Americans, striving to poison the minds of your people against England. She secretly buys, owns, controls newspapers which are used as vehicles for that propaganda.

"She is debauching the Irish here who are discontented with England's rule; she spends vast sums of money in teaching treachery in your schools, in arousing suspicion among farmers, in subsidising mercantile firms.

"Garry, I tell you that a Hun is always a Hun; a Boche is always a Boche, call him what else you will.

"The Germans are the monkeys of the world; they have imitated the human race. But, Garry, they are still what they always have been at heart, barbarians who have no business in Europe.

"In their hearts—and for all their priests and clergymen and cathedrals and churches—they still believe in their old gods which they themselves created—fierce, bestial supermen, more cruel, more powerful, more treacherous, more beastly than they themselves.

"That is the German. That is the Hun under all his disguises. No white man can meet him on his own ground; no white man can understand him, appeal to anything in common between himself and the Boche. He is brutal and contemptuous to women; he is tyrannical to the weak, cringing to the strong, fundamentally bestial, utterly selfish, intolerant of any civilisation which is not his conception of civilisation—his monkey-like conception of Christ—whom, in his pagan soul, he secretly sneers at—not always secretly, now!"

She straightened up with a quick little gesture of

contempt. Her face was brightly flushed; her eyes brilliant with scorn.

"Garry, has not America heard enough of 'the good German,' the 'kindly Teuton,' the harmless, sentimental and 'excellent citizen,' whose morally edifying origin as a model emigrant came out of his own sly mouth, and who has, by his own propaganda alone, become an accepted type of good-natured thrift and erudition in your Republic?

"Let me say to you what a French girl thinks! A hundred years ago you were a very small nation, but you were homogeneous and the average of culture was far higher in America then than it is at present. For now, your people's cultivation and civilisation is diluted by the ignorance of millions of foreigners to whom you have given hospitality. And, of these, the Germans have done you the most deadly injury, vulgarising public taste in art and literature, affronting your clean, sane intelligence by the new decadence and perversion in music, in painting, in illustration, in fiction.

"Whatever the normal Hun touches he vulgarises; whatever the decadent Boche touches he soils and degrades and transforms into a horrible abomination. This he has done under your eyes in art, in literature, in architecture, in modern German music.

"His filthy touch is even on your domestic life—this Barbarian who feeds grossly, whose personal habits are a by-word among civilised and cultured people, whose raw ferocity is being now revealed to the world day by day in Europe, whose proverbial clumsiness and stupidity have long furnished your stage with its oafs and clowns.

"This is the thing that is now also invading you with thousands of spies, betraying you with millions of traitors, and which will one day turn on you and tear you and trample you like an enraged hog, unless you and your people awake to what is passing in the world you live in!"

She was on her feet now, flushed, lovely, superb in her deep and controlled excitement.

"I'll tell you this much," she said. "It is Germany that wishes my destruction. Germany trapped me; Germany would have destroyed me in the trap had I not escaped. Now, Germany is afraid of me, knowing what I know. And her agents follow me, spy on me, thwart me, prevent me from earning my living, until I—I can scarcely endure it—this hounding and persecution——" Her voice broke; she waited to control it:

"I am not a spy. I never was one. I never betrayed a human soul—no, nor any living thing that ever trusted me! These people who hound me know that I am not guilty of that for which another Government is ready to try me—and condemn me. They fear that I shall prove to this other Government my innocence. I can't. But they fear I can. And the Hun is afraid of me. Because, if I ever proved my innocence, it would involve the arrest and trial and certain execution of men high in rank in the capital of this other country. So—the Hun dogs me everywhere I go. I do not know why he does not try to kill me. Possibly he lacks courage, so far. Possibly he has not had any good opportunity, because I am very careful, Garry."

"But this—this is outrageous!" broke out Barres. "You can't stand this sort of thing, Thessa! It's a matter for the police——"

"Don't interfere!"

"But——"

"Don't interfere! The last thing I want is publicity. The last thing I wish for is that your city, state, or national government should notice me at all or have any curiosity concerning me or any idea of investigating my affairs."

"Why?"

"Because, although as soon as your country is at war with Germany, my danger from Germany ceases, on the other hand another very deadly danger begins at once to threaten me."

"What danger?"

"It will come from a country with which your country will be allied. And I shall be arrested here as a *German* spy, and I shall be sent back to the country which I am supposed to have betrayed. And there nothing in the world could save me."

"You mean—court-martial?"

"A brief one, Garry. And then the end."

"Death?"

She nodded.

After a few moments she moved toward the door. He went with her, picking up his hat.

"I can't let you go with me," she said with a faint smile.

"Why not?"

"You are involved sufficiently already."

"What do I care for——"

"Hush, Garry. Do you wish to displease me?"

"No, but I——"

"Please! Call me a taxicab. I wish to go back alone."

In spite of argument she remained smilingly firm. Finally he rang up a taxi for her. When it signalled he walked down stairs, through the dim hall and out to the grilled gateway beside her.

"Good-bye," she said, giving her hand. He detained it:

"I can't bear to have you go alone——"

"I'm perfectly safe, mon ami. I've had a delightful time at your party—really I have. This affair of the letter does not spoil it. I'm accustomed to similar episodes. So now, good-night."

"Am I to see you again soon?"

"Soon? Ah, I can't tell you that, Garry."

"When it is convenient then?"

"Yes."

"And will you telephone me on your safe arrival home to-night?"

She laughed:

"If you wish. You're so sweet to me, Garry. You always have been. Don't worry about me. I am not in the least apprehensive. You see I'm rather a clever girl, and I know something about the Boche."

"You had your letter stolen."

"Only half of it!" she retorted gaily. "She is a gallant little thing, your friend Dulcie. Please give her my love. As for your other friends, they were amusing. . . . Mr. Mandel spoke to me about an engagement."

"Why don't you consider it? Corot Mandel is the most important producer in New York."

"Is he, really? Well, if I'm not interfered with perhaps I shall go to call on Mr. Mandel." She began to laugh mischievously to herself: "There was one man there who never gave me a moment's peace until I promised to lunch with him at the Ritz."

"Who the devil——"

"Mr. Westmore," she said demurely.

"Oh, Jim Westmore! Well, Thessa, he's a corker.

He's really a splendid fellow, but look out for him! He's also a philanderer."

"Oh, dear. I thought he was just a sculptor and a rather strenuous young man."

"I wasn't knocking him," said Barres, laughing, "but he falls in love with every pretty woman he meets. I'm merely warning you."

"Thank you, Garry," she smiled. She gave him her hand again, pulled the rose-coloured cloak around her bare shoulders, ran across the sidewalk to the taxi, and whispered to the driver.

"You'll telephone me when you get home?" he reminded her, baffled but smiling.

She laughed and nodded. The cab wheeled out into the street, backed, turned, and sped away eastward.

Half an hour later his telephone rang:

"Garry, dear?"

"Is it you, Thessa?"

"Yes. I'm going to bed. . . . Tell Mr. Westmore that I'm not at all sure I shall meet him at the Ritz on Monday."

"He'll go, anyway."

"Will he? What devotion. What faith in woman! What a lively capacity for hope eternal! What vanity! Well, then, tell him he may take his chances."

"I'll tell him. But I think you might make a date with me, too, you little fraud!"

"Maybe I will. Maybe I'll drop in to see you unexpectedly some morning. And don't let me catch you philandering in your studio with some pretty woman!"

"No fear, Thessa."

"I'm not at all sure. And your little model, Dulcie, is dangerously attractive."

"Piffle! She's a kid!"

"Don't be too sure of that, either! And tell Mr. Westmore that I may keep my engagement. And then again I may not! Good-night, Garry, dear!"

"Good-night!"

Walking slowly back to extinguish the lights in the studio before retiring to his own room for the night, Barres noticed a piece of paper on the table under the lamp, evidently a fragment from the torn letter.

The words "Ferez Bey" and "Murtagh" caught his eye before he realised that it was not his business to decipher the fragment.

So he lighted a match, held the shred of letter paper to the flame, and let it burn between his fingers until only a blackened cinder fell to the floor.

But the two names were irrevocably impressed on his mind, and he found himself wondering who these men might be, as he stood by his bed, undressing.

XIV

THE weather was turning hot in New York, and by the middle of the week the city sweltered.

Barres, dropping his brushes and laying aside a dozen pictures in all stages of incompletion; and being, otherwise, deeply bitten by the dangerously enchanting art of Madship—dangerous as inspiration but enchanting to gaze upon—was very busy making out of wax a diminutive figure of the running Arethusa.

And Dulcie, poor child, what with being poised on the ball of one little foot and with the other leg slung up in a padded loop, almost perished. Perspiration spangled her body like dew powdering a rose; sweat glistened on the features and shoulder-bared arms of the impassioned sculptor, even blinding him at times; but he worked on in a sort of furious exaltation, reeking of ill-smelling wax. And Dulcie, perfectly willing to die at her post, thought she was going to, and finally fainted away with an alarming thud.

Which brought Barres to his senses, even before she had recovered hers; and he proclaimed a vacation for his overworked Muse and his model, too.

"Do you feel better, Sweetness?" he enquired, as she opened her eyes when Selinda exchanged a wet compress for an ice-bag.

Dulcie, flat on the lounge, swathed in a crash bathrobe, replied only by a slight but reassuring flutter of one hand.

Esmé Trenor sauntered in for a gossip, wearing his celebrated lilac-velvet jacket and Louis XV slippers.

"Oh, the devil," he drawled, looking from Dulcie to the Arethusa; "she's worth more than your amateurish statuette, Garry."

"You bet she is. And here's where her vacation begins."

Esmé turned to Dulcie, lifting his eyebrows:

"You go away with him?"

The idea had never before entered Barres's head. But he said:

"Certainly; we both need the country for a few weeks."

"You'll go to one of those damned artists' colonies, I suppose," remarked Esmé; "otherwise, washed and unwashed would expel shrill cries."

"Probably not in my own home," returned Barres, coolly. "I shall write my family about it to-day."

Corot Mandel dropped in, also, that morning—he and Esmé were ever prowling uneasily around Dulcie in these days—and he studied the Arethusa through a foggy monocle, and he loitered about Dulcie's couch.

"You know," he said to Barres, "there's nothing like dancing to recuperate from all this metropolitan pandemonium. If you like, I can let Dulcie in on that thing I'm putting on at Northbrook."

"That's up to her," said Barres. "It's her vacation, and she can do what she likes with it——"

Esmé interposed with characteristic impudence:

"Barres imitates Manship with impunity; I'd like to have a plagiaristic try at Sorolla and Zuloaga, if Dulcie says the word. Very agreeable job for a girl in hot weather," he added, looking at Dulcie, "—an easy swimming pose in some nice cool little Adirondack lake——"

187

"Seriously," interrupted Mandel, twirling his monocle impatiently by its greasy string, "I mean it, Barres." He turned and looked at the lithely speeding Arethusa. "If that is Dulcie, I can give her a good part in——"

"You hear, Dulcie?" enquired Barres. "These two kind gentlemen have what they consider attractive jobs for you. All I can offer you is liberty to tumble around the hayfields at Foreland Farms, with my sketching easel in the middle distance. Now, choose your job, Sweetness."

"The hayfields and——"

Dulcie's voice faded to a whisper; Barres, seated beside her, leaned nearer, bending his head to listen.

"And *you*," she murmured again, "——if you want me."

"I always want you," he whispered laughingly, in return.

Esmé regarded the scene with weariness and chagrin.

"Come on," he said languidly to Mandel, "we'll buy her some flowers for the evil she does us. She'll need 'em; she'll be finished before this amateur sculptor finishes his blooming Arethusa."

Mandel lingered:

"I'm going up to Northbrook in a day or two, Barres. If you change—change Dulcie's mind for her, just call me up at the Adolf Gerhardt's."

"Dulcie will call you up if she changes my mind."

Dulcie laughed.

When they had gone, Barres said:

"You know I haven't thought about the summer. What was your idea about it?"

"My—idea?"

"Yes. You'd want a couple of weeks in the country somewhere, wouldn't you?"

"I don't know. I never went away," she replied vaguely.

It occurred to him, now, that for all his pleasant toleration of Soane's little daughter during the two years and more of his residence in Dragon Court, he had never really interested himself in her well-being, never thought to enquire about anything which might really concern her. He had taken it for granted that most people have some change from the stifling, grinding, endless routine of their lives—some respite, some quiet interval for recovery and rest.

And so, returning from his own vacations, it never occurred to him that the shy girl whom he permitted within his precincts, when convenient, never knew any other break in the grey monotony—never left the dusty, soiled, and superheated city from one year's summer to another.

Now, for the first time, he realised it.

"We'll go up there," he said. "My family is accustomed to models I bring there for my summer work. You'll be very comfortable, and you'll feel quite at home. We live very simply at Foreland Farms. Everybody will be kind and nobody will bother you, and you can do exactly as you please, because we all do that at Foreland Farms. Will you come when I'm ready to go up?"

She gave him a sweet, confused glance from her grey eyes.

"Do you think your family would mind?"

"Mind?" He smiled. "We never interfere with one another's affairs. It's not like many families, I fancy. We take it for granted that nobody in the family could do anything not entirely right. So we take that for granted and it's a jolly sensible arrangement."

She turned her face on the pillow presently; the ice-bag slid off; she sat up in her bathrobe, stretched her arms, smiled faintly:

"Shall I try again?" she asked.

"Oh, Lord!" he said, "*would* you? Upon my word, I believe you would! No more posing to-day! I'm not a murderer. Lie there until you're ready to dress, and then ring for Selinda."

"Don't you want me?"

"Yes, but I want you alive, not dead! Anyway, I've got to talk to Westmore this morning, so you may be as lazy as you like—lounge about, read——" He went over to her, patted her cheek in the smiling, absent-minded way he had with her: "Tell me, ducky, how are you feeling, anyway?"

It confused her dreadfully to blush when he touched her, but she always did; and she turned her face away now, saying that she was quite all right again.

Preoccupied with his own thoughts, he nodded:

"That's fine," he said. "Now, trot along to Selinda, and when you're fixed up you can have the run of the place to yourself."

"Could I have my slippers?" She was very shy even about her bare feet when she was not actually posing.

He found her slippers for her, laid them beside the lounge, and strolled away. Westmore rang a moment later, but when he blew in like a noisy breeze Dulcie has disappeared.

"My little model toppled over," said Barres, taking his visitor's outstretched hand and wincing under the grip. "I shall cut out work while this weather lasts."

Westmore turned toward the Arethusa, laughed at the visible influence of Manship.

"All the same, Garry," he said, "there's a lot in your running nymph. It's nice; it's knowing."

"That is pleasant to hear from a sculptor."

"Sculptor? Sometimes I feel like a sculpin—prickly heat, you know." He laughed heartily at his own witticism, slapped Barres on the shoulder, lighted a pipe, and flung himself on the couch recently vacated by Dulcie.

"This damned war," he said, "takes the native gaiety out of a man—takes the laughter out of life. Over two years of it now, Garry; and it's as though the sun is slowly growing dimmer every day."

"I know," nodded Barres.

"Sure you feel it. Everybody does. By God, I have periods of sickness when the illustrated London periodicals arrive, and I see those dead men pictured there—such fine, clean fellows—our own kind—half of them just kids!—well, it hurts me to look at them, and, for the sheer pain of it, I'm always inclined to shirk and turn that page quickly. But I say to myself, 'Jim, they're dead fighting Christ's own battle, and the least you can do is to read their names and ages, and look upon their faces.' . . . And I do it."

"So do I," nodded Barres, sombrely gazing at the carpet.

After a silence, Westmore said:

"Well, the Boche has taken his medicine and canned Tirpitz—the wild swine that he is. So I don't suppose we'll get mixed up in it."

"The Hun is a great liar," remarked Barres. "There's no telling."

"Are you going to Plattsburg again this year?" enquired Westmore.

"I don't know. Are you?"

"In the autumn, perhaps. . . . Garry, it's discouraging. Do you realise what a gigantic task we have ahead of us if the Hun ever succeeds in kicking us into

191

this war? And what a gigantic mess we've made of two years' inactivity?"

Barres, pondering, scowled at his own thoughts.

"And now," continued the o'''er, "the Guard is off to the border, and here we s . . . stripped clean, with the city lousy with Germans and every species of Hun deviltry hatching out fires and explosions and disloyal propaganda from the Atlantic to the Pacific, from the Lakes to the Gulf!

"A fine mess!—no troops, nothing to arm them with, no modern artillery, no preparations; the Boche growing more insolent, more murderous, but slyer; a row on with Mexico, another brewing with Japan, all Europe and Great Britain regarding us with contempt—I ask you, can you beat it, Garry? Are there any lower depths for us?—any sub-cellars of iniquity into which we can tumble, like the basket of jelly-fish we seem to be!"

"It's a nightmare," said Barres. "Since Liège and the *Lusitania*, it's been a bad dream getting worse. We'll have to wake, you know. If we don't, we're of no more substance than the dream itself:—we *are* the dream, and we'll end like one."

"I'm going to wait a bit longer," said Westmore restlessly, "and if there's nothing doing, it's me for the other side."

"For me, too, Jim."

"Is it a bargain?"

"Certainly. . . . I'd rather go under my own flag, of course. . . . We'll see how this Boche backdown turns out. I don't think it will last. I believe the Huns have been stirring up the Mexicans. It wouldn't surprise me if they were at the bottom of the Japanese menace. But what angers me is to think that we have received with innocent hospitality these hundreds of thousands of Huns in America, and that now, all over the land, this vast, acclimated nest of snakes rises hissing at us, menacing us with their filthy fangs?"

"Thank God our police is still half Irish," growled Westmore, puffing at his pipe. "These dirty swine might try to rush the city if war comes while the Guard is away."

"They're doing enough damage as it is," said Barres, "with their traitorous press, their pacifists, their agents everywhere inciting labour to strike, teaching disorganisation, combining commercially, directing blackmail, bomb outrages, incendiaries, and infesting the Republic with a plague of spies——"

The studio bell rang sharply. Barres, who stood near the door, opened it.

"Thessa!" he exclaimed, astonished and delighted.

XV

BLACKMAIL

SHE came in swiftly, stirring the sultry stillness of the studio with a little breeze from her gown, faintly fragrant.

"Garry, dear!—" She gave him both her hands and looked at him; and he saw the pink tint of excitement in her cheeks and her dark eyes brilliant.

"Thessa, this is charming of you——"

"No! I came——" She cast a swift glance around her, beheld Westmore, gave him one hand as he came forward:

"How do you do?" she said, almost breathlessly, plainly controlling some inward excitement.

But Westmore retained her hand and laid the other over it.

"You *said* you'd come to the Ritz——"

"I'm sorry. . . . I have been—bothered—with matters—affairs——"

"You are bothered now," he said. "If you have something to say to Garry, I'll go about my business. . . . Only I'm sorry it's not your business, too."

He released her hand and reached for the door-knob: her dark eyes were resting on him with a strained, intent expression. On impulse she thrust out her arm and closed the door, which he had begun to open:

"Please—Mr. Westmore. . . . I do want to see you. I'm trying to think clearly—" She turned and looked at Barres.

194

"Is it serious?" he said in a low voice.

"I—suppose so. . . . Garry, I wish to—to come here . . . and stay."

"What!"

She nodded.

"Is it all right?"

"All right," he replied pleasantly, bewildered and almost inclined to laugh.

She said in a low, tense voice:

"I'm really in trouble, Garry. I told you once that the word was not in my vocabulary. . . . I've had to include it."

"I'm so sorry! Tell me all about——"

He checked himself: she turned to Westmore—a deeper flush came into her cheeks—then she said gravely:

"I scarcely know Mr. Westmore, but if he is like you, Garry—your sort—perhaps he——"

"He'd do anything for you, Thessa, if you'll let him. Have you confidence in me?"

"You know I have."

"Then you can have the same confidence in Jim. I suggest it because I have a hazy idea what your trouble is. And if you came to ask advice, then I think that you'll get double value if you include Jim Westmore in your confidence."

She stood silent and with heightened colour for a moment, then her expression became humorous, and, partly turning, she put out her gloved hand behind her and took hold of Westmore's sleeve. It was at once an appeal and an impulsive admission of her confidence in this young man whom she had liked from the beginning, and who must be trustworthy because he was the friend of Garret Barres.

"I'm scared half to death," she remarked, without a

quaver in her voice, but her smile had now become
forced, and a quick, uneven little sigh escaped her as
she passed her arms through Barres' and Westmore's,
and, moving across the carpet between them, suffered
herself to be installed among the Chinese cushions upon
the lounge by the open window.

In, her distractingly pretty summer hat and gown,
and with her white gloves and gold-mesh purse in her
lap—her fresh, engaging face and daintily rounded
figure—Thessalie Dunois seemed no more mature, no
more experienced in worldly wisdom, than the charming young girls one passes on Fifth Avenue on a golden
morning in early spring.

But Westmore, looking into her dark eyes, divined,
perhaps, something less inexperienced, less happy in
their lovely, haunted depths. And, troubled by he
knew not what, he waited in silence for her to speak.

Barres said to her:

"You are being annoyed, Thessa, dear. I gather
that much from what has already happened. Can Jim
and I do anything?"

"I don't know. . . . It's come to a point where I—
I'm afraid—to be alone."

Her gaze fell; she sat brooding for a few moments,
then, with a quick intake of breath:

"It humiliates me to come to you. Would you believe that of me, Garry, that it has come to a point
where I am actually afraid to be alone? I thought I
had plenty of what the world calls courage."

"You have!"

"I had. I don't know what's become of it—what has
happened to me. . . . I don't want to tell you more
than I have to——"

"Tell us as much as you think necessary," said
Barres, watching her.

"Thank you. . . . Well, then, some years ago I earned the enmity of a man. And, through him, a European Government blacklisted me. It was a terrible thing. I did not fully appreciate what it meant at the time." She turned to Westmore in her pretty, impulsive way: "This European Government, of which I speak, believes me to be the agent of another foreign government—believes that I betrayed its interests. This man whom I offended, to punish me and to cover his own treachery, furnished evidence which would have convicted me of treachery and espionage."

The excited colour began to dye her cheeks again; she stretched out one arm in appeal to Westmore:

"Please believe me! I am no spy. I never was. I was too young, too stupid, too innocent in such matters to know what this man was about—that he had very cleverly implicated me in this abhorrent matter. Do you believe me, Mr. Westmore?"

"Of course I do!" he said with a fervour not, perhaps, necessary. "If you'll be kind enough to point out that gentleman——"

"Wait, Jim," interposed Barres, nodding to Thessalie to proceed.

She had been looking at Westmore, apparently much interested in his ardour, but she came to herself when Barres interrupted, and sat silent again as though searching her mind concerning what further she might say. Slowly the forced smile curved her lips again. She said:

"I don't know just what that enraged European Government might have done to me had I been arrested, because I ran away . . . and came here. . . . But the man whom I offended discovered where I was and never for a day even have his agents ceased to watch me, annoy me——"

There was a quick break in her voice; she set her
lips in silence until the moment's emotion had passed,
then, turning to Westmore with winning dignity: "I
am a dancer and singer—an entertainer of sorts, by
profession. I——"

"Tell Westmore a little more, Thessa," said Barres.

"If you think it necessary."

"I'll tell him. Miss Dunois was the most celebrated
entertainer in Europe when this happened. Since she
came here the man she has mentioned has, somehow,
managed to interfere and spoil every business arrangement which she has attempted." He looked at Thessa.
"I don't know whether, if Thessalie had cared to use
the name under which she was known all over Europe——"

"I didn't dare, Garry. I thought that, if some
manager would only give me a chance I could make a
new name for myself. But wherever I went I was
dogged, and every arrangement was spoiled. . . . I had
my jewels. . . . You remember some of them, Garry.
I gave those away—I think I told you why. But I
had other jewels—unset diamonds given to my mother
by Prince Haledine. Well, I sold them and invested
the money. . . . And my income is all I have—quite a
tiny income, Mr. Westmore, but enough. Only I could
have done very well here, I think, if I had not been
interfered with."

"Thessa," said Barres, "why not tell us both a little
more? We're devoted to you."

The girl lifted her dark eyes, and unconsciously they
were turned to Westmore. And in that young man's
vigorous, virile personality perhaps she recognised
something refreshing, subtlely compelling, for, still
looking at him, she began to speak quite naturally of

things which had long been locked within her lonely heart:

"I was scarcely more than a child when General Count Klingenkampf killed my father. The Grand Duke Cyril hushed it up.

"I had several thousand roubles. I had—trouble with the Grand Duke. . . . He annoyed me . . . as some men annoy a woman. . . . And when I put him in his place he insulted the memory of my mother because she was a Georgian. . . . I slapped his face with a whip. . . . And then I had to run away."

She drew a quick, uneven breath, smiling at Westmore from whose intent gaze her own dark eyes never wandered.

"My father had been a French officer before he took service in Russia," she said. "I was educated in Alsace and then in England. Then my father sent for me and I returned to St. Peters—I mean Petrograd. And because I loved dancing my father obtained permission for me to study at the Imperial school. Also, I had it in me to sing, and I had excellent instruction.

"And because I did such things in my own way, sometimes my father permitted me to entertain at the gay gatherings patronised by the Grand Duke Cyril."

She smiled in reminiscence, and her gaze became remote for a moment. Then, coming back, she lifted her eyes once more to Westmore's:

"I ran away from Cyril and went to Constantinople, where Von-der-Goltz Pasha and others whom I had met at the Grand Duke's parties, when little more than a child, were stationed. I entertained at the German Embassy, and at the Yildiz Palace. . . . I was successful. And my success brought me opportunities—of the wrong kind. Do you understand?"

Westmore nodded.

"So," she continued, with a slight movement of disdain, "I didn't quite see how I was to get to Paris all alone and begin a serious career. And one evening I entertained at the German Embassy—tell me, do you know Constantinople?"

"No."

"Well, it is nothing except a vast mass of gossip and intrigue. One breakfasts on rumours, lunches on secrets, and dines on scandals. And my maid told me enough that day to make certain matters quite clear to me.

"And so I entertained at the Embassy. . . . Afterward it was no surprise when his Excellency whispered to me that an honest career was assured me if I chose, and that I might be honestly launched in Paris without paying the price which I would not pay.

"Later I was not surprised, either, when Ferez Bey, a friend of my father, and a man I had known since childhood, presented me to—to——" She glanced at Barres; he nodded; she concluded to name the man: "—the Count d'Eblis, a Senator of France, and owner of the newspaper called *Le Mot d'Ordre.*"

After a silence she stole another glance at Barres; a smile hovered on her lips. He, also, smiled; for he, too, was thinking of that moonlit way they travelled together on a night in June so long ago.

Her glance asked:

"Is it necessary to tell Mr. Westmore this?"

He shook his head very slightly.

"Well," she went on, her eyes reverting again to Westmore, "the Count d'Eblis, it appeared, had fallen in love with me at first sight. . . . In the beginning he misunderstood me. . . . When he realised that I would endure no nonsense from any man he proved to be sufficiently infatuated with me to offer me marriage."

She shrugged:

"At that age one man resembled another to me. Marriage was a convention, a desirable business arrangement. The Count was in a position to launch me into a career. Careers begin in Paris. And I knew enough to realise that a girl has to pay in one way or another for such an opportunity. So I said that I would marry him if I came to care enough for him. Which merely meant that if he were ordinarily polite and considerate and companionable I would ultimately become his wife.

"That was the arrangement. And it caused much trouble. Because I was a—" she smiled at Barres, "—a success from the first moment. And d'Eblis immediately began to be abominably jealous and unreasonable. Again and again he broke his promise and tried to interfere with my career. He annoyed me constantly by coming to my hotel at inopportune moments; he made silly scenes if I ventured to have any friends or if I spoke twice to the same man; he distrusted me—he and Ferez Bey, who had taken service with him. Together they humiliated me, made my life miserable by their distrust.

"I warned d'Eblis that his absurd jealousy and unkindness would not advance him in my interest. And for a while he seemed to become more reasonable. In fact, he apparently became sane again, and I had even consented to our betrothal, when, by accident, I discovered that he and Ferez were having me followed everywhere I went. And that very night was to have been a gay one—a party in honour of our betrothal—the night I discovered what he and Ferez had been doing to me.

"I was so hurt, so incensed, that—" She cast an involuntary glance at Barres; he made a slight movement

of negation, and she concluded her sentence calmly:
"—I quarrelled with d'Eblis. . . . There was a very
dreadful scene. And it transpired that he had sold a
preponderating interest in *Le Mot d'Ordre* to Ferez
Bey, who was operating the paper in German interests
through orders directly from Berlin. And d'Eblis
thought I knew this and that I meant to threaten him,
perhaps blackmail him, to shield some mythical lover
with whom, he declared, I had become involved, and
who was betraying him to the British Ambassador."

She drew a deep, long breath:
"Is it necessary for me to say that there was not a
particle of truth in his hysterical accusations?—that
I was utterly astounded? But my amazement became
anger and then sheer terror when I learned from his
own lips that he had cunningly involved me in his trans-
actions with Ferez and with Berlin. So cunningly, so
cleverly, so seriously had he managed to compromise
me as a German agent that he had a mass of evidence
against me sufficient to have had me court-martialled
and shot had it been in time of war.

"To me the situation seemed hopeless. I never would
be believed by the French Government. Horror of arrest overwhelmed me. In a panic I took my unset
jewels and fled to Belgium. And then I came here."

She paused, trembling a little at the memory of it
all. Then:

"The agents of d'Eblis and Ferez discovered me and
have given me no peace. I do not appeal to the police
because that would stir up secret agents of the French
Government. But it has come now to a place where—
where I don't know what to do. . . . And so—being
afraid at last—I am here to—to ask—advice——"

She waited to control her voice, then opened her
gold-mesh bag and drew from it a letter.

"Three weeks ago I received this," she said. "I ignored it. Two weeks ago, as I opened the door of my room to go out, a shot was fired at me, and I heard somebody running down stairs. . . . I was badly scared. But I went out and did my shopping, and then I went to the writing room of a hotel and wrote to Garry. . . . Somebody watching me must have seen me write it, because an attempt was made to steal the letter. A man wearing a handkerchief over his face tried to snatch it out of the hands of Dulcie Soane. But he got only half of the letter.

"And when I got home that same evening I found that my room had been ransacked. . . . That was why I did not go to meet you at the Ritz; I was too upset. Besides, I was busy moving my quarters. . . . But it was no use. Last night I was awakened by hearing somebody working at the lock of my bedroom. And I sat up till morning with a pistol in my hand. . . . And —I don't think I had better live entirely alone—until it is safer. Do you, Garry?"

"I should think not!" said Westmore, turning red with anger.

"Did you wish us to see that letter?" asked Barres.

She handed it to him. It was typewritten; and he read it aloud, leisurely and very distinctly, pausing now and then to give full weight to some particularly significant and sinister sentence:

"MADEMOISELLE:

"For two years and more it has been repeatedly intimat d to you that your presence in America is not desirable to certain people, except under certain conditions, which conditions you refuse to consider.

"You have impudently ignored these intimations.

"Now, you are beginning to meddle. Therefore, this warning is sent to you: *Mind your business and cease your meddling!*

"Moreover, you are invited to leave the United States at your early convenience.

"France, England, Russia, and Italy are closed to you. Without doubt you understand that. Also, doubtless you have no desire to venture into Germany, Austria, Bulgaria, or Turkey. Scandinavia remains open to you, and practically no other country except Spain, because we do not permit you to go to Mexico or to Central or South America. Do you comprehend? *We* do not permit it.

"Therefore, hold your tongue and control your *furor scribendi* while in New York. And make arrangements to take the next Danish steamer for Christiania.

"This is a friendly warning. For if you are still here in the United States two weeks after you have received this letter, other measures will be taken in your regard which will effectually dispose of your troublesome presence.

"The necessity which forces us to radical action in this affair is regrettable, but entirely your own fault.

"You have, from time to time during the last two years, received from us overtures of an amicable nature. You have been approached with discretion and have been offered every necessary guarantee to cover an understanding with us.

"You have treated our advances with frivolity and contempt. And what have you gained by your defiance?

"Our patience and good nature has reached its limits. We shall ask nothing further of you; we deliver you our orders hereafter. And our orders are to leave New York immediately.

"Yet, even now, at the eleventh hour, it may not be too late for us to come to some understanding if you change your attitude entirely and show a proper willingness to negotiate with us in all good faith.

"But that must be accomplished within the two weeks' grace given you before you depart.

"You know how to proceed. If you try to play us false you had better not have been born. If you deal honestly with us your troubles are over.

"This is final.

"THE WATCHER."

XVI

"THE WATCHER," repeated Barres, studying the typewritten signature for a moment longer. Then he looked at Westmore: "What do you think of that, Jim?"

Westmore, naturally short tempered, became very red, got to his feet, and began striding about the studio as though some sudden blaze of inward anger were driving him into violent motion.

"The thing to do," he said, "is to catch this 'Watcher' fellow and beat him up. That's the way to deal with blackmailers—catch 'em and beat 'em up—vermin of this sort—this blackmailing fraternity!—I haven't anything to do; I'll take the job!"

"We'd better talk it over first," suggested Barres. "There seem to be several ways of going about it. One way, of course, is to turn detective and follow Thessa around town. And, as you say, spot any man who dogs her and beat him up very thoroughly. That's your way, Jim. But Thessa, unfortunately, doesn't desire to be featured, and you can't go about beating up people in the streets of New York without inviting publicity."

Westmore came back and stood near Thessalie, who looked up at him from her seat on the Chinese couch with visible interest:

"Mr. Westmore?"

"Yes?"

"Garry is quite right about the way I feel. I don't want notoriety. I can't afford it. It would mean stirring up every French Government agent here in New York. And if America should ever declare war on Germany and become an ally of France, then your own Secret Service here would instantly arrest me and probably send me to France to stand trial."

She bent her pretty head, adding in a quiet voice:

"Extradition would bring a very swift end to my career. With the lying evidence against me and a Senator of France to corroborate it by perjury—ask yourselves, gentlemen, how long it would take a military court to send me to the parade in the nearest caserne!"

"Do you mean they'd shoot you?" demanded Westmore, aghast.

"Any court-martial to-day would turn me over to a firing squad!"

"You see," said Barres, turning to Westmore, "this is a much more serious matter than a case of ordinary blackmail."

"Why not go to our own Secret Service authorities and lay the entire business before them?" asked Westmore excitedly.

But Thessalie shook her head:

"The evidence against me in Paris is overwhelming. My dossier alone, as it now stands, would surely condemn me without corroborative evidence. Your people here would never believe in me if the French Government forwarded to them a copy of my dossier from the secret archives in Paris. As for my own Government——" She merely shrugged.

Barres, much troubled, glanced from Thessalie to Westmore.

"It's rather a rotten situation," he said. "There must be, of course, some sensible way to tackle it, though I don't quite see it yet. But one thing is very plain to me: Thessa ought to remain here with us for the present. Don't you think so, Jim?"

"How can I, Garry?" she asked. "You have only one room, and I couldn't turn you out——"

"I can arrange that," interposed Westmore, turning eagerly to Barres with a significant gesture toward the door at the end of the studio. "There's the solution, isn't it?"

"Certainly," agreed Barres; and to Thessalie, in explanation: "Westmore's two bedrooms adjoin my studio—beyond that wall. We have merely to unlock those folding doors and throw his apartment into mine, making one long suite of rooms. Then you may have my room and I'll take his spare room."

She still hesitated.

"I am very grateful, Garry, and I admit that I am becoming almost afraid to remain entirely alone, but——"

"Send for your effects," he insisted cheerfully. "Aristocrates will move my stuff into Westmore's spare room. Then you shall take my quarters and be comfortable and well guarded with Aristocrates and Selinda on one side of you, and Jim and myself just across the studio." He cast a sombre glance at Westmore: "I suppose those rats will ultimately trail her to this place."

Westmore turned to Thessalie:

"Where are your effects?" he asked.

She smiled forlornly:

"I gave up my lodgings this morning, packed everything, and came here, rather scared." A little flush came over her face and she lifted her dark eyes and met Westmore's intent gaze. "You are very kind," she said. "My trunks are at the Grand Central Station

207

—if you desire to make up my disconcerted mind for me. Do you really want me to come here and stay a few days?"

Westmore suppressed himself no longer:

"I won't *let* you go!" he said. "I'm worried sick about you!" And to Barres, who sat slightly amazed at his friend's warmth:

"Do you suppose any of those dirty dogs have traced the trunks?"

Thessalie said:

"I've never yet been able to conceal anything from them."

"Probably, then," said Barres, "they have traced your luggage and are watching it."

"Give me your checks, anyway," said Westmore. "I'll go at once and get your baggage and bring it here. If they're watching for you it will jolt them to see a man on the job."

Barres nodded approval; Thessalie opened her purse and handed Westmore the checks.

"You both are so kind," she murmured. "I have not felt so sheltered, so secure in many, many months."

Westmore, extremely red again, controlled his emotions—whatever they were—with a visible effort:

"Don't worry for one moment," he said. "Garry and I are going to settle this outrageous business for you. Now, I'm off to find your trunks. And if you could give me a description of any of these fellows who follow you about——"

"Please—you are not to beat up anybody!" she reminded him, with a troubled smile.

"I'll remember. I promise you not to."

Barres said:

"I think one of them is a tall, bony, one-eyed man,

who has been hanging around here pretending to peddle artists' materials."

Thessalie made a quick gesture of assent and of caution:

"Yes! His name is Max Freund. I have found it impossible to conceal my whereabouts from him. This man, with only one eye, appears to be a friend of the superintendent, Soane. I am not certain that Soane himself is employed by this gang of blackmailers, but I believe that his one-eyed friend 'y pay him for any scraps of information concerning me."

"Then we had better keep an eye on Soane," growled Westmore. "He's no good; he'll take graft from anybody."

"Where is his daughter, Dulcie?" asked Thessalie. "Is she not your model, Garry?"

"Yes. She's in my room now, lying down. This morning it was pretty hot in here, and Dulcie fainted on the model stand."

"The poor child!" exclaimed Thessalie impulsively. "Could I go in and see her?"

"Why, yes, if you like," he replied, surprised at her warm-hearted interest. He added, as Thessalie rose: "She is really all right again. But go in if you like. And you might tell Dulcie she can have her lunch in there if she wants it; but if she's going to dress she ought to be about it, because it's getting on toward the luncheon hour."

So Thessalie went swiftly away down the corridor to knock at the door of the bedroom, and Barres walked out with Westmore as far as the stairs.

"Jim," he said very soberly, "this whole business looks ugly to me. Thessa seems to be seriously entangled in the meshes of some blackmailing spider who is sewing her up tight."

"It's probably a tighter web than we realise," growled Westmore. "It looks to me as though Miss Dunois has been caught in the main net of German intrigue. And that the big spider in Berlin did the spinning."

"That's certainly what it looks like," admitted the other in a grave voice. "I don't believe that this is merely a local matter—an affair of petty, personal vengeance: I believe that the Hun is actually afraid of her—afraid of the evidence she might be able to furnish against certain traitors in Paris."

Westmore nodded gloomily:

"I'm pretty sure of it, too. They've tried, apparently, to win her over. They've tried, also, to drive her out of this country. Now, they mean to force her out, or perhaps kill her! Good God! Garry, did you ever hear of such filthy impudence as this entire German propaganda in America?"

"Go and get her trunks," said Barres, deeply worried. "By the time you fetch 'em back here, lunch will be ready. Afterward, we'd all better get together and talk over this unpleasant situation."

Westmore glanced at his watch, turned and went swinging away in his quick, energetic stride. Barres walked slowly back to the studio.

There was nobody there. Thessalie had not yet returned from her visit to Dulcie Soane.

The Prophet, however, came in presently, his tail politely hoisted. An agreeable aroma from the kitchen had doubtless allured him; he made an amicable remark to Barres, suffered himself to be caressed, then sprang to the carved table—his favourite vantage point for observation—and gazed solemnly toward the dining-room.

For half an hour or more, Barres fussed and pot-tered about in the rather aimless manner of all artists, shifting canvases and stacking them against the wall, twirling his wax Arethusa around to inspect her from every possible and impossible angle, using clouds of fixitive on such charcoal studies as required it, scraping away meditatively at a too long neglected palette.

He was already frankly concerned about Thessalie, and the more he considered her situation the keener grew his apprehension.

Yet he, like all his fellow Americans, had not yet actually persuaded himself to believe in spies.

Of course he read about them and their machinations in the daily papers; the spy scare was already well developed in New York; yet, to him and to the great majority of his fellow countrymen, people who made a profession of such a dramatic business seemed unreal —abstract types, not concrete examples of the human race—and he could not believe in them—could neither visualise such people nor realise that they existed outside melodrama or the covers of a best-seller.

There is an incredulity which knows yet refuses to believe in its own knowledge. It is very American and it represented the paradoxical state of mind of this deeply worried young man, as he stood there in the studio, scraping away mechanically at his crusted palette.

Then, as he turned to lay it aside, through the open studio door he saw a strange, bespectacled man looking in at him intently.

An unpleasant shock passed through him, and his instinct started him toward the open door to close it.

"Excuse," said he of the thick spectacles; and Barres stopped short:

"Well, what is it?" he asked sharply.

The man, who was well dressed and powerfully built,

squinted through his spectacles out of little, inflamed and pig-like eyes.

"Miss Dunois iss here?" he enquired politely. "I haff a message——"

"What is your name?"

"Excuse, please. My name iss not personally known to Miss Dunois——"

"Then what is your business with Miss Dunois?"

"Excuse, please. It iss of a delicacy—of a nature quite private, iff you please."

Barres inspected him in hostile silence for a moment, then came to a swift conclusion.

"Very well. Step inside," he said briefly.

"I thank you, I will wait here——"

"Step inside!" snapped Barres.

Startled into silence, the man only blinked at him. Under the other's searching, suspicious gaze, the small, pig-like eyes were now shifting uneasily; then, as Barres took an abrupt step forward, the man shrank away and stammered out something about a letter which he was to deliver to Miss Dunois in private.

"You say you have a letter for Miss Dunois?" demanded Barres, now determined to get hold of him.

"I am instructed to giff it myself to her in private, all alone——"

"Give it to me!"

"I am instruc——"

"Give it to me, I tell you!—and come inside here! Do you hear what I'm saying to you?"

The spectacled man lost most of his colour as Barres started toward him.

"Excuse!" he faltered, backing off down the corridor. "I giff you the letter!" And he hastily thrust his hand into the side pocket of his coat. But it was a pistol he poked under the other's nose—a shiny, lumpy weapon, clutched most unsteadily.

"Hands up and turn me once around your back!" whispered the man hoarsely. "Quick!—or I shoot you!"—as the other, astounded, merely gazed at him. The man had already begun to back away again, but as Barres moved he stopped and cursed him:

"Put them up your hands!" snarled the spectacled man, with a final oath. "Keep your distance or I kill you!"

Barres heard himself saying, in a voice not much like his own:

"You can't do this to me and get away with it! It's nonsense! This sort of thing doesn't go in New York!"

Suddenly his mind grew coldly, terrible clear:

"No, you *can't* get away with it!" he concluded aloud, in the calm, natural voice of conviction. "Your stunt is scaring women! You try to keep clear of men—you dirty, blackmailing German crook! I've got your number! You're the 'Watcher'!—you murderous rat! You're afraid to shoot!"

It was plain that the spectacled man had not discounted anything of this sort—plain now, to Barres, that if, indeed, murder actually had been meant, it was not his own murder that had been planned with that big, blunt, silver-plated pistol, now wavering wildly before his eyes.

"I blow your face off!" whispered the stranger, beginning to back away again, and ghastly pale.

"Keep out of thiss! I am not looking for you. Get you back; step once again inside that door away!——"

But Barres had already jumped for him, had almost caught him, was reaching for him—when the man hurled the pistol straight at his face. The terrific impact of the heavy weapon striking him between the eyes dazed him; he stumbled sideways, colliding with the wall, and he reeled around there a second.

But that second's leeway was enough for the bespectacled stranger. He turned and ran like a deer. And when Barres reached the staircase the whitewashed hall below was still echoing with the slam of the street grille.

Nevertheless, he hurried down, but found the desk-chair empty and Soane nowhere visible, and continued on to the outer door, more or less confused by the terrific blow on the head.

Of course the bespectacled man had disappeared amid the noonday foot-farers now crowding both sidewalks east and west, on their way to lunch.

Barres walked slowly back to the desk, still dazed, but now thoroughly enraged and painfully conscious of a heavy swelling where the blow had fallen on his forehead.

In the superintendent's quarters he found Soane, evidently just awakened after a sodden night at Grogan's, trying to dress.

Barres said:

"There is nobody at the desk. Either you or Miss Kurtz should be on duty. That is the rule. Now, I'm going to tell you something: If I ever again find that desk without anybody behind it, I shall go to the owners of this building and tell them what sort of superintendent you are! And maybe I'll tell the police, also!"

"Arrah, then, Misther Barres——"

"That's all!" said Barres, turning on his heel. "Anything more from you and you'll find yourself in trouble!"

And he went up stairs.

The lumpy pistol still lay there in the corridor; he picked it up and took it into the studio. The weapon was fully loaded. It seemed to be of some foreign make—German or Austrian, he judged by the marking which had been almost erased, deliberately obliterated, it appeared to him.

He placed it in his desk, seated himself, explored his bruises gingerly with cautious finger-tips, concluded that the bridge of his nose was not broken, then threw himself back in his armchair for some grim and concentrated thinking.

XVII

THE elegantly modulated accents of Aristocrates, announcing the imminence of luncheon, aroused Barres from disconcerted but wrathful reflections.

As he sat up and tenderly caressed his battered head, Thessalie and Dulcie came slowly into the studio together, their arms interlaced.

Both exclaimed at the sight of the young man's swollen face, but he checked their sympathetic enquiries drily:

"Bumped into something. It's nothing. How are you, Dulcie? All right again?"

She nodded, evidently much concerned about his disfigured forehead; so to terminate sympathetic advice he went away to bathe his bruises in witch hazel, and presently returned smelling strongly of that time-honoured panacea, and with a saturated handkerchief adorning his brow.

At the same time, there came a considerable thumping and bumping from the corridor; the bell rang, and Westmore appeared with the trunks—five of them. These a pair of brawny expressmen rolled into the studio and carried thence to the storeroom which separated the bedroom and bath from the kitchen.

"Any trouble?" enquired Barres of Westmore, when the expressmen had gone.

"None at all. Nobody looked at me twice. What's happened to your noddle?"

"Bumped it. Lunch is ready."

Thessalie came over to him:

"I have included Dulcie among my confidants," she said in a low voice.

"You mean you've told her——"

"Everything. And I am glad I did."

Barres was silent; Thessalie passed her arm around Dulcie's waist; the two men walked behind together.

The table was a mass of flowers, over which netted sunlight played. Three cats assisted—the Prophet, always dignified, blinked pleasantly from a window ledge; the blond Houri, beside him, purred loudly. Only Strindberg was impossible, chasing her own tail under the patient feet of Aristocrates, or rolling over and over beneath the table in a mindless assault upon her own hind toes.

Seated there in the quiet peace and security of the pleasant room, amid familiar things, with Aristocrates moving noiselessly about, sunlight lacing wall and ceiling, and the air aromatic with the scent of brilliant flowers, Barres tried in vain to realise that murder could throw its shadow over such a place—that its terrible menace could have touched his threshold, even for an instant.

No, it was impossible. The fellow could not have intended murder. He was merely a blackmailer, suddenly detected and instantly frightened, pulling a gun in a panic, and even then failing in the courage to shoot.

It enraged Barres to even think about it, but he could not bring himself to attach any darker significance to the incident than just that—a blackmailer, ready to display a gun, but not to use it, had come to bully a woman; had found himself unexpectedly trapped, and had behaved according to his kind.

Barres had meant to catch him. But he admitted to himself that he had gone about it very unskilfully. This added disgust to his smouldering wrath, but he realised that he ought to tell the story.

And after the rather subdued luncheon was ended, and everybody had gone out to the studio, he did tell it, deliberately including Dulcie in his audience, because he felt that she also ought to know.

"And this is the present state of affairs," he concluded, lighting a cigarette and flinging one knee across the other, "—that my friend, Thessalie Dunois, who came here to escape the outrageous annoyance of a gang of blackmailers, is followed immediately and menaced with further insult on my very threshold.

"This thing must stop. It's going to be stopped. And I suggest that we discuss the matter now and decide how it ought to be handled."

After a silence, Westmore said:

"You had your nerve, Garry. I'm wondering what I might have done under the muzzle of that pistol."

Dulcie's grey eyes had never left Barres. He encountered her gaze now; smiled at its anxious intensity.

"I made a botch of it, Sweetness, didn't I?" he said lightly. And, to Westmore: "The moment I suspected him he was aware of it. Then, when I tried to figure out how to get him into the studio, it was too late. I made a mess of it, that's all. And it's too bad, Thessa, that I haven't more sense."

She gently shook her head:

"You haven't any sense, Garry. That man might easily have killed you, in spite of your coolness and courage——"

"No. He was just a rat——"

"In a corner! You couldn't tell what he'd do——"

"Yes, I could. He *didn't* shoot. Moreover, he

legged it, which was exactly what I was certain he meant to do. Don't worry about me, Thessa; if I didn't have brains enough to catch him, at least I was clever enough to know it was safe to try." He laughed. "There's nothing of the hero about me; don't think it!"

"I think that Dulcie and I know what to call your behaviour," she said quietly, taking the silent girl's hand in hers and resting it in her lap.

"Sure; it was bull-headed pluck," growled Westmore. "The drop is the drop, Garry, and you're no mind-reader."

But Barres persisted in taking it humorously:

"I read that gentleman's mind correctly, and his character, too." Then, to Thessalie: "You say you don't recognise him from my description?"

She shook her head thoughtfully.

"Garry," said Westmore impatiently, "if we're going to discuss various ways of putting an end to this business, what way do you suggest?"

Barres lighted another cigarette:

"I've been thinking. And I haven't a notion how to go about it, unless we turn over the matter to the police. But Thessa doesn't wish publicity," he added, "so whatever is to be done we must do by ourselves."

Thessalie leaned forward from her seat on the lounge by Dulcie:

"I don't ask that of you," she remonstrated earnestly. "I only wanted to stay here for a little while——"

"You shall do that too," said Westmore, "but this matter seems to involve something more than annoyance and danger to you. Those miserable rascals are Germans and they are carrying on their impudent intrigues, regardless of American laws and probably to the country's detriment. How do we know what they

are about? What else may they be up to? It seems
to me that somebody had better investigate their activities—this one-eyed man, Freund—this handy gun-
man in spectacles—and whoever it was who took a shot
at you the other day——"

"Certainly," said Barres, "and you and I are going
to investigate. But how?"

"What about Grogan's?"

"It's a German joint now," nodded Barres. "One
of us might drop in there and look it over. Thessa,
how do you think we ought to go about this affair?"

Thessalie, who sat on the sofa with Dulcie's hand
clasped in both of hers—a new intimacy which still
surprised and pleasantly perplexed Barres—said that
she could not see that there was anything in particular
for them to do, but that she herself intended to cease
living alone for a while and refrain from going about
town unaccompanied.

Then it suddenly occurred to Barres that if he and
Dulcie went to Foreland Farms, Thessalie should be
invited also; otherwise, she'd be alone again, except for
the servants, and possibly Westmore. And he said so.

"This won't do," he insisted. "We four ought to
remain in touch with one another for the present. If
Dulcie and I go to Foreland Farms, you must come, too,
Thessa; and you, Jim, ought to be there, too."

Nobody demurred; Barres, elated at the prospect,
gave Thessalie a brief sketch of his family and their
home.

"There's room for a regiment in the house," he
added, "and you will feel welcome and entirely at home.
I'll write my people to-night, if it's settled. Is it,
Thessa?"

"I'd adore it, Garry. I haven't been in the country
since I left France."

"And you, Jim?"

"You bet. I always have a wonderful time at Foreland."

"Now, this is splendid!" exclaimed Barres, delighted. "If you disappear, Thessa, those German rats may become discouraged and give up hounding you. Anyway, you'll have a quiet six weeks and a complete rest; and by that time Jim and I ought to devise some method of handling these vermin."

"Nobody," said Thessalie, smiling, "has asked Dulcie's opinion as to how this ma' 'er ought to be handled."

Barres turned to meet Dulcie's shy gaze.

"Tell us what to do, Sweetness!" he said gaily. "It was stupid of me not to ask for your views."

For a few moments the girl remained silent, then, the lovely tint deepening in her cheeks, she suggested diffidently that the people who were annoying Thessalie had been hired to do it by others more easy to handle, if discovered.

There was a moment's silence, then Barres struck his palm with doubled fist:

"*That*," he said with emphasis, "is the right way to approach this business! Hired thugs can be handled in only two ways—beat 'em up or call in the police. And we can do neither.

"But the men higher up—the men who inspire and hire these rats—they can be dealt with in other ways. You're right, Dulcie! You've started us on the only proper path!"

Considerably excited, now, as vague ideas crowded in upon him, he sat smiting his knees, his brows knit in concentrated thought, aware that they were on the right track, but that the track was but a blind trail so far.

Dulcie ventured to interrupt his frowning cogitation:

"People of position and influence who hire men to do unworthy things are cowards at heart. To discover them is to end the whole matter, I think."

"You're absolutely right, Sweetness! Wait! I begin to see—to see things—see something—interesting——"

He looked up at Thessalie:

"D'Eblis, Ferez Bey, Von-der-Goltz Pasha, Excellenz, Berlin—all these were mixed up with this German-American banker, Adolf Gerhardt, were they not?"

"It was Gerhardt's money, I am sure, that bought the *Mot d'Ordre* from d'Eblis for Ferez—that is, for Berlin," she said.

"Do you mean," asked Westmore, "the New York banker, Adolf Gerhardt, of Gerhardt, Klein & Schwartzmeyer, who has that big show place at Northbrook?"

Barres smiled at him significantly:

"What do you know about that, Jim! If we go to Foreland we're certain to be asked to the Gerhardt's! They're part of the Northbrook set; they're received everywhere. They entertain the personnel of the German and Austrian Embassies. Probably their place, Hohenlinden, is a hotbed of German intrigue and propaganda! Thessa, how about you? Would you care to risk recognition in Gerhardt's drawing-room, and see what information you could pick up?"

Thessalie's cheeks grew bright pink, and her dark eyes were full of dancing light:

"Garry, I'd adore it! I told you I had never been a spy. And that is absolutely true. But if you think I am sufficiently intelligent to do anything to help my country, I'll try. And I don't care how I do it," she added, with her sweet, reckless little laugh, and squeezed Dulcie's hand tightly between her fingers.

"Do you suppose Gerhardt would remember you?" asked Westmore.

"I don't think so. I don't believe anybody would recollect me. If anybody there ever saw Nihla Quellen, it wouldn't worry me, because Nihla Quellen is merely a memory if anything, and only Ferez and d'Eblis know I am alive and here——"

"And their hired agents," added Westmore.

"Yes. But such people would not be guests of Adolf Gerhardt at Northbrook."

"Ferez Bey might be his guest."

"What of it!" she laughed. "I was never afraid of Ferez—never! He is a jackal always. A threatening gesture and he flees! No, I do not fear Ferez Bey, but I think he is horribly afraid of me. . . . I think, perhaps, he has orders to do me very serious harm— and dares not. No, Ferez Bey comes sniffing around after the fight is over. He does no fighting, not Ferez! He slinks outside the smoke. When it clears away and night comes he ventures forth to feed furtively on what is left. That is Ferez—my Ferez on whom I would not use a dog-whip—no!—merely a slight gesture— and he is gone like a swift shadow in the dark!"

Fascinated by the transformation in her, the other three sat gazing at Thessalie in silence. Her colour was high, her dark eyes sparkled, her lips glowed. And the superb young figure so celebrated in Europe, so straight and virile, seemed instinct with the reckless gaity and courage which rang out in her full-throated laughter as she ended with a gesture and a snap of her white fingers.

"For my country—for France, whose generous mind has been poisoned against me—I would do anything—

anything!" she said. "If you think, Garry, that I have wit enough to balk d'Eblis, check Ferez, confuse the plotters in Berlin—well, then!—I shall try. If you say it is right, then I shall become what I never have been —a spy!"

She sat for a moment smiling in her flushed excitement. Nobody spoke. Then her expression altered, subtlely, and her dark eyes grew pensive.

"Perhaps," she said wistfully, "if I could serve my country in some little way, France might believe me loyal. . . . I have sometimes wished I might have a chance to prove it. There is nothing I would not risk if only France would come to believe in me. . . . But there seemed to be no chance for me. It is death for me to go there now, with that dossier in the secret archives and a Senator of France to swear my life away——"

"If you like," said Westmore, very red again, "I'll go into the business, too, and help you nail some of these Hun plotters. I've nothing better to do; I'd be delighted to help you land a Hun or two."

"I'm with you both, heart and soul!" said Barres. "The whole country is rotten with Boche intrigue. Who knows what we may uncover at Northbrook?"

Dulcie rose and came over to where Barres sat, and he reached up without turning around, and gave her hand a friendly little squeeze.

She bent over beside him:

"Could I help?" she asked in a low voice.

"You bet, Sweetness! Did you think you were being left out?" And he drew her closer and passed one arm absently around her as he began speaking again to Westmore:

"It seems to me that we ought to stumble on something at Northbrook worth following up, if we go about it circumspectly, Jim—with all that Austrian and German Embassy gang coming and going during the summer, and this picturesque fellow, Murtagh Skeel, being lionised by——"

Dulcie's sudden start checked him and he looked up at her.

"Murtagh Skeel, the Irish poet and patriot," he repeated, "who wants to lead a Clan-na-Gael raid into Canada or head a death-battalion to free Ireland. You've read about him in the papers, Dulcie?"

"Yes. . . . I want to talk to you alone——" She blushed and dropped a confused little curtsey to Thessalie: "Would you please pardon my rudeness——"

"You darling!" said Thessalie, blowing her a swift, gay kiss. "Go and talk to your best friend in peace!"

Barres rose and walked away slowly beside Dulcie. They stood still when out of earshot. She said:

"I have a few of my mother's letters. . . . She knew a young man whose name was Murtagh Skeel. . . . He was her dear friend. But only in secret. Because I think her father and mother disliked him. . . . It would seem so from her letters and his. . . . And she was—in love with him. . . . And he with mother. . . . Then—I don't know. . . . But she came to America with father. That is all I know. Do you believe he can be the same man?"

"Murtagh Skeel," repeated Barres. "It's an unusual name. Possibly he is the same man whom your mother knew. I should say he might have been about your mother's age, Dulcie. He is a romantic figure now—one of those dreamy, graceful, impractical patriots—an enthusiast with one idea and that an impossible one!—the freedom of Ireland wrenched by force from the traditional tyrant, England."

He thought a moment, then:

"Whatever the fault, and wherever lies the blame for Ireland's unrest to-day, this is no time to start rebellion. Who strikes at England now strikes at all Freedom in the world. Who conspires against England to-day conspires with barbarism against civilisation.

"My outspoken sympathy of yesterday must remain unspoken to-day. And if it be insisted on, then it will surely change and become hostility. No, Dulcie; the line of cleavage is clean: it is Light against Darkness, Right against Might, Truth against Falsehood, and Christ against Baal!

"This man, Murtagh Skeel, is a dreamer, a monomaniac, and a dangerous fanatic, for all his winning and cultivated personality and the personal purity of his character. . . . It is an odd coincidence if he was once your mother's friend—and her suitor, too."

Dulcie stood before him, her head a trifle lowered, listening to what he said. When he ended, she looked up at him, then across the studio where Westmore had taken her place on the sofa beside Thessalie. They both seemed to be absorbed in a conversation which interested them immensely.

Dulcie hesitated, then ventured to take possession of Barres' arm:

"Could you and I sit down over here by ourselves?" she asked.

He smiled, always amused by her increasing confidence and affection, and always a little touched by it, so plainly she revealed herself, so quaintly—sometimes very quietly and shyly, sometimes with an ardent impulse too swift for self-conscious second thoughts which might have checked her.

So they seated themselves in the carved compartments of an ancient choir-stall and she rested one elbow on the partition between them and set her rounded chin in her palm.

"You pretty thing," he said lightly.

At that she blushed and smiled in the confused way she had when teased. And at such times she never looked at him—never even pretended to sustain his laughing gaze or brave out her own embarrassment.

"I won't torment you, Sweetness," he said. "Only you ought not to let me, you know. It's a temptation to make you blush; you do it so prettily."

"Please——" she said, still smiling but vividly disconcerted again.

"There, dear! I won't. I'm a brute and a bully. But honestly, you ought not to let me."

"I don't know how to stop you," she admitted, laughing. "I could kill myself for being so silly. Why is it, do you suppose, that I blu——"

She checked herself, scarlet now, and sat motionless with her head bent over her clenched palm, and her lip bitten till it quivered. Perhaps a flash of sudden insight had answered her own question before she had even finished asking it. And the answer had left her silent, rigid, as though not daring to move. But her bitten lip trembled, and her breath, which had stopped, came swiftly now, desperately controlled. But there seemed to be no control for her violent little heart, which was racing away and setting every pulse a faster pace.

Barres, more uneasy than amused, now, and having before this very unwillingly suspected Dulcie of an exaggerated sentiment concerning him, inspected her furtively and sideways.

"I won't tease you any more," he repeated. "I'm sorry. But you understand, Sweetness; it's just a friendly tease—just because we're such good friends."

"Yes," she nodded breathlessly. "Don't notice me, please. I don't seem to know how to behave myself when I'm with you——"

"What nonsense, Dulcie! You're a wonderful comrade. We have bully times when we're together. Don't we?"

"Yes."

"Well, then, for the love of Mike! What's a little teasing between friends? Buck up, Sweetness, and don't ever let me upset you again."

"No." She turned and looked at him, laughed. But there was a wonderful beauty in her grey eyes and he noticed it.

"You little kiddie," he said, "your eyes are all starry like a baby's! You are not growing up as fast as you think you are!"

She laughed again deliciously:

"How wise you are," she said.

"Aha! So you're joshing me, now!"

"But aren't you very, very wise?" she asked demurely.

"You bet I am. And I'm going to prove it."

"How, please?"

"Listen, irreverent youngster! If you are going to Foreland Farms with me, you will require various species of clothes and accessories."

At that she was frankly dismayed:

"But I can't afford——"

"Piffle! I advance you sufficient salary. Thessalie had better advise you in your shopping——" He hesitated, then: "You and Thessa seem to have become excellent friends rather suddenly."

"She was so sweet to me," explained Dulcie. "I hadn't cared for her very much—that evening of the party—but to-day she came into your room, where I was lying on the bed, and she stood looking at me for a moment and then she said, 'Oh, you darling!' and dropped on her knees and drew me into her arms. . . . Wasn't that a curious thing to happen? I—I was too surprised to speak for a minute; then the loveliest shiver came over me and I—I cuddled up close to her—because I had never remembered being in mother's arms—and it seemed wonderful—I had wanted it so —dreamed sometimes—and awoke and cried myself to sleep again. . . . She was so sweet to me. . . . We talked. . . . She told me, finally, about the reason of her visit to you. Then she told me about herself. . . . So I became her friend very quickly. And I am sure that I am going to love her dearly. . . . And when I love"—she looked steadily away from him—"I would die to serve—my friend."

The girl's quiet ardour, her simplicity and candour, attracted and interested him. Always he had seemed to be aware, in her, of hidden forces—of something fresh and charmingly impetuous held in leash—of controlled impulses, restless, uneasy, bitted, curbed, and reined in.

Pride, perhaps, a natural reticence in the opposite sex—perhaps the habit of control in a girl whose childhood had had no outlet—some of these, he concluded, accounted for her subdued air, her restraint from demonstration. Save for the impulsive little hand on his arm at times, the slightest quiver of lip and voice, there was no sign of the high-strung, fresh young force that he vaguely divined within her.

"Dulcie," he said, "how much do you know about the romance of your mother?"

She lifted her grey eyes to his:

"What romance?"

"Why, her marriage."

"Was that a romance?"

"I gather, from your father, that your mother was very much above him in station."

"Yes. He was a gamekeeper for my grandfather."

"What was your mother's name?"

"Eileen."

"I mean her family name."

"Fane."

He was silent. She remained thoughtful, her chin resting between two fingers.

"Once," she murmured, as though speaking to herself, "when my father was intoxicated, he said that Fane is my name, not Soane. . . . Do you know what he meant?"

"No. . . . His name is Soane, isn't it?"

"I suppose so."

"Well, what do you suppose he meant, if he meant anything?"

"I don't quite know."

"He is your father, isn't he?"

She shook her head slowly:

"Sometimes, when he is intoxicated, he says that he isn't. And once he added that my name is not Soane but Fane."

"Did you question him?"

"No. He only cries when he is that way. . . . Or talks about Ireland's wrongs."

"Ask him some time."

"I have asked him when he was sober. But he denied ever saying it."

"Then ask him when he's the other way. I—well, to be frank, Dulcie, you haven't the slightest resemblance to your father—not the slightest—not in any mental or physical particular."

"He says I'm like mother."

"And her name was Eileen Fane," murmured Barres. "She must have been beautiful, Dulcie."

"She was——" A bright blush stained her face, but this time she looked steadily at Barres and neither of them smiled.

"She was in love with Murtagh Skeel," said Dulcie. "I wonder why she did not marry him."

"You say her family objected."

"Yes, but what of that, if she loved him?"

"But even in those days he may have been a trouble-maker and revolutionist——"

"Does that matter if a girl is in love?"

In Dulcie's voice there was again that breathless tone through which something rang faintly—something curbed back, held in restraint.

"I suppose," he said, smiling, "that if one is in love nothing else matters."

"Nothing matters," she said, half to herself. And he looked askance at her, and looked again with increasing curiosity.

Westmore called across the room:

"Thessalie and I are going shopping! Any objections?"

A sudden and totally unexpected dart seemed to penetrate the heart region of Garret Barres. It was jealousy and it hurt.

"No objection at all," he said, wondering how the devil Westmore had become so familiar with her name in such a very brief encounter.

Thessalie rose and came over:

"Dulcie, will you come with us?" she asked gaily.

"That's a first rate idea," said Barres, cheering up. "Dulcie, tell her what things you have and she'll tell you what you need for Foreland Farms."

"Indeed I will," cried Thessalie. "We'll make her

perfectly adorable in a most economical manner. Shall we, dear?"

And she held out her hand to Dulcie, and, smiling, turned her head and looked across the room at Westmore.

Which troubled Barres and left him rather silent there in the studio after they had gone away. For he had rather fancied himself as the romance in Thessalie's life, and, at times, was inclined to sentimentalise a little about her.

And now he permitted himself to wonder how much there really might be to that agreeable sentiment he entertained for, perhaps, the prettiest girl he had ever met in his life, and, possibly, the most delightful.

XVIII

THE double apartment in Dragon Court, swept by such vagrant July breezes as wandered into the heated city, had become lively with preparations for departure.

Barres fussed about, collecting sketching paraphernalia, choosing brushes, colours, canvases, field kits, and costumes from his accumulated store, and boxing them for transportation to Foreland Farms, with the languid assistance of Aristocrates.

Westmore had only to ship a modelling stand, a handful of sculptors' tools, and a ton or two of Plasteline, an evil-smelling composite clay, very useful to work with.

But the storm centre of preparation revolved around Dulcie. And Thessalie, enchanted with her new rôle as adviser, bargainer, and purchaser, and always attaching either Westmore or Barres to her skirts when she and Dulcie sallied forth, was selecting and accumulating a charming and useful little impedimenta. For the young girl had never before owned a single pretty thing, except those first unpremeditated gifts of Barres', and her happiness in these expeditions was alloyed with trepidation at Thessalie's extravagance, and deep misgivings concerning her ultimate ability to repay out of the salary allowed her as a private model.

Intoxicated by ownership, she watched Thessalie and Selinda laying away in her brand-new trunk the lovely things which had been selected. And one day, thrilled but bewildered, she went into the studio, where Barres sat opening his mail, and confessed her fear that only lifelong devotion in his service could ever liquidate her overwhelming financial obligations to him.

He had begun to laugh when she opened the subject:

"Thessa is managing it," he said. "It looks like a lot of expense, but it isn't. Don't worry about it, Sweetness."

"I *do* worry——"

"Now, what a ridiculous thing to do!" he interrupted. "It's merely advanced salary—your own money. I told you to blow it; I'm responsible. And I shall arrange it so you won't notice that you are repaying the loan. All I want you to do is to have a good time about it."

"I am having a good time—when it doesn't scare me to spend so much for——"

"Can't you trust Thessa and me?"

The girl dropped to her knees beside his chair in a swift passion of gratitude:

"Oh, I trust you—I do——" But she could not utter another word, and only pressed her face against his arm in the tense silence of emotions which were too powerful to express, too deep and keen to comprehend or to endure.

And she sprang to her feet, flushed, confused, turning from him as he retained one hand and drew her back:

"Dear child," he said, in his pleasant voice, "this is really a very little thing I do for you, compared to the help you have given me by hard, unremitting, uncomplaining physical labour and endurance. There is no harder work than holding a pose for painter or sculptor—nothing more cruelly fatiguing. Add to that your cheerfulness, your willingness, your quiet, loyal, unobtrusive companionship—and the freshness and inspiration and interest ever new which you always awake in me—tell me, Sweetness, are you really in my debt, or am I in yours?"

"I am in yours. You made me."

"You always say that. It's foolish. You made yourself, Dulcie. You are making yourself all the while. Why, good heavens!—if you hadn't had it in you, somehow, to ignore your surroundings—take the school opportunities offered you—close your eyes and ears to the sights and sounds and habits of what was supposed to be your home——"

He checked himself, thinking of Soane, and his brogue, and his ignorance and his habits.

"How the devil you escaped it all I can't understand," he muttered to himself. "Even when I first knew you, there was nothing resembling your—your father about you—even if you were almost in rags!"

"I had been with the Sisters until I went to high school," she murmured. "It makes a difference in a child's mind what is said and thought by those around her."

"Of course. But, Dulcie, it is usually the unfortunate rule that the lower subtly contaminates the higher, even in casual association—that the weaker gradually undermines the stronger until it sinks to lesser levels. It has not been so with you. Your clear mind remained untarnished, your aspiration uncontaminated. Somewhere within you had been born the quality of recognition; and when your eyes opened on better things you recognised them and did not forget after they disappeared——"

Again he ceased speaking, aware, suddenly, that for

the first time he was making the effort to analyse this girl for his own information. Heretofore, he had accepted her, sometimes curious, sometimes amused, puzzled, doubtful, even uneasy as her mind revealed itself by degrees and her character glimmered through in little fitful gleams from that still hidden thing, herself.

He began to speak again, before he knew he was speaking—indeed, as though within him somewhere another man were using his lips and voice as vehicles:

"You know, Dulcie, it's not going to end—our companionship. Your real life is all ahead of you; it's already beginning—the life which is properly yours to shape and direct and make the most of.

"I don't know what kind of life yours is going to be; I know, merely, that your career doesn't lie down stairs in the superintendent's lodgings. And this life of ours here in the studio is only temporary, only a phase of your development toward clearer aims, higher aspiration, nobler effort.

"Tranquillity, self-respect, intelligent responsibility, the happiness of personal independence are the prizes: the path on which you have started leads to the only pleasure man has ever really known—labour."

He looked down at her hand lying within his own, stroked the slender fingers thoughtfully, noticing the whiteness and fineness of them, now that they had rested for three months from their patient martyrdom in Soane's service.

"I'll talk to my mother and sister about it," he concluded. "All you need is a start in whatever you're going to do in life. And you bet you're going to get it, Sweetness!"

He patted her hand, laughed, and released it. She

couldn't speak just then—she tried to as she stood there, head averted and grey eyes brilliant with tears—but she could not utter a sound.

Perhaps aware that her overcharged heart was meddling with her voice, he merely smiled as he watched her moving slowly back to Thessalie's room, where the magic trunk was being packed. Then he turned to his letters again. One was from his mother:

"Garry darling, anybody you bring to Foreland is always welcome, as you know. Your family never inquires of its members concerning any guests they may see fit to invite. Bring Miss Dunois and Dulcie Soane, your little model, if you like. There's a world of room here; nobody ever interferes with anybody else. You and your guests have two thousand acres to roam about in, ride over, fish over, paint over. There's plenty for everybody to do, alone or in company.

"Your father is well. He looks little older than you. He's fishing most of the time, or busy reforesting that sandy region beyond the Foreland hills.

"Your sister and I ride as usual and continue to improve the breeds of the various domestic creatures in which we are interested and you are not.

"The pheasants are doing well this year, and we're beginning to turn them out with their foster-mothers.

"Your father wishes me to tell you and Jim Westmore that the trout fishing is still fairly good, although it was better, of course, in May and June.

"The usual parties and social amenities continue in Northbrook. Everybody included in that colony seems to have arrived, also the usual influx of guests, and there is much entertaining, tennis, golf, dances—the invariable card always offered there.

"Claire and I go enough to keep from being too completely forgotten. Your father seldom bothers himself.

"Also, the war in Europe has made us, at Foreland, disinclined to frivolity. Others, too, of the older society in Northbrook are more subdued than usual, devote themselves to quieter pursuits. And those among us who have sons of military age are prone to take life soberly in these strange, oppressive days when even under sunny skies in this land aloof from war, all are conscious of the tension, the vague foreboding, the brooding stillness that sometimes heralds storms.

"But all north-country folk do not feel this way. The Gerhardts, for example, are very gay with a house full of guests and overflowing week-ends. The German Embassy, as always, is well represented at Hohenlinden. Your father won't go there at all now. As for Claire and myself, we await political ruptures before we indulge in social ones. And it doesn't look like war, now that Von Tirpits has been sent to Coventry.

"This, Garry darling, is my budget of news. Bring your guests whenever you please. You wouldn't bring anybody you oughtn't to; your family is liberal, informal, pleasantly indifferent, and always delightfully busy with its individual manias and fads; so come as soon as you please—sooner, please—because, strange as it may seem, your mother would like to see you."

The letter was what he had expected. But, as always, it made him very grateful.

"Wonderful mother I have," he murmured, opening another letter from his father:

"DEAR GARRET:

"Why the devil don't you come up? You've missed the cream of the fishing. There's nothing doing in the streams now, but at sunrise and toward evening they're breaking nicely in the lake.

"I've put in sixty thousand three-year transplants this year on that sandy stretch. They are white, Scotch and Austrian. Your children will enjoy them.

"The dogs are doing well. There's one youngster, the litter-tyrant of Goldenrod's brood, who ought to make a field winner. But there's no telling. You and I'll have 'em out on native woodcock.

"There are some grouse, but we ought to let them alone for the next few years. As for the pheasants, they're everywhere now, in the brake, silver-grass, and weeds, peeping, scurrying, creeping—cunning little beggars and growing wild as quail.

"The horses are all right. The crops promise well. Labour is devilish scarce, and unsatisfactory when induced to accept preposterous wages. What we need are coolies, if these lazy, native slackers continue to handicap the farmers who have to employ them. The American 'hired man'! He makes me sick. With few exceptions, he is incredibly stupid, ignorant, unwilling, lazy.

"He's sometimes a crook, too; he takes pay for what he doesn't do; he steals your time; he cares absolutely nothing about your interests or convenience; he will leave you stranded in harvest time, without any notice at all; decent treatment he does not appreciate; he'll go without a warning even, leaving your horses unfed, your cattle unwatered, your crops rotting!

"He's a degenerate relic of those real men who broke up the primæval wilderness. He is the reason for high prices, the cause of agricultural and industrial distress, the inert, sodden, fermenting, indigestible mass in the belly of the body-politic!

"The American hired man! If the country doesn't spew him up, he'll kill it!

"Perhaps you've heard me before on this subject, Garret. I'm likely to air my views, you know.

"Well, my son, I look forward to your arrival. I am glad that Westmore is coming with you. As for your other guests, they are welcome, of course.

"Your father,
"REGINALD BARRES."

He laughed; this letter so perfectly revealed his father.

"Dad and his trout and his birds and his pines and his eternally accursed hired help," he said to himself, "Dad and his monocle and his immaculate attire—the finest man who ever fussed!" And he laughed tenderly to himself as he broke the seal of his sister's brief note:

"Garry dear, I've been so busy schooling horses and dancing that I've had no time for letter writing. So glad you're coming at last. Bring along any good novels you see. My best to Jim. Your guests can be well mounted, if they ride. Father is wild because there are more foxes than usual, but he's promised not to treat them as vermin, and the Northbrook pack is to hunt our territory this season, after all. Poor Dad! He is a brick, isn't he?"
"Affectionately,

"Lee."

Barres pocketed his sheaf of letters and began to stroll about the studio, whistling the air of some recent musical atrocity.

Westmore, in his own room, composing verses—a secret vice unsuspected by Barres—bade him "Shut up!"—the whistling no doubt ruining his metre.

But Barres, with politest intentions, forgot himself so many times that the other man locked up his "Lines to Thessalie when she was sewing on a button for me," and came into the studio.

"Where is she?" he inquired naïvely.

"Where's who?" demanded Barres, still sensitive over the increasing intimacy of this headlong young man and Thessalie Dunois.

"Thessa."

"In there fussing with Dulcie's togs. Go ahead in, if you care to."

"Is your stuff packed up?"

Barres nodded:

"Is yours?"

"Most of it. How many trunks is Thessa taking?"

"How do I know?" said Barres, with a trace of irritation. "She's at liberty to take as many as she likes."

Westmore didn't notice the irritation; his mind was entirely occupied by Thessalie—an intellectual condition which had recently become rather painfully apparent to Barres, and, doubtless, equally if not painfully apparent to Thessalie herself.

Probably Dulcie noticed it, too, but gave no sign, except when the serious grey eyes stole toward Barres at times, as though vaguely apprehensive that he might not be entirely in sympathy with Westmore's enchanted state of mind.

As for Thessalie, though Westmore's naïve and increasing devotion could scarcely escape her notice, it was utterly impossible to tell how it affected her—whether, indeed, it made any impression at all.

For there seemed to be no difference in her attitude toward these two men; it was plain enough that she liked them both—that she believed in them implicitly, was happy with them, tranquil now in her new security, and deeply penetrated with gratitude for their kindness to her in her hour of need.

"Come on in," coaxed Westmore, linking his arm in Barres', and counting on the latter to give him countenance.

The arm of Barres remained rigid and unresponsive, but his legs were reluctantly obliging and carried him along with Westmore to what had been his own room before Thessalie had installed herself there.

And there she was on her knees, amid a riot of lingerie and feminine effects, while Dulcie lovingly smoothed out and folded object after object which Selinda placed between layers of pale blue tissue paper in the trunks.

"How are things going, Thessa?" inquired Westmore, in the hearty, cheerful voice of the intruder who hopes to be made welcome. But her attitude was discouraging.

"You know you are only in the way," she said. "Drive him out, Dulcie!"

Dulcie laughed and looked at them both with shyly friendly eyes:

"Is my trousseau not beautiful?" she asked. "If you'll step outside I'll put on a hat and gown for you——"

"Oh, Dulcie!" protested Thessalie, "I want you to dawn upon them, and a dress rehearsal would spoil it all!"

Westmore tiptoed around amid lovely, frail mounds of fabrics, until ordered to an empty chair and forbidden further motion. It was all the same to him, so long as his fascinated gaze could rest on Thessalie.

Which further annoyed Barres, and he backed out and walked to the studio, considerably disturbed in his mind.

"That man," he thought, "is making an ass of himself, hanging around Thessa like a half-witted child. She can't help noticing it, but she doesn't seem to do anything about it. I don't know why she doesn't squelch him—unless she likes it——" But the idea was so unpleasant to Barres that he instantly abandoned that train of thought and prepared for himself a comfortable nest on the lounge, a pipe, and an uncut volume of flimsy summer fiction.

In the middle of these somewhat sullen preparations, there came a ring at his studio door. Only the superintendent or strangers rang that bell as a rule, and Barres went to his desk, slipped his loaded pistol into his coat pocket, then walked to the door and opened it.

Soane stood there, his face a shiny-red from drink, his legs steady enough. As usual when drunk, he was inclined to be garrulous.

"What's the matter?" inquired Barres in a low voice:

"Wisha, Misther Barres, sorr, av ye're not too busy f'r to——"

"S-h-h! Don't bellow at the top of your voice. Wait a moment!"

He picked up his hat and came out into the corridor, closing the studio door behind him so that Dulcie, if she appeared on the scene, should not be humiliated before the others.

Soane began again, but the other cut him short:

"Don't start talking here," he said. "Come down to your own quarters if you're going to yell your head off!" And he led the way, impatiently, down the stairs, past the desk where Miss Kurtz sat stolid and mottled-faced as a lump of uncooked sausage, and into Soane's quarters.

"Now, you listen to me first!" he said when Soane had entered and he had closed the door behind them. "You keep out of my apartment and out of Dulcie's way, too, when you're drunk! You're not going to last very long on this job; I can see that plainly——"

"Faith, sorr, you're right! I'm fired out entirely this blessed minute!"

"You've been discharged?"

"I have that, sorr!"

"What for? Drunkenness?"

"Th' divil do I know phwat for! Wisha, then, Misther Barres, is there anny harrm av a man——"

"Yes, there is! I told you Grogan's would do the trick for you. Now you're discharged without a reference, I suppose."

Soane smiled airily:

"Misther Barres, dear, don't lave that worrit ye! I want no riference from anny landlord. Sure, landlords is tyrants, too! An' phwat the divil should I be wantin'——"

"What are you going to do then?"

Soane hooked both thumbs into the armholes of his vest, and swaggered about the room:

"God bless yer kind heart, sorr, I've a-plenty to do and more for good measure!" He came up to confront Barres, and laid a mysterious finger alongside his over-red nose and began to brag:

"There's thim in high places as looks afther the likes o' me, sorr. There's thim that thrusts me, thim that depinds on me——"

"Have you another job?"

Soane's scorn was superb:

"A job is ut? Misther Barres, dear, I was injuced f'r to accept a *position* of *grave* importance!"

"Here in town?"

"Somewhere around tin thousand miles away or thereabouts," remarked Soane airily.

"Do you mean to take Dulcie with you?"

"Musha, then, Misther Barres, 'tis why I come to ye above f'r to ax ye will ye look afther Dulcie av I go away on me thravels!"

"Yes, I will! . . . Where are you going? What is all this stuff you're talking, anyway——"

"Shtuff? God be good to you, it's no shtuff I talk, Misther Barres! Sure, can't a decent man thravel f'r to see the wurruld as God made it an' no harrm in——"

"Be careful what company you travel in," said Barres, looking at him intently. "You have been travelling around New York in very suspicious company, Soane. I know more about it than you think I do. And it wouldn't surprise me if you have a run-in with the police some day."

"The po-lice, sorr! Arrah, then, me fut in me hand an' me tongue in me cheek to the likes o' thim! An' lave them go hoppin' afther me av they like. The po-lice is ut! Open y'r two ears, asthore, an' listen here!—there'll be nary po-lice, no nor constabulary, nor excise, nor landlords the day that Ireland flies her flag on Dublin Castle! Sure, that will be the grand sight, with all the rats a-runnin', an' all the hurryin' and scurryin' an' the futther and mutther——"

"What are you gabbling about, Soane? What's all this boasting about?"

"Gabble is ut? Is it boastin' I am? Sorra the day! An' there do be grand gintlemen and gay ladies to-day that shall look for a roof an' a sup o' tay this day three weeks, when th' fut o' the tyrant is lifted from the neck of Ireland an' the landlords is runnin' for their lives——"

"I thought so!" exclaimed Barres, disgusted.

"An' phwat was ye thinkin', sorr?"

"That your German friends at Grogan's are stirring up trouble among the Irish. What's all this nonsense, anyway? Are they trying to persuade you to follow the old Fenian tactics and raid Canada? Or is it an armed expedition to the Irish coast? You'd better be careful; they'll only lock you up here, but it's a hanging matter over there!"

"Is it so?" grinned Soane.

"It surely is."

"Well, then, be aisy, Misther Barres, dear. Av there's hangin' to be done this time, 'twill not be thim as wears the green that hangs!"

Barres slowly shook his head:

"This is German work. You're sticking your neck into the noose."

"Lave the noose for the Clan-na-Gael to pull, sorr, an' 'twill shqueeze no Irish neck!"

"You're a fool, Soane! These Germans are exploiting such men as you. Where's your common sense? Can't you see you're playing a German game? What do they care what becomes of you or of Ireland? All they want is for you to annoy England at any cost. And the cost is death! Do you dream for an instant that you and your friends stand a ghost of a chance if you are crazy enough to invade Canada? Do you suppose it possible to land an expedition on the Irish coast?"

Soane deliberately winked at him. Then he burst into laughter and stood rocking there on heel and toe while his mirth lasted.

But the inevitable Celtic reaction presently sobered him and switched him into a sombre recapitulation of Erin's wrongs. And this tragic inventory brought the inevitable tears in time. And Woe awoke in him the memory of the personal and pathetic.

The world had dealt him a wretched hand. He had sat in a crooked game from the beginning. The cards had been stacked; the dice were cogged. And now he meant to make the world disgorge—pay up the living that it owed him.

Barres attempted to stem the flow of volubility, but it instantly became a torrent.

Nobody knew the sorrows of Ireland or of the Irish. Tyranny had marked them for its own. As for himself—once a broth of a boy—he had been torn from the sacred precincts of his native shanty and consigned to a loveless, unhappy marriage.

Then Barres listened without interrupting. But the woes of Soane became vague at that point. Veiled references to being "thrampled on," to "th' big house," to "thim that was high an' shtiff-necked," abounded in an unconnected way. There was something about being a servant at the fireside of his own wife—a footstool on the hearth of his own home—other incomprehensible plaints and mutterings, many scalding tears, a blub or two, and a sort of whining silence.

Then Barres said:

"Who is Dulcie, Soane?"

The man, seated now on his bed, lifted a congested and stupid visage as though he had not comprehended.

"Is Dulcie your daughter?" demanded Barres.

Soane's blue eyes wandered wildly in an agony of recollection:

"Did I say she was *not*, sorr?" he faltered. "Av I told ye that, may the saints forgive me——"

"Is it true?"

"Ah, what was I afther sayin', Misther——"

"Never mind what you said or left unsaid! I want to ask you another question. Who was Eileen Fane?"

Soane bounded to his feet, his blue eyes ablaze:

"Holy Mother o' God! What have I said!"

"Was Eileen Fane your wife?"

"Did I say her blessed name!" shouted Soane. "Borra the sup I tuk that loosed the tongue o' me this cursed day! 'Twas the dommed whishkey inside o' me that told ye that—not me—not Larry Soane! Wurra the day I said it! An' listen, now, f'r the love o' God! Take pride to yourself, sorr, for all the goodness ye done to Dulcie.

"An' av I go, and I come no more to vex her, I thank God 'tis in a gintleman's hands the child do be——" He choked; his marred hands dropped by his side, and he stared dumbly at Barres for a moment. Then:

"Av I come no more, will ye guard her?"

"Yes."

"Will ye do fair by her, Misther Barres?"

"Yes."

"Call God to hear ye say ut!"

"So—help me—God."

Soane dropped on to the bed and took his battered face and curly head between his hands

"I'll say no more," he said thickly. "Nor you nor she shall know no more. An' av ye have guessed it out, kape it locked in. I'll say no more. . . . I was good to her—in me own way. But ye cud see—anny wan with half a cock-eye cud see. . . . I was—honest— with her mother. . . . She made the bargain. . . . I tuk me pay an' held me tongue. . . . 'Tis whishkey talks, not me. . . . I tuk me pay an' I kept to the bargain. . . . Wan year. . . . Then—she was dead of it—like a flower, sorr—like the rose ye pull an' lave lyin' in the sun. . . . Like that, sorr—in a year. . . . An' I done me best be Dulcie. . . . I done me best. An' held to the bargain. . . . An' done me best be Dulcie—little Dulcie—the wee baby that had come at last—her baby—Dulcie Fane! . . ."

XIX

A CHANCE ENCOUNTER

A SINGLE shaded lamp illuminated the studio, making the shapes of things vague where outline and colour were lost in the golden dusk. Dulcie, alone at the piano, accompanied her own voice with soft, scarcely heard harmonies, as she hummed, one after another, old melodies she had learned from the Sisters so long ago—"The Harp," "Shandon Bells," "The Exile," "Shannon Water"—songs of that sort and period:

> *"The Bells of Shandon,*
> *They sound so grand on*
> *The pleasant waters of the River Lee."*

Thessalie sat by the open window and Westmore squatted at her feet on the sill of the little balcony, doing, as usual, all the talking while she lay deep in her arm-chair waving her fan, listening, responding with a low-voiced laugh or word now and again. Dulcie sang:

> *"On the banks of the Shannon*
> *When Mary was nigh."*

From that she changed to a haunting, poignant little song; and Barres looked up from his desk under the lamp. Then he sealed and stamped the three letters which he had written to his Foreland kinfolk, and, holding them in one hand, took his hat from the table with the other, as though preparing to rise. Dulcie half turned her head, her hands still idling over the shadowy keys:

"Are you going out?"

"Just to the corner."

"Why don't you mail your letters down stairs?"

"I'll step around to the branch post office; they'll go quicker. . . . What was that air you were playing just now?"

"It is called 'Mea Culpa.'"

"Play it again."

She turned to the keys, recommenced the Celtic air, and sang in a clear, childish voice:

> "Wake, little maid!
> Red dawns the morn,
> The last stars fade,
> The day is born;
> Now the first lark wings high in air,
> And sings the Virgin's praises there!
>
> "I am afraid
> To see the morn;
> I lie dismayed
> Beside the thorn,
> Gazing at God with frightened eyes,
> Where larks are singing in the skies.
>
> II
>
> "Why, mourn, dear maid,
> Alone, forlorn,
> White and afraid
> Beside the thorn,
> With weeping eyes and sobbing breath
> And fair sweet face as pale as death?

"For love repayed
By Mary's scorn,
I weep, betrayed
By one unborn!
Where can a poor lass hide her head
Till day be done and she be dead!"

The voice and playing lingered among the golden shadows, hushed to a whisper, ceased.

"Is it very old, that sad little song?" he asked at last.

"My mother wrote it. . . . There is the *Mea Culpa*, still, which ends it. Shall I sing it?"

"Go on," he nodded.

So she sang the *Mea Culpa:*

III

"Winds in the whinns
    Shall kene for me—
(*For Love is Love though men be men!*)
    Till all my sins
    Forgiven be—
(*Maxima culpa, Lord. Amen.*)
    And Mary's grace my fault shall purge,
    While skylarks plead my cause above,
    And breezy rivers sing my dirge,
    Because I loved and died of Love.
(*I love, and die of Love!*)
        Amen."

When the soft cadence of the last notes was stilled, Dulcie turned once more toward him in the uncertain light.

"It's very lovely," he said, "and dreadfully triste. The air alone is enough to break your heart."

"My mother, when she wrote it, was unhappy, I imagine——" She swung slowly around to face the keys again.

"Do you know why she was so unhappy?"

"She fell in love," said the girl over her shoulder. "And it saddened her life, I think."

He sat motionless for a while. Dulcie did not turn again. Presently he rose and walked slowly out and down stairs, carrying his letters with him.

The stolid, mottled-faced German girl was on duty at the desk, and she favoured him with a sour look, as usual.

"There was a gen'l'man to see you," she mumbled.

"When?"

"Just now. I didn't know you was in."

"Well, why didn't you ring up the apartment and find out?" he demanded.

She gave him a sullen look:

"Here's his card," she said, shoving it across the desk.

Barres picked up the card. "Georges Renoux, Architect," he read. "Hotel Astor" was pencilled in the corner.

Barres knit his brows, trying to evoke in his memory a physiognomy to fit a name which seemed hazily familiar.

"Did the gentleman leave any message?" he asked.

"No."

"Well, please don't make another mistake of this kind," he said.

She stared at him like a sulky sow, her little eyes red with malice.

"Where is Soane?" he inquired.

"Out."

"Where did he go?"

"I didn't ask him," she replied, with a slight sneer.

"I wish to see him," continued Barres patiently.

"Could you tell me whether he was likely to go to Grogan's?"

"What's Grogan's?"

"Grogan's Café on Third Avenue—where Soane hangs out," he managed to explain calmly. "You know where it is. You have called him up there."

"I don't know nothin' about it," she grunted, resuming the greasy novel she had been reading.

But when Barres, now thoroughly incensed, turned to leave, her small, pig-like eyes peeped slyly after him. And after he had disappeared through the corridor into the street she hastily unhooked the transmitter and called Grogan's.

"This is Martha. . . . Martha Kurtz. Yes, I want Frank Lehr. . . . Is that you, Frank? . . . The artist, Barres, who was pumping Soane the other night, is after him again. I told you how I listened at the door, and how I heard that Irish souse blabbing and bragging. . . . What? . . . Sure! . . . Barres was at the desk just now inquiring if Soane had gone to Grogan's. . . . You bet! . . . Barres is leery since *K17* hit him with a gun. Sure; he's stickin' his nose into everything. . . . Look out for him, if he comes around Grogan's askin' for Soane. . . . And say; there was a French guy here callin' on Barres. I knew he was in, but I said he was out. I was just goin' to call you when Barres came down. . . . Yes, I got his name. . . . Wait, I copied it out. . . . Here it is, 'Georges Renoux, Architect.' And he wrote 'Hotel Astor' in the corner.

"Yes, he said tell Barres to call him up. Naw, I didn't give him the message. . . . You don't say! Is that right? He's one o' them nosey Frenchman? *A captain!* . . . Gee! . . . What's his lay? . . . In New York? Well, you better watch out then. . . .

Sure, I'll ring you if he comes back! . . . No, there
ain't no news. . . . Yes, I was to the Astor grille last
night, and I talked to *K17*. . . . There was a guy
higher up there. I don't know who. He looked like
he was a dark complected Jew. . . . *Foxx Boy!* . . .
Gee! . . . You expect Skeel? To-night? Doin' what?
You think this man Renoux is watchin' the Clan-na-
Gael? Well, you better tell Soane to shut his mouth
then.

"Yes, that Dunois girl is here still. It's a pity *K17*
lost his nerve. . . . Well, you better look out for her
and for Barres, too. They're as thick as last year
honey!

"All right, I'll let you know anything. Bye-bye."

Barres, walking leisurely up the street, kept watching for Soane somewhere along the block; but could
see nobody in the darkness, resembling him.

Outdoors the July night was cooler; young girls,
hatless, in summer frocks, gathered on stoops or
strolled through the lamplit dark. Somewhere a piano
sounded, not unpleasantly.

In the branch post office he mailed his letters, turned
to go out, and caught sight of Soane passing along the
sidewalk just outside.

And with him was the one-eyed man, Max Freund—
the man who, perhaps, had robbed Dulcie of half the
letter.

His first emotion was sheer anger, and it started him
toward the door, bent on swift but unconsidered vengeance.

But before this impulse culminated in his collaring
the one-eyed man, sufficient common sense came to the
rescue. A row meant publicity, and an inquiry by

authority would certainly involve the writer of the partly stolen letter—Thessalie Dunois.

Cool and collected now, but mad all through, Barres continued to follow Soane and Freund, dropping back several yards to keep out of sight, and trying to make up his mind what he ought to do.

The cross street was fairly well lighted; there seemed to be plenty of evening strollers abroad, so that he was not particularly conspicuous on the long block between Sixth and Fifth Avenues.

The precious pair, arriving at Fifth Avenue, halted, blocked by the normal rush of automobiles, unchecked now by a traffic policeman.

So Barres halted, too, and drew back alongside a shop window.

And, as he stopped and stepped aside, he saw a man pause on the sidewalk across the street and move back cautiously into the shadow of a façade opposite.

There was nothing significant in the occurrence; Barres merely happened to notice it; then he turned his eyes toward Soane and Freund, who now were crossing Fifth Avenue. And he went after them, with no definite idea in his head.

Soane and Freund walked on eastward; a tramcar on Madison Avenue stopped them once more; and, as Barres also halted behind them and stepped aside into the shadows, there, just across the street, he saw the same man again halt, retire, and stand motionless in a recess between two shop windows.

Barres tried to keep one eye on him and the other on Soane and Freund. The two latter were crossing Madison Avenue; and as soon as they had crossed, still headed east, the man on the other side of the street came out of his shadowy recess and started eastward, too.

Then Barres also started, but now he was watching the man across the street as well as keeping Soane and Freund in view—watching the former solitary individual with increasing curiosity.

Was that man keeping an eye on him? Was he following Soane and Freund? Was he, in fact, following anybody, and had the lively imagination of Barres begun to make something out of nothing?

At Park Avenue Freund and Soane paused, not apparently because of any vehicular congestion impeding their progress, but they seemed to be engaged in vehement conversation, Soane's excitable tones reaching Barres, where he had halted again beside the tradesmen's gate of a handsome private house.

And once more, across the street the solitary figure also halted and stood unstirring under a porte-cochère.

Barres, straining his eyes, strove to make out details of his features and dress. And presently he concluded that, though the man did turn and glance in his direction occasionally, his attention was principally fixed on Soane and Freund.

His movements, too, seemed to corroborate this idea, because as soon as they started across Park Avenue the man on the opposite side of the street was in instant motion. And Barres, now intensely curious, walked eastward once more, following all three.

At Lexington Avenue Soane sheered off and, despite the clutch of Freund, went into a saloon. Freund finally followed.

As usual, across the street the solitary figure had stopped. Barres, also immobile, kept him in view. Evidently he, too, was awaiting the reappearance of Soane and Freund.

Suddenly Barres made up his mind to have a good look at him. He walked to the corner, walked over to the south side of the street, turned west, and slowly sauntered past the man, looking him deliberately in the face.

As for the stranger, far from shrinking or avoiding the scrutiny, he on his part betrayed a very lively interest in the physiognomy of Barres; and as that young man approached he found himself scanned by a brilliant and alert pair of eyes, as keen as a fox-terrier's.

In frank but subtly hostile curiosity their glances met and crossed. Then, in an instant, a rather odd smile glimmered in the stranger's eyes, twitched at his pleasant mouth, just shaded by a tiny moustache:

"If you please, sir," he said in a low, amused voice, "you will not—as they say in New York—butt in."

Barres, astonished, stood quite still. The young man continued to regard him with a very intelligent and slightly ironical expression:

"I do not know, of course," he said, "whether you are of the city police, the State service, the Post Office, the Department of Justice, the Federal Secret Service"—he shrugged expressive shoulders—"but this I do know very well, that through lack of proper co-ordination in the branches of all your departments of City, State, and Federal surety, there is much bungling, much working at cross purposes, much interference, and many blunders.

"Therefore, I beg of you not to do anything further in the matter which very evidently occupies you." And he bowed and glanced across at the saloon into which Soane and Freund had disappeared.

Barres was thinking hard. He drew out his cigarette case, lighted a cigarette, came to his conclusions:

"You are watching Freund and Soane?" he asked bluntly.

MICROCOPY RESOLUTION TEST CHART

(ANSI and ISO TEST CHART No. 2)

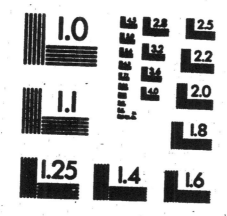

APPLIED IMAGE Inc

1653 East Main Street
Rochester, New York   14609   USA
(716) 482 - 0300 - Phone
(716) 288 - 5989 - Fax

"And you, sir? Are you observing the stars?" inquired the young man, evidently amused at something or other unperceived by Barres.

The latter said, frankly and pleasantly:

"I *am* following those two men. It is evident that you are, also. So may I ask, have you any idea where they are going?"

"I can guess, perhaps."

"To Grogan's?"

"Of course."

"Suppose," said Barres quietly, "I put myself under your orders and go along with you."

The strange young man was much diverted:

"In your kind suggestion there appears to be concealed a germ of common sense," he said. "In which particular service are you employed, sir?"

"And you?" inquired Barres, smilingly.

"I imagine you may have guessed," said the young man, evidently greatly amused at something or other.

Sheer intuition prompted Barres, and he took a chance.

"Yes, I have ventured to guess that you are an Intelligence Officer in the French service, and secretly on duty in the United States."

The young man winced but forced a very bland smile.

"My compliments, whether your guess is born of certainty or not. And you, sir? May I inquire your status?"

"I'm merely a civilian with a season's Plattsburg training as my only professional experience. I'm afraid you won't believe this, but it's quite true. I'm not in either Municipal, State, or Federal service. But I don't believe I can stand this Hun business much longer without enlisting with the Canadians."

"Oh. May I ask, then, why you follow that pair yonder?"

"I'll tell you why. I am a painter. I live at Dragon Court. Soane, an Irishman, is superintendent of the building. I have reason to believe that German propagandists have been teaching him disloyalty under promise of aiding Ireland to secure political independence.

"Coming out of the branch post office this evening, where I had taken some letters, I saw Soane and that fellow, Freund. I really couldn't tell you exactly what my object was in following them, except that I itched to beat up the German and refrained because of the inevitable notoriety that must follow.

"Perhaps I had a vague idea of following them to Grogan's, where I knew they were bound, just to look over the place and see for myself what that German rendezvous is like.

"Anyway, what kept me on their trail was noticing *you;* and your behaviour aroused my curiosity. That is the entire truth concerning myself and this affair. And if you believe me, and if you think I can be of any service to you, take me along with you. If not, then I shall certainly not interfere with whatever you are engaged in."

For a few moments the young Intelligence Officer looked intently at Barres, the same amused, inexplicable smile on his face. Then:

"Your name," he said, with malicious gaiety, "is Garret Barres."

At that Barres completely lost countenance, but the other man began to laugh:

"Certainly you are Garry Barres, a painter, a celebrated Beaux Arts man of——"

"Good heavens!" exclaimed Barres, "*you* are

259

Renoux! You are little Georges Renoux, of the atelier Ledoux!—on the architect's side!—you are that man who left his card for me this evening! I've seen you often! You were a little devil of a nouveau!—but you were always the centre of every bit of mischief in the rue Bonaparte! You put the whole Quarter en charette! I saw you do it."

"I saw *you*," laughed Renoux, "on one notorious occasion, teaching jiu-jitsu to a policeman! Don't talk to me about my escapades!"

Cordially, firmly, in grinning silence, they shook hands. And for a moment the intervening years seemed to melt away; the golden past became the present; and Renoux even thrilled a little at the condescension of Barres in shaking hands with him—the nouveau honoured by the *ancien!*—the reverence never entirely forgotten.

"What are you, anyway, Renoux?" asked Barres, still astonished at the encounter, but immensely interested.

"My friend, you have already guessed. I am Captain: Military Intelligence Department. You know? There are no longer architects or butchers or bakers in France, only soldiers. And of those soldiers I am a very humble one."

"On secret duty here," nodded Barres.

"I need not ask an old Beaux Arts comrade to be discreet and loyal."

"My dear fellow, France is next in my heart after my own country. Tell me, you are following that Irishman, Soane, and his boche friend, Max Freund, are you not?"

"It happens to be as you say," admitted Renoux, smilingly. "A job for a 'flic,' is it not?"

"Shall I tell you what I know about those two men?
—what I suspect?"

"I should be very glad——" But at that moment
Soane came out of the saloon across the way, and
Freund followed.

"May I come with you?" whispered Barres.

"If you care to. Yes, come," nodded Renoux, keeping his clear, intelligent eyes on the two across the
street, who now stood under a lamp-post, engaged in
some sort of drunken altercation.

Renoux, watching them all the while, continued in
a low voice:

"Remember, Barres, if we chance to meet again here
in America, I am merely Georges Renoux, an architect and a fellow Beaux Arts man."

"Certainly. . . . Look! They're starting on, those
two!"

"Come," whispered Renoux.

Soane, unsteady of leg and talkative, was now making for Third Avenue beside Freund, who had taken
him by the arm, in hopes, apparently, of steadying
them both.

As Renoux and Barres followed, the latter cautiously requested any instructions which Renoux might
think fit to give.

Renoux said in his cool, agreeable voice:

"You know it's rather unusual for an officer to
bother personally with this sort of thing. But my
people—even the renegade Germans in our service—
have been unable to obtain necessary information for
us in regard to Grogan's.

"It happened this afternoon that certain information was brought to me which suggested that I myself take a look at Grogan's. And that is what I was going to do when I saw you on the street, carefully stalking two well-known suspects."

They both laughed cautiously.

Grogan's was now in sight on the corner, its cherrywood magnificence and its bilious imitation of stained glass aglow with electricity. And into its "Family Entrance" swaggered Soane, followed by the lank figure of Max Freund.

Renoux and Barres had halted fifty yards away. Neither spoke. And presently came to them a short, dark, powerfully built man, who strolled up casually, puffing a large, rank cigar.

Renoux named him to Barre :

"Emile Souchez, one of my men." He added: "Anybody gone in yet?"

"Otto Klein, of Gerhardt, Klein & Schwartzmeyer went in an hour ago," replied Souchez.

"Oho," nodded Renoux softly. "That signifies something really interesting. Who else went in?"

"Small fry—Dave Sendelbeck, Louis Hochstein, Terry Madigan, Dolan, McBride, Clancy—all Clanna-Gael men."

"Skeel?"

"No. He's still at the Astor. Franz Lehr came out about half an hour ago and took a taxi west. Jacques Alost is following in another."

Renoux thought a moment:

"Lehr has probably gone to see Skeel at the Hotel Astor," he concluded. "We're going to have our chance, I think."

Then, turning to Barres:

"We've decided to take a sport-chance to-night. We have most reliable information that this man Lehr, who now owns Grogan's, will carry here upon his person papers of importance to my Government—and to yours, too, Barres.

"The man from whom he shall procure these papers is an Irish gentleman named Murtagh Skeel, just arrived from Buffalo and stopping overnight at the Hotel Astor.

"Lehr, we were informed, was to go personally and get those papers. . . . Do you really wish to help us?"

"Certainly."

"Very well. I expect we shall have what you call a mix-up. You will please, therefore, walk into Grogan's—not by the family entrance, but by the swinging doors on Lexington Avenue. Kindly refresh yourself there with some Munich beer; also eat a sandwich at my expense, if you care to. Then you will give yourself the pains to inquire the way to the washroom. And there you will possess your soul in amiable patience until you shall hear me speak your name in a very quiet, polite tone."

Barres, recognising the familiar mock seriousness of student days in Paris, began to smile. Renoux frowned and continued his instructions:

"When you hear me politely pronounce your name, mon vieux, then you shall precipitate yourself valiantly to the aid of Monsieur Souchez and myself—and perhaps Monsieur Alost—and help us to hold, gag and search the somewhat violent German animal whom we corner inside the family entrance of Herr Grogan!"

Barres had difficulty in restraining his laughter. Renoux was very serious, with the delightful mock gravity of a witty and perfectly fearless Frenchman.

"Lehr?" inquired Barres, still laughing.

"That is the animal under discussion. There will be a taxicab awaiting us——" He turned to Souchez:

"Dis, donc, Emile, faut employer ton coup du Père François pour nous assurer de cet animal là."

"B'en sure," nodded Souchez, fishing furtively in the side pocket of his coat and displaying the corner of a red silk handkerchief. He stuffed it into his pocket again; Renoux smiled carelessly at Barres.

"Mon vieux," he said, "I hope it will be like a good fight in the Quarter—what with all those Irish in there. You desire to get your head broken?"

"You bet I do, Renoux!"

"Bien! So now, if you are quite ready?" he suggested. "Merci, monsieur, et à bientôt!" He bowed profoundly.

Barres, still laughing, walked to Lexington Avenue, crossed northward, and entered the swinging doors of Grogan's, perfectly enchanted to have his finger in the pie at last, and aching for an old-fashioned Latin Quarter row, the pleasures of which he had not known for several too respectable years.

XX

THE material attraction of Grogan's was principally German beer; the æsthetic appeal of the place was also characteristically Teutonic and consisted of peculiarly offensive decorations, including much red cherry, much imitation stained glass, many sprawling brass fixtures, and many electric lights. Only former inmates of the Fatherland could have conceived and executed the embellishments of Grogan's.

There was a palatial bar, behind which fat, white-jacketed Teutons served slopping steins of beer upon a perforated brass surface. There was a centre table, piled with those barbarous messes known to the undiscriminating Hun as "delicatessen"—raw fish, sour fish, smoked fish, flabby portions of defunct pig in various guises—all naturally nauseating to the white man's olfactories and palate, and all equally relished by the beer-swilling boche.

A bartender with Pekinese and apoplectic eyes and the scorbutic facial symptoms of a Strassburg liver, took the order from Barres and set before him a frosty glass of Pilsner, incidentally drenching the bar at the same time with swipes, which he thriftily scraped through the perforated brass strainer into a slop-bucket underneath.

Being a stranger there, Barres was furtively scrutinised at first, but there seemed to be nothing particularly suspicious about a young man who stopped in for a glass of Pilsner on a July night, and nobody paid him any further attention.

Besides, two United States Secret Service men had just gone out, followed, as usual, by one Johnny Klein; and the Germans at the tables at the bar, and behind the bar were still sneeringly commenting on the episode—now a familiar one and of nightly occurrence.

So only very casual attention was paid to Barres and his Pilsner and his rye-bread and sardine sandwich, which he took over to a vacant table to desiccate and discuss at his leisure.

People came and went; conversation in Hunnish gutturals became general; soiled evening newspapers were read, raw fish seized in fat red fingers and suckingly masticated; also, skat and pinochle were resumed with unwiped hands, and there was loud slapping of cards on polished table tops, and many porcine noises.

Barres finished his Pilsner, side-stepped the sandwich, rose, asked a bartender for the wash-room, and leisurely followed the direction given.

There was nobody in there. He had, for company, a mouse, a soiled towel on a roller, and the remains of some unattractive soap. He lighted a cigarette, surveyed himself in the looking glass, cast a friendly glance at the mouse, and stood waiting, flexing his biceps muscles with a smile of anticipated pleasure in renewing the use of them after such a very long period wasted in the peaceful pursuit of art.

For he was still a boy at heart. All creative minds retain something of those care-free, irresponsible years as long as the creative talent lasts. As it fails, worldly caution creeps in like a thief in the night, to steal the spontaneous pleasures of the past and leave in their places only the old galoshes of prudence and the finger-prints of dull routine.

Barres stood by the open door of the wash-room, listening. The corridor which passed it led on into another corridor running at right angles. This was the Family Entrance.

Now, as he waited there, he heard the street door open, and instantly the deadened shock of a rush and struggle.

As he started toward the Family Entrance, straining his ears for the expected summons, a man in flight turned the corner into his corridor so abruptly that he had him by the throat even before he recognised in him the man with the thick eye-glasses who had hit him between the eyes with a pistol—the "Watcher" of Dragon Court!

With a swift sigh of gratitude to Chance, Barres folded the fleeing Watcher to his bosom and began the business he had to transact with him—an account too long overdue.

The Watcher fought like a wildcat, but in silence —fought madly, using both fists, feet, baring his teeth, too, with frantic attempts to use them. But Barres gave him no opportunity to kick, bite, or to pull out any weapon; he battered the Watcher right and left, swinging on him like lightning, and his blows drummed on him like the tattoo of fists on a punching bag until one stinging crack sent the Watcher's head snapping back with a jerk, and a terrific jolt knocked him as clean and as flat as a dead carp.

There were papers in his coat, also a knuckle-duster, a big clasp-knife, and an automatic pistol. And Barres took them all, stuffed them into his own pockets, and, dragging his still dormant but twitching victim by the collar, as a cat proudly lugs a heavy rat, he started for the Family Entrance, where Donnybrook had now broken loose.

But the silence of the terrific struggle in that narrow entry, the absence of all yelling, was significant. No Irish whoops, no Teutonic din of combat shattered the stillness of that dim corridor—only the deadened sounds of blows and shuffling of frantic feet. It was very evident that nobody involved desired to be interrupted by the police, or call attention to the location of the battle field.

Renoux, Souchez, and a third companion were in intimate and desperate conflict with half a dozen other men—dim, furious figures fighting there under the flickering gas jet from which the dirty globe had been knocked into fragments.

Into this dusty maelstrom of waving arms and legs went Barres—first dropping his now inert prey—and began to hit out enthusiastically right and left, at the nearest hostile countenance visible.

His was a flank attack and totally unexpected by the the attackees; and the diversion gave Renoux time to seize a muscular, struggling opponent, hold him squirming while Souchez passed his handkerchief over his throat and the third man turned his pockets inside out.

Then Renoux called breathlessly to Barres:

"All right, mon vieux! Face to the rear front! March!"

For a moment they stiffened to face a battering rush from the stairs. Suddenly a pistol spoke, and an Irish voice burst out:

"Whist, ye domm fool! G'wan wid yer fightin' an' can th' goon-play!"

There came a splintering crash as the rickety banisters gave way and several Teutonic and Hibernian warriors fell in a furious heap, blocking the entry with an unpremeditated obstacle.

Instantly Souchez, Barres and the other man backed out into the street, followed nimbly by Renoux and his plunder.

Already a typical Third Avenue crowd was gathering—though the ominous glimmer of a policeman's buttons had not yet caught the lamplight from the street corner.

Then the door of Grogan's burst open and an embattled Irishman appeared. But at first glance the hopelessness of the situation presented itself to him; a taxi loaded with French and American franc-tireurs was already honking triumphantly away westward; an excited and rapidly increasing throng pressed around the Family Entrance; also, the distant glitter of a policeman's shield and buttons now extinguished all hope of pursuit.

Soane glared at the crowd out of enraged and bloodshot eyes:

"G'wan home, ye bunch of bums!" he said thickly, and slammed the door to the Family Entrance of Grogan's notorious café.

At 42d Street and Madison Avenue the taxi stopped and Souchez and Alost got out and went rapidly across the street toward the Grand Central depot. Then the taxi proceeded west, north again, then once more west.

Renoux, busy with a bleeding rose, remarked carelessly that Souchez and Alost were taking a train and were in a hurry, and that he himself was going back to the Astor.

"You do not mind coming with me, Barres?" he added. "In my rooms we can have a bite and a glass together, and then we can brush up. That was a nice little fight, was it not, mon ami?"

"Fine," said Barres with satisfaction.

"Quite like the old and happy days," mused Renoux,

surveying wilted collar and rumpled tie of his comrade. "You came off well; you have merely a bruised cheek." His eyes began to sparkle and he laughed: "Do you remember that May evening when your very quarrelsome atelier barricaded the Café de la Source and forbade us to enter—and my atelier marched down the Boul' Mich' with its Kazoo band playing our atelier march, determined to take your café by assault? Oh, my! What a delightful fight that was!"

"Your crazy comrades stuffed me into the fountain among the goldfish. I thought I'd drown," said Barres, laughing.

"I know, but your atelier gained a great victory that night, and you came over to Müller's with your Kazoo band playing the Fireman's March, and you carried away our palms and bay-trees in their green tubs, and you threw them over the Pont-au-Change into the Seine!——"

They were laughing like a pair of schoolboys now, quite convulsed and holding to each other.

"Do you remember," gasped Barres, "that girl who danced the Carmagnole on the Quay?"

"Yvonne Tête-de-Linotte!"

"And the British giant from Julien's, who threw everybody out of the Café Montparnasse and invited the Quarter in to a free banquet?"

"McNeil!"

"What ever became of that pretty girl, Doucette de Valmy?"

"Oh, it was she who cheered on your atelier to the assault on Müllers!——"

Laughter stifled them.

"What crazy creatures we all were," said Renoux, staunching the last crimson drops oozing from his nose. Then, more soberly: "We French have a grimmer affair

over there than the joyous rows of the Latin Quarter.
I'm sorry now that we didn't throw every waiter in
Müller's after the bay-trees. There would have been
so many fewer spies to betray France."

The taxi stopped at the 44th Street entrance to the
Astor. They descended, Renoux leading, walked
through the corridor to Peacock Alley, turned to the
right through the bar, then to the left into the lobby,
and thence to the elevator.

In Renoux's rooms they turned on the electric light,
locked the door, closed the transom, then spread their
plunder out on a table.

To Renoux's disgust his own loot consisted of sealed
envelopes full of clippings from German newspapers
published in Chicago, Milwaukee, and New York.

"That animal, Lehr," he said with a wry face, "has
certainly played us a filthy turn. These clippings
amount to nothing——" His eyes fell on the packet
of papers which Barres was now opening, and he leaned
over his shoulder to look.

"Thank God!" he said, "here they are! Where on
earth did you find these papers, Barres? They're the
documents we were after! They ought to have been
in Lehr's pockets!"

"He must have passed them to the fellow who
bumped into me near the washroom," said Barres, enchanted at his luck. "What a fortunate chance that
you sent me around there!"

Renoux, delighted, stood under the electric light unfolding document after document, and nodding his
handsome, mischievous head with satisfaction.

"What luck, Barres! What did you do to the fellow?"

"Thumped him to sleep and turned out his pockets.
Are these really what you want?"

"I should say so! This is precisely what we are looking for!"

"Do you mind if I read them, too?"

"No, I don't. Why should I? You're my loyal comrade and you understand discretion. . . . *What do you think of this!*" displaying a typewritten document marked "Copy," enclosing a sheaf of maps.

It contained plans of all the East River and Harlem bridges, a tracing showing the course of the new aqueduct and the Ashokan Dam, drawings of the Navy Yard, a map of Iona Island, and a plan of the Welland Canal.

The document was brief:

"Included in report by *K17* to Diplomatic Agent controlling Section 7-4-11-B. Recommended that detail plan of DuPont works be made without delay.

"SKEEL."

Followed several sheets in cipher, evidently some intricate variation of those which are always ultimately solved by experts.

But the documents that were now unfolded by Captain Renoux proved readable and intensely interesting.

These were the papers which Renoux read and which Barres read over his shoulder:

"(Copy)

Berlin Military Telegraph Office
Telegram

Berlin. Political Division of the General
Staff
Nr. Pol. 6431.
(SECRET)
8, Moltkestrasse,
Berlin, NW, 40.
March 20, 1916.

272

"FERES BEY,
        N. Y.

"Referring to your correspondence and conversations with Colonel Skeel, I most urgently request that the necessary funds be raised through the New York banker, Adolf Gerhardt; also that Bernstorff be immediately informed through Boy-Ed, so that plans of Head General Staff of Army on campaign may not be delayed.

"Begin instantly enlist and train men, secure and arm power-boat assemble equipment and explosives, Welland Canal Exp'd'n. War Office No. 159-16, Secret U. K.:— T, S, P."

                                    "Foreign Office, Berlin,
                                        "Dec. 28, 1914.

"DEAR SIR ROGER:—I have the honour to acknowledge receipt of your letter of the 23d inst., in which you submitted to his Imperial Majesty's Government a proposal for the formation of an Irish brigade which would be pledged to fight only for the cause of Irish nationalism, and which is to be composed of any Irish prisoners of war willing to join such a regiment.

"In reply I have the honour to inform you that his Imperial Majesty's Government agrees to your proposal and also to the conditions under which it might be possible to train an Irish brigade. These conditions are set out in the declaration enclosed in your letter of the 13th inst., and are given at foot. I have the honour to be, dear Roger, your obedient servant,

                            "(Signed) ZIMMERMAN,
        "Under Secretary of State for the Foreign Office.

    "To HIS HONOUR, SIR ROGER CASEMENT,
    "Eden Hotel, Kurfürstendamm, Berlin."

                    "(SECRET)

"COLONEL MURTAGH SKEEL,
    "Flying Division, Irish Expeditionary Corps,
    "New York.

"For your information I enclose Zimmerman's letter to Sir Roger, and also the text of Articles 6 and 7, being part of our first agreement with Sir Roger Casement.

"You will note particularly the Article numbered 7.

"This paragraph, unfortunately, still postpones your suggested attempt to seize on the high seas a British or neutral steamer loaded with arms and munitions, and make a landing from her on the Irish Coast.

"But, in the meantime, is it not possible for you to seize one of the large ore steamers on the Great Lakes, transfer to her sufficient explosives, take her into the Welland Canal and blow up the locks?

"No more valuable service could be performed by Irishmen; no deadlier blow delivered at England.

' "I am, my dear Skeel, your sincere friend and comrade,

"(Signed)   VON PAPEN.

"P. S.—Herewith appended are Articles 6 and 7 included in the Casement convention:

"(SECRET)

"Text of Articles 6 and 7 of the convention concluded between Sir Roger Casement and the German Government:

"6.   The German Imperial Government undertakes 'under certain circumstances' to lend the Irish Brigade adequate military support, and to send it to Ireland abundantly supplied with arms and ammunition, in order that once there it may equip any Irish who would like to join it in making an attempt to re-establish Ireland's national liberty by force of arms.

"The 'special circumstances' stipulated above are as follows:

"In case of a German naval victory which would make it possible to reach the Irish coast, the German Imperial Government pledges itself to despatch the Irish Brigade and a German expeditionary corps commanded by German officers, in German troopships, to attempt a landing on the Irish coast.

"7. It will be impossible to contemplate a landing in Ireland unless the German Navy can gain such a victory as to make it really likely that an attempt to reach Ireland by sea would succeed. Should the German Navy not win such a victory, then a use will be found for the Irish Brigade in Germany or elsewhere. But in no case will it be used except in such ways as Sir Roger Casement shall approve, as being completely in accordance with Article 2.

"In this case the Irish Brigade might be sent to Egypt to lend assistance in expelling the English and re-establishing Egyptian independence.

"Even if the Irish Brigade should not succeed in fighting for the liberation of Ireland from the English yoke, nevertheless a blow dealt at the British intruders in Egypt and intended to help the Egyptians to recover their freedom would be a blow struck for a cause closely related to that of Ireland."

Another paper read as follows:

> "Halbmondlager,
> "Aug. 20th, 1915.

"(SECRET)"

"To MURTAGH SKEEL, COLONEL,
  "Irish Exp. Force,
    "N. Y.

"REPORT

"On June 7, fifty Irishmen, with one German subaltern, were handed over to this camp, to be temporarily accommodated here. On June 16 five more Irishmen arrived, one of whom, having a broken leg, was sent to the camp hospital. There are, therefore, fifty-four Irishmen now here, one Sergeant Major, one Deputy Sergeant Major, three Sergeants, three Corporals, three Lance Corporals, and forty-three privates.

"They were accommodated as well as could be among the Indian battalion, an arrangement which gives rise to much trouble, which is inevitable, considering the tasks imposed upon Half Moon Camp.

"The Irish form an Irish brigade, which was constituted after negotiations between the Foreign Office and Sir Roger Casement, the champion of Irish independence.

"Enclosed is the Foreign Office communication of Dec. 28, 1914, confirming the conditions on which the Irish brigade was to be formed.

"The members of the Irish brigade are no longer German prisoners of war, but receive an Irish uniform; and, according to orders, instructions are to be issued to treat the Irish as comrades in arms.

"The Irish are under the command of a German officer, First Lieut. Boehm, the representative of the Grand General Staff (Political Division) which is in direct communication with the subaltern in charge of the Irish. This subaltern has been receiving money direct, which he expends in the interests of the Irish; 250 marks were given him through the Commandant's office, Zossen, and 250 marks by First Lieut. Boehm.

"Promotions, also, are made known by being directly communicated to the subaltern in question. As will appear from the enclosed copy, dated July 20, these promotions were as follows: (1) Sergeant Major, (2) Deputy Sergeant Major, and (3) Sergeants.

"The uniforms arrived between the end of July and the beginning of August. Their coming was announced in a letter dated July 20 (copy enclosed), and their distribution was ordered. The box of uniforms was addressed to Zossen, whence it was brought here. The uniforms consist of a jacket, trousers, and cap in Irish style, and are of huntsman's green cloth. Altogether, uniforms arrived for fifty men, and they have since been given out. Three non-commissioned officers brought their uniforms with them from Limburg on July 16. Two photographs of the Irish are annexed.

"A few Irish are in correspondence with Sir Roger Casement, who, in a letter from Munich, dated Aug. 16, says that he hears that the Irish are shortly to be transferred from here to another place. In a letter dated July 17 he complains of his want of success, only fifty men having sent in their names as wishing to join the brigade.

"Six weeks ago Sir Roger Casement was here with First Lieutenant Boehm. Since then, however, neither of these gentlemen has personally visited the Irish.

"Since the 18th of June the commandant's office has allowed every penniless Irishman two marks a week—a sum which is now being paid out to fifty-three men.

"On Aug. 6 the subaltern in charge of the Irish brigade was given a German soldier to help him.

"In this camp every possible endeavour is made to

help to attain the important objects in view, but owing
to the Irish being accommodated with coloured races within
the precincts of a closed camp, it is inevitable that serious
dissensions and acts of violence should take place. Moreover, a German subaltern is not suited for dealing inde-
pendently with Irishmen.

"(Sgd.) HAUPTMANN, d. R. a. D.,
"(Retired Captain on the Reserve List)."

The last paper read as follows:

"(COPY)

"(Wireless via Mexico)

"Berlin (no date).

"FRANZ,
"N. Y.
"Necessary close Nihla Quellen case immediately. Evidently useless expect her take service with us. Hold you
responsible. Advise you take secret measures to end menace to our interests in Paris. D'Eblis urges instant action.
Bolo under suspicion. Ex-minister also suspected. Only
drastic and final action on your part can end danger. You
know what to do. Do it."
The telegram was signed with a string of letters and
numerals.

Renoux glanced curiously at Barres, who had turned
very red and was beginning to re-read the wireless.
When he finished, Renoux folded all the documents
and placed them in the breast pocket of his coat.
"Mon ami, Barres," he said pleasantly, "you and
I have much yet to say to each other."
"In the meanwhile, let us wash the stains of combat
from our persons. What is the number of your col-
lar?"
"Fifteen and a half."
"I can fit you out. The bathroom is this way, old
top!"

XXI

THE WHITE BLACKBIRD

REFRESHED by icy baths and clean linen, and now further fortified against the slings and arrows of outrageous fortune by a supper of cold fowl and Moselle, Captain Renoux and Garret Barres sat in the apartment of the former gentleman, gaily exchanging Latin Quarter reminiscences through the floating haze of their cigars.

But the conversation soon switched back toward the far more serious business which alone accounted for their being there together after many years. For, as the French officer had remarked, a good deal remained to be said between them. And Barres knew what he meant, and was deeply concerned at the prospect.

But Renoux approached the matter with careless good humour and by a leisurely, circuitous route, which polite pussy-footing was obviously to prepare Barres for impending trouble.

He began by referring to his mission in America, admitting very frankly that he was a modest link in the system of military and political intelligence maintained by all European countries in the domains of their neighbours.

"I might as well say so," he remarked, "because it's known to the representatives of enemy governments here as well as to your own Government, that some of us are here; and anybody can imagine why.

"And, in the course of my—studies," he said deliberately, while his clear eyes twinkled, "it has come to my knowledge, and to the knowledge of the French Ambassador, that there is, in New York, a young woman who already has proven herself a dangerous enemy to my country."

"That is interesting, if true," said Barres, reddening to the temples. "But it is even more interesting if it is not true. . . . And it isn't!"

"You think not?"

"I don't think anything about it, Renoux; I *know*."

"I am afraid you have been misled, Barres. And it is natural enough."

"Why?"

"Because," said Renoux serenely, "she is very beautiful, very clever, very young, very appealing. . . . Tell me, my friend, where did you meet her?"

Barres looked him in the eyes:

"Where did you learn that I had ever met her?"

"Through the ordinary channels which, if you will pardon me, I am not at liberty to discuss."

"All right. It is sufficient that you know I have met her. Now, where did I meet her?"

"I don't know," said Renoux candidly.

"How long have I known her then?"

"Possibly a few weeks. Our information is that your acquaintance with her is not of long duration."

"Wrong, my friend: I met her in France several years ago; I know her intimately."

"Yes, the intimacy has been reported," said Renoux, blandly. "But it doesn't take long, sometimes."

Barres reddened again and shook his head:

"You and your agents are all wrong, Renoux. So is your Government. Do you know what it's doing —what you and your agents are doing? You're playing a German game for Berlin!"

This time Renoux flushed and there was a slight quiver to his lips and nostrils; but he said very pleasantly:

"That would be rather mortifying, mon ami, if it were true."

"It is true. Berlin, the traitor in Paris, the conspirator in America, the German, Austrian, and Turkish diplomatic agents here ask nothing better than that you manage, somehow, to eliminate the person in question."

"Why?" demanded Renoux.

"Because more than one of your public men in Paris will face charges of conspiracy and treason if the person in question ever has a fair hearing and a chance to prove her innocence of the terrible accusations that have been made against her."

"Naturally," said Renoux, "those accused bring counter charges. It is always the history of such cases, mon ami."

"Your mind is already made up, then?"

"My mind is a real mind, Barres. Reason is what it seeks—the logical evidence that leads to truth. If there is anything I don't know, then I wish to know it, and will spare no pains, permit no prejudice to warp my judgment."

"All right. Now, let's have the thing out between us, Renoux. We are not fencing in the dark; we understand each other and are honest enough to say so. Now, go on."

Renoux nodded and said very quietly and pleasantly:

"The reference in one of these papers to the celebrated Nihla Quellen reminds me of the first time I ever saw her. I was quite bowled over, Barres, as you may easily imagine. She sang one of those Asiatic

songs—and then the dance!—a miracle!—a delight—
apparently entirely unprepared, unpremeditated even
—you know how she did it?—exquisite perfection—
something charmingly impulsive and spontaneous—a
caprice of the moment! Ah—there is a wonderful ar-
tiste, Nihla Quellen!"

Barres nodded, his level gaze fixed on the French
officer.

"As for the document," continued Renoux, "it does
not entirely explain itself to me. You see, this Eurasian, Ferez Bey, was a very intimate friend of Nihla
Quellen."

"You are quite mistaken," interposed Barres. But
the other merely smiled with a slight gesture of defer-
ence to his friend's opinion, and went on.

"This Ferez is one of those persistent, annoying
flies which buzz around chancelleries and stir up dip-
lomats to pernicious activities. You know there isn't
much use in swatting, as you say, the fly. No. Better find the manure heap which hatched him and burn
that!"

He smiled and shrugged, relighted his cigar, and
continued:

"So, mon ami, I am here in your charming and hos-
pitable city to direct the necessary sanitary measures,
sub rosa, of course. You have been more than kind.
My Government and I have you to thank for this batch
of papers——" He tapped his breast pocket and
made salutes which Frenchmen alone know how to
make.

"Renoux," said Barres bluntly, "you have learned
somehow that Nihla Quellen is under my protection.
You conclude I am her lover."

The officer's face altered gravely, but he said nothing.

Barres leaned forward in his chair and laid a hand on his comrade's shoulder:

"Renoux, do you trust me, personally?"

"Yes."

"Very well. Then I shall trust you. Because there is nothing you can tell me about Nihla Quellen that I do not already know—nothing concerning her *dossier* in your secret archives, nothing in regard to the evidence against her and the testimony of the Count d'Eblis. And that clears the ground between you and me."

If Renoux was surprised he scarcely showed it.

Barres said:

"As long as you know that she is under my protection, I want you to come to my place and talk to her. I don't ask you to accept my judgment in regard to her; I merely wish you to listen to what she has to say, and then come to your own conclusions. Will you do this?"

For a few moments Renoux sat quite still, his clear, intelligent eyes fixed on the smoking tip of his cigar. Without raising them he said slowly:

"As we understand it, Nihla Quellen has been a spy from the very beginning. Our information is clear, concise, logical. We know her history. She was the mistress of Prince Cyril, then of Ferez, then of d'Eblis—perhaps of the American banker, Gerhardt, also. She came directly from the German Embassy at Constantinople to Paris, on Gerhardt's yacht, the *Mirage*, and under his protection and the protection of Comte Alexandre d'Eblis.

"Ferez was of the party. And that companionship of conspirators never was dissolved as long as Nihla Quellen remained in Europe."

"That Nihla Quellen has ever been the mistress of

any man is singularly untrue," said Barres coolly. "Your Government has to do with a chaste woman; and it doesn't even know that much!"

Renoux regarded him curiously:

"You have seen her dance?" he enquired gravely.

"Often. And, Renoux, you are too much a man of the world to be surprised at the unexpected. There are white blackbirds."

"Yes, there are."

"Nihla Quellen is one."

"My friend, I desire to believe it if it would be agreeable to you."

"I know, Renoux; I believe in your good-will. Also, I believe in your honesty and intelligence. And so I do not ask you to accept my word for what I tell you. Only remember that I am absolutely certain concerning my belief in Nihla Quellen. . . . I have no doubt that you think I am in love with her. . . . I can't answer you. All Europe was in love with her. Perhaps I am. . . . I don't know, Renoux. But this I do know; she is clean and sweet and honest from the crown of her head to the sole of her foot. In her heart there has never dwelt treachery. Talk to her to-night. You're like the best of your compatriots, clear minded, logical, intelligent, and full of that legitimate imagination without which intellect is a machine. You know the world; you know men; you don't know women and you know you don't. Therefore, you are equipped to learn the truth—to divine it—from Nihla Quellen. Will you come over to my place now?"

"Yes," said Renoux pleasantly.

The orchestra was playing as they passed through the hotel; supper rooms, corridors, café and lobby were crowded with post-theatre throngs in search of food and drink and dance music; and although few theatres were open in July, Long Acre blazed under its myriad lights and the sidewalks were packed with the audiences filtering out of the various summer shows and into all-night cabarets.

They looked across at the distant war bulletins displayed on Times Square, around which the usual gesticulating crowd had gathered, but kept on across Long Acre, and west toward Sixth Avenue.

Midway in the block, Renoux touched his comrade silently on the arm, and halted.

"A few minutes, mon ami, if you don't mind—time for you to smoke a cigarette while waiting."

They had stopped before a brownstone house which had been converted into a basement dwelling, and which was now recessed between two modern shops constructed as far as the building line.

All the shades and curtains in the house were drawn and the place appeared to be quite dark, but a ring at the bell brought a big, powerfully built porter, who admitted them to a brightly lighted reception room. Then the porter replaced the chains on the door of bronze.

"Just a little while, if you will be amiable enough to have patience," said Renoux.

He went away toward the rear of the house and Barres seated himself. And in a few moments the burly porter reappeared with a tray containing a box of cigarettes and a tall glass of Moselle.

"Monsieur Renoux will not be long," he said, bringing a sheaf of French illustrated periodicals to the little table at Barres' elbow; and he retired with a bow and resumed his chair in the corridor by the bronze door.

Through closed doors, somewhere from the rear of

the silent house came the distant click of a typewriter. At moments, too, looking over the war pictures in the periodicals, Barres imagined that he heard a confused murmur as of many voices.

Later it became evident that there were a number of people somewhere in the house, because, now and then, the porter unlatched the door and drew the chains to let out some swiftly walking man.

Once two men came out together. One carried a satchel; the other halted in the hallway to slip a clip into an automatic pistol before dropping it into the side pocket of his coat.

And after a while Renoux appeared, bland, debonaire, evidently much pleased with whatever he had been doing.

Two other men appeared in the corridor behind him; he said something to them in a low voice; Barres imagined he heard the words, "Washington" and "Jusserand."

Then the two men went out, walking at a smart pace, and Renoux sauntered into the tiny reception room.

"You don't know," he said, "what a very important service you have rendered us by catching that fellow to-night and stripping him of his papers."

Barres rose and they walked out together.

"This city," added Renoux, "is fairly verminous with disloyal Huns. The streets are crawling with them; every German resort, saloon, beer garden, keller, café, club, society—every German drug store, delicatessen shop, music store, tobacconist, is lousy with the treacherous swine.

"There are two great hotels where the boche gathers and plots; two great banking firms are centres of German propaganda; three great department stores, dozens of downtown commercial agencies; various buildings and piers belonging to certain transatlantic steamship lines, the offices of certain newspapers and periodicals. . . . Tell me, Barres, did you know that the banker, Gerhardt, owns the building in which you live?"

"Dragon Court!"

"You didn't know it, evidently. Yes, he owns it."

"Is he really involved in pro-German intrigue?" asked Barres.

"That is our information."

"I ask," continued Barres thoughtfully, "because his summer home is at Northbrook, not far from my own home. And to me there is something peculiarly contemptible about disloyalty in the wealthy who owe every penny to the country they betray."

"His place is called Hohenlinden," remarked Renoux.

"Yes. Are you having it watched?"

Renoux smiled. Perhaps he was thinking about other places, also—the German Embassy, for example, where, inside the Embassy itself, not only France but also the United States Government was represented by a secret agent among the personnel.

"We try to learn what goes on among the boches," he said carelessly. "They try the same game. But, Barres, they are singularly stupid at such things—not adroit, merely clumsy and brutal. The Hun cannot camouflage his native ferocity. He reveals himself.

"And in that respect it is fortunate for civilisation that it is dealing with barbarians. Their cunning is of the swinish sort. Their stench ultimately discovers them. You are discovering it for yourselves; you detected Dernberg; you already sniff Von Papen, Boy-ed, Bernstorff. All over the world the nauseous effluvia from the vast Teutonic hog-pen is being detected and recognised. And civilisation is taking sanitary measures to abate the nuisance. . . . And your country, too, will one day send out a sanitary brigade to help clean up the world, just as you now supply our details with the necessary chlorides and antiseptics."

Barres laughed:

"You are very picturesque," he said. "And I'll tell you one thing, if we don't join the sanitary corps now operating, I shall go out with a bottle of chloride myself."

They entered Dragon Court a few moments later. Nobody was at the desk, it being late.

"To-morrow," said Barres, as they ascended the stairs, "my friends, Miss Soane, Miss Dunois, and Mr. Westmore are to be our guests at Foreland Farms. You didn't know that, did you?" he added sarcastically.

"Oh, yes," replied Renoux, much amused. "Miss Dunois, as you call her, sent her trunks away this evening."

Barres, surprised and annoyed, halted on the landing:

"Your people didn't interfere, I hope."

"No. There was nothing in them of interest to us," said Renoux naïvely. "I sent a report when I sent on to Washington the papers which you secured for us."

Barres paused before his studio door, key in hand. They could hear the gramophone going inside. He said:

"I don't have to ask you to be fair, Renoux, because the man who is unfair to others swindles himself, and you are too decent, too intelligent to do that. I am going to present you to Thessalie Dunois, which happens to be her real name, and I am going to tell her in your presence who you are. Then I shall leave you alone with her."

He fitted his latchkey and opened the door.

Westmore was trying fancy dancing with Dulcie on one side, and Thessalie on the other—the latter evidently directing operations.

"Garry!" exclaimed Thessalie.

"You're a fine one! Where have you been?" began Westmore. Then he caught sight of Renoux and became silent.

Barres led his comrade forward and presented him:

"A fellow student of the Beaux Arts," he explained, "and we've had a very jolly evening together. And, Thessa, there is something in particular that I should like to have you explain to Monsieur Renoux, if you don't mind. . . ." He turned and looked at Dulcie: "If you will pardon us a moment, Sweetness."

She nodded and smiled and took Westmore's arm again, and continued the dance alone with him while Barres, drawing Thessalie's arm through his, and passing his other arm through Renoux's, walked leisurely through his studio, through the now open folding doors, past his bedroom and Westmore's, and into the latter's studio beyond.

"Thessa, dear," he said very quietly, "I feel very certain that the worst of your troubles are about to end——" He felt her start slightly. "And," he continued, "I have brought my comrade, Renoux, here to-night so that you and he can clear up a terrible misunderstanding.

"And Monsieur Renoux, once a student of architecture at the Beaux Arts, is now Captain Renoux of the Intelligence Department in the French Army——"

Thessalie lost her colour and a tremor passed through the arm which lay within his.

But he said calmly:

288

"It is the only way as well as the best way, Thessa. I know you are absolutely innocent. I am confident that Captain Renoux is going to believe it, too. If he does not, you are no worse off. Because it has already become known to the French Government that you are here. Renoux knew it."

They had halted; Barres led Thessalie to a seat. Renoux, straight, deferential, correct, awaited her pleasure.

She looked up at him; his keen, intelligent eyes met hers.

"If you please, Captain Renoux, will you do me the honour to be seated?" she said in a low voice.

Barres went to her, bent over her hand, touched it with his lips.

"Just tell him the truth, Thessa, dear," he said.

"Everything?" she smiled faintly, "including our first meeting?"

Barres flushed, then laughed:

"Yes, tell him about that, too. It was too charming for him not to appreciate."

And with a half mischievous, half amused nod to Renoux he went back to find the dancers, whom he could hear laughing far away in his own studio.

It was nearly one o'clock when Dulcie, who had been sleeping with Thessalie, whispered to Barres that she was ready to retire.

"Indeed, you had better," he said, releasing her as the dance music ran down and ceased. "If you don't get some sleep you won't feel like travelling to-morrow."

"Will you explain to Thessa?"

"Of course. Good-night, dear."

She gave him her hand in silence, turned and offered it to Westmore, then went away toward her room.

Westmore, who had been fidgeting a lot since Thessalie had retired for a tête-à-tête with a perfectly unknown and alarmingly good-looking young man whom he never before had laid eyes on, finally turned short in his restless pacing of the studio.

"What the deuce can be keeping Thessa?" he demanded. "And who the devil is that black-eyed young sprig of France you brought home with you?"

"Sit down and I'll tell you," said Barres crisply, instinctively resenting his friend's uncalled for solicitude in Thessalie's behalf.

So Westmore seated himself and Barres told him all about the evening's adventures. And he was still lingering unctuously over the details of the battle at Grogan's, the recital of which, Westmore demanding, he had begun again, when at the farther end of the studio Thessalie appeared, coming toward them.

Renoux was beside her, very deferential and graceful in his attendance, and with that niceness of attitude which confesses respect in every movement.

Thessalie came forward; Barres advanced to meet her with the unspoken question in his eyes, and she gave him both her hands with a tremulous little smile of happiness.

"Is it all right?" he whispered.

"I think so."

Barres turned and grasped Renoux by one hand. The latter said:

"There is not the slightest doubt in my mind, mon ami. You were perfectly right. A frightful injustice has been done in this matter. Of that I am absolutely convinced."

"You will do what you can to set things right?"

"Of course," said Renoux simply.

There was a moment's silence, then Renoux smiled:

"You know," he said lightly, "we French have a horror of any more mistakes like the Drevfus case. We are terribly sensitive. Be assured that my Government will take up this affair instantly upon receiving my report."

He turned to Barres:

"Would you, perhaps, offer me a day's hospitality at your home in the country, if I should request it by telegram sometime this week or next?"

"You bet," replied Barres cordially.

Then Renoux made his adieux, as only such a Frenchman can make them, saying exactly the right thing to each, in exactly the right manner.

When he was gone, Barres took Thessalie's hands and pressed them:

"Pretty merle-blanc, your little friend Dulcie is already asleep. Tell us to-morrow how you convinced him that you are what you are—the dearest, sweetest girl in the world!"

She laughed demurely, then glanced apprehensively, sideways, at Westmore.

And the mute but infuriated expression on that young man's countenance seemed to cause her the loss of all self-possession, for she cast one more look at him and fled with a hasty "good-night!"

XXII

TOWARD three o'clock on the following afternoon the sun opened up like a searchlight through the veil of rain, dissolving it to a golden haze which gradually grew thinner and thinner, revealing glimpses of rolling country against a horizon of low mountains.

About the same time the covered station wagon turned in between the white gates of Foreland Farms, proceeded at a smart trot up the drive, and stopped under a dripping porte-cochère, where a smiling servant stood waiting to lift out the luggage.

A trim looking man of forty odd, in soft shirt and fawn coloured knickers, and wearing a monocle in his right eye and a flower in his buttonhole, came out on the porch as Barres and his guests descended.

"Well, Garry," he said, "I'm glad you're home at last! But you're rather late for the fishing." And to Westmore:

"How are you, Jim? Jolly to have you back! But I regret to inform you that the fishing is very poor just now."

His son, who stood an inch or two taller than his debonaire parent, passed one arm around his shoulders and patted them affectionately while the easy presentations were concluded.

At the same moment two women, beautifuly mounted

and very wet, galloped up to the porch and welcomed Garry's guests from their saddles in the pleasant, informal, incurious manner characteristic of Foreland Farm folk—a manner which seemed too amiably certain of itself to feel responsibility for anybody or anything else.

Easy, unconcerned, slender and clean-built women these—Mrs. Reginald Barres, Garry's mother, and her daughter, Lee. And in their smart, rain-wet riding clothes they might easily have been sisters, with a few years' difference between them, so agreeably had Time behaved toward Mrs. Barres, so closely her fair-haired, fair-skinned daughter resembled her.

They swung carelessly out of their saddles and set spurred foot to turf, and, with Garret and his guests, sauntered into the big living hall, where a maid waited with wine and biscuits and the housekeeper lingered to conduct Thessalie and Dulcie to their rooms.

Dulcie Soane, in her pretty travelling gown, walked beside Mrs. Reginald Barres into the first great house she had ever entered. Composed, but shyly enchanted, an odd but delightful sensation possessed her that she was where she belonged—that such environment, such people should always have been familiar to her—were logical and familiar to her now.

Mrs. Barres was saying:

"And if you like parties, there is always gaiety at Northbrook. But you don't have to go anywhere or do anything you don't wish to."

Dulcie said, diffidently, that she liked everything, and Mrs. Barres laughed.

"Then you'll be very popular," she said, tossing her riding crop onto the table and stripping off her wet gloves.

Barres senior was already in serious confab with

Westmore concerning piscatorial conditions, the natural low water of midsummer, the capricious conduct of the trout in the streams and in the upper and lower lakes.

"They won't look at anything until sunset," he explained, "and then they don't mean business. You'll see, Jim. I'm sorry; you should have come in June."

Lee, Garret's boyishly slim sister, had already begun to exchange opinions about horses with Thessalie, for both had been familiar with the saddle since childhood, though the latter's Cossack horsemanship and mastery of the haute école, incident to her recent and irregular profession, might have astonished Lee Barres.

Mrs. Barres was saying to Dulcie:

"We don't try to entertain one another here, but everybody seems to have a perfectly good time. The main thing is that we all feel quite free at Foreland. You'll lose yourself indoors at first. The family for a hundred years has been adding these absurd two-story wings, so that the house wanders at random over the landscape, and you may have to inquire your way about in the beginning."

She smiled again at Dulcie and took her hand in both of hers:

"I'm sure you will like the Farms," she said, linking her other arm through her son's. "I'm rather wet, Garry," she added, "but I think Lee and I had better dry out in the saddle." And to Dulcie again: "Tea at five, if anybody wishes it. Would you like to see your room?"

Thessalie, conversing with Lee, turned smilingly to be included in the suggestion; and the maid came forward to conduct her and Dulcie through the intricacies of the big, casual, sprawling house, where rooms and corridors and halls rambled unexpectedly and irrelevantly in every direction, and one vista seemed to terminate in another.

When they had disappeared, the Barres family turned to inspect its son and heir with habitual and humorous insouciance, commenting frankly upon his personal appearance and concluding that his health still remained all that could be desired by the most solicitous of parents and sisters.

"There are rods already rigged up in the workroom," remarked his father, "if you and your guests care to try a dry-fly this evening. As for me, you'll find me somewhere around the upper lake, if you care to look for me——"

He fished out of his pocket a bewildering tangle of fine mist-leaders, and, leisurely disentangling them, strolled toward the porch, still talking:

"There's only one fly they deign to notice, now—a dust-coloured midge tied in reverse with no hackle, no tinsel, a May-fly tail, and barred canary wing——" He nodded wisely over his shoulder at his son and Westmore, as though sharing with them a delightful secret of world-wide importance, and continued on toward the porch, serenely interested in his tangled leaders.

Garret glanced at his mother and sister; they both laughed. He said:

"Dad is one of those rarest of modern beings, a genuine angler of the old school. After all the myriad trout and salmon he has caught in a career devoted to fishing, the next fish he catches gives him just as fine a thrill as did the very first one he ever hooked! It's quite wonderful, isn't it, mother?"

"It's probably what keeps him so youthful," remarked Westmore. "The thing to do is to have something to do. That's the elixir of youth. Look at your mother, Garry. She's had a busy handful bringing you up!"

Garret looked at his slender, attractive mother and laughed again:

"Is that what keeps you so young and pretty, mother?—looking after me?"

"Alas, Garry, I'm over forty, and I look it!"

"Do you?—you sweet little thing!" he interrupted, picking her up suddenly from the floor and marching proudly around the room with her. "Gaze upon my mother, Jim! Isn't she cunning? Isn't she the smartest little thing in America? Behave yourself, mother! Your grateful son is showing you off to the appreciative young gentleman from New York——"

"You're ridiculous! Jim! Make him put me down!"

But her tall son swung her to his shoulder and placed her high on the mantel shelf over the huge fireplace; where she sat beside the clock, charming, resentful, but helpless, her spurred boots dangling down.

"Come on, Lee!" cried her brother, "I'm going to put you up beside her. That mantel needs ornamental bric-a-brac and objets d'art——"

Lee turned to escape, but her brother cornered and caught her, and swung her high, seating her beside his indignant mother.

"Just as though we were two Angora kittens," remarked Lee, sidling along the stone shelf toward her mother. Then she glanced out through the open front door. "Lift us down, quick, Garry. You'd better! The horses are in the flower beds and there'll be no more bouquets for the table in another minute!"

So he lifted them off the mantel and they hastily departed, each administering correction with her riding crop as she dodged past him and escaped.

"If your guests want horses you know where to find

them!" called back his sister from the porch. And presently she and his mother, securely mounted, went cantering away across country, where grass and fern and leaf and blossom were glistening in the rising breeze, weighted down with diamond drops of rain.

Westmore walked leisurely toward his quarters, to freshen up and don knickers. Garret followed him into the west wing, whistling contentedly under his breath, inspecting each remembered object with great content as he passed, nodding smilingly to the servants he encountered, lingering on the landing to acknowledge the civilities of the ancient family cat, who recognised him with effusion but coyly fled the advances of Westmore, ignoring all former and repeated introductions.

Their rooms adjoined and they conversed through the doorway while engaged in ablutions.

Presently, from behind his sheer sash-curtains, Westmore caught sight of Thessalie on the west terrace below. She wore a shell-pink frock and a most distractingly pretty hat; and he hurried his dressing as much as he could without awaking Garret's suspicions.

A few minutes later, radiant in white flannels, he appeared on the terrace, breathing rather fast but wreathed in persuasive smiles.

"I know this place; I'll take you for a walk where you won't get your shoes wet. Shall I?" he suggested, with all his guile an' cunning quite plain to Thessalie, and his purpose perfectly transparent to her smiling eyes.

But she consented prettily, and went with him without demurring, picking her way over the stepping-stone walk with downcast gaze and the trace of a smile on her lips—a smile as delicately indefinable as the fancy which moved her to accept this young man's headlong advances—which had recognized them and accepted them from the first. But why, she did not even yet understand.

"Agreeable weather, isn't it?" said Westmore, fatuously revealing his present paucity of ideas apart from those which concerned the wooing of her. And he was an intelligent young man at that, and a sculptor of attainment, too. But now, in his infatuated head, there remained room only for one thought, the thought of this girl who walked so demurely and daintily beside him over the flat, grass-set stepping stones toward the three white pines on the little hill.

For it had been something or other at first sight with Westmore—love, perhaps—anyway that is what he called the mental chaos which now disorganised him. And it was certain that something happened to him the first time he laid eyes on Thessalie Dunois. He knew it, and she could not avoid seeing it, so entirely naïve his behaviour, so utterly guileless his manœuvres, so direct, unfeigned and childish his methods of approach.

At moments she felt nervous and annoyed by his behaviour; at other times apprehensive and helpless, as though she were responsible for something that did not know how to take care of itself—something immature, irrational, and entirely at her mercy. And it may have been the feminine response to this increasing sense of obligation—the confused instinct to guide, admonish and protect—that began being the matter with her.

Anyway, from the beginning the man had a certain fascination for her, unwillingly divined on her part, yet specifically agreeable even to the point of exhilaration. Also, somehow or other, the girl realised he had a brain.

And yet he was a pitiably hopeless case; for even now he was saying such things as:

"Are you quite sure that your feet are dry? I

should never forgive myself, Thessa, if you took cold.
. . . Are you tired? . . . How wonderful it is to be
here alone with you, and strive to interpret the mystery
of your mind and heart! Sit here under the pines.
I'll spread my coat for you. . . . Nature *is* wonderful, isn't it, Thessa?"

And when she gravely consented to seat herself he
dropped recklessly onto the wet pine needles at her
feet, and spoke with imbecile delight again of nature
—of how wonderful were its protean manifestations,
and how its beauties were not meant to be enjoyed
alone but in mystic communion with' another who understood.

It was curious, too, but this stuff seemed to appeal
to her, some commonplace chord within her evidently
responding. She sighed and looked at the mountains.
They really were miracles of colour—masses of pur-
est cobalt, now, along the horizon.

But perhaps the trite things they uttered did not
really matter; probably it made no difference to them
what they said. And even if he had murmured:
"There are milestones along the road to Dover," she
might have responded: "There was an old woman
who lived in a shoe"; and neither of them would have
heard anything at all except the rapid, confused, and
voiceless conversation of two youthful human hearts
beating out endless questions and answers that never
moved their smiling lips. There was the mystery, if
any—the constant wireless current under the haphaz-
ard flow of words.

There was no wind in the pines; meadow and pas-
ture, woodland and swale stretched away at their feet
to the distant, dark-blue hills. And all around them
hung the rain-washed fragrance of midsummer under
a still, cloudless sky.

"It seems impossible that there can be war anywhere in the world," she said.

"You know," he began, "it's getting on my nerves the way those swine from the Rhine are turning this decent green world into a bloody wallow! Unless we do something about it pretty soon, I think I'll go over."

She looked up:

"Where?"

"To France."

She remained silent for a while, merely lifting her dark eyes to him at intervals; then she grew preoccupied with other thoughts that left her brows bent slightly inward and her mouth very grave.

He gazed reflectively out over the fields and woods:

"Yes, I can't stand it much longer," he mused aloud.

"What would you do there?" she inquired.

"Anything. I could drive a car. But if they'll take me in some Canadian unit—or one of the Foreign Legions—it would suit me. . . . You know a man can't go on just living in the world while this beastly business continues—can't go on eating and sleeping and shaving and dressing as though half of civilisation were not rolling in agony and blood, stabbed through and through——"

His voice caught—he checked himself and slowly passed his hand over his smoothly shaven face.

"Those splendid poilus," he said; "where they stand we Americans ought to be standing, too. . . . God knows why we hesitate. . . . I can't tell you what we think. . . . Some of us—don't agree—with the Administration."

His jaws snapped on the word; he stared out through the sunshine at the swallows, now skimming the uncut hay fields in their gusty evening flight.

"Are you really going?" she asked, at length.

"Yes. I'll wait a little while longer to see what my country is going to do. If it doesn't stir during the next month or two, I shall go. I think Garry will go, too."

She nodded.

"Of course," he remarked, "we'd prefer our own flag, Garry and I. But if it is to remain furled——" He shrugged, picked a spear of grass, and sat brooding and breaking it into tiny pieces.

"The only thing that troubles me," he went on presently, keeping his gaze riveted on his busy fingers, "the only thing that worries me is you!"

"Me?" she exclaimed softly. And an inexplicable little thrill shot through her.

"You," he repeated. "You worry me to death."

She considered him a moment, her lips parted as though she were about to say something, but it remained unsaid, and a slight colour came into her cheeks.

"What am I to do about you?" he went on, apparently addressing the blade of grass he was staring at. "I can't leave you as matters stand."

She said:

"Please, you are not responsible for me, are you?" And tried to laugh, but scarcely smiled.

"I want to be," he muttered. "I desire to be entirely——"

"Thank you. You have been more than kind. And very soon I hope I shall be on happy terms with my own Government again. Then your solicitude should cease."

"If your Government listens to reason——"

"Then I also could go to France!" she interrupted. "Merely to think of it excites me beyond words!"

He looked up quickly:

"You wish to go back?"

"Of course!"

"Why?"

"How can you ask that! If you had been a disgraced exile as I have been, as I still am—and falsely accused of shameful things—annoyed, hounded, blackmailed, offered bribes, constantly importuned to become what I am not—a traitor to my own people—would you not be wildly happy to be proven innocent? Would you not be madly impatient to return and prove your devotion to your own land?"

"I understand," he said in a low voice.

"Of course you understand. Do you imagine that I, a French girl, would have remained here in shameful security if I could have gone back to France and helped? I would have done anything—anything, I tell you—scrubbed the floors of hospitals, worked my fingers to the bone——"

"I'll wait till you go," he said. . . . "They'll clear your record very soon, I expect. I'll wait. And we'll go together. Shall we, Thessa?"

But she had not seemed to hear him; her dark eyes grew remote, her gaze swept the sapphire distance. It was his hand laid lightly over hers that aroused her, and she, withdrew her fingers with a frown of remonstrance.

"Won't you let me speak?" he said. "Won't you let me tell you what my heart tells me?"

She shook her head slowly:

"I don't desire to hear yet—I don't know where my own heart—or even my mind is—or what I think about —anything. Please be reasonable." She stole a look at him to see how he was taking it, and there was concern enough in her glance to give him a certain amount of hope had he noticed it.

"You like me, Thessa, don't you?" he urged.

"Have I not admitted it? Do you know that you are becoming a serious responsibility to me? You worry me, too! You are like a boy with all your emotions reflected on your features and every thought perfectly unconcealed and every impulse followed by unconsidered behaviour.

"Be reasonable. I have asked it a hundred times of you in vain. I shall ask it, probably, innumerable times before you comply with my request. Don't show so plainly that you imagine yourself in love. It embarrasses me, it annoys Garry, and I don't know what his family will think——"

"But if I *am* in love, why not——"

"Does one advertise all one's most intimate and secret and—and sacred emotions?" she interrupted in sudden and breathless annoyance. "It is not the way that successful courtship is conducted, I warn you! It is not delicate, it is not considerate, it is not sensible. . . . And I *do* want you to—to be always—sensible and considerate. I *want* to like you."

He looked at her in a sort of dazed way:

"I'll try to please you," he said. "But it seems to confuse me—being so suddenly bowled over—a thing like that rather knocks a man out—so unexpected, you know!—and there isn't much use pretending," he went on excitedly. "I can't see anybody else in the world except you! I can't think of anybody else! I'm madly in love—blindly, desperately——"

"Oh, please, *please!*" she remonstrated. "I'm not a girl to be taken by storm! I've seen too much—lived too much! I'm not a Tzigane to be galloped alongside of and swung to a man's saddle-bow! Also, I shall tell you one thing more. Happiness and laughter are necessities to me! And they seem to be becoming extinct in you."

"Hang it!" he demanded tragically, "how can I laugh when I'm in love!"

At that a sudden, irresponsible little peal of laughter parted her lips.

"Oh, dear!" she said, "you *are* funny! Is it a matter of prayer and fasting, then, this gloomy sentiment which you say you entertain for me? I don't know whether to be flattered or vexed—you are *so* funny!" And her laughter rang out again, clear and uncontrolled.

The girl was quite irresistible in her care-free gaiety; her lovely face and delicious laughter no man could utterly withstand, and presently a faint grin became visible on his features.

"Now," she cried gaily, "you are becoming human and not a Grecian mask or a gargoyle! Remain so, mon ami, if you expect me to wish you good luck in your love—your various affairs——" She blushed as she checked herself. But he said very quickly:

"Will you wish me luck, Thessa, in my various love affairs?"

"How many have you on hand?"

"Exactly one. Do you wish me a sporting chance? Do you, Thessa?"

"Why—yes——"

"Will you wish me good luck in my courtship of you?"

The quick colour again swept her cheeks at that, but she laughed defiantly:

"Yes," she said, "I wish you luck in that, also. Only remember this—whether you win or lose you must laugh. *That* is good sportsmanship. Do you promise? Very well! Then I wish you the best of luck in your—various—courtships! And may the girl you win at least know how to laugh!"

"She certainly does," he said so naïvely that they both gave way to laughter again, finding each other delightfully absurd.

"It's the key to my heart, laughter—in case you are looking for the key," she said daringly. "The world is a grim scaffold, mon ami; mount it gaily and go to the far gods laughing. Tell me, is there a better way to go?"

"No; it's the right way, Thessa. I shan't be a gloom any more. Come on; let's walk! What if you do get your bally shoes wet! I'm through mooning and fussing and worrying over you, young lady! You're as sturdy and vigorous as I am. After all, it's a comrade a man wants in the world—not a white mouse in cotton batting! Come! Are you going for a brisk walk across country? Or are you a white mouse?"

She stood up in her dainty shoes and frail gown and cast a glance of hurt reproach at him.

"Don't be brutal," she said. "I'm not dressed to climb trees and fences with you."

"You won't come?"

Their eyes met in silent conflict for a few moments. Then she said: "Please don't make me. . . . It's such a darling gown, Jim."

A wave of deep happiness enveloped him and he laughed: "All right," he said, "I won't ask you to spoil your frock!" And he spread his coat on the pine needles for her once more.

She considered the situation for a few moments before she sat down. But she did seat herself.

"Now," he said, "we are going to discuss a situation. This is the situation: I am deeply in love. And you're quite right, it's no funeral; it's a joyous thing to be in love. It's a delight, a gaiety, a happy enchantment. Isn't it?"

She cast a rather shy and apprehensive glance at him, but nodded slightly.

"Very well," he said, "I'm in love, and I'm happy and proud to be in love. What I wish then, naturally, is marriage, a home, children——"

"Please, Jim!"

"But I can't have 'em! Why? Because I'm going to France. And the girl I wish to marry is going also. And while I bang away at the boche she makes herself useful in canteens, rest-houses, hospitals, orphanages, everywhere, in fact, where she is needed."

"Yes."

"And after it's all over—all over—and ended——"

"Yes?"

"Then—then if she finds out that she loves me——"

"Yes, Jim—if she finds that out. . . . And thank you for—asking me—so sweetly." . . . She turned sharply and looked out over a valley suddenly blurred.

For it had been otherwise with her in years gone by, and men had spoken then quite as plainly but differently. Only d'Eblis, burnt out, done for, and obsessed, had wearily and unwillingly advanced that far. . . . And Ferez, too; but that was unthinkable of a creature in whom virtue and vice were of the same virus.

Looking blindly out over the valley she said:

"If my Government deals justly with me, then I shall go to France with you as your comrade. If I ever find that I love you I will be your wife. . . . Until then——" She stretched out her hand, not looking around at him; and they exchanged a quick, firm clasp.

And so matters progressed between these two—rather ominously for Barres, in case he entertained any really serious sentiments in regard to Thessalie. And, recently, he had been vaguely conscious that he entertained something or other concerning the girl which caused him to look with slight amazement and unsympathetic eyes upon the all too obvious behaviour of his comrade Westmore.

At present he was standing in the summer house which terminated the blossoming tunnel of the rose arbour, watching water falling into a stone basin from the fishy mouth of a wall fountain, and wondering where Thessalie and Westmore had gone.

Dulcie, in a thin white frock and leghorn hat, roaming entranced and at hazard over lawn and through shrubbery and garden, encountered him there, still squinting abstractedly at the water spout.

It was the first time the girl had seen him since their arrival at Foreland Farms. And now, as she paused under the canopy of fragrant rain-drenched roses and looked at this man who had made all this possible for her, she suddenly felt the change within herself, fitting her for it all—a subtle metamorphosis completing itself within her—the final accomplishment of a transmutation, deep, radical, permanent.

For her, the stark, starved visage which Life had worn had relaxed; in the grim, forbidding wall which had closed her horizon, a door opened, showing a corner of a world where she knew, somehow, she belonged.

And in her heart, too, a door seemed to open, and her youthful soul stepped out of it, naked, fearless, quite certain of itself and, for the first time during their brief and earthly partnership, quite certain of the body wherein it dwelt.

He was thinking of Thessalie when Dulcie came

up and stood beside him, looking down into the water where a few goldfish swam.

"Well, Sweetness," he said, brightening, "you look very wonderful in white, with that big hat on your very enchanting red hair."

"I feel both wonderful and enchanted," she said, lifting her eyes. "I shall live in the country some day."

"Really?" he said smiling.

"Yes, when I earn enough money. Do you remember the crazy way Strindberg rolls around? Well, I feel like doing it on that lawn."

"Go ahead and do it," he urged. But she only laughed and chased the goldfish around the basin with gentle fingers.

"Dulcie," he said, "you're unfolding, you're blossoming, you're developing feminine snap and go and pep and je-ne-sais-quoi."

"You're teasing. But I believe I'm very feminine —and mature—though you don't think so."

"Well, I don't think you're exactly at an age called well-preserved," he said, laughing. He took her hands and drew her up to confront him. "You're not too old to have me as a playmate, Sweetness, are you?"

She seemed to be doubtful.

"What! Nonsense! And you're not too old to be bullied and coaxed and petted——"

"Yes, I am."

"And you're not too old to pose for me——"

She grew pink and looked down at the submerged goldfish. And, keeping her eyes there:

"I wanted to ask you," she said, "how much longer you think you would require me—that way."

There was a silence. Then she looked at him out of her frank grey eyes.

"You know I'll do what you wish," she said. "And

I know it is quite all right. . . ." She smiled at him. "I belong to you: you made me. . . . And you know all about me. So you ought to use me as you wish."

"You don't want to pose?" he said.

"Yes, except——"

"Very well."

"Are you annoyed?"

"No, Sweetness. It's all right."

"You are annoyed—disappointed! And I won't have it. I—I couldn't stand it—to have you displeased——"

He said pleasantly:

"I'm not displeased, Dulcie. And there's no use discussing it. If you have the slightest feeling that way, when we go back to town I'll do things like the Arethusa from somebody else——"

"Please don't!" she exclaimed in such naïve alarm that he began to laugh and she blushed vividly.

"Oh, you are feminine, all right!" he said. "If it isn't to be you it isn't to be anybody."

"I didn't mean that. . . . *Yes*, I did!"

"Oh, Dulcie! Shame! *You* jealous!—even to the verge of sacrificing your own feelings——"

"I don't know what it is, but I'd rather you used me for your Arethusa. You know," she added wistfully, "that we began it together."

"Right, Sweetness. And we'll finish it together or not at all. Are you satisfied?"

She smiled, sighed, nodded. He released her lovely, childlike hands and she walked to the doorway of the summer house and looked out over the wall-bed, where tall thickets of hollyhock and blue larkspur stretched away in perspective toward a grove of trees and a little pond beyond.

His painter's eye, already busy with the beauty of

her face and figure against the riot of flowers, and
almost mechanically transposing both into terms of
colour and value, went blind suddenly as she turned
and looked at him.

And for the first time—perhaps with truer vision
—he became aware of what else this young girl was
besides a satisfying combination of tint and contour
—this lithe young thing palpitating with life—this
slender, gently breathing girl with her grey eyes meeting his so candidly—this warm young human being
who belonged more truly in the living scheme of things
than she did on painted canvas or in marble.

From this unexpected angle, and suddenly, he found
himself viewing her for the first time—not as a play-
thing, not as a petted model, not as an object appealing to his charity, not as an experiment in altruism
—nor sentimentally either, nor as a wistful child without a childhood.

Perhaps, to him, she had once been all of these. He
looked at her with other eyes now, beginning, possibly,
to realise something of the terrific responsibility he
was so lightly assuming.

He got up from his bench and went over to her;
and the girl turned a trifle pale with excitement and
delight.

"Why did you come to me?" she asked breathlessly.

"I don't know."

"Did you know I was trying to make you get up
and come to me?"

"What?"

"Yes! Isn't it curious? I looked at you and kept
thinking, 'I want you to get up and come to me! I
want you to come! I want you!' And suddenly you
got up and came!"

He looked at her out of curious, unsmiling eyes:

"It's your turn, after all, Dulcie."

"How is it my turn?"

"I drew you—in the beginning," he said slowly.

There was a silence. Then, abruptly, her heart began to beat very rapidly, scaring her dumb with its riotous behaviour. When at length her consternation subsided and her irregular breathing became composed, she said, quite calmly:

"You and all that you are and believe in and care for very naturally attracted me—drew me one evening, to your open door. . . . It will always be the same—you, and what of life and knowledge you represent—will never fail to draw me."

"But—though I am just beginning to divine it— you also drew *me*, Dulcie."

"How could that be?"

"You did. You do still. I am just waking up to that fact. And that starts me wondering what I'd do without you."

"You don't have to do without me," she said, instinctively laying her hand over her heart; it was beating so hard and, she feared, so loud. "You can always have me when you wish. You know that."

"For a while, yes. But some day, when——"

"Always!"

He laughed without knowing why.

"You'll marry some day, Sweetness," he insisted.

She shook her head.

"Oh, yes you will——"

"No!"

"Why?"

But she only looked away and shook her head. And the silent motion of dissent gave him an odd sense of relief.

XXIII

WITH the decline of day came enough of a
chill to spin a delicate cobweb of mist across
the country and cover forests and hills with
a bluish bloom.

The sunset had become a splashy crimson affair, perhaps a bit too theatrical. In the red blaze Thessalie
and Westmore came wandering down from the three
pines on the hill, and found Barres on the lawn, scowling at the celestial conflagration in the west, and Dulcie seated near on the fountain rim, silent, distrait,
watching the scarlet ripples spreading from the plash-
ing central jet.

"You can't paint a thing like that, Garry," remarked Westmore. Barres looked around:

"I don't want to. Where have you been, Thessa?"

"Under those pines over there. We supposed you'd
see us and come up."

Barres glanced at her with an inscrutable expression; Dulcie's grey eyes rested on Barres. Thessalie
walked over to the reddened pool.

"It's like a prophecy of blood, that water," she
said. "And over there the world is in flames."

"The Western World," added Westmore, "I hope
it's an omen that we shall soon catch fire. How long
are you going to wait, Garry?"

Barres started to answer, but checked himself, and
glanced across at Dulcie without knowing exactly why.

"I don't know," he said irresolutely. "I'm fed up now. . . . But——" he continued to look vaguely at Dulcie, as though something of his uncertainty remotely concerned her.

"I'm ready to go over when you are," remarked Westmore, placidly smiling at Thessalie, who immediately presented her pretty profile to him and settled down on the fountain rim beside Dulcie.

"Darling," she said, "it's about time to dress. Are you going to wear that enchanting white affair we discovered at Mendel's?"

Barres senior came sauntering out of the woods and through the wall gate, switching a limber rod reflectively. He obligingly opened his creel and displayed half a dozen long, slim trout.

"They all took that midge fly I described to you this afternoon," he said, with the virtuous satisfaction of all prophets.

Everybody inspected the crimson-flecked fish while Barres senior stood twirling his monocle.

"Are we dining at home?" inquired his son.

"I believe so. There is a guest of honour, if I recollect—some fellow they're lionising—I don't remember. . . . And one or two others—the Gerhardts, I believe."

"Then we'd better dress, I think," said Thessalie, encircling Dulcie's waist.

"Sorry," said Barres senior, "hoped to take you young ladies out on the second lake and let you try for a big fish this evening."

He walked across the lawn beside them, switching his rod as complacently as a pleased cat twitches its tail.

"We'll try it to-morrow evening," he continued reassuringly, as though all their most passionate hopes had been bound up in the suggested sport; "it's rather

annoying—I can't remember who's dining with us—
some celebrated Irishman—poet of sorts—literary
chap—guest of the Gerhardts—neighbours, you know.
It's a nuisance to bother with dinner when the trout
rise only after sunset."

"Don't you ever dine willingly, Mr. Barres, while
the trout are rising?" inquired Thessalie, laughing.

"Never willingly," he replied in a perfectly sincere
voice. "I prefer to remain near the water and have
a bit of supper when I return." He smiled at Thessalie indulgently. "No doubt it amuses you, but I
wager that you and little Miss Soane here will feel
exactly as I do after you've caught your first big
trout."

They entered the house together, followed by Garry
and Westmore.

A dim, ruddy glow still lingered in the quiet rooms;
every window glass was still lighted by the sun's smouldering ashes sinking in the west; no lamps had yet
been lighted on the ground floor.

"It's the magic hour on the water," Barres senior
confided to Dulcie, "and here I am, doomed to a stiff
shirt and table talk. In other words, nailed!" And
he gave her a mysterious, melancholy, but significant
look as though she alone were really fitted to understand the distressing dilemmas of an angler.

"Would it be too late to fish after dinner?" ventured Dulcie. "I'd love to go with you——"

"Would you, really!" he exclaimed, warmly grateful. "That is the spirit I admire in a girl! It's human, it's discriminating! And yet, do you know, nobody except myself in this household seems to care
very much about angling? And, actually, I don't believe there is another soul in this entire house who

would care to miss dinner for the sake of landing the finest trout in the second lake!—unless you would?"

"I really would!" said Dulcie, smiling. "Please try me, Mr. Barres."

"Indeed, I shall! I'll give you one of my pet rods, too! I'll——"

The rich, metallic murmur of a temple gong broke out in the dim quiet of the house. It was the dressing bell.

"We'll talk it over at dinner—if they'll let me sit by you," whispered Barres senior. And with the smile and the cautionary gesture of the true conspirator, he went away in the demi-light.

Thessalie came from the bay window, where she had been with Westmore and Garry, and she and Dulcie walked away toward the staircase hall, leisurely followed by the two men who, however, turned again into the western wing.

Dulcie was the first to reappear and descend the stairs of the north wing—a willowy white shape in the early dusk, slim as a young spirit in the lamplit silence.

Nobody else had come down; a maid was turning up a lamp here and there; the plebeian family cat came out of the shadows from somewhere and made advances as though divining that this quiet stranger was a friend to cats.

So Dulcie stooped to pet her, then wandered on through the place and finally into the music room, where she seated herself at the piano and touched the keys softly in the semi-dusk.

Among the songs—words and music—which her mother had left in manuscript, was one which she had learned recently,—"Blue Eyes"—and she played the air now, seated there all alone in the subdued lamp light.

Presently people began to appear from above—Mrs. Barres, who motioned her not to rise, and who seated herself near, watching the girl's slender fingers moving on the keys; then Lee, who came and stood beside her, followed in a few moments by Thessalie and the two younger men.

"What is that lovely little air you are playing?" inquired Mrs. Barres.

"It is called 'Blue Eyes,'" said Dulcie, absently.

"I have never before heard it."

The girl looked up:

"No, my mother wrote it."

After a silence:

"It is really exquisite," said Mrs. Barres. "Are there words to it?"

Some people had come into the entrance hall beyond; there was the low whirring of an automobile outside.

"Yes, my mother made some verses for it," replied Dulcie.

"Will you sing them for me after dinner?"

"Yes, I shall be happy to."

Mrs. Barres turned to welcome her new guests, now entering the music room convoyed by Barres senior, who was arrayed in the dreaded "stiff shirt" and already indulging in "table talk."

"They took," he was explaining, "a midge-fly with no hackle—Claire, here are the Gerhardts and Mr. Skeel!" And while his wife welcomed them and introductions were effected, he continued explaining the construction of the midge to anybody who listened.

At the first mention of Murtagh Skeel's name, the glances of Westmore, Garry and Thessalie crossed like lightning, then their attention became riveted on this tall, graceful, romantic looking man of early middle age, who was being lionised at Northbrook.

The next moment Garry stepped back beside Dulcie Soane, who had turned white as a flower and was gazing at Skeel as though she had seen a ghost.

"Do you suppose he can be the same man your mother knew?" he whispered, dropping his arm and taking her trembling hand in a firm clasp.

"I don't know. . . . I seem to feel so. . . . I can't explain to you how it pierced my heart—the sound of his name. . . . Oh, Garry!—suppose it is true—that he is the man my mother knew—and cared for!"

Before he could speak, cocktails were served, and Adolf Gerhardt, a large, bearded, pompous man, engaged him in explosive conversation:

"Yes, this fellow Corot Mandel is producing a new spectacle-play on my lawn to-morrow evening. Your family and your guests are invited, ? course. And for the dance, also——" He inclu Dulcie in a pompous bow, finished his cocktail wit another flourish:

"You will find my friend Skeel very attractive," he went on. "You know who he is?—*the* Murtagh Skeel who writes those Irish poems of the West Coast—and is not, I believe, very well received in England just now—a matter of nationalism—patriotism, eh? Why should it surprise your Britisher, eh?—if a gentleman like Murtagh Skeel displays no sympathy for England?—if a gentleman like my friend, Sir Roger Casement, prefers to live in Germany?"

Garry, under his own roof, said pleasantly:

"It wouldn't do for us to discuss those things, I fear, Mr. Gerhardt. And your Irish lion seems to be very gentle and charming. He must be fascinating to women."

Gerhardt threw up his hands:

"Oh, Lord! They would like to eat him! Or be eaten by him! You know? It is that way always between the handsome poet and the sex. Which eats which is of no consequence, so long as they merge. Eh?" And his thunderous laughter set the empty glasses faintly ringing on the butler's silver tray.

Garry spoke to Mrs. Gerhardt, a large, pallid, slabby German who might have been somebody's kitchen maid, but had been born a *von*.

Later, as dinner was announced, he contrived to speak to Thessalie aside:

"Gerhardt," he whispered, "doesn't recognise you, of course."

"No; I'm not at all apprehensive."

"Yet, it was on his yacht——"

"He never even looked twice at me. You know what he thought me to be? Very well, he had only social ambitions then. I think that's all he has now. You see what he got with his Red Eagle," nodding calmly toward Mrs. Gerhardt, who now was being convoyed out by the monocled martyr in the "stiff shirt."

The others passed out informally; Lee had slipped her arm around Dulcie. As Garry and Thessalie turned to follow, he said in a low voice:

"You feel quite secure, then, Thessa?"

She halted, put her lips close to his ear, unnoticed by those ahead:

"Perfectly. The Gerhardts are what you call fat-heads—easily used by anybody, dangerous to no one, governed by greed alone, without a knowledge of any honour except the German sort. But that Irish dreamer over there, *he* is dangerous! That type always is. He menaces the success of any enterprise to which his quixotic mind turns, because it instantly becomes a fixed idea with him—an obsession, a monomania!"

She took his arm and walked on beside him.

"I know that fascinating, hot-headed, lovable type of mystic visionary," she said, "handsome, romantic, illogical, governed entirely by emotion, not fickle yet never to be depended on; not faithless, but absolutely irresponsible and utterly ignorant of fear! . . . My father was that sort. *Not* the hunting cheetah Cyril and Ferez pretended. And it was in *defence* of a woman that my father died. . . . Thank God!"

"Who told you?"

"Captain Renoux—the other night."

"I'm so glad, Thessa!"

She held her flushed head high and smiled at him.

"You see," she said, "after all it is in my blood to be decent."

The Gerhardts, racially vulgar and socially blunt —for the inherent vulgarity of the Teutonic peoples is an axiom among the civilised—made themselves characteristically conspicuous at the flower-laden table; but it was on Murtagh Skeel that all eyes became ultimately focused to the limit of good-breeding. He was the lode-star—he was the magnet, the vanishing point for all curiosity, all surmises, all interest.

Perfect breeding, perfect unconsciousness of self, were his minted marks to guarantee the fineness of his metal. He was natural without effort, winning in voice, in manner, in grace of mind and body, this fascinating Irishman of letters—a charming listener, a persuasive speaker, modest, light hearted, delightfully deferential.

Seated on the right of Mrs. Barres, his smiling hostess very quickly understood the situation and made it pleasantly plain to everybody that her guest of honour was not to be privately monopolised.

So almost immediately all currents of conversation flowed from all sides toward this dark-eyed, handsome man, and in return the silver-tongued tide of many currents—the Irish Sea at its sparkling flood—flowed prettily and spread out from its perennial source within him, and washed and rippled gently over every separate dinner plate, so that nobody seemed neglected, and there was jetsam and beach-combing for all.

And it was inevitable, presently, that Murtagh Skeel's conversation should become autobiographical in some degree, and his careless, candid, persuasive phrases turn into little gemlike memories. For he came ultimately, of course, to speak of Irish nationalism and what it meant; of the Celt as he had been and must remain—utterly unchanged, as long as the last Celt remained alive on earth.

The subject, naturally, invaded the fairy lore, wild legend and lovely mysticism of the West Coast; and centred about his own exquisite work of interpreting it.

He spoke of it very modestly, as his source of inspiration, as the inception of his own creative work in that field. But always, through whatever he said, rang low and clear his passionate patriotism and the only motive which incited him to creative effort—his longing for national autonomy and the re-gathering of a scattered people in preparation for its massed journey toward its Destiny.

His voice was musical, his words unconscious poetry. Without effort, without pains, alas!—without logic —he held every ear enthralled there in the soft candle-light and subdued glimmer of crystal and of silver.

His was the magic of shadow and half-lights, of vague nuances and lost outlines, and the valued degrees of impinging shade. No sharp contours, no stark, uncompromising shapes, no brutality of raw daylight, and—alas!—no threat of uncompromising logic invaded his realm of dreamy demi-lights and faded fantasies.

He reigned there, amid an enchanted twilight of his own creation, the embodiment of Irish romance, tender, gay, sweet-minded, persuasive, gallant—and tragic, when, at some unexpected moment, the frail veil of melancholy made his dark eyes less brilliant.

All yielded to his charm—even the stuffed Teutons, gorging gravy; all felt his sway over mind and heart, nor cared to analyse it, there in the soft light of candles and the scent of old-fashioned flowers.

There arose some question concerning Sir Roger Casement.

Murtagh Skeel spoke of him with the pure enthusiasm of passionate belief in a master by a humble disciple. And the Teutons grunted assent.

The subject of the war had been politely avoided, yet, somehow, it came out that Murtagh Skeel had served in Britain's army overseas, as an enlisted man in some Irish regiment—a romantic impulse of the moment, involving a young man's crazy plan to foment rebellion in India. Which little gem of a memoire presently made the fact of his exile self-explanatory. Yet, he contrived that the ugly revelation should end in laughter—an outbreak of spontaneous mirth through which his glittering wit passed like lightning, cauterising the running sore of treason. . . .

Coffee served, the diners drifted whither it suited them, together or singly.

Like an errant spirit, Dulcie moved about at hazard amid the softened lights, engaged here, approached there, pausing, wandering on, nowhere in particular, yet ever listlessly in motion.

Encountering her near the porch, Barres senior had paused to whisper that there was no hope for any fishing that evening; and she had lingered to smile after him, as, unreconciled, he took his stiff-shirted way toward the pallid, bejewelled, unanimated mass of Mrs. Gerhardt, settled in the widest armchair and absorbing cordial.

A moment later the girl encountered Garry. He remained with her for a while, evidently desiring to be near her without finding anything in particular to say. And when he, in turn, moved elsewhere, obeying some hazy mandate of hospitality, he became conscious of a reluctance to leave her.

"Do you know, Sweetness," he said, lingering, "that you wear a delicate beauty to-night lovelier than I have ever seen in you? You are not only a wonderful girl, Dulcie; you are growing into an adorable woman."

The girl looked back at him, blushing vividly in her sheer surprise—watched him saunter away out of her silent sphere of influence before she found any word to utter—if, indeed, she had been seeking any, so deeply, so painfully sweet had sunk his words into every fibre of her untried, defenceless youth.

Now, as her cheeks cooled, and she came to herself and moved again, there seemed to grow around her a magic and faintly fragrant radiance through which she passed—whither, she paid no heed, so exquisitely her breast was thrilling under the hurrying pulses of her little heart. . . . And presently found herself on the piano bench, quite motionless, her gaze remote, her fingers resting on the keys. . . . And, after a long

while, she heard an old air stealing through the silence, and her own voice,—à *demi-voix*—repeating her
mother's words:

I

"Were they as wise as they are blue—
    My eyes—
They'd teach me not to trust in you!—
If they were wise as they are blue.

But they're as blithe as they are blue—
    My eyes—
They bid my heart rejoice in you,
Because they're blithe as well as blue.

Believe and love! my gay heart cries;
Believe him not! my mind replies;
 What shall I do
When heart affirms and sense denies
All I reveal within my eyes
 To you?

II

"If they were black instead of blue—
    My eyes—
Perhaps they'd prove unkind to you!
If they were black instead of blue.

But God designed them blithe and blue—
    My eyes—
Designed them to be kind to you,
And made them tender, gay and true.

Believe me, love, no maid is wise
When from the windows of her eyes,
 Her heart looks through!
Alas! My heart, to its surprise,
Has learned to look; and now it sighs
 For you!"

She became conscious of somebody near, as she
ended. She turned and saw Murtagh Skeel at her

elbow—saw his agitated, ashen face—looked beyond him and discovered other people gathered in the tinted light beyond, listening; then she lifted her clear, still gaze again to the white-faced man beside her, and saw his shaken soul staring at her through the dark windows of his eyes.

"Where did you learn it?" he asked with a futile effort at that control so difficult for any Celt to grasp where the heart is involved.

"The song I sang? 'Blue Eyes'?" she inquired.

"Yes—that."

"I have the manuscript of the composer."

"Could you tell me where you got it—and—and who wrote those words you sang?"

"The manuscript came to me from my mother. . . . She wrote it. . . . I think you knew her."

His strong, handsome hand dropped on the piano's edge, gripped it; and under his pale skin the quick blood surged to his temples.

"What was your—your mother's name, Miss Soane?"

"She was Eileen Fane."

The throbbing seconds passed and still they looked into each other's eyes in silence. And at last:

"So you did know my mother," she said under her breath; and the hushed finality of her words set his strong hand trembling.

"Eileen's little daughter," be repeated. "Eileen Fane's child. . . . And grown to womanhood. . . . Yes, I knew your mother—many years ago. . . . When I enlisted and went abroad. . . . Was it Sir Terence Soane who married your mother?"

She shook her head. He stared at her, striving to concentrate, to think. "There were other Soanes," he muttered, "the Ellet Water folk—no?—— But there were many Soanes among the landed gentry in the East and North. . . . I cannot seem to recollect—the sudden shock—hearing a song unexpectedly——"

His white forehead had grown damp under the curly hair now clinging to it. He passed his handkerchief over his brow in a confused way, then leaned heavily on the piano with both hands grasping it. For the ghost of his youth was interfering, disputing his control over his own mind, filling his ear with forgotten words, taking possession of his memory and tormenting it with the distant echoes of a voice long dead.

Through the increasing chaos in his brain his strained gaze sought to fix itself on this living, breathing face before him—the child of Eileen Fane.

He made the effort:

"There were the Soanes of Colross——" But he got no farther that way, for the twin spectres of his youth and *hers* were busy with his senses now; and he leaned more heavily on the piano, enduring with lowered head the ghostly whirlwind rushing up out of that obscurity and darkness where once, under summer skies, he had sowed a zephyr.

The girl had become rather white, too. One slim hand still rested on the ivory keys, the other lay inert in her lap. And after a while she raised her grey eyes to this man standing beside her:

"Did you ever hear of my mother's marriage?"

He looked at her in a dull way:

"No."

"You heard—nothing?"

"I heard that your mother had left Fane Court."

"What was Fane Court?"

Murtagh Skeel stared at her in silence.

"I don't know," she said, trembling a little. "I

know nothing about my mother. She died when I was a few months old."

"Do you mean that you don't know who your mother was? You don't know who she married?" he asked, astounded.

"No."

"Good God!" he said, gazing at her. His tense features were working now; the battle for self-control was visible to her, and she sat there dumbly, looking on at the mute conflict which suddenly sent the tears flashing into his dark eyes and left his sensitive mouth twitching.

"I shall not ask you anything now," he said unsteadily; "I shall have to see you somewhere else—where there are no people—to interrupt. . . . But I shall tell you all I know about—your mother. . . . I was in trouble—in India. Somehow or other I heard indirectly that your mother had left Fane Court. Later it was understood that she had eloped. . . . Nobody could tell me the man's name. . . . My people in Ireland did not know. . . . And I was not on good terms with your grandfather. So there was no hope of information from Fane Court. . . . I wrote, indeed, begging, beseeching for news of your mother. Sir Barry—your grandfather—returned my letters unopened. . . . And that is all I have ever heard concerning Eileen Fane—your mother—with whom I—fell in love—nearly twenty years ago."

Dulcie, marble pale, nodded.

"I knew you cared for my mother," she said.

"How did you learn it?"

"Some letters of hers written to you. Letters from you to her. I have nothing else of hers except some verses and little songs—like the one you recognised."

"Child, she wrote it as I sat beside her!——" His

voice choked, broke, and his lips quivered as he fought for self-control again. . . . "I was not welcome at Fane Court. . . . Sir Barry would not tolerate me. . . . Your mother was more kind. . . . She was very young. And so was I, Dulcie. . . . There were political troubles. I was always involved. God knows which was the stronger passion—it must have been love of country—the other seeming hopeless—with the folk at Fane Court my bitter enemies—only excepting your mother. . . . So I went away. . . . And which of the Soanes your mother eloped with I have never learned. . . . Now, tell me—for you surely know that much."

She said:

"There is a man called Soane who tells me sometimes that he was once a game-keeper at what he calls 'the big house.' I have always supposed him to be my father until within the last year. But recently, when he has been drinking heavily, he sometimes tells me that my name is not Soane but Fane. . . . Did you ever know of such a man?"

"No. There were game-keepers about. . . . No. I cannot recall—and it is impossible! A game-keeper! And your *mother!* The man is mad! What in God's name does all this mean!——"

He began to tremble, and his white forehead under the clustering curls grew damp and pinched again.

"If you are Eileen's daughter——" But his face went dead white and he got no further.

People were approaching from behind them, too; voices grew distinct in conversation; somebody turned up another lamp.

"Do sing that little song again—the one you sang for Mr. Skeel," said Lee Barres, coming up to the piano on her brother's arm. "Mrs. Gerhardt has been waiting very patiently for an opportunity to ask you."

XXIV

THE guests from Hohenlinden had departed from Foreland Farms; the family had retired. Outside, under a sparkling galaxy of summer stars, tall trees stood unstirring; indoors nothing stirred except the family cat, darkly prowling on velvet-shod feet in eternal search of those viewless things which are manifest only to the feline race—sorcerers all, whether quadruped or human.

In various bedrooms upstairs lights went out, one after another, until only two windows remained illuminated, one in the west wing, one in the north.

For Dulcie, in her negligée and night robe, still sat by the open window, chin resting on palm, her haunted gaze remotely lost somewhere beyond the July stars.

And, in his room, Garry had arrived only as far as removing coat and waistcoat in the process of disrobing for the night. For his mind was still deeply preoccupied with Dulcie Soane and with the strange expression of her face at the piano—and with the profoundly altered visage of Murtagh Skeel.

And he was asking himself what could have happened between those two in such a few minutes there at the piano in the music-room. For it was evident to him that Skeel was labouring under poorly controlled emotion, was dazed by it, and was recovering self-possession only by a mighty effort.

And when Skeel had finally taken his leave and had

gone away with the Gerhardts, he suddenly stopped on the porch, returned to the music-room, and, bending down, had kissed Dulcie's hand with a grace and reverence which made the salute more of a serious ceremony than the impulsive homage of a romantic poet's whim.

Considered by itself, the abrupt return and quaintly perfect salute might have been taken as a spontaneous effervescence of that delightful Celtic gallantry so easily stirred to ebullition by youth and beauty. And for that it was accepted by the others after Murtagh Skeel was gone; and everybody ventured to chaff Dulcie a little about her conquest—merely the gentle humour of gentlefolk—a harmless word or two, a smile in sympathy.

Garry alone saw in the girl's smile no genuine response to the light badinage, and he knew that her serenity was troubled, her careless composure forced.

Later, he contrived to say good-night to her alone, and gave her a chance to speak; but she only murmured her adieux and went slowly away up the stairs with Thessalie, not looking back.

Now, sitting there in his dressing-gown, briar pipe alight, he frowned and pondered over the matter in the light of what he already knew of Dulcie, of the dead mother who bore her, of the grotesquely impossible Soane, of this man, Murtagh Skeel.

What had he and Dulcie found in common to converse about so earnestly and so long there in the music-room? What had they talked about to drive the colour from Dulcie's cheeks and alter Skeel's countenance so that he had looked more like his own wraith than his living self?

That Dulcie's mother had known this man, had once, evidently, been in love with him more or less, doubtless was revealed in their conversation at the piano. Had Skeel enlightened Dulcie any further? And on what subject? Soane? Her mother? Her origin—in case the child had admi ter ignorance of it? Was Dulcie, now, in possession of new facts concerning herself? Were they agreeable facts? Were they depressing? Had she learned anything definite in regard to her birth? Her parentage? Did she know, now, who was her real father? Was the obvious absurdity of Soane finally exploded? Had she learned what the drunken Soane meant by asserting that her name was not Soane but Fane?

His pipe burned out and he laid it aside, but did not rise to resume his preparation for bed.

Then, somewhere from the unlighted depths of the house came the sound of the telephone bell—at that hour of night always a slightly ominous sound.

He got up and went down stairs, not troubling to switch on any light, for the lustre of the starry night outside silvered every window and made it possible for him to see his way.

At the clamouring telephone, finally, he unhooked the receiver:

"Hello?" he said. "Yes! Yes! Oh, is that you, Renoux? Where on earth are you? . . . At North-brook? . . . Where? . . . At the Summit House? Well, why didn't you come here to us? . . . Oh! . . . No, it isn't very late. We retire early at Foreland. . . . Oh, yes, I'm dressed. . . . Certainly. . . . Yes, come over. . . . Yes! . . . Yes! . . . I'll wait for you in the library. . . . In an hour? . . . You bet. No, I'm not sleepy. . . . Sure thing! . . . Come on!"

He hung up the receiver, turned, and made his way through the dusk toward the library which was op-posite the music-room across the big entrance hall.

Before he turned on any light he paused to look out at the splendour of the stars. The night had grown warmer; there was no haze, now, only an argentine clarity in which shadowy trees stood mysterious and motionless and the dim lawn stretched away to the distant avenue and wall, lost against their looming border foliage.

Once he thought he heard a slight sound somewhere in the house behind him, but presently remembered that the family cat held sway among the mice at such an hour.

A little later he turned from the window to light a lamp, and found himself facing a slim, white figure in the starry dusk.

"Dulcie!" he exclaimed under his breath.

"I want to talk to you."

"Why on earth are you wandering about at this hour?" he asked. "You made me jump, I can tell you."

"I was awake—not in bed yet. I heard the telephone. Then I went out into the west corridor and saw you going down stairs. . . . Is it all right for me to sit here in my night dress with you?"

He smiled:

"Well, considering——"

"Of course!" she said hastily, "only I didn't know whether outside your studio——"

"Oh, Dulcie, you're becoming self-conscious! Stop it, Sweetness. Don't spoil things. Here—tuck yourself into this big armchair!—curl up! There you are. And here I am——" dropping into another wide, deep chair. "Lord! but you're a pretty thing, Dulcie, with your hair down and all glimmering with starlight! We'll try painting you that way some day—I wouldn't know how to go about it offhand, either. Maybe a screened arc-lamp in a dark partition, and a peep-hole—I don't know——"

He lay back in his chair, studying her, and she watched him in silence for a while. Presently she sighed, stirred, placed her feet on the floor as though preparing to rise. And he came out of his impersonal abstraction:

"What is it you want to say, Sweetness?"

"Another time," she murmured. "I don't——"

"You dear child, you came to me needing the intimacy of our comradeship—perhaps its sympathy. My mind was wandering—you are so lovely in the starlight. But you ought to know where my heart is."

"Is it open—a little?"

"Knock and see, Sweetness."

"Well, then, I came to ask you—Mr. Skeel is coming to-morrow—to see me—alone. Could it be contrived—without offending?"

"I suppose it could. . . . Yes, of course. . . . Only it will be conspicuous. You see, Mr. Skeel is much sought after in certain circles—beginning to be pursued and——"

"He asked me."

"Dear, it's quite all right——"

"Let me tell you, please. . . . He did know my mother."

"I supposed so."

"Yes. He was the man. I want you to know what he told me. . . . I always wish you to know everything that is in my—mind—always, for ever."

She leaned forward in her chair, her pretty, bare feet extended. One silken sleeve of her negligee had fallen to the shoulder, revealing the perfect symmetry of her arm. But he put from his mind the ever latent artistic delight in her, closed his painter's eye to her protean possibilities, and resolutely concentrated his mental forces upon what she was now saying:

"He turns out to be the same man my mother wrote to—and who wrote to her. . . . They were in love, then. He didn't say why he went away, except that my mother's family disliked him. . . . She lived at a house called Fane Court. . . . He spoke of my mother's father as Sir Barry Fane. . . ."

"That doesn't surprise me, Sweetness."

"Did *you* know?"

"Nothing definite." He looked at the lovely, slender-limbed girl there in the starry dusk. "I knew nothing definite," he repeated, "but there was no mistaking the metal from which you had been made—or the mould, either. And as for Soane——" he smiled.

She said:

"If my name is really Fane, there can be only one conclusion; some kinsman of that name must have married my mother."

He said:

"Of course," very gravely.

"Then who was he? My mother never mentioned him in her letters. What became of him? He must have been my father. Is he living?"

"Did you ask Mr. Skeel?"

"Yes. He seemed too deeply affected to answer me. He must have loved my mother very dearly to show such emotion before me."

"What did you ask him, Dulcie?"

"After we left the piano?"

"Yes."

"I asked him that. I had only a few more moments alone with him before he left. I asked him about my mother—to tell me how she looked—so I could think

of her more clearly. He has a picture of her on ivory.
He is to bring it to me and tell me more about her.
That is why I must see him to-morrow—so I may
ask him again about my father."

"Yes, dear. . . ." He sat very silent for a while,
then rose, came over, and seated himself on the padded
arm of Dulcie's chair, and took both her hands into
his:

"Listen, Sweetness. You are what you are to me
—my dear comrade, my faithful partner sharing our
pretty partnership in art; and, more than these, Dulcie, you are my friend. . . . Never doubt that. Never
forget it. Nothing can alter it—nothing you learn
about your origin can exalt that friendship. . . .
Nothing lessen it. Do you understand? *Nothing* can
lessen it, save only if you prove untrue to what you
are—your real self."

She had rested her cheek against his arm while he
was speaking. It lay there now, pressed closer.

"As for Murtagh Skeel," he said, "he is a charming,
cultivated, fascinating man. But if he attempts to
carry out his agitator's schemes and his revolution-
ary propaganda in this country, he is headed for most
serious trouble."

"Why does he?"

"Don't ask me why men of his education and character do such things. They do; that's all I know.
Sir Roger Casement is another man not unlike Skeel.
There are many, hot-hearted, generous, brave, irrational. There is no use blaming them—no justice in
it, either. The history of British rule in Ireland is
a matter of record.

"But, Dulcie, he who strikes at England to-day
strikes at civilisation, at liberty, at God! This is no
time to settle old grievances. And to attempt to do,

it by violence, by propaganda—to attempt a reckoning of ancient wrongs in any way, to-day, is a crime—the crime of treachery against Christ's teachings—of treason against Lord Christ Himself!"

After a long interval:

"You are going to this war quite soon. Mr. Westmore said so."

"I am going—with my country or without it."

"When?"

"When I finally lose patience and self-respect. . . . I don't know exactly when, but it will be pretty soon."

"Could I go with you?"

"Do you wish to?"

She pressed her cheek against his arm in silence.

He said:

"That has troubled me a lot, Dulcie. Of course you could stay here; I can arrange—I had come to a conclusion in regard to financial matters——"

"I can't," she whispered.

"Can't what?"

"Stay here—take anything from you—accept without service in return."

"What would you do?"

"I wouldn't care—if you—leave me here alone."

"But, Dulcie——"

"I know. You said it this evening. There will come a time when you would not find it convenient to have me—around——"

"Dear, it's only because a man and a woman in this world cannot continue anything of enduring intimacy without business as an excuse. And even then, the pleasant informality existing now could not be continued with anything except very serious disadvantage to you."

"You will grow tired of painting me," she said under her breath.

"No. But your life is all before you, Dulcie. Girls usually marry sooner or later."

"Men do too."

"That's not what I meant——"

"You will marry," she whispered.

Again, at her words, the same odd uneasiness began to possess him as though something obscure, unformulated as yet, must some day be cleared up by him and decided.

"Don't leave me—yet," she said.

"I couldn't take you with me to France."

"Let me enlist for service. Could you be patient for a few months so that I might learn something— anything!—I don't care what, if only I can go with you? Don't they require women to scrub and do unpleasant things—humble, unclean, necessary things?"

"You couldn't—with your slender youth and delicate beauty——"

"Oh," she whispered, "you don't know what I could do to be near you! That is all I want—all I want in the world!—just to be somewhere not too far away. I couldn't stand it, now, if you left me. . . . I couldn't live——"

"Dulcie!"

But, suddenly, it was a hot-faced, passionate, sobbing child who was clinging desperately to his arm and staunching her tears against it—saying nothing more, merely clinging close with quivering lips.

"Listen," he said impulsively. "I'll give you time. If there's anything you can learn that will admit you to France, come back to town with me and learn it. . . . Because I don't want to leave you, either. . . . There ought to be some way—some way——" He checked himself abruptly, stared at the bowed head under its torrent of splendid hair—at the desperate white little hands holding so fast to his sleeve, at the slender body gathered there in the deep chair, and all aquiver now.

"We'll go—together," he said unsteadily. . . . "I'll do what I can; I promise. . . . You must go upstairs to bed, now. . . . Dulcie! . . . dear girl . . ."

She released his arm, tried to get up from her chair obediently, blinded by tears and groping in the starlight.

"Let me guide you——" His voice was strained, his touch feverish and unsteady, and the convulsive closing of her fingers over his seemed to burn to his very bones.

At the stairs she tried to speak, thanking him, asking pardon for her tears, her loss of self-command, penitent, afraid that she had lowered herself, strained his friendship—troubled him——'

"No. I—want you," he said in an odd, indistinct, hesitating voice. . . . "Things must be cleared up—matters concerning us—affairs——" he muttered.

She closed her eyes a moment and rested both hands on the banisters as though fatigued, then she looked down at him where he stood watching her:

"If you had rather go without me—if it is better for you—less troublesome——"

"I've told you," he said in a dull voice, "I want you. You must fit yourself to go."

"You are so kind to me—so wonderful——"

He merely stared at her; she turned almost wearily to resume her ascent.

"Dulcie!"

She had reached the landing above. She bent over, looking down at him in the dusk.

"Did you understand?"

"I—yes, I think so."

"That I want you?"

"Yes."

"It is true. I want you always. I'm just beginning to understand that myself. Please don't ever forget what I say to you now, Dulcie; I want you. I shall always want you. Always! As long as I live."

She leaned heavily on the newel-post above, looking down.

He could not see that her eyes were closed, that her lips moved in voiceless answer. She was only a vague white shape there in the dusk above him—a mystery which seemed to have been suddenly born out of some poignant confusion of his own mind.

He saw her turn, fade into the darkness. And he stood there, not moving, aware of the chaos within him, of shapeless questions being evolved out of this profound disturbance—of an inner consciousness groping with these questions—questions involving other questions and menacing him with the necessity of decision.

After a while, too, he became conscious of his own voice sounding there in the darkness:

"I am very near to love. . . . I have been close to it. . . . It would be very easy to fall in love to-night. . . . But I am wondering—about to-morrow. . . . And afterward. . . . But I have been very near—very near to love, to-night. . . ."

The front doorbell rang through the darkness.

XXV

WHEN Barres opened the front door he saw Renoux standing there in the shadow of the porch, silhouetted against the starlight. They exchanged a silent grip; Renoux stepped inside; Barres closed the front door.

"Shall I light up?" he asked in a low voice.

"No. There are complications. I've been followed, I think. Take me somewhere near a window which commands the driveway out there. I'd like to keep my eye on it while we are talking."

"Come on," said Barres, under his breath. He guided Renoux through the shadowy entrance hall to the library, moved two padded armchairs to the window facing the main drive, motioned Renoux to seat himself.

"When did you arrive?" he asked in a cautious voice.

"This morning."

"What! You got here before we did!"

"Yes. I followed Souchez and Alost. Do you know who *they* were following?"

"No."

"One of your guests at dinner this evening."

"Skeel!"

Renoux nodded:

"Yes. You saw them start for the train. Skeel was on the train. But the conference at your studio delayed me. So I came up by automobile last night."

"And you've been here all day?"

Renoux nodded, but his keen eyes were fixed on the drive, shining silver-grey in the starlight. And his gaze continually reverted to it while he continued speaking:

"My friend, things are happening. Let me first tell you what is the situation. Over this entire hemisphere German spies are busy, German intrigue and propaganda are being accelerated, treason is spreading from a thousand foci of infection.

"In South America matters are very serious. A revolution is being planned by the half million Germans in Brazil; the neutrality of Argentine is being most grossly violated and Count Luxburg, the boche Ambassador, is already tampering with Chile and other Southern Republics.

"Of course, the Mexican trouble is due to German intrigue which is trying desperately to involve that Republic and yours and also drag in Japan.

"In Honolulu the German cruiser which your Government has interned is sending out wireless information while her band plays to drown the crackle of the instrument.

"And from the Golden Gate to the Delaware capes, and from the Soo to the Gulf, the spies of Germany swarm in your great Republic, planning your destruction in anticipation of the war which will surely come."

Barres reddened in the darkness and his heart beat more rapidly:

"You think it really will come?"

"War with Germany? My friend, I am certain of it. Your Government may not be certain. It is, if you permit a foreigner to say so—an—unusual Administration. . . . In this way, for example: it is cognisant of almost everything treasonable that is happening; it maintains agents in close contact with every mischief-hatching German diplomat in this hemisphere; it even has agents in the German Embassies—agents unsuspected, who daily rub elbows with German Ambassadors themselves!

"It knows what Luxburg is doing; it is informed every day concerning Bernstorff's dirty activities; the details of the Mexican and Japanese affairs are familiar to Mr. Lansing; all that happens aboard the *Geier*, the interned German liners—all that occurs in German consulates, commercial offices, business houses, clubs, cafés, saloons, is no secret to your Government.

"Yet, nothing has been done, nothing is being done except to continue to collect data of the most monstrous and stupendous conspiracy that ever threatened a free nation! I repeat that nothing is being done; no preparation is being made to face the hurricane which has been looming for two years and more, growing ever blacker over your horizon. All the world can see the lightning playing behind those storm clouds.

"And, my God!—not an umbrella! Not an order for overshoes and raincoats! . . . I am not, perhaps, in error when I suggest that the Administration is an—unusual one."

Barres nodded slowly.

Renoux said:

"I am sorry. The reckoning will be heavy."

"I know."

"Yes, you know. Your great politician, Mr. Roosevelt, knows; your great Admiral, Mahan, knew; your great General, Wood, knows. Also, perhaps some million or more sane, clear thinking American citizens know." He made a hopeless gesture. "It is a pity, Barres, my friend. . . . Well—it is, of course, the affair of your people to decide. . . . We French can only

wait. . . . But we have never doubted your ultimate
decision . . . . Lafayette did not live in vain. York-
town was not merely a battle. Your Washington
lighted a torch for your people and for ours to hold
aloft eternally. Even the rain of blood drenching our
Revolution could not extinguish it. It still burned at
Gravelotte, at Metz, at Sedan. It burned above the
smoke and dust of the Commune. It burned at the
Marne. It still burns, mon ami."

"Yes."

"Alors——" He sat silent for a few moments, his
gaze intent on the starry obscurity outdoors. Then,
slow and pleasantly:

"The particular mess, the cooking of which interests my Government, the English Government, and
yours, is now on the point of boiling over. It's this
Irish stew I speak of. Poor devils—they must be
crazy, every one of them, to do what they are already
beginning to do. . . . You remember the papers which
you secured?"

"Yes."

"Well, what we did last night at Grogan's has pre-
maturely dumped the fat into the fire. They know
they've been robbed; they know that their plans are
in our hands. Do you suppose that stops them? No!
On the contrary, they are at this very moment attempting, as you say in New York, to beat us to it."

"How do you mean?"

"This way: the signal for an Irish attempt on Canada is to be the destruction of the Welland Canal.
You remember the German suggestion that an ore
steamer be seized? They're going to try it. And if
that fails, they're to take their power boat into the
canal anyway and blow up a lock, even if they blow
up themselves with it. Did you ever hear of such mad-

ness?' Mon dieu, if only we had those men under your flag on our western front!"

"Do you know who these men are?" asked Barres.

"Your dinner guest—Murtagh Skeel—leads this company of Death."

"When?"

"Now! To-morrow! That's why I'm here! That's why your Secret Service men are arriving. I tell you the mess is on the point of boiling over. The crew is already on its way to take over the launch. They're travelling west singly, by separate trains and routes."

"Do you know who they are—these madmen?"

"Here is the list—don't strike a light! I can recall their names, I think—some of them anyway——"

"Are any of them Germans?"

"Not one. Your German doesn't blow himself up with anything but beer. Not he! No; he lights a fuse and legs it! I don't say he's a coward. But self-immolation for abstract principle isn't in him. There have been instances resembling it at sea—probably not genuine—not like that poor sergeant of ours in 1870, who went into the citadel at Laon and shoved a torch into the bin of loose powder under the magazine. . . . Because the city had surrendered. And Paris was not many miles away. . . . So he blew himself up with citadel, magazine, all the Prussians in the neighbourhood, and most of the town. . . . Well—these Irish are planning something of that sort on the Welland Canal. . . . Murtagh Skeel leads them. The others I remember are Madigan, Cassidy, Dolan, McBride—and that fellow Soane!——"

"Is *he* one of them?"

"He surely is. He went west on the same train that brought Skeel here. And now I'll tell you what has been done and why I'm here.

"We haven't located the power-boat on the lake. But the Canadians are watching for it and your agents are following these Irishmen. When the crew assembles they are to be arrested and their power-boat and explosives seized.

"I and my men have no official standing here, of course—would not be tolerated in any co-operation, *officially*. But we have a certain understanding with certain authorities."

Barres nodded.

"You see? Very well. Then, with delicacy and discretion, we keep in touch with Mr. Skeel. . . . And with other people. . . . You see? . . . He is abed in the large house of Mr. Gerhardt over yonder at North-brook. . . . Under surveillance. . . . He moves? We move—very discreetly. You see?"

"Certainly."

"Very well, then. But I am obliged to tell you, also, that the hunting is not done entirely by our side. No! In turn, I and my men, and also your agents, are being hunted by German agents. . . . It is that which annoys and hampers us, because these German agents continually dog us and give the alarm to these Irishmen. You see?"

"Who are the German agents? Do you know?"

"Very well indeed. Bernstorff is the head; Von Papen and Boy-ed come next. Under them serve certain so-called 'Diplomatic Agents of Class No. 1'—Adolf Gerhardt is one of them; his partners, Otto Klein and Joseph Schwartzmeyer are two others.

"They, in turn, have under them diplomatic agents of the second class—men such as Ferez Bey, Franz Lehr, called *K17*. You see? Then, lower still in the scale, come the spies who actually investigate under orders; men like Dave Sendelbeck, Johnny Klein, Louis

Hochstein, Max Freund. And, then, lowest of all in
rank, are the rank and file—the secret 'shock-troops'
who carry out desperate enterprises under some leader.
Among the Germans these are the men who sneak about
setting fires, lighting the fuses of bombs, scuttling ships,
defacing Government placards, poisoning Red Cross
bandages to be sent to the Allies—that sort. But
among them are no battalions of Death. *Non pas!*
And, for that, you see, they use these Irish. You understand now?"

"Yes, I do."

"Well, then! I trust you absolutely, Barres. And
so I came over to ask you—and your clever friends,
Mademoiselle Dunois, Miss Soane, Mr. Westmore, to
keep their eyes on this man Skeel to-morrow afternoon
and also to-morrow evening. Because they will be
guests at the Gerhardts'. Is it not so?"

"Yes."

"Well, your Government's agents will be there. They
will also be in the neighbourhood, watching roads and
railway stations. I have one man in service with the
Gerhardts—their head chauffeur. If anything happens—if Skeel tries to slip away—if you miss him—
I would be very grateful if you and your friends notify
the head chauffeur, Menard."

"We'll try to do it."

"That's all I want. Just get word to Menard that
Skeel seems to be missing. That will be sufficient. Will
you say this to your friends?"

"Yes, I will, Renoux. I'll be glad to. I'll be particularly happy to offer to Miss Dunois this proof of
your confidence in her integrity."

Renoux looked very grave.

"For me," he sa⬤ "Miss Dunois is what she pretends to be. I have so informed my Government at home and its representatives at Washington."

"Have you heard anything yet?"

"Yes, a telegram in cipher from Washington late this afternoon."

"Favourable to her?"

"Yes. Our Ambassador is taking up immediately the clues Miss Dunois furnished me last night. Also, he has cabled at length to my home Government. At this hour, no doubt, d'Eblis, Bolo, probably an ex-minister or two, are being watched. And in this country your Government is now in possession of facts which must suggest a very close surveillance of the activities of Ferez Bey."

"Where is he?"

Renoux shook his head:

"He *was* in New York. But he gave us the slip. An eel!" he added, rising. "Oh, we shall pick up his slimy traces again in time. But it is mortifying. . . . Well, thank you, mon ami. I must go." And he started toward the hall.

"Have you a car anywhere?" asked Barres.

"Yes, up the road a bit." He glanced through the sidelight of the front door, carelessly. "A couple of men out yonder dodging about. Have you noticed them, Barres?"

"No! Where?"

"They're out there in the shadow of your wall. I imagined that I'd be followed." He smiled and opened the front door.

"Wait!" whispered Barres. "You are not going out there alone, are you?"

"Certainly. There's no danger."

"Well, I don't like it, Renoux. I'll walk as far as your car——"

"Don't trouble! I have no personal apprehension——"

"All the same," muttered the other, continuing on down the front steps beside his comrade.

Renoux shrugged good-humouredly his disapproval of such precaution, but made no further protest. Nobody was visible anywhere on the grounds. The big iron gates were still locked, but the wicket was open. Through this they stepped out onto the macadam.

A little farther along stood a touring car with two men in it.

"You see?" began Renoux—when his words were cut by the crack of a pistol, and the red tail-light of the car crashed into splinters and went dark.

"Well, by God!" remarked Renoux calmly, looking at the woods across the road and leisurely producing an automatic pistol.

Then, from deeper in the thicket, two bright flames stabbed the darkness and the crash of the shots re-echoed among the trees.

Both men in the touring car instantly turned loose their pistols; Renoux said, in a voice at once perplexed and amused:

"Go home, Barres. I don't want people to know you are out here. . . . I'll see you again soon."

"Isn't there anything——"

"Nothing. Please—you would oblige me by keeping clear of this if you really desire to help me."

There were no more shots. Renoux stepped leisurely into the tonneau.

"Well, what the devil do you gentlemen make of this?" Barres heard him say in his cool, humorous voice. "It really looks as though the boches were getting nervous."

The car started. Barres could see Renoux and an-

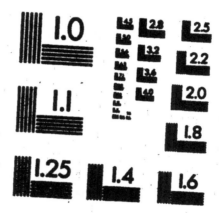

APPLIED IMAGE Inc

1853 East Main Street
Rochester, New York 14609 USA
(716) 482 – 0300 – Phone
(716) 288 – 5989 – Fax

other man sitting with pistols levelled as the car glided along the fringe of woods. But there were no more shots on either side, and, after the car had disappeared, Barres turned and retraced his way.

Then, as he entered his own gate by the side wicket, and turned to lock it with his own key, an electric torch flashed in his face, blinding him.

"Let him have it!" muttered somebody behind the dazzling light.

"That's not one of them!" said another voice distinctly. "Look out what you're doing! Douse your glim!"

Instantly the fierce glare faded to a cinder. Barres heard running feet on the macadam, the crash of shrubbery opposite. But he could see nobody; and presently the footsteps in the woods were no longer audible.

There seemed to be nothing for him to do in the matter. He lingered by the wicket for a while, peering into the night, listening. He saw nothing; heard nothing more that night.

XXVI

'BE-N EIRINN I!

BARRES senior rose with the sun. Also with determination, which took the form of a note slipped under his wife's door as he was leaving the house:

"DARLING:

"I lost last night's fishing and I'm hanged if I lose it to-night! So don't ask me to fritter away a perfectly good evening at the Gerhardt's party, because the sun is up; I'm off to the woods; and I shall remain there until the last trout breaks.

"Tell the little Soane girl that I left a rod for her in the work-room, if she cares to join me at the second lake. Garry can bring her over and leave her if he doesn't wish to fish. Don't send a man over with a lot of food and shawls. I've a creel full of provisions, and I am sufficiently clad, and I hate to be disturbed and I am never grateful to people who try to be good to me. However, I love you very dearly.

"Your husband,
"REGINALD BARRES."

'At half past seven trays were sent to Mrs. Barres and to Lee; and at eight-thirty they were in the saddle and their horses fetlock deep in morning dew.

Dulcie, sipping her chocolate in bed, marked their departure with sleepy eyes. For the emotions of the night before had told on her, and when a maid came to remove the tray she settled down among her pillows again, blinking unresponsively at the invitation of the sun, which cast over her a fairy net of gold.

Thessalie, in negligee, came in later and sat down on the edge of her bed.

"You sleepy little thing," she said, "the men have breakfasted and are waiting for us on the tennis court."

"I don't know how to play," said Dulcie. "I don't know how to do anything."

"You soon will, if you get up, you sweet little lazybones!"

"Do you think I'll ever learn to play tennis and golf and to ride?" inquired Dulcie. "You know how to do everything so well, Thessa."

"Dear child, it's all locked up in you—the ability to do everything—be anything! The only difference between us is that I had the chance to try."

"But I can't even stand on my head," said Dulcie wistfully.

"Did you ever try?"

"N-no."

"It's easy. Do you want to see me do it?"

"Oh, please, Thessa!"

So Thessalie, calmly smiling, rose, cast herself lightly upon her hands, straightened her lithe figure leisurely, until, amid a cataract of tumbling silk and chiffon, her rose silk slippers pointed toward the ceiling. Then, always with graceful deliberation, she brought her feet to the floor, forming an arc with her body; held it a moment, and slowly rose upright, her flushed face half-buried in her loosened hair.

Dulcie, in raptures, climbed out of bed and insisted on immediate instruction. Down on the tennis court, Garry and Westmore heard their peals of laughter and came across the lawn under the window to remonstrate.

"Don't trouble! I have no personal apprehension——"

"All the same," muttered the other, continuing on down the front steps beside his comrade.

Renoux shrugged good-humouredly his disapproval of such precaution, but made no further protest. Nobody was visible anywhere on the grounds. The big iron gates were still locked, but the wicket was open. Through this they stepped out onto the macadam.

A little farther along stood a touring car with two men in it.

"You see?" began Renoux—when his words were cut by the crack of a pistol, and the red tail-light of the car crashed into splinters and went dark.

"Well, by God!" remarked Renoux calmly, looking at the woods across the road and leisurely producing an automatic pistol.

Then, from deeper in the thicket, two bright flames stabbed the darkness and the crash of the shots re-echoed among the trees.

Both men in the touring car instantly turned loose their pistols; Renoux said, in a voice at once perplexed and amused:

"Go home, Barres. I don't want people to know you are out here. . . . I'll see you again soon."

"Isn't there anything——"

"Nothing. Please—you would oblige me by keeping clear of this if you really desire to help me."

There were no more shots. Renoux stepped leisurely into the tonneau.

"Well, what the devil do you gentlemen make of this?" Barres heard him say in his cool, humorous voice. "It really looks as though the boches were getting nervous."

The car started. Barres could see Renoux and another man sitting with pistols levelled as the car glided along the fringe of woods. But there were no more shots on either side, and, after the car had disappeared, Barres turned and retraced his way.

Then, as he entered his own gate by the side wicket, and turned to lock it with his own key, an electric torch flashed in his face, blinding him.

"Let him have it!" muttered somebody behind the dazzling light.

"That's not one of them!" said another voice distinctly. "Look out what you're doing! Douse your glim!"

Instantly the fierce glare faded to a cinder. Barres heard running feet on the macadam, the crash of shrubbery opposite. But he could see nobody; and presently the footsteps in the woods were no longer audible.

There seemed to be nothing for him to do in the matter. He lingered by the wicket for a while, peering into the night, listening. He saw nothing; heard nothing more that night.

'BE-N EIRINN I!

BARRES senior rose with the sun. Also with determination, which took the form of a note slipped under his wife's door as he was leaving the house:

"DARLING:

"I lost last night's fishing and I'm hanged if I lose it to-night! So don't ask me to fritter away a perfectly good evening at the Gerhardt's party, because the sun is up; I'm off to the woods; and I shall remain there until the last trout breaks.

"Tell the little Soane girl that I left a rod for her in the work-room, if she cares to join me at the second lake. Garry can bring her over and leave her if he doesn't wish to fish. Don't send a man over with a lot of food and shawls. I've a creel full of provisions, and I am sufficiently clad, and I hate to be disturbed and I am never grateful to people who try to be good to me. However, I love you very dearly.

"Your husband,
"REGINALD BARRES."

At half past seven trays were sent to Mrs. Barres and to Lee; and at eight-thirty they were in the saddle and their horses fetlock deep in morning dew.

Dulcie, sipping her chocolate in bed, marked their departure with sleepy eyes. For the emotions of the night before had told on her, and when a maid came to remove the tray she settled down among her pillows again, blinking unresponsively at the invitation of the sun, which cast over her a fairy net of gold.

Thessalie, in negligee, came in later and sat down on the edge of her bed.

"You sleepy little thing," she said, "the men have breakfasted and are waiting for us on the tennis court."

"I don't know how to play," said Dulcie. "I don't know how to do anything."

"You soon will, if you get up, you sweet little lazy-bones!"

"Do you think I'll ever learn to play tennis and golf and to ride?" inquired Dulcie. "You know how to do everything so well, Thessa."

"Dear child, it's all locked up in you—the ability to do everything—be anything! The only difference between us is that I had the chance to try."

"But I can't even stand on my head," said Dulcie wistfully.

"Did you ever try?"

"N-no."

"It's easy. Do you want to see me do it?"

"Oh, please, Thessa!"

So Thessalie, calmly smiling, rose, cast herself lightly upon her hands, straightened her lithe figure leisurely, until, amid a cataract of tumbling silk and chiffon, her rose silk slippers pointed toward the ceiling. Then, always with graceful deliberation, she brought her feet to the floor, forming an arc with her body; held it a moment, and slowly rose upright, her flushed face half-buried in her loosened hair.

Dulcie, in raptures, climbed out of bed and insisted on immediate instruction. Down on the tennis court, Garry and Westmore heard their peals of laughter and came across the lawn under the window to remonstrate.

"Aren't you ever going to get dressed!" called up Westmore. "If you're going to play doubles with us you'd better get busy, because it's going to be a hot day!"

So Thessalie went away to dress and Dulcie tiptoed into her bath, which the maid had already drawn.

But it was an hour before they appeared on the lawn, cool and fresh in their white skirts and shoes, and found Westmore and Barres, red and drenched, hammering each other across the net in their second furious set.

So Dulcie took her first lesson under Garry's auspices; and she took to it naturally, her instinct being sound, but her technique as charmingly awkward as a young bird's in its first essay at flying.

To see her all in white, with sleeves tucked up, throat bare, and the sun brilliant on her ruddy, rippling hair, produced a curious impression on Barres. As far as the East is from the West, so far was this Dulcie of the tennis court separated from the wistful, shabby child behind the desk at Dragon Court.

Could they possibly be the same—this lithe, fresh, laughing girl, with white feet flashing and snowy skirts awhirl?—and the pale, grey-eyed slip of a thing that had come one day to his threshold with a faltering request for admittance to that wonderland wherein dwelt only such as he?

Now, those grey eyes had turned violet, tinged with the beauty of the open sky; the loosened hair had become a net entangling the very sunlight; and the frail body, now but one smooth, soft symmetry, seemed fairly lustrous with the shining soul it masked within it.

She came over to the net, breathless, laughing, to shake hands with her victorious opponents.

"I'm so sorry, Garry," she said, turning penitently to him, "but I need such a lot of help in the world before I'm worth anything to anybody."

"You're all right as you are. You always have been all right," he said in a low voice. "You never were worth less than you are worth now; you'll never be worth more than you are worth to me at this moment."

They were walking slowly across the lawn toward the northern veranda. She halted a moment on the grass and cast a questioning glance at him:

"Doesn't it please you to have me learn things?"

"You always please me."

"I'm so glad. . . . I try. . . . But don't you think you'd like me better if I were not so ignorant?"

He looked at her absently, shook his head:

"No. . . . I couldn't like you better. . . . I couldn't care more—for any girl—than I care for you. . . . Did you suspect that, Dulcie?"

"No."

"Well, it's true."

They moved slowly forward across the grass—he distrait, his handsome head lowered, swinging his tennis-bat as he walked; she very still and lithe and slender, moving beside him with lowered eyes fixed on their mingled shadows on the grass.

"When are you to see Mr. Skeel?" he asked abruptly.

"This afternoon. . . . He asked if he might hope to find me alone. . . . I didn't know exactly what to say. So I told him about the rose arbour. . . . He said he would pay his respects to your mother and sister and then ask their permission to see me there alone."

They came to the veranda; Dulcie seated herself on the steps and he remained standing on the grass in front of her.

"Remember," he said quietly, "that I can never care

less for you than I do at this moment. . . . Don't forget what I say, Dulcie."

She looked up at him, happy, wondering, even perhaps a little apprehensive in her uncertainty as to his meaning.

He did not seem to care to enlighten her further. His mood changed, too, even as she looked at him, and she saw the troubled gravity fade and the old gaiety glimmering in his eyes:

"I've a mind to put you on a horse, Sweetness, and see what happens," he remarked.

"Oh, Garry! I don't want to tumble off before *you!*"

"Before whom had you rather land on that red head of yours?" he inquired. "I'd be more sympathetic than many."

"I'd rather have Thessa watch me break my neck. Do you mind? It's horrid to be so sensitive, I suppose. But, Garry, I couldn't bear to have you see me so shamefully awkward and demoralised."

"Fancy your being awkward! Well, all right——"

He looked across the lawn, where Thessalie and Westmore sat together, just outside the tennis court, under a brilliant lawn umbrella.

Oddly enough, the spectacle caused him no subtle pang, although their heads were pretty close together and their mutual absorption in whatever they were saying appeared evident enough.

"Let 'em chatter," he said after an instant's hesitation. "Thessa or my sister can ride with you this afternoon when it's cooler. I suppose you'll take to the saddle as though born there."

"Oh, I hope so!"

"Sure thing. All Irish girls—of your quality—take to it."

"My—quality?"

"Yours. . . . It's merely happened so," he added irrelevantly, "—but the contrary couldn't have mattered . . . as long as you are *you!* Nothing else matters one way or another. You *are* you: that answers all questions, fulfils all requirements——"

"I *don't* quite understand what you say, Garry!"

"Don't you, Sweetness? Don't you understand why you've always been exactly what you appear like at this moment?"

She looked at him with her lovely, uncertain smile:

"I've always been myself, I suppose. You are teasing me dreadfully!"

He laughed in a nervous, excited way, not like himself:

"You bet you have always been yourself, Sweetness! —in spite of everything you've always been *yourself*. I am very slow in discovering it. But I think I realise it now."

"Please," she remonstrated, "you are laughing at me and I don't know why. I think you've been talking nonsense and expecting me to pretend to understand. . . . If you don't stop laughing at me I shall retire to my room and—and——

"What, Sweetness?" he demanded, still laughing.

"Change to a cooler gown," she said, humorously vexed at her own inability to threaten or punish him for his gaiety at her expense.

"All right; I'll change too, and we'll meet in the music-room!"

She considered him askance:

"Will you be more respectful to me, Garry?"

"Respectful? I don't know."

"Very well, then, I'm not coming back."

But when he entered the music-room half an hour later, Dulcie was seated demurely before the piano, and when he came and stood behind her she dropped her head straight back and looked up at him.

"I had a wonderful icy bath," she said, "and I'm ready for anything. Are you?"

"Almost," he said, looking down at her.

She straightened up, gazed silently at the piano for a few moments; sounded a few chords. Then her fingers wandered uncertainly, as though groping for something that eluded them—something that they delicately sought to interpret. But apparently she did not discover it; and her search among the keys ended in a soft chord like a sigh. Only her lips could have spoken more plainly.

At that moment Westmore and Thessalie came in breezily and remained to gossip a few minutes before bathing and changing.

"Play something jolly!" said Westmore. "One of those gay Irish things, you know, like 'The Honourable Michael Dunn,' or 'Finnigan's Wake,' or——"

"I don't know any," said Dulcie, smiling. "There's a song called 'Asthore.' My mother wrote it——"

"Can you sing it?"

The girl ran her fingers over the keys musingly:

"I'll remember it presently. I know one or two old songs like 'Irishmen All.' Do you know that song?" And she sang it in her gay, unembarrassed way:

"Warm is our love for the island that bore us,
Ready are we as our fathers before us,
 Genial and gallant men,
 Fearless and valiant men,
Faithful to Erin we answer her call,
 Ulster men, Munster men,
 Connaught men, Leinster men,
Irishmen all we answer her call!"

"Fine!" cried Westmore. "Try it again, Dulcie!"

"Maybe you'll like this better," she said:

> "Our Irish girls are beautiful,
> As all the world will own;
> An Irish smile in Irish eyes
> Would melt a heart of stone;
> But all their smiles and all their wiles
> Will quickly turn to sneers
> If you fail to fight for Erin
> In the Irish Volunteers!"

"Hurrah!" cried Westmore, beating time and picking up the chorus of the "Irish Volunteers," which Dulcie played to a thunderous finish amid frantic applause.

She sang for them "The West's Awake!", "The Risin' of the Moon," "Clare's Dragoons," and "Paddy Get Up!" And after Westmore had exercised his lungs sufficiently in every chorus, he and Thessalie went off to their respective quarters, leaving Barres leaning on the piano beside Dulcie.

"Your people are a splendid lot—given half a chance," he said.

"My people?"

"Certainly. After all, Sweetness, you're Irish, you know."

"Oh."

"Aren't you?"

"I don't know what I am," she murmured half to herself.

"Whoever you are it's the same to me, Dulcie." ... He took a few short, nervous turns across the room; walked slowly back to her: "Has it come back to you yet—that song of your mother's you were trying to remember?"

Even while he was speaking the song came back to her memory—her mother's song called "Asthore"—startling her with its poignant significance to herself.

"Do you recollect it?" he asked again.

"Y-yes. . . . I can't sing it."

"Why?"

"I don't wish to sing 'Asthore'——" She bent her head and gazed at the keyboard, the painful colour dyeing her neck and cheeks.

When at length she looked up at him out of lovely, distressed eyes, something in his face—something—some new expression which she dared not interpret—set her heart flying. And, scarcely knowing what she was saying in her swift and exquisite confusion:

"The words of my mother's song would mean nothing to you, Garry," she faltered. "You could not understand them——"

"Why not?"

"B-because you could not be in sympathy with them."

"How do you know? Try!"

"I can't——"

"Please, dear!"

The smile edging her lips glimmered in her eyes now —a reckless little glint of humour, almost defiant.

"Do you insist that I sing 'Asthore'?"

"Yes."

He seemed conscious of a latent excitement in her to which something within himself was already responsive.

"It's about a lover," she said, "—one of the old-fashioned, head-long, hot-headed sort—Irish, of course! —you'd not understand—such things——" Her tongue and colour were running random riot; her words outstripped her thoughts and tripped up her tongue, scaring her a little. She drummed on the keys a rollicking trill or two, hesitated, stole a swift, uncertain glance at him.

A delicate intoxication enveloped her, stimulating, frightening her a little, yet hurrying her into speech again:

"I'll sing it for you, Garry asthore! And if I were a lad I'd be singing my own gay credo!—if I were the lad—and you but a lass, asthore!"

Then, though her gray eyes winced and her flying colour betrayed her trepidation, she looked straight at him, laughingly, and her clear, childish voice continued the little prelude to "Asthore":

I

"I long for her, who e'er she be—
The lass that Fate decrees for me;
Or dark or white and fair to see,
My heart is hers 'be n-Eirinn i!

I care not, I,
Who ever she be,
I could not love her more!
* 'Be n-Eirinn i—
'Be n-Eirinn i—
'Be n-Eirinn i Asthore!

II

"I know her tresses unconfined,
In wanton ringlets woo the wind—
Or rags or silk her bosom bind
It's one to me; my eyes are blind!

I care not, I,
Who ever she be,
Or poor, or rich galore!
'Be n-Eirinn i—
'Be n-Eirinn i—
'Be n-Eirinn i Asthore!

III

"At noon, some day, I'll climb a hill,
And find her there and kiss my fill;
And if she won't, I think she will,
For every Jack must have his Jill!

I care not, I,
Who ever she be,
The lass that I adore!
'Be n-Eirinn i—
'Be n-Eirinn i—
'Be n-Eirinn i Asthore!"

Dulcie's voice and her flushed smile, too, faded, died
out. She looked down at the keyboard, where her
white hands rested idly; she bent lower—a little lower;
laid her arms on the music-rest, her face on her crossed
arms. And, slowly, the tears fell without a tremor,
without a sound.

He had leaned over her shoulders; his bowed head was
close to hers—so close that he became aware of the
hot, tearful fragrance of her breath; but there was
not a sound from her, not a stir.

"What is it, Sweetness?" he whispered.

"I—don't know. . . . I didn't m-mean to—cry.
. . . And I don't know why I should. . . . I'm very
h-happy——" She withdrew one arm and stretched it
out, blindly, seeking him; and he took her hand and
held it close to his lips.

"Why are you so distressed, Dulcie?"

* The refrain, pronounced Bay-nayring-ee, is common to a number of Irish love-songs written during the last century. It should
be translated: "Whoever she be."
In writing this song, it is evident that Eileen Fane was inspired by Blind William of Tipperary; and that she was beho . .n
to Carroll O'Daly for her "Eileen, my Treasure," although not
to Robin Adair of County Wicklow.

AUTHOR.

"I'm not. I'm happy. . . . You know I am. . . .
My heart was very full; that is all. . . . I don't seem
to know how to express myself sometimes. . . . Perhaps it's because I don't quite dare. . . . So something
gives way. . . . And this happens—tears. Don't mind
them, please. . . . If I could reach my handkerchief——" She drew the tiny square of sheer stuff
from her bosom and rested her closed eyes on it.

"It's silly, isn't it, Garry? . . . W-when a girl is
so heavenly contented. . . . Is anybody coming?"

"Westmore and Thessa!"

She whisked her tears away and sat up swiftly. But
Thessa merely called to them that she and Westmore
were off for a walk, and passed on through the hall
and out through the porch.

"Garry," she murmured, looking away from him.

"Yes, dear?"

"May I go to my room and fix my hair? Because
Mr. Skeel will be here. Do you mind if I leave you?"

He laughed:

"Of course not, you charming child!" Then, as he
looked down at her hand, which he still retained, his
expression altered; he inclosed the slender fingers, bent
slowly and touched the fragrant palm with his lips.

They were both on their feet the next second; she
passing him with a pale, breathless little smile, and
swiftly crossing the hall; he dumb, confused by the sudden tumult within him, standing there with one hand
holding to the piano as though for support, and looking after the slim, receding figure till it disappeared beyond the library door.

His mother and sister returned from their morning
ride, lingered to chat with him, then went away to dress
for luncheon. Murtagh Skeel had not yet arrived.

Westmore and Thessalie returned from their walk in

the woods by the second lake, reporting a distant view of Barres senior, fishing madly from a canoe.

Dulcie came down and joined them in the library. Later Mrs. Barres and Lee appeared, and luncheon was announced.

Murtagh Skeel had not come to Foreland Farms, and there was no word from him.

Mrs. Barres spoke of his absence during luncheon, for Garry had told her he was coming to talk to Dulcie about her mother, whom he had known very well in Ireland.

Luncheon ended, and the cool north veranda became the popular rendezvous for the afternoon, and later for tea. People from Northbrook drove, rode, or motored up for a cheering cup, and a word or two of gossip. But Skeel did not come.

By half-past five the north veranda was thronged with a gaily chattering and very numerous throng from neighbouring estates. The lively gossip was of war, of the coming elections, of German activities, of the Gerhardts' promised moonlight spectacle and dance, of Murtagh Skeel and the romantic interest he had aroused among Northbrook folk.

So many people were arriving or leaving and such a delightful and general informality reigned that Dulcie, momentarily disengaged from a vapid but persistent dialogue with a chuckle-headed but persistent youth, ventured to slip into the house, and through it to the garden in the faint hope that perhaps Murtagh Skeel might have avoided the tea-crush and had gone directly there.

But the rose arbour was empty; only the bubble of the little wall fountain and a robin's evening melody broke the scented stillness of the late afternoon.

Her mind was full of Murtagh Skeel, her heart of

Garry Barres, as she stood there in that blossoming solitude, listening to the robin and the fountain, while her eyes wandered across flower-bed, pool, and clipped greensward, and beyond the garden wall to the hill where three pines stood silver-green against the sky.

Little by little the thought of Murtagh Skeel faded from her mind; fuller and fuller grew her heart with confused emotions new to her—emotions too perplexing, too deep, too powerful, perhaps, for her to understand—or to know how to resist or to endure. For the first vague sweetness of her thoughts had grown keen to the verge of pain—an exquisite spiritual tension which hurt her, bewildered her with the deep emotions it stirred.

To love, had been a phrase to her; a lover, a name. For beyond that childish, passionate adoration which Barres had evoked in her, and which to her meant friendship, nothing more subtly mature, more vital, had threatened her unawakened adolescence with any clearer comprehension of him or any deeper apprehension of herself.

And even now it was not knowledge that pierced her, lighting little confusing flashes in her mind and heart. For her heart was still a child's heart; and her mind, stimulated and rapidly developing under the warm and magic kindness of this man who had become her only friend, had not thought of him in any other way. . . . Until to-day.

What had happened in her mind, in her heart, she had not analysed—probably was afraid to, there at the piano in the music-room. And later, in her bedroom, when she had summoned up innocent courage sufficient for self-analysis, she didn't know how to question herself—did not realise exactly what had happened to her, and never even thought of including him in the en-

chanted cataclysm which had befallen her mind and
heart and soul.

Thessalie and Westmore appeared on the lawn by
the pool. Behind the woods the sky was tinted with
pale orange.

It may have been the psychic quality of the Celt in
Dulcie—a pale glimmer of clairvoyance—some momentary and vague premonition wirelessed through the evening stillness which set her sensitive body vibrating;
for she turned abruptly and gazed northward across
the woods and hills—remained motionless, her grey
eyes fixed on the far horizon, all silvery with the hidden
glimmer of unlighted stars.

Then she slowly said aloud to herself:

"He will not come. He will never come again—this
man who loved my mother."

Barres approached across the grass, looking for her.
She went forward through the arbour to meet him.

"Hasn't he come?" he asked.

"He is not coming, Garry."

"Why? Have you heard anything?"

She shook her head:

"No. But he isn't coming."

"Probably he'll explain this evening at the Gerhardts'."

"I shall never see him again," she said absently.

He turned and gave her a searching look. Her gaze
was remote, her face a little pale.

They walked back to the house together in silence.

A servant met them in the hall with a note on a tray.
It was for Barres; Dulcie passed on with a pale little
smile of dismissal; Barres opened the note:

"The pot has boiled over, mon ami. Something has
scared Skeel. He gave us the slip very cleverly, leaving

THE MOONLIT WAY

Gerhardt's house before sunrise and motoring north at crazy speed. Where he will strike the railway I have no means of knowing. Your Government's people are trying to cover Lake Erie and Lake Ontario. On the Canada side the authorities have been notified and are alert I hope.

"Gerhardt's country house is a nest of mischief hatchers. One in particular is under surveillance and will be arrested. His name is Tauscher.

"Because, mon ami, it has just been discovered that there are *two* plots to blow up the Welland Canal! One is Skeel's. The other is Tauscher's. It is a purely German plot. They don't intend to blow themselves up these Huns. Oh no! They expect to get away.

"Evidently Bernstorff puts no faith in Skeel's mad plan. So, in case it doesn't pan out, here is Tauscher with another plan, made in Germany, and very, very thorough. Isn't it characteristic? Here is the report I received this morning:

"'Captain Franz von Papen, Military Attaché on the ambassadorial staff of Count von Bernstorff, and Captain Hans Tauscher, who, besides being the Krupp agent in America, is also, by appointment of the German War Office, von Papen's chief military assistant in the United States, have plotted the destruction of the Welland Canal in Canada.

"'Captain Hans Tauscher will be arrested and indicted for violation of Section 13 of the United States Criminal Code, for setting on foot a military enterprise against Canada during the neutrality of the United States.

"'Tauscher is a German reserve officer and is subject to the orders of Captain Franz von Papen, Military Attaché of Count von Bernstorff. His indictment will be brought about by reason of an attempt to blow up parts of the Welland Canal, the waterway connecting Lakes Erie and Ontario. A small party of Germans, under command of one von der Golts, have started from New York for the purpose of committing this act of sabotage, and, incidentally, of assassination of all men, women and children who might be involved in the explosion at the point to be selected by the plotters.

"'Tauscher bought and furnished to this crowd of assassins the dynamite which was to be used for the purpose.

864

The fact that Tauscher had bought the dynamite has become known to the United States authorities and he will be called upon to make an explanation.

" 'Captain Tauscher is said to be an agreeable companion, but he had the ordinary predilection of a German officer for assassinating women and children.'

"Now, then, mon ami, this is the report. I expect that United States Secret Service men will arrest Tauscher to-night. Perhaps Gerhardt, also, will be arrested.

"At any rate, at the dance to-night you need not look for Skeel. But may I suggest that you and Mr. Westmore keep your eyes on Mademoiselle Dunois. Because, at the railway station to-day, the German agents, Frans Lehr and Max Freund, were recognised by my men, disguised as liveried chauffeurs, but in whose service we have not yet been able to discover.

"Therefore, it might be well for you and Mr. Westmore to remain near Mademoiselle Dunois during the evening.

"Au revoir! I shall see you at the dance.

"RENOUX."

XXVII

THE MOONLIT WAY

BARRES whistled and sang alternately as he tied his evening tie before his looking glass.

> *"And I care not, I,*
> *Who ever she be*
> *I could not love her more!"*

he chanted gaily, examining the effect and buttoning his white waistcoat.

Westmore, loitering near and waiting for him, referred again, indignantly, to Renoux's report concerning the presence of Freund and Lehr at the Northbrook railway station.

"If I catch them hanging around Thessa," he said, "I'll certainly beat them up, Garry.

"Deal with anything of that sort directly; that's always the best way. No use arguing with a Hun. When he misbehaves, beat him up. It's the only thing he understands."

"Well, it's all right for us to do it now, as long as the French Government knows where Thessa is," remarked Barres, drawing a white clove-carnation through his button-hole. "But what do you think of that dirty swine, Tauscher, planning wholesale murder like that? Isn't it the fine flower of Prussianism? There's the real and porcine boche for you, sombre, savage, stupidly ferocious, swinishly persistent, but never quite cunning enough, never sufficiently subtle in planning his filthy and murderous holocausts."

Westmore nodded:

"Quite right. The *Lusitania* and Belgium cost the Hun the respect of civilisation, and are driving the civilised world into a common understanding. We'll go in before long; don't worry."

They descended the stairs together just as dinner was announced.

Mrs. Barres said laughingly to her son:

"Your father is still fishing, I suppose, so in spite of his admonition to me by letter this morning, I sent over one of the men with some thermos bottles and a very nice supper. He grumbles, but he always likes it."

"I wonder what Mr. Barres will think of me," ventured Dulcie. "He left such a pretty little rod for me. Thessa and I have been examining it. I'd like to go, only—" she added with a wistful smile, "I have never been to a real party."

"Of course you're going to the Gerhardts'," insisted Lee, laughing. "Dad is absurd about his fishing. I don't believe any girl ever lived who'd prefer fishing on that foggy lake at night to dancing at such a party as you are going to to-night."

"Aren't you going?" asked Thessalie, but Lee shook her head, still smiling.

"We have two young setters down with distemper, and mother and I always sit up with our dogs under such circumstances."

Personal devotion of this sort was new to Thessalie. Mrs. Barres and Lee told her all about the dreaded contagion and how very dreadful an epidemic might be in a kennel of such finely bred dogs as was the well-known Foreland Kennels.

Dog talk absorbed everybody during dinner. Mrs. Barres and Lee were intensely interested in Thessalie's description of the Grand Duke Cyril's Russian wolf-hounds, with which she had coursed and hunted as a child.

Once she spoke, also, of those strange, pathetic, melancholy Ishmaelites, pitiable outcasts of their race —the pariah dogs of Constantinople. For, somehow, while dressing that evening, the distant complaint of a tethered beagle had made her think of Stamboul. And she remembered that night so long ago on the moonlit deck of the *Mirage*, where she had stood with Feres Bey while, from the unseen, monstrous city close at hand, arose the endless wailing of homeless dogs.

How strange it was, too, to think that the owner of the *Mirage* should this night be her host here in the Western World, yet remain unconscious that he had ever before entertained her.

Before coffee had been served in the entrance hall, the kennel master sent in word that one of the pups, a promising Blue Belton, had turned very sick indeed, and would Mrs. Barres come to the kennels as soon as convenient.

It was enough for Mrs. Barres and for Lee; they both excused themselves without further ceremony and went away together to the kennels, apparently quite oblivious of their delicate dinner gowns and slippers.

"I've seen my mother ruin many a gown on such errands," remarked Garry, smiling. "No use offering yourself as substitute; my mother would as soon abandon her own sick baby to strangers as turn over an ailing pup to anybody except Lee and herself."

"I think that is very splendid," murmured Dulcie,

relinquishing her coffee cup to Garry and suffering
a maid to invest her with a scarf and light silk wrap.

"My mother is splendid," said Garry in a low voice.
"You will see her prove it some day, I hope."

The girl turned her lovely head, curiously, not understanding. Garry laughed, but his voice was not
quite steady when he said:

"But it all depends on you, Dulcie, how splendid
my mother may prove herself."

"On me!"

"On your—kindness."

"My—kindness!"

Thessalie came up in her pretty carnation-rose cloak,
esquired by the enraptured Westmore, expressing admiration for the clothing adorning the very obvious
object of his devotion:

"All girls can't wear a thing like that cloak," he was
explaining proudly; "now it would look like the devil
on you, Dulcie, with your coppery hair and——"

"What exquisite tact!" shrugged Thessalie, already
a trifle restive under his constant attendance and unremitting admiration. "Can't you, out of your richly
redundant vocabulary, find something civil to say to
Dulcie?"

But Dulcie, still preoccupied with what Barres had
said, merely gave her an absent-minded smile and walked
slowly out beside her to the porch, where the head-
lights of a touring car threw two broad beams of gold
across the lawn.

It was a swift, short run through the valley northward among the hills, and very soon the yellow lights
of Northbrook summer homes dotted the darkness
ahead, and cars were speeding in from every direction
—from Ilderness, Wythem, East and South Gorloch—

carrying guests for the Gerhardts' moonlight spectacle and dance.

Apropos of the promised spectacle, Barres observed to Dulcie that there happened to be no moon, and consequently no moonlight, but the girl, now delightfully excited by glimpses of Hohenlinden festooned with electricity, gaily reproached him for being literal.

"If one is happy," she said, "a word is enough to satisfy one's imagination. If they call it a moonlight spectacle, I shall certainly see moonlight whether it's there or not!"

"They may call it heaven, too, if they like," he said, "and I'll believe it—if you are there."

At that she blushed furiously:

"Oh, Garry! You don't mean it, and it's silly to say it!"

"I mean it all right," he muttered, as the car swung in through the great ornamental gates of Hohenlinden. "The trouble is that I mean so much—and *you* mean so much to me—that I don't know how to express it."

The girl, her face charmingly aglow, looked straight in front of her out of enchanted eyes, but her heart's soft violence in her breast left her breathless and mute; and when the car stopped she scarcely dared rest her hand on the arm which Barres presented to guide her in her descent to earth.

It may have been partly the magnificence of Hohenlinden that so thrillingly overwhelmed her as she seated herself with Garry on the marble terrace of an amphitheatre among brilliant throngs already gathered to witness the eagerly discussed spectacle.

And it really was a bewilderingly beautiful scene, there under the summer stars, where a thousand rosy lanterns hung tinting the still waters of the little stream that wound through the clipped greensward which was the stage.

The foliage of a young woodland walled in this vernal scene; the auditorium was a semi-circle of amber marble—rows of low benches, tier on tier, rising to a level with the lawn above.

The lantern light glowed on pretty shoulders and bare arms, on laces and silks and splendid jewels, and stained the sombre black of the men with vague warm hues of rose.

Westmore, leaning over to address Barres, said with an amused air:

"You know, Garry, it's Corot Mandel who is putting this thing for the Gerhardts."

"Certainly I know it," nodded Barres. "Didn't he try to get Thessa for it?"

Thessalie, whose colour was high and whose dark eyes, roaming, had grown very brilliant, suddenly held out her hand to one of two men who, traversing the inclined aisle beside her, halted to salute her.

"Your name was on our lips," she said gaily. "How do you do, Mr. Mandel! How do you do, Mr. Trenor! Are you going to amaze us with a miracle in this enchanting place?"

The two men paid their respects to her, and, with unfeigned astonishment and admiration, to Dulcie, whom they recognised only when Thessalie named her with delighted malice.

"Oh, I say, Miss Soane," began Mandel, leaning on the back of the marble seat, "you and Miss Dunois might have helped me a lot if I'd known you were to be in this neighbourhood."

Esmé Trenor bent over Barres, dropping his voice:

"We had to use a couple of Broadway hacks—you'll recognise 'em through their paint—you understand?—

the two that New York screams for. It's too bad. Corot wanted something unfamiliarly beautiful and young and fresh. But these Northbrook amateurs are incredibly amateurish."

Thessalie was chattering away with Corot Mandel and Westmore; Esmé Trenor gazed upon Dulcie in wonder not unmixed with chagrin:

"You've never forgiven me, Dulcie, have you?"

"For what?" she inquired indifferently.

"For not discovering you when I should have."

She smiled, but the polite effort and her detachment of all interest in him were painfully visible to Esmé.

"I'm sorry you still remember me so unkindly," he murmured.

"But I never do remember you at all," she explained so candidly that Barres was obliged to avert his amused face, and Esmé Trenor reddened to the roots of his elaborate hair. Mandel, with a wry grin, linked his arm in Trenor's and drew him away toward the flight of steps which was the stage entrance to the dressing rooms below.

"Good-bye!" he said, waving his hat. "Hope you'll like my moonlight frolic!"

"Where's your bally moon!" demanded Westmore.

As he spoke, an unseen orchestra began to play "*Au Claire de la Lune*," and, behind the woods, silhouetting every trunk and branch and twig, the glittering edge of a huge, silvery moon appeared.

Slowly it rose, flashing a broad path of light across the lawn, reflected in the still little river. And when it was in the position properly arranged for it, some local Joshua—probably Corot Mandel—arrested its further motion, and it hung there, flooding the stage with a witching lustre.

All at once the stage swarmed with supple, glimmer-

ing shapes: Oberon and Titania came flitting down
through the trees; Puck, scintillating like a dragon-fly,
dropped on the sward, seemingly out of nowhere.

It was a wonderfully beautiful ballet, with an unseen chorus singing from within the woods like a thousand seraphim.

As for the play itself, which began with the calm
and silvered river suddenly swarming alive with water-
nymphs, it had to do, spasmodically, with the love of
the fairy crown-prince for the very attractive water-
nymph, Ythali. This nimble lady, otherwise, was
fiercely wooed by the King of the Mud-turtles, a most
horrid and sprawling shape, but a clever foil—with
his army of river-rats, minks and crabs—to the
nymphs and wood fairies.

Also, the music was refreshingly charming, the singing excellent, and the story interesting enough to keep
the audience amused until the end.

There was, of course, much moonlight dancing, much
frolicking in the water, few clothes on the Broadway
principals, fewer on the chorus, and apparently no
scruples about discarding even these.

But the whole spectacle was so unreal, so spectral,
that its shadowy beauty robbed it of offence.

That sort of thing had made Corot Mandel famous.
He calculated to the width of a moonbeam just how
far he could go. And he never went a hair's breadth
farther.

Thessalie looked on with flushed cheeks and parted
lips, absorbed in it all with the savant eyes of a professional. She also had once coolly decided how far
her beauty and talent and adolescent effrontery could
carry her gay disdain of man. And she had flouted him
with indifferent eyes and dainty nose uplifted—mocked
him and his conventions, with a few roubles in her

dressing-room—slapped the collective face of his sex with her insolent loveliness, and careless smile.

Perhaps, as she sat there watching the fairy scene, she remembered her ostrich and the German Embassy, and the aged Von-der-Goltz Pasha, all over jewels and gold, peeping at her through thick spectacles under his red fez.

Perhaps she thought of Ferez, too, and maybe it was thought of him that caused her smooth young shoulders the slightest. of shivers, as though a harsh breeze had chilled her skin.

As for Dulcie, she was in the seventh heaven, thrilled with the dreamy beauty of it all and the exquisite phantoms floating on the greensward under her enraptured eyes.

No other thought possessed her save sheer delight in this revelation of pure enchantment.

So intent, so still she became, leaning a little forward in her place, that Barres found her far more interesting and wonderful to watch than Mandel's cunningly contrived illusions in the artificial moonlight below.

And now Titania's trumpets sounded from the woods, warning all of the impending dawn. Suddenly the magic fairy moon vanished like the flame of a blown-out candle; a faint, rosy light grew through the trees, revealing an empty stage and a river on which floated a single swan.

Then, from somewhere, a distant cock-crow rang through the dawn. The play was ended.

Two splendid orchestras were alternating on the vast marble terraces of Hohenlinden, where hundreds of dancers moved under the white radiance of a huge silvery moon overhead—another contrivance of Mandel's—for the splendid sphere aglow with white fire had somehow been suspended above the linden trees so that no poles and no wires were visible against the starry sky.

And in its milky flood of light the dancers moved amid a wilderness of flowers or thronged the supper-rooms within, where Teutonic architectural and decorative magnificence reigned in one vast, incredible, indigestible gastronomic apotheosis of German kultur.

Barres, for the moment, dancing with Thessalie, pressed her fingers with mischievous tenderness and whispered:

"The moonlit way once more with you, Thessa! Do you remember our first dance?"

"Can I ever thank God enough for that night's folly!" she said, with such sudden emotion that his smile altered as he looked into her dark eyes.

"Yet that dance by moonlight exiled you," he said.

"Do you realise what it saved me from, too? And what it has given me?"

He wondered whether she included Westmore in the gift. The music ceased at that moment, and, though the other orchestra began, they strolled along the flowering balustrade of the terrace together until they encountered Dulcie and Westmore.

"Have you spoken to your hostess?" inquired Westmore. "She's over yonder on a dais, enthroned like Germania or a Metropolitan Opera Valkyrie. Dulcie and I have paid our homage."

So Barres and Thessalie went away to comply with the required formality; and, when they returned from the rite, they found Esmé Trenor and Corot Mandel cornering Dulcie under a flowering orange tree while Westmore, beside her, chatted with a most engaging woman who proved, later, to be a practising physician.

Esmé was saying languidly, that anybody could fly into a temper and kick his neighbours, but that indifference to physical violence was a condition of mind attained only by the spiritual intellect of the psychic adept.

"Passivism," he added with a wave of his lank fingers, "is the first plane to be attained on the journey toward Nirvana. Therefore, I am a pacifist and this silly war does not interest me in the slightest."

The very engaging woman, who had been chatting with Westmore, looked around at Esmé Trenor, evidently much amused.

"I imagined that you were a pacifist," she said. "I fancy, Mr. Mandel, also, is one."

"Indeed, I am, madam!" said Corot Mandel. "I've plenty to do in life without strutting around and bawling for blood at the top of my lungs!"

"Thank heaven," added Esmé, "the President has kept us out of war. This business of butchering others never appealed to me—except for the slightly unpleasant sensations which I experience when I read the details."

"Oh. Then unpleasant sensations so appeal to you?" inquired Westmore, very red.

"Well, they *are* sensations, you know," drawled Esmé. "And, for a man who experiences few sensations of any sort, even unpleasant ones are pleasurable."

Mandel yawned and said:

"The war is an outrageous bore. All wars are stupid to a man of temperament. Therefore, I'm a pacifist. And I had rather live under Prussian domination than rush about the country with a gun and sixty pounds of luggage on my back!"

He looked heavily at Dulcie, who had slipped out of the corner on the terrace, where he and Esmé had penned her.

"There are other things to do more interesting than jabbing bayonets into Germans," he remarked. "Did you say you hadn't any dance to spare us, Miss Soane? Nor you either, Miss Dunois? Oh, well." He cast a disgusted glance at Barres, squinted at Westmore through his greasy monocle in hostile silence; then, taking Esmé's arm, made them all a too profound obeisance and sauntered away along the terrace.

"What a pair of beasts!" said Westmore. "They make me actually ill!"

Barres shrugged and turned to the very engaging lady beside him:

"What do you think of that breed of human, doctor?" he inquired.

She smiled at Barres and said:

"Several of my own patients who are suffering from the same form of psycho-neurotic trouble are also peace-at-any-price pacifists. They do not come to me to be cured of their pacifism. On the contrary, they cherish it most tenderly. In examining them for other troubles I happened upon what appeared to me a very close relation between the peculiar attitude of the peace-at-any-price pacifist and a certain type of unconscious pervert."

"That passivism is perversion does not surprise me," remarked Barres.

"Well," she said, "the pacifist is not conscious of his real desires and therefore cannot be termed a true pervert. But the very term, passivism, is usually significant and goes very deep psychologically. In analysing my patients I struck against a buried impulse in them to suffer tyrannous treatment from an omnipotent master. The impulse was so strong that it amounted to a craving and tried to absorb all the psychic material within its reach. They did not recognise the original impulse, because that had long ago been crushed down by the exactions of civilised life. Nevertheless, they were tortured and teased, made unsettled and wretched by a something which continually baffled them. Deep under the upper crust of their personalities was concealed a seething desire to be completely, inevitably, relentlessly, unreservedly overwhelmed by a subjugation from which there was no escape."

She turned to Westmore:

"It's purely pathological, the condition of those two self-confessed pacifists. The pacifist loves suffering. The ordinary normal person avoids suffering when possible. He endures it only when something necessary or desirable cannot be gained in any other way. He may undergo agony at the mere thought of it. His bravery consists in facing danger and pain in spite of fear. But the extreme passivist, who is really an unconscious pervert, loves to dream of martyrdom and suffering. It must be a suffering, however, which is forced upon him, and it must be a personal matter, not impersonal and general, as in war. And he loves to contemplate a condition of complete captivity—of irresponsible passivity, in which all resistance is in vain."

"Do you know, they disgust me, those two!" said Westmore angrily. "I never could endure anything abnormal. And now that I know Esmé is—and that big lout, Mandel—I'll keep away from them. Do you blame me, doctor?"

"Well," she said, much amused and turning to go, "they're very interesting to physicians, you know— these non-resisting, pacifistic perverts. But outside a sanatorium I shouldn't expect them to be very popular." And she laughed and joined a big, good-looking man who had come to seek her, and who wore, in his buttonhole, the button of the French Legion of Honour.

Thessalie had strolled forward along the terrace by herself, interested in the pretty spectacle and the play of light on jewels and gowns.

Westmore, busy in expressing to Barres his opinion of Esmé and Mandel, did not at the moment miss Thessalie, who continued to saunter on along the balustrade of the terrace, under the blossoming row of orange trees.

Just below her was another terrace and an oval pool set with tiny jets which seemed to spray the basin with liquid silver. Silvery fish, too, were swimming in it near the surface, sometimes flinging themselves clear out of water as though intoxicated by the unwonted lustre which flooded their crystal pool.

To see them nearer, Thessalie ran lightly down the steps and walked toward the shimmering basin. And at the same time the head and shoulders of a man in evening dress, his bosom crossed by a sash of watered red silk, appeared climbing nimbly from a still lower level.

She watched him step swiftly upon the terrace and cross it diagonally, walking in her direction toward the stone stairs which she had just descended. Then, paying him no further attention, she looked down into the water.

He came along very near to where she stood, gazing into the pool—peered at her curiously—was already passing at her very elbow—when something made her lift her head and look around at him.

The mock moonlight struck full across his features; and the shock of seeing him drove every vestige of colour from her own face.

The man halted, staring at her in unfeigned amazement. Suddenly he snarled at her, baring his teeth in her shrinking face.

"*Kismet dir!*" he whispered, "it ees *you!* . . . Nihla Quellen! *Now* I begin onderstan'! . . . Yas, I now onders⁺an' who arrange it that they haf arrest my good frien', Tauscher! It ees *you*, then! Von Igel he has tol' me, look out once eef she escape—thees yoong leopardess——"

"Ferez!" Thessalie's young figure stiffened and the colour flamed in her cheeks.

"You leopardess!" he repeated, every tooth a-grin again with rage, "you misbegotten slut of a hunting cheetah! So thees is 'ow you strike! . . . Ver' well. Yas, I see 'ow it ees you strike at——"

"Ferez!" she cried. "Listen to *me!*"

"I 'ear you! Alles!"

"Ferez Bey! I am not afraid of you!"

"Ees it so?"

"Yes, it is so. I *never* have been afraid of you! Not even there on the deck of the *Mirage*, that night when you tapped the hilt of your Kurdish knife and spoke of Seraglio Point! Nor when your scared spy shot at me in the corridor of the Tenth Street house; nor afterward at Dragon Court! Nor now! Do you understand, Eurasian jackal! Nor *now!* Anybody can see what *Heruli* whelped you! What are you doing in America? Kassim Pasha is your den, where your *rayah* loll and scratch in the sun! It is their *Keyeff!* And yours!"

She took a quick step toward him, her eyes flashing, her white hand clenched:

"*Allah Kerim*—do you say? *El Hamdu Lillah!* Do you take yourself for the *muezzin* of all jackals, then, howling blasphemies from some *minaret* in the hills? Do you understand what they'd do to you in the *Hirka-i-Sherif Jamesi?* Because you are *nothing;* do you hear?—nothing but an Eurasian assassin! And Moslem and Christian alike know where *you* belong among the lost pariahs of Stamboul!"

The girl was utterly transfigured. Whatever of the Orient was in her, now blazed white hot.

"What have I done to you, Ferez? What have I ever done to you that you, even from my childhood, come always stepping noiselessly at my skirt's edge? —always padding behind me at my heels, silent, sinister, whimpering with bared teeth for the courage to bite which God denies you!"

The man stood almost motionless, moistening his dry lips with his tongue, but his eyes moved continually, stealing uneasy glances around him and upward, where, on the main terrace above them, the heads of the throng passed and repassed.

"Nihla," he said, "for all thees scorn and abuse of me, you know, in the false heart of you, why it ees so if I have seek you."

"You dealer in lies! You would have sold me to d'Eblis! You thought you *had* sold me! You were paid for it, too!"

"An' still!" He looked at her furtively.

"What do you mean? You conspired with d'Eblis to ruin me, soul and body! You involved me in your treacherous propaganda in Paris. Through you I am an exile. If I go back to my own country, I shall go to a shameful death. You have blackened my honour in my country's eyes. But that was not enough. No! You thought me sufficiently broken, degraded, terrified to listen to any proposition from you. You sent your agents to me with offers of money if I would betray my country. Finding I would not, you whined and threatened. Then, like the Eurasian dog you are, you tried to bargain. You were eager to offer me anything if I would keep quiet and not interfere——"

"Nihla!"

"What?" she said, contemptuously.

"In spite of thees—of all you say—I have love you!"

"Liar!" she retorted wrathfully. "Do you dare say that to me, whom you have already tried to murder?"

"I say it. Yas. Eef it has not been so then you were dead long time."

"You—you are trying to tell me that you spared me?" she demanded scornfully.

"It ees so. Alexandre—d'Eblis, you know?—long time since he would have safety for us all—thees way. Non! Je ne pourrais pas vous tuer, moi! It ees not in my heart, Nihla. . . . Because I have love you long time—ver' long time."

"Because you have *feared* me long time, ver' long time!" she mocked him. "That is why, Feres—because you are afraid; because you are only a jackal. And jackals never kill. No!"

"You say thees-a to me, Nihla?"

"Yes, I say it. You're a coward! And I'll tell you something more. I am going to make a complete statement to the French Government. I shall relate everything I know about d'Eblis, Bolo Effendi, a certain bureaucrat, an Italian politician, a Swiss banker, old Von-der-Goltz Pasha, Heimholz, Von-der-Hohe Pasha, and you, my Feres—and you, also!

"Do you know what France will do to d'Eblis and his scoundrel friends? Do you guess what these duped Americans will do to Bolo Effendi? And to you? And to Von Papen and Boy-ed and Von Igel—yes, and to Bernstorff and his whole murderous herd of Germans? And can you imagine what my own doubly duped

HE CAME TOWARD HER STEALTHILY

Government will surely, surely do, some day, to you, Ferez!"

She laughed, but her dark eyes fairly glittered

"*My* martyrdom is ending, God be thanked! And then I shall be free to serve where my heart is . . . in Alsace! . . . Alsace!—forever French!"

In the white light she saw the sweat break out on the man's forehead—saw him grope for his handkerchief—and draw out a knife instead—never taking his eyes off her.

She turned to run; but he had already blocked the way to the stone steps; and now he came creeping toward her, white as a cadaver, distracted from sheer terror, and rubbing the knife flat against his thigh.

"So you shall do thees—a filth to me—eh, Nihla?" he whispered with blanched lips. "It ees on me, your frien', you spring to keel me, eh, my leopardess? Ver' well. But firs' I teach you somethings you don' know! —thees-a way, my Nihla!"

He came toward her stealthily, moving more swiftly as she put the stone basin of the pool between them and cast an agonised glance up at the distant terrace.

"Jim!" she cried frantically. "Jim! Help me, Jim!"

The gay din of the music above drowned her cry; she fled as Ferez darted toward her, but again he doubled and sprang back to bar the stone steps, and she halted, white and breathless, yet poised for instant flight.

Again and again she called out desperately for aid; the noise of the orchestra smothered her cry. And if, indeed, anybody from the terrace above chanced to glance down, it is likely that they supposed these two were skylarking merrymakers at some irresponsible game of catch-who-can.

Suddenly Thessalie remembered the lower level, where the automobiles were parked, and from which Ferez had first appeared. She could escape that way. There were the steps, not very far behind her. The next instant she turned and ran like a deer.

And after her sped Ferez, his broad, thin-bladed knife pressed flat against the crimson sash across his breast, his dead-white visage distorted with that blind, convulsive fear which makes murderers out of cowards.

XXVIII

GREEN JACKETS

THOROUGHLY worried by this time over the sudden disappearance of Thessalie Dunois, and unable to discover her anywhere on the terrace or in the house, Westmore, Barres and Dulcie Soane had followed the winding main drive as far as the level, where their car was waiting among scores of other cars.

But Thessalie was not there; the chauffeur had not seen her.

"Where in the world could she have gone?" faltered Dulcie. "She was standing up there on the terrace with us, a moment ago; then, the very next second, she had vanished utterly."

Westmore, grim and pallid, walked back along the drive; Dulcie followed with Barres. As they overtook Westmore, he cast one more glance back at the ranks of waiting cars, then stared up at the terraced hill above them, over which the artificial moon hung above the lindens, glowing with pallid, lambent fires.

There was a vague whitish object on one of the grassy slopes—something in motion up there—something that was running erratically but swiftly—as though in pursuit—or *pursued!*

"My God! What's that, Garry!" he burst out. "That thing up there on the hillside!"

He sprang for the steps, Barres after him, taking

385

the ascent at incredible speed, up, up, then out along a shrub-set grassy slope.

"Thessa!" shouted Westmore. "Thessa!"

But the girl was flat on her back on the grass now, fighting sturdily for life—twisting, striking, baffling the whining, panting thing that knelt on her, holding her and trying to drive a knife deep into the lithe young body which always slipped and writhed out of his trembling clutch.

Again and again he tore himself free from her grasp; again and again his armed hand sought to strike, but she always managed to seize and drag it aside with the terrible strength of one dying. And at last, with a last crazed, superhuman effort, she wrested the knife from his unnerved fist, tore it out of his spent fingers.

It fell somewhere near her on the grass; he strove to reach it and pick it up, but already her dauntless resistance began to exhaust him, and he groped for the knife in vain, trying to pin her down with one hand while, with desperate little fists, she rained blows on his bloodless face that dazed him.

But there was still another way—a much better way, in fact. And, as the idea came to him, he ripped the red-silk sash from his breast and, in spite of her struggles, managed to pass it around her bare neck.

"Now!" he panted. "I keep my word at last. C'est fini, ma petite Nihla."

"Jim! Help me!" she gasped, as Ferez pulled savagely at the silk noose, tightened it with all his strength, knotted it. And in that same second he heard Westmore crashing through the shrubbery, close to him.

Instantly he rose to his knees on the grass; bounded to his feet, leaped over the low shrubs, and was off down the slope—gone like a swift hawk's shadow on the hillside. Barres was after him.

The soul of Thessalie Dunois was very near to its escape, now, brightening, glistening within its unconscious chrysalis, stretching its glorious limbs and wings; preparing to arise from its spectral tenement and soar aloft to its myriad sisters, where they swarmed glittering in the zenith.

Had it not been for the knife lying beside her on the grass—the blade very bright in the starlight—truly the youthful soul of Thessalie had been sped.

At the edge of the Gerhardts' pine woods, Barres, at fault, baffled, furious, out of breath and glaring around him in the dark, sullenly gave up the hopeless chase, turned in his tracks, and came back. Thessalie, lying in Dulcie's arms, unclosed her eyes and looked up at him.

"Are you all right?" he asked, kneeling and bending over her.

"Yes. . . . Jim came."

Westmore's voice was shaky.

"We worked her arms—Dulcie and I—started respiration. She was nearly gone. That beast strangled her——"

"I lost him in those woods below. Who was he?"

"Ferez Bey!"

Thessalie sighed, closed her eyes.

"She's about all in," whispered Westmore. And, to Dulcie: "Let me take her. I'll carry her to the car."

At that Thessalie opened her eyes again and the old, faintly humorous smile glimmered out at him as he stooped and lifted her from the grass.

"Can I really trust myself to your arms, Jim?" she murmured.

"You'd better get used to 'em," he retorted. "You'll never get away from them again—I can tell you that right now!"

"Oh. . . . In that case, I hope they'll be—comfortable—your arms."

"Do you think they will be, Thessa?"

"Perhaps." She gazed into his eyes very seriously from where she lay cradled in his powerful arms.

"I'm tired, Jim. . . . So sore and bruised. . . . When he was choking me I tried to think of you—believing it was the end—my last conscious thought——"

"My darling!——"

"I'm so tired," she breathed, "so lonely. . . . I shall be—contented—in your arms. . . . Always——" She turned her head and rested her cheek against his breast with a deep sigh.

He held her in his arms in the car all the way to Foreland Farms. Dulcie, however, had possessed herself of Thessalie's left hand, and when she stroked it and pressed it to her lips the girl's tightening fingers responded, and she always smiled.

"I'm just tired and sore," she explained languidly. "Ferez battered me about so dreadfully! . . . It was so mortifying. I despised him all the time. It made me furious to be handled by such a contemptible and cowardly creature."

"It's a matter for the police, now," remarked Barres gloomily.

"Oh, Garry!" she exclaimed. "What a very horrid ending to the moonlit way we took together so long ago!—the lovely silvery path of Pierrot!"

"The story of Pierrot is a tragedy, Thessa! We have been luckier on our moonlit way."

"Than Pierrot and Pierrette?"

"Yes. Death always saunters along the path of the moon, watching for those who take it. . . . You are very fortunate, Pierrette."

"Yes," she murmured, "I am fortunate. . . . Am I not, Jim?" she added, looking up wistfully into his shadowy face above her.

"I don't know about that," he said, "but there'll be no more moonlight business for you unless I'm with you. And under those circumstances," he added, "I'll knock the block off Old Man Death if he tries to flirt with you!"

"How brutal! Garry, do you hear his language to me?"

"I hear," said Barres, laughing. "Your young man is a very matter of fact young man, Thessa, and I fancy he means what he says."

She looked up at Westmore; her lips barely moved: "Do you—dear?"

"You bet I do," he whispered. "I'll pull this planet to pieces looking for you if you ever again steal away to a rendezvous with Old Man Death."

When the car arrived at Foreland Farms, Thessalie felt able to proceed to her room upon her own legs, and with Dulcie's arm around her.

Westmore bade her good-night, kissing her hand—awkwardly—not being convincing in any rôle requiring attitudes.

He wanted to take her into his arms, but seemed to know enough not to do it. Probably she divined his irresolute state of mind, for she extended her hand in a pretty manner quite unmistakable. And the romantic education of James H. Westmore began.

Barres lingered at the door after Westmore departed, obeying a whispered aside from Dulcie. She

c*me out in a few moments, carefully closing the bedroom door, and stood so, one hand behind her still resting on the knob.

"Thessa is crying. It's only the natural relaxation
from that horrible tension. I shall sleep with her to-
night."

"Is there anything——"

"Oh, no. She will be all right. . . . Garry, are
they—are they—in *love?*"

"It rather looks that way, doesn't it?" he said, smiling.

She gazed at him questioningly, almost fearfully.

"Do *you* believe that Thessa is in love with Mr.
Westmore?" she whispered.

"Yes, I do. Don't you?"

"I didn't know. . . . I thought so. But——"

"But what?"

"I didn't—didn't know—what you would think of
it. . . . I was afraid it might—might make you—
unhappy."

"Why?"

"Don't you *care* if Thessa loves somebody else?"
she asked breathlessly.

"Did you think I did, Dulcie?"

"Yes."

"Well, I don't."

There was a strained silence; then the girl smiled at
him in a confused manner, drew a swift, sudden breath,
and, as he stepped forward to detain her, turned
sharply away, pressing her forearm across her eyes.

"Dulcie! Did you understand me?" he said in a low,
unsteady voice.

She was already trying to open the door, but he
dropped his right hand over her fingers where they
were fumbling with the knob, and felt them trembling.

At the same moment, the sound of Thessalie's smothered and convulsive sobbing came to him; and Dulcie's nervous hand slipped from his.

"Dulcie!" he pleaded. "Will you come back to me if I wait?"

She had stopped; her back was still toward him, but she nodded slightly, then moved on toward the bed, where Thessalie lay all huddled up, her face buried in the tumbled pillows.

Barres noiselessly closed the door.

He had already started along the corridor toward his own room, when the low sound of voices in the staircase hall just below arrested his attention—his sister's voice and Westmore's. And he retraced his steps and went down to where they stood together by the library door.

Lee wore a nurse's dress and apron, such as a kennel-mistress affects, and her strong, capable hands were full of bottles labelled "Grover's Specific"—the same being dog medicine of various sorts.

"Mother is over at the kennels, Garry," she said. "She and I are going to sit up with those desperately sick pups. If we can pull them through to-night they'll probably get well, eventually, unless paralysis sets in. I was just telling Jim that a very attractive young Frenchman was here only a few minutes before you arrived. His name is Renoux. And he left this letter for you—fish it out of my apron pocket, there's a dear——"

Her brother drew out the letter; his sister said:

"Mr. Renoux went away in a car with two other men. He asked me to say to you that there was no time to lose—whatever he meant by that! Now, I must hurry away!" She turned and sped through the hall and out through the swinging screen door on the north ·

porch. Garry had already opened the note from Renoux, glanced over it; then he read it aloud to Westmore:

"MY DEAR COMRADE:

"The fat's in the fire! Your agents took Tauscher in charge to-day. Max Freund and Frans. Lehr have just been arrested by your excellent Postal authorities. Warrants are out for Sendelbeck, Johann Klein, and Louis Hochstein. I think the latter are making for Mexico, but your Secret Service people are close on their heels.

"Recall for von Papen and Boy-ed is certain to be demanded by your Government. Mine will look after Bolo Effendi and d'Eblis and their international gang of spies and crooks. Feres Bey, however, still eludes us. He is somewhere in this vicinity, but of course, even when we locate him again, we can't touch him. All we can do is to point him out to your Government agents, who will then keep him in sight.

"So far so good. But now I am forced to ask a very great favour of you, and, if I may, of your friend, Mr. Westmore. It is this: Skeel, contrary to what was expected of him, did not go to the place which is being watched. Nor have any of his men appeared at that rendezvous where there lies the very swift and well-armed launch, *Togue Rouge*, which we had every reason to suppose was to be their craft in this outrageous affair.

"As a matter of fact, this launch is Tauscher's. But it, and the pretended rendezvous, are what you call a plant. Skeel never intended to assemble his men there; never intended to use that particular launch. Tauscher merely planted it. Your men and the Canadian agents, unfortunately, are covering that vicinity and are still watching for Skeel, who has a very different plan in his crazy head.

"Now, this is Skeel's plan, and this is the situation, learned by me from papers discovered on Tauscher:

"The explosives bought and sent there by Tauscher himself are on a big, fast power-boat which is lying at anchor in a little cove called Saibling Bay. The boat flies the Quebec Yacht Club ensign, and a private pennant to which it has no right.

"Two of Skeel's gang are already aboard—a man named Con McDermott and another, Kelly Walsh. Skeel joins the others at a hamlet near the Lake shore, known as Three Ponds. The tavern is a notorious and disreputable old brick hotel—what you call a speak-easy. That is their rendezvous.

"Well, then, I have wired to your people, to Canada, to Washington. But Three Ponds is not a very long drive from here, if one ignores speed limits. Yes? Could you help us maintain a close surveillance over that damned tavern to-night? Is it too much to ask?

"And if you and Mr. Westmore are graciously inclined to aid us, would you be so kind as to come armed? Because, mon ami, unless your Government people arrive in time, I shall certainly try to keep Skeel and his gang from boarding that boat.

"Au revoir, donc! I am off with Jacques Alost and Emile Souches for that charming summer resort, the Three Ponds Tavern, where, from the neighbouring roadside woods, I shall hope to flag your automobile by sunrise and welcome you and your amiable friend, Mr. Westmore, as our brothers in arms.

"RENOUX, your comrade and friend."

There was a silence. Then Westmore looked at his watch.

"We ought to hustle," he remarked. "I'll get on some knickers and stick a couple of guns in my pocket. You'd better telephone to the garage."

As they hastened up the stairs together, Barres said:

"Have I time for a word with Dulcie?"

"That's up to you. I'm not going to say anything to Thessa. I wouldn't care to miss this affair. If we arrived too late and they had already dynamited the Welland Canal, we'd never forgive ourselves."

Barres ran for his room.

They were dressed, armed and driving out of the Foreland Farms gates inside of ten minutes. Barres

had the wheel; Westmore sat beside him shoving new
clips into two automatics and dividing the remaining
boxes of ammunition.

"The crazy devils," he said to Barres, raising his
voice to make himself heard. "Blow up the Canal,
will they! What's the matter with these Irishmen!
The rest are not like 'em. Look at the Flanders fighting, Garry! Look at the magnificent record of the
Irish regiments! Why don't our Irish play the
game?"

"It's their blind hatred of England," shouted Barres,
in his ear. "They're monomaniacs. They can't see
anything else—can't see what they're doing to civilisation—cutting the very throat of Liberty every time
they jab at England. What's the use? You can't
talk to them. They're lunatics. But when they start
things over here they've got to be put into strait-
jackets."

"They *are* lunatics," repeated Westmore. "If they
weren't, they wouldn't risk the wholesale murder of
women and children. That is a purely German pe-
culiarity; it's what the normal boche delights in. But
the Irish are white men. And it's only when they're
crazy they'd try a thing like this."

After a long silence:
"How fast, Garry?"
"Around fifty."
"How far is it?"
"About twenty-five miles further."

The car rushed on through the night under the brilliant July stars and over a perfect road. In the hol-
lows, where spring brooks ran under stone bridges, a
slight, chilling mist hung, but otherwise the night was
clear and warm.

Woods, fields, farms, streamed by in the darkness;

Lightning Source UK Ltd.
Milton Keynes UK
UKHW02n1904120218
317777UK00003B/80/P